"DO AS YOU ARE TOLD AND ON THE MORROW YOU WILL BE A WOMAN."

Nicola slid across the mattress to where the bed met the wall. Only when the serving women were gone did she cry after them, "When have I ever done as I was told?"

The night candle flickered, its meager illumination barely penetrating the thick darkness. His form but an uncertain shadow, Gilliam moved to shut the door. At the heavy clank of the lock, Nicola's heart exploded in panic. Oh, sweet Mary, but he was locking her in to assure his success. Once again this chamber became a prison.

Rage came roaring in after panic. Damn him, but she'd not let him take all she had left. The mattress dipped as he sat on its edge. Nicola eased back until she felt the cold wall against her shoulders. Drawing new strength from the stones of her home, she tensed in preparation for the coming battle. . . .

ANNOUNCING THE

TOPAZ FREQUENT READERS CLUB
COMMEMORATING TOPAZ'S I YEAR ANNIVERSARY!

THE MORE YOU BUY, THE MORE YOU GET

Redeem coupons found here and in the back of all new Topaz titles for FREE Topaz gifts:

Send in:

 2 coupons for a free TOPAZ novel (choose from the list below);

- ☐ THE KISSING BANDIT, Margaret Brownley
- ☐ BY LOVE UNVEILED, Deborah Martin
- ☐ TOUCH THE DAWN, Chelley Kitzmiller
- ☐ WILD EMBRACE, Cassie Edwards

 4 coupons for an "I Love the Topaz Man" on-board sign

 6 coupons for a TOPAZ compact mirror

 8 coupons for a Topaz Man T-shirt

Just fill out this certificate and send with original sales receipts to:

TOPAZ FREQUENT READERS CLUB-IST ANNIVERSARY
Penguin USA • Mass Market Promotion; Dept. H.U.G.
375 Hudson St., NY, NY I0014

Name_____

Address_____

City_____State_____Zip_____

Offer expires 5/31/1995

This certificate must accompany your request. No duplicates accepted. Void where prohibited, taxed or restricted. Allow 4-6 weeks for receipt of merchandise. Offer good only in U.S., its territories, and Canada.

SPRING'S FURY

by

Denise Domning

A TOPAZ BOOK

TOPAZ
Published by the Penguin Group
Penguin Books USA Inc., 375 Hudson Street,
New York, New York 10014, U.S.A.
Penguin Books Ltd, 27 Wrights Lane,
London W8 5TZ, England
Penguin Books Australia Ltd, Ringwood,
Victoria, Australia
Penguin Books Canada Ltd, 10 Alcorn Avenue,
Toronto, Ontario, Canada M4V 3B2
Penguin Books (N.Z.) Ltd, 182–190 Wairau Road,
Auckland 10, New Zealand

Penguin Books Ltd, Registered Offices:
Harmondsworth, Middlesex, England

First published by Topaz, an imprint of Dutton Signet,
a division of Penguin Books USA Inc.

First Printing, April, 1995
10 9 8 7 6 5 4 3 2 1

Prologue

Late June, 1194

Something heavy hit the bed, and the door slammed. John of Ashby jerked, startled out of his fever-glazed musing. From his hall, which lay outside and to the left of his bedchamber door, folk screamed in terror. An attack!

He wrenched himself upright. The gash on his side reopened, destroying all his daughter's fine needlework. Fiery pain erupted from the wound as the bandages swathing his massive middle grew damp with blood. Blackness whirled in on him, but the ache was a vicious reminder; it was the memory of his sin that kept John conscious.

Oath breaker, he cursed himself. He leaned gingerly against the headboard, and stared in depression at the dark draperies curtaining his bed. What he heard happening in his hall was no enemy assault. 'Twas Rannulf of Graistan's rightful retribution on the vassal who dared raise a murderous sword against his overlord.

Shame burned in John's gut, hotter than the infection that ate at him. Even if this wound did not take him, his life was over. He'd done worse than shatter his vow of loyalty to Rannulf, he had violated every principle he held dear.

Lord God, but he was a thickheaded fool. His new wife had curled her sweet body around him until he was besotted with lust and blinded to her lies. How easily she had molded his quick temper and slow wits into her weapon. At least what he heard in the hall suggested her plot to kill Rannulf had failed.

John listened in helpless sorrow as the terror-filled screams grew to a louder pitch. Every soul within Ashby's walls would pay for his mindless rage. Threaded into the sounds of panic were a paltry few voices raised in command. His daughter would be one of these.

Nicola. John's eyes closed, and tears filled their leathery corners. Of all the pains he bore just now, the realization that he had killed his daughter dug the deepest. When she was dead, their family line would be no more. Such was a traitor's fate.

How much longer did he have before Graistan's men reached him? John slumped in sorrow, only to have his soul cry out in protest. This was no way to finish his life. Be damned if they'd find him hiding abed like some craven coward. John buried his hands into the thick drapes, and slowly shifted his huge bulk across the straw-filled mattress, each movement an agony. The bedclothes spilled over the bed's edge before him.

By the time he set feet to the floor, John was again blinking away darkness. Cold metal touched a calf. He glanced down. His sword lay tilted against the bed frame, hilt upward and blade bared. Who had been so careless with his precious weapon?

He closed a hand about the familiar grip, its leather wrap long since softened into the shape of his palm, then lay the heavy blade across his lap. John stared at it in regret. Would that he could meet his end with

weapon in hand, but a traitor had no right to so honor-
able a demise.

When he again raised his gaze, it was to glance
around his bedchamber in loving farewell. Extending
from a small, stone keep tower, his home was little
more than a barn, with wooden walls and thatch to
keep out the rain. Still, the wide window with its dusty
shutters in the eastern wall, his armor chest beneath it,
even the rising pegs in the warped floorboard were all
friends of long acquaintance.

When he was dead, his lord Rannulf would give this
place to another man. This new vassal would be the
one to collect Ashby's plentiful harvests and hunt in its
thick forests. So, too, would Ashby's new lord marry
and watch his children take life in this bed, just as he
had watched his children come into the world.

John sighed. God had cheated him in his offspring.
His son had been a weakling who died five years past,
while his daughter was a warrior witch who had
learned to use her sword at his knee. From her eighth
year, Nicola had burned with the desire to hold Ashby
as her own fief. She still clung to that childish dream,
refusing to believe it was not possible.

He should have forced her to give it up, and insisted
on marriage long ago. Many men had offered for her,
even though Nicola was overly tall and plain, her manner lacking even the slightest trace of feminine softness. Aye, if he had found her an acceptable husband,
he would never have remarried and the events of this
day would not have occurred.

John's breath hissed from him in the tiniest hint of
laughter. How foolish of him. God's teeth, despite the
rich contract he and Hugh de Ocslade had drawn be-

tween them, Nicola vowed to murder the man if he insisted on marriage.

Nay, forcing his daughter to the altar would have created an equally violent outcome. It would have destroyed John to watch some man beat the spirit out of Nicola. Or—he lifted a brow in brief amusement—shamed him to watch her beat someone like de Ocslade into a bloody pulp. 'Twas best Nicola died in this battle, for, were she to live without her father's indulgent protection, her life would surely be someone's hell.

Now at peace with his life's end, John turned his attention to the bedchamber's door, then squinted at it in closer study. Gray tendrils of smoke curled into the room from between door and lintel. Fine wisps snaked up the plastered wall, touching and lifting, as if testing for weakness. Even as he watched, a misty cloud began to puddle beneath the reed ceiling. With it came a new, deep rumbling from the hall. Its volume swiftly grew until it was a wicked, rasping roar.

John stiffened in terror. Ashby burned! Jesus God, 'twas better to hang than burn. Even in that short instant, the fire's voice strengthened, drowning out all other sound. The need to escape shot through him.

With his sword's tip braced against the floor, John levered himself off the bed, only to sway weakly in exhaustion once he was on his feet. How in God's holy name was he to escape a fiery death if the simple act of standing was beyond him? The answer was simple; he wasn't. John bowed his head in understanding. He would burn.

When he looked up again, it was to stare at the smoke above him. It had grown thicker and darker. Smoldering reeds added an acrid tang to wood smoke, and he coughed as the smell stung his nose. The bedchamber door flew open, ancient leather hinges croaking in startled protest.

Coughing violently, Nicola leapt into the room, a coil of rope over her shoulder. Her hazel eyes were round in fear, her thin face was streaked with soot, her gowns charred. She hurled the rope across the room and slammed the door behind her. It rebounded. She caught it with her back and threw her weight against it, her feet braced to force it shut.

John stared at the rope by the window. His daughter meant to rescue him. Her care for him was deeply touching, but what she wanted to do was impossible. Not only did he weigh more than twenty stone, but the rope would finish what Rannulf's gash had started; he would be torn in two. "Daughter," he said to her, "you cannot save me."

"Papa?" Nicola yelped in hoarse surprise. In that instant, the door exploded open behind her, striking her mid-back. She tumbled across the room to land, facedown and stunned, near the window.

In the doorway stood a knight, tall to the point of being a giant. His surcoat was foul with blood, and his sword rusty with the lives of Ashby's folk. Although his mail coif and his helmet concealed his face, John knew him. His great size alone named him Gilliam FitzHenry, brother to Rannulf of Graistan. The young knight silently entered the room, his blade held defensively before him.

So, Rannulf had set Ashby afire, not content to simply destroy its folk. John's overlord meant to expunge from this earth all trace of him. Such was a traitor's fate.

John relaxed, ready for death. His grip on his weapon eased. He'd not compound the sin of attacking his overlord by resisting his rightful execution at the hand of that man's brother. At the very least, it was a far swifter death than the fire offered.

"Here is where the traitor hides," Gilliam FitzHenry said, stopping a blow's length away. His deep voice was thick from smoke. He pointed with his sword toward the bloody bandages around John's middle. "So, my brother was not as helpless as you might have wished him, eh? Lift your weapon and taste the steel of another of Graistan's sons." The words were cold and hard.

John only stared in disbelief at the young knight, certain he had misheard. An executioner's victim did not put up a defense. In the hall, walls howled in pain, beams groaned in agony. John's lungs spasmed at the bitter smoke. Time was very short. Why did the lad not strike?

Across the room, Nicola stirred, gasping for breath as she returned to her senses. She fought her way onto her hands and knees, elbows trembling. "Nay," she coughed out, "stop!" Her voice was choked and tight.

Gilliam FitzHenry paid her no heed. "Raise your sword," he demanded of the older man, "unless you'd rather burn."

At his words, John's heart tore between sadness and elation. Lord Rannulf's youngest brother was offering this godforsaken traitor an awesome gift: the chance to die like the man of honor John had once been.

It took every bit of his remaining strength to lift his sword tip from the floor. John strove to hold his shoulders level, thus offering the knight a clear target. In doing so, he also assured himself a swift and nearly painless exit from life.

Gilliam nodded once, that simple motion communicating respect for his opponent's courage in facing death. It was enough to restore John's shattered soul. He closed his eyes, his spirit soaring free even before the sword bit into his neck.

Chapter One

God be damned. De Ocslade had to come. Only the contract they'd drawn last spring could save her.

Nicola of Ashby gave an angry huff, her breath clouding in the chill air. She chided herself for doubting. She needed to believe her suckling sister had not failed to deliver the message, else there'd be naught for Nicola but forced marriage to the man who had murdered her father and destroyed her village and home.

'Twas better she died than to make Gilliam Fitz-Henry Ashby's lord. Nay, 'twas better *he* died.

Four long strides took her from one side of the tiny chamber to its door, and she stared at its handle. Pride demanded she try; the latch did not lift. Since Lord Rannulf had held her prisoner for four of the five months she'd been his ward, this was hardly surprising.

With a sharp turn that set her unbound hair bouncing around her hips in lively brown ringlets, Nicola started back across the room. Past the stool and chamber pot, past the coarse straw pallet that was last night's bed, she went. The skirts of her expensive gold and green gowns, created for a wedding that she refused to allow, flew wide with each long step. Her warden should have returned her everyday gowns if he'd wanted these

finer garments to remain unmarred. She'd slept in them
last night apurpose.

Nicola halted at the tower chamber's far wall. Here,
the thick stone was pierced by a slender arrow loop.
Neither it nor its mate in the adjoining wall had a shut-
ter. She put her face into the narrow, defensive opening
and peered out into a world beyond her reach.

Although dawn had come over an hour ago, the day
was yet dull and gray, and the sky unreadable, thick
with early November clouds. The loop let her see a
segment of the town clinging to Graistan keep's outer
wall. Houses were crammed one against the other in a
degree of closeness a country girl like herself could
never abide. Even still, she envied them. These townsfolk had what she did not; their own homes, beds, and
clothing, while she was trapped in someone else's
house with nothing of her own save a bit of jewelry.

The heavens chose that moment to release a gentle
veil of mist. It turned slate roofs to silver, and woke
the tangy scent of gardens slumbering beneath a blanket of mulch. Nicola breathed deeply in homesickness.
'Twas this smell, the scent of growing things, that reminded her most of Ashby's woodlands and rolling
hills.

She sighed against her heartache. Home called to
her. In all her life, she'd spent no more than two weeks
away from Ashby. To have been separated from it now,
during the time her folk needed her most, was almost
more than she could bear. Who knew better how to rebuild the place, she or that buffoon who had destroyed
it?

Guilt, sudden and swift, stabbed through her. If not
for her, there'd be no need to rebuild at all. Aye, her
stepmother had urged Papa to attack Lord Rannulf, but

it had been at Nicola's command that the gates remained shut when Gilliam FitzHenry came knocking.

Nicola slammed her fist against the stone wall and let rage wash away self-blame. Ashby's fall was not her fault. All she had ever wanted was to keep her home as hers, alone.

Rage grew. Aye, if the world were a just place, she would never have attempted subterfuge in order to trick Lord Rannult into ceding her Ashby. She could have been as good a lord to her home as any man. Damn the laws that saw no value in a woman save for the property she brought with her. Why should Lord Rannulf have control over every aspect of her life, simply because she was female?

Keys clanked at the other side of the thick, oaken door. Nicola leapt into the chamber's deepest corner, every muscle tensed in expectation of battle. The door groaned open.

Two burly men, dressed in steel-sewn hauberks and metal caps upon their heads, stepped inside the door. They were armed far beyond the norm for simple guard duty, their hands upon their sword hilts and their eyes wary. Then, again, she had knocked one of them senseless on her last try at escaping. Nicola let a tiny smile touch her mouth.

"Cowards," she jeered at them. "Are you so frightened of one, defenseless maiden?"

"Have a care with your tongue, vixen," one snarled, "or we'll not let the girl in."

Nicola straightened in surprise. Graistan was empty just now, the household having moved to Upwood for the season. Yesterday, her maid had been a grandmother from a local merchant's household, and she'd expected the same woman today. Her overlord chose this elderly servant deliberately, certain Nicola would not attack the helpless; he was right, she saved her violence for her captors. "What girl?"

They stepped back to reveal Tilda of Ashby on the landing behind them, a tray of foods on one arm and a bucket of water over her other arm. Nicola's heart leapt, and she bit back the urge to scream in joy and relief. But if her warden learned that Tilda was her ally, he would swiftly exile the girl.

Her gaolers leered as the petite commoner entered the room, their masculine appreciation of her lush form and fine features written clearly on their faces. Drab gowns did not dim Tilda's honey and cream coloring, and her hood was thrown back to reveal her wealth of tawny hair. Brown eyes were bright with carefully subdued amusement.

"Put your cocks back into your chausses," Nicola called, her voice scornful. "I'm certain she wants none of what you'd offer her."

"Good morrow, Lady Ashby," Tilda said in her horrible French. "My grandmama sends her excuses this day, for she is ill. I hope you can tolerate my presence in her stead."

Nicola coughed to hide her laugh. Although her friend knew the Norman tongue, she and Tilda had always spoken English. Tilda's mother, Agnes, had been Nicola's nurse, and the girls had been inseparable ever since that time. The commoner set her tray down on the stool, then turned on the men. "A little privacy, if you please. I would see to the lady's personal needs."

" 'Tis not allowed," one replied. "Make haste completing what you must do." The two retreated to block the exit and watch that nothing untoward happened.

Tilda turned her back on them with a casual shrug.

"Here, now, Lady Ashby, you've gotten yourself all atangle," she said, her accent making mincemeat of her words. "Lift your arm so I can rearrange your laces."

Nicola did as asked, and the girl loosened the knot. But, instead of drawing the string tighter, Tilda pulled it free of the gown altogether. She drew a breath and glanced over her shoulder at the guards. Where any woman would have recognized this as unnecessary and a blatant attempt to stall, it flew unnoticed over the heads of men.

She looked back at Tilda and saw the pretty girl's lips rise in a triumphant smile. Four months of separation had dimmed Nicola's recall of how much her closest companion enjoyed tweaking those who thought they could control her. And, God forbid that Tilda came to hate someone; her revenge could be vicious.

As the smaller girl smoothed and patted the creases from the now loose garments, Nicola bent her head as if to watch. "Will de Ocslade come?" she whispered.

"Do I look like a nobleman's confidante?" Tilda hissed into the folds of the gown as she rethreaded the lace. "You asked no more of me than to deliver your message." She glanced up with a disbelieving frown. "Why do you care? You surely do not mean to marry him." Her words were barely audible.

"I must," Nicola breathed. "I cannot give Ashby to FitzHenry. Hugh, I can control."

"Nay, not. Too canny." Tilda's whispered warning came around the string in her mouth as she drew its frayed end into a point.

Nicola let a lift of her brows shrug for her. "Then, I'll marry the little man and make myself a widow." A widowed noblewoman sometimes bought control of her estate from the king. Only in that way could a woman manage her own properties with no man at her side.

Tilda blinked, arms outstretched as she evened the string in its eyelets. "Let me straighten your collar, Lady Ashby." She stood on tiptoe to do so, leaning close to whisper, "You are mad. Those women have hair on their chin and grown heirs."

Nicola clenched her fists, not wanting to hear that her plot was flawed; she already knew that. "Little maid," she said aloud, "do you know my tale? Although I tell Lord Rannulf I am betrothed to Hugh de Ocslade, my warden would force me to wed his brother, Gilliam FitzHenry. It matters naught to him that this is the man who murdered my father. Tell me, am I the only one who sees no justice in this?"

"Lady Ashby," one of the guards called, "say no more or I shall remove the maid."

"Consider me muzzled," Nicola said, shooting the man a hard look.

Tilda smoothed the gowns over Nicola's slender waist and hips. "There, that is much better. Now, you sit and eat, while I comb your hair."

She handed the tall girl her tray, and Nicola settled onto the stool facing the wall opposite the door. Tilda stood behind her, her back to the guards. "Why, Lady Ashby, you have no eating knife."

When Nicola looked up, there was no surprise in her friend's face. "Aye, my warden keeps me disarmed, not even allowing me something as puny as a table knife." She tilted her head to one side, her fingers caressing the pin that held her mantle in place.

This piece was the only thing of her father's that she knew to survive her home's destruction. Its garnet-studded head was as thick as two fingers, and it fit into

her palm like a dagger's hilt. The narrow tongue that
kept the pin fastened in her mantle's shoulder was
longer than her hand, and sharpened to a fine point.
She was hardly disarmed. "I manage well enough
without one."

"I can see that you do," Tilda said, slowly drawing
her comb through Nicola's hair. With her second
stroke, she leaned forward and whispered, "I have your
pack."

Her words brought Nicola around so suddenly, the
petite commoner took a startled step back. The guards
leapt toward them, hands on hilts. Nicola glanced at
them and clapped a hand to her head.

"Have a care," she chided in her most arrogant tone.
"How much will my bridegroom like me if I am bald?"
The men relaxed and stepped back into the doorway.

"My pardon, Lady Ashby," Tilda said with a gay
laugh, "but you have difficult hair."

Nicola could not restrain her smile. Now, that was
an understatement. Although she valued the stuff as
her most feminine feature, it had a life of its own. Like
her, it hated to be bound even in something as sensible
as a plait.

Tilda once again placed her body between Nicola
and the guards. "I have a new life outside of Ashby,"
she whispered. "Join me in it."

Nicola drew a quick breath of surprise. But Ashby
was their home. Her questions would have to wait. If
de Ocslade would not come to her, the contents of that
pack offered Nicola the freedom to go to him. Pilfered
last July from Graistan's overloaded coffers, it included everything she needed to transform herself. In
this new identity, she could even run anywhere without
attracting the slightest attention.

Tilda stood back to admire the far more sober tresses. A guard called to her, "You are finished now. Go."

"At your command," the commoner replied in English as Nicola came to her feet, then continued in French to the noblewoman. "My lady, I have always enjoyed weddings. Are you not marrying this day at Tierce? Might I come to witness?"

She smiled, the lilt of her mouth saying she could not wait to taste danger's spice, then angled her head to one side, displaying her even features to their best advantage. This was a blatant taunt. The exchange of marriage vows was always a public event, held where any and all could witness. Tilda meant her words to stick in the guards' minds, stinging them after the fact for not recognizing what went forward beneath their noses.

"Of course you may attend," Nicola replied, "but the abbot has delayed the ceremony until midday. It will please me to look for you in the crowd, for yours is a friendly face and I am among enemies here."

"I will be there." Still smiling, Tilda walked out the door. The men stepped swiftly from the room and shut the door quietly behind them.

Nicola crossed the room to the door, where she stared at the latch. Pride demanded she try. The latch would not lift; it was locked.

Chapter Two

Elbows braced on his knees, Gilliam FitzHenry sat on a bench before the farthest of the twin hearths in Graistan's empty hall. He stared into the flames leaping on the raised stone platform. Firelight gleamed off the fine golden embroidery trimming the sleeves of his best blue gown. It also marked the damage done by yesterday's wrestle with the vixen.

Anger was hardly the sign of a happy bridegroom. Nor was so hurried an affair the mark of a love match. That thought made the corners of his mouth lift slightly. No one doubted that this would be a marriage made in hell, but fate and pride left him no other choice.

His thoughts returned to his bride's claim of betrothal. An obvious lie. Now, why did she do so when all she could win was a delay? Gilliam blinked. Of course. 'Twas only the opportunity for escape she sought.

His worry eased. This he could prevent. Aye, no complaint or threat could stop him from becoming Lord Ashby in name as well as deed. At long last, he would gain the one thing a youngest son never dared dream to have: a home of his own.

A winner's howl of success rose from the depths of

the hall behind Gilliam's back, echoing into the high roof. The few men he'd brought from Ashby had joined Graistan's off-duty garrison at the other hearth in a friendly game of dice. Winter was the keep's period of rest, replenishing its stores during the season. When the wedding was done, these soldiers would be the keep's only occupants.

"Lord Gilliam, 'tis Lord Geoffrey." The porter's call came from the door at the room's opposite end, floating over the shouts of the losers on the last roll.

"Better late than never, my mother's oldest son," Gilliam muttered to himself. Where Rannulf occupied a father's place in Gilliam's life and Temric that of a disapproving uncle, Geoff was a friend and the sibling least likely to treat him as a child. Burying his discontent beneath the expression of the carefree youth that always seemed expected of him, Gilliam came to his feet.

Geoffrey, Lord Coudray, strode past the tall screens guarding the hall from the door's draft. Although he was fully armed in a chain-mail tunic over leggings of the same metal mesh, he had removed his helmet and shucked his metal hood and cap before entering the room. Fisted in one of his ungloved hands was the cloak of a small and bony lad.

Travel in November's blustery weather had burned the boy's pale skin raw and streaked his cheeks with dirt. Knotted spikes of fine brown hair thrust up over his generous forehead to stand above his hood, snarled into place by the wind. What with the child's wide-set brown eyes, the whole came together to give him a mummer's astonished look.

"Geoff, I am here," Gilliam called out, the power of his deep voice nigh on lifting the painted linen panels that covered the stone walls. "Is this a wedding gift you bring me?"

"Nay, the bed is my gift, my mother's youngest son. Taking on a squire is work and I'll not have you complaining that I make gift of work," Geoff retorted. His easy stride made the boy trot as they crossed the expanse of rush-covered floor.

"Ah, but the bed's too short."

"It wouldn't be if you'd stopped growing before you were too tall for it."

Gilliam laughed, truly pleased to have his brother here. "Come close, let me have a look."

Although Geoff obligingly thrust the boy out before him, it wasn't the lad Gilliam wanted to see. If he and Geoff were different in height and build, they were startlingly alike in appearance, or had been until little less than a year ago. They shared their golden hair color and shape of face, even the same inability to grow a proper beard. 'Twas the missing eye and scars, gifts from Geoff's wife, now blessedly deceased, that made them different. At least the scars had healed flat, and a patch could cover the eye.

"They mend well enough," Geoff said softly as he recognized Gilliam's interest, the pain in his voice not physical. His remaining eye, a slightly darker blue than Gilliam's own pale eye color, grew darker still against it.

Gilliam instantly shifted subjects. "So, will you stay for the wedding?"

"What?" Geoff asked in confusion. "Here I was coming with apologies on my lips for being late, thinking the deed was done yesterday. Did I get the day wrong?"

"There were complications." Gilliam managed to

swallow his anger behind a wry grin. "My beloved claims to be betrothed to Ashby's neighbor."

"That is not possible," Geoff instantly protested.

Gilliam gave a lift of his brows. "Ah, but the new abbot seeks ways to break free of Rannulf's influence, and my bride gave him just the tool he wanted. This Abbot Simon insisted on sending to Ocslade, demanding the man's appearance so he might decide whose claim is valid."

His brother's single-faceted gaze sparked with sudden amusement. "Rannulf must be nigh on mad with rage. I warned him he expected too much of the abbey, and that the monks resented him for it."

"Aye, he's there right now, using all his diplomacy and tact to ease the situation. He'll manage, he always does," Gilliam said with an unconcerned shrug. "Now, why not introduce me to this gift of mine. A boy is far better than a bed." Knowing how intimidating his great height could be, Gilliam sat on the bench, then winked at the boy. The lad only turned his face to the side.

"Jocelyn," Geoffrey said mildly, "come put out your hand and greet my brother, the new Lord Ashby. Lord Ashby, this is Jocelyn, heir to the manor at Freyne, wishing to be fostered in your home."

Bottom lip trembling, Jocelyn reluctantly thrust out his hand, his eyes now focused on the floor. "Well met, my lord. 'Tis kind of you to offer me hearth and home," he mumbled. It was obvious that he'd been coached to make the statement; there was no gratitude in his voice.

Gilliam curled his large hand around the boy's thin fingers and found no strength in the child's grip. "Well met, it is. 'Tis an honor to have you join my family."

When he released the boy's hand, he pointed to the

far table where an array of cold dishes had been laid for the morning meal. The simplicity reflected the fact that there was only one harried cook in the kitchen. "Take yourself to yon table and find a bite to eat. 'Twill be a long day of waiting for you, for we'll not be leaving for Ashby until the morrow's morn."

Where the boy Gilliam had been would have raced eagerly toward the prospect of any meal, this one dragged his feet as if going to his execution. He watched Jocelyn as he made his limp-kneed way around the table, then turned on the bench to look up at his brother.

"Geoff, when you asked me to take him as my squire, I admit I thought you addlepated," he said softly to be certain the child did not overhear. "While I had no doubt I could teach him a warrior's skills, my house is only half rebuilt, and I, not yet married. Now I understand. How old is he, ten? Eleven? He cannot even close his hand around mine to greet me. If he were sent to a house with other boys, they would eat him alive, no?"

Geoff sank to sit beside him, then stretched his legs out before him. " 'Tis worse than that. He's nigh on thirteen. He should already be riding at quintains and have his first set of armor. His parents interpreted his small size to mean he could have no life but the Church."

"What has size to do with power?"

"Is that my giant of a brother I hear speaking those words?" Geoff asked with a breath of amusement.

"Size and strength help," Gilliam admitted with a smile, "but 'tis the mingling of skill, stamina, and numbers that carry the day. Nor is holiness any imped-iment. There are more than a few churchmen who can swing a right powerful morning star, Hugh of Durham being a case in point." It had been the holy Bishop of Durham's siege at Tickhill that helped end John Lackland's recent insurrection against his brother and monarch, Richard, called the Lionheart.

Geoff only shook his head and stared into the fire. "Nay, Jocelyn's dam meant for him to be a scholar. In her effort to keep her son from a life she sees as violent, she's turned him into a milksop, afraid of any physical activity. Is it not just like fate to remove both his father and elder brother and make him Freyne's heir? Now, neither his dam nor he have any choice in the matter. Knight he will be, and after that, Freyne's lord." He turned his head to offer his brother a small smile, aimed at life's ironies.

Gilliam looked beyond Geoff to the boy. Jocelyn sat with an adult's stillness at the table, his arms crossed tightly before him as if to keep the world at bay. "What's his temper like?"

"He is a dour child, joyless and playless. When I urge him to make an effort, he cries and says he cannot because he is too weak and small. 'Tis but an echo of his mother's excuses for him. Gilliam, if anyone can teach him to find what is fun in this life he must live, you can."

"Is that a compliment or a chide?" Gilliam replied, his laugh meant to hide his hurt over this seeming jibe.

"Now, Gilliam," Geoff said, a spark of laughter in his eye, "I wouldn't have entrusted him to you if I did not think you man enough to be his foster father. Your nature is just that, your nature. I, for one, am glad of it. Besides, 'tis either you or I who will make of him a knight; I would rather it be you." He smiled. "His mother grows hysterical when it comes to Jocelyn destroying every bit of good I achieve with him. Jesu, Gilliam, her tears could fill my moat. I only hope I survive her presence until her babe is born. Dear God, I never expected to play nursemaid to a pregnant widow, but such is my duty." It was a disgusted aside.

Gilliam managed a chagrined look. "My pardon, brother. I happily accept this responsibility. 'Tis only that I sometimes think none of you remember I am a man full grown."

Geoff laughed. "Now who is misjudging others? Did you not prove yourself last June when you took down Ashby's walls in only one day to free Rannulf? If ever we questioned, we do so no longer." He paused a moment, then shot his brother a sidelong look. Gilliam tensed at what lay in his gaze. Geoff was going to speak of the past.

"Which brings me to a question that's been plaguing me. Why have you hurried this wedding of yours?"

Gilliam sagged in relief. It wasn't the question he expected. "In short, I need Ashby's lady and what she knows. Where Rannulf sees only a virago, her folk tell another tale of her. Their lady is loyal and true, using her healing arts to care for them and their families. Those who serve the manor say that without her household skills, we'll all starve this winter."

"So, they have convinced you she will be a caring wife?" Geoff's brows lifted as he awaited his answer.

"They have convinced me she is a right fine lady, who holds her folks concerns first in her heart." It was a hedge. He accepted his wife would never love him, but he craved her cooperation like a drowning man craved air. There had to be a way to make her see beyond their past to Ashby's future.

"Rannulf says she threatens you with murder. This is not a woman likely to add your care to her heart's work. Why her, Gilliam?" Geoff asked softly. "Rannulf offered you another suitable property where there was no heiress to marry."

"I did not find the place to my liking," Gilliam retorted, his jaw stiff.

Geoff turned his gaze to the fire. "I see the word 'penance' written all over this wedding." It was a gentle sneer.

Gilliam tried to send his brother a quelling look, but Geoff stared at his boots as if they were fascinating. "Do you not wish to disarm and prepare for the ceremony?" he asked stiffly. "Rannulf should be here shortly, and it will be time to fetch my bride."

"Nay," his brother said quietly, "I think I would rather know why you tie yourself to a woman who wishes you dead, when you could have property without marriage."

"I want Ashby." Gilliam scowled at the flames. "These past five months have turned the place into my heart and home, making its folk mine own. I am loath to begin the process anew at some other manor. As for the woman," he managed a mirthless laugh, "you know I have a way with dangerous creatures."

"Aye, with admirable success," Geoff said, his voice still gentle and his attention yet focused at his feet, "but this is a woman, not one of your pets. I find myself thinking of Isotte and your son."

Gilliam's stomach clenched at the mention of Rannulf's second wife and the child Gilliam had set in her. If there was any man on earth who did not deserve a loving wife, 'twas he. "So, among the three of you,

you were the one elected to speak to me," he snapped. "Well, I will not discuss it, not even with you."

"If Rannulf has released the past, why do you yet cling to it?"

Gilliam turned his head away from his brother, so Geoff could not see his face. "Jesus God, what I did stained my soul forever," he hissed. "I do not cling to it, it clings to me like the stench of offal. Leave it be."

"I cannot. I must know why you keep punishing yourself when all is forgiven." His brother kept his voice calm, refusing to react to Gilliam's anger.

"Forgiven by Rannulf, mayhap, but I hurt more than he." Suddenly, rage and festering pain drove his carefully buried words from him. "Tell me, Geoff, how I can forgive myself for committing adultery and incest with my brother's wife? Murder, as well, for the child I made in her killed her. Brother, my sins pile, one atop the other.

"Even Ashby's destruction lies upon my doorstep. If not for my youthful sin with Isotte, her sister could never have worked her evil on John of Ashby. If it was my misdeed that caused Ashby's destruction, should it not be I who restores the place? I accept the heiress's hate as my rightful penance." His voice faded to a whisper as his stomach turned. He bowed his head and fought the sickness. "Jesu, I've said too much."

"I never thought you capable of such pain," his brother murmured after a long moment of silence. "Vow to me, Gilliam. Say you'll not make my mistake. Do not place so high a value on your pride that you forget to see the sort of woman you acquire."

Gilliam looked up to find Geoff watching him, worry marking his expression. "I do not. If I seek no love or caring in my marriage, neither is she a mad-woman, else her folk would not cherish her so."

"What if she attempts to make good on her vow of murder?" Geoff did not add "as my wife nearly did," but the unspoken words hung between them.

"I have installed a lock on our chamber door," Gilliam said, his voice without inflection. "I will keep her prisoner to protect myself."

"For how long? I know you. You cannot stand to chain your dog."

Gilliam rubbed a hand against his brow. "Ah, Geoff, I refuse to believe it will come to that. When you see her, you'll understand why I hope for her acceptance. Nicola of Ashby may well be the only woman I can embrace without worrying over doing damage to her."

The moment the words were out, Gilliam's native humor returned and he laughed at himself. "There I go, making impossible wishes, once more. Gain the home I've longed for and I begin counting on a wife strong enough to warm my nights. My men are wagering she'll gut me before our wedding night is over. I have matched their bets, calculating that if they win, I'll be dead and they cannot collect." He shot his brother a broad grin.

"You are doing this on a dare?" There was astonishment in his brother's quiet voice.

"Nay, Geoff," Gilliam said, his own tone firm in determination. "You have heard my reasons for setting my hand around Ashby. It is mine, and I'll not release it to any man—or woman. The dare only makes the possibility of failure and a life filled with domestic war easier to swallow."

Geoffrey nodded slowly as he digested his brother's

words. "Your reasons I accept." Coudray's lord came to his feet and signaled to his men, who had joined the other gaming soldiers. "Robert, bring my pack so I may change. Who is gathering the wagers on this wedding?"

One man threw up a hand. " 'Tis I, Lord Geoffrey."

"I'll lay three marks on my brother's survival," he said. The men all groaned at so rich a sum, hinting they thought he'd soon be parted from it. "Brother or no, my money's well placed," Lord Coudray insisted.

"How can you believe so when you've not seen my opponent?" Gilliam laughed, feeling easier about this wedding now. Perhaps this speech with Geoff was a good thing, after all.

"I learned my lesson last June, when I wagered against your chances of taking down Ashby's walls with a ballista. Never again, my mother's youngest son," Geoff said with a quick smile. "I cannot afford to underestimate you."

The porter cried sharply in surprise from his post at the doorway. Gilliam leapt to his feet as Geoff turned, his hand on his sword hilt. Dressed in a gown of fine red wool trimmed in silver and gold, Rannulf FitzHenry, Lord Graistan, stormed into the room.

"I'll cram this marriage down that godforsaken churchman's throat or die trying," he bellowed. "No sanctimonious little monk tells me who I take as my vassal. Gilliam, fetch the vixen you so desire."

On the landing atop the spiraling stairs leading to the north tower chamber, Gilliam raised a hand in greeting to the guards. His smile was not forced. "A fine day, my lads. Your lord has declared that my wed-

ding begins this moment. I've come to fetch me a
bride."

"By yourself?" one scoffed.

"Aye," the other agreed. "Where are your ropes?
Yestermorn, you had to hold her whilst we bound her."

"Ah, but today is different." Gilliam wagged a finger at the man. " 'Tis my guess that our prisoner plots
escape, fearing the abbot cannot or will not prevent our
marriage. If I am right, she'll not let herself be bound.
Stand back now and let us see."

The guards smiled skeptically, and the door opened.
Gilliam stepped past them, ducking beneath the lintel
to enter the small room.

Nicola of Ashby was pressed into the room's far
wall, prepared for battle. As always, her height surprised him. She nearly looked him in the eye when he
was the tallest man he knew. Strong, too. 'Twas truly
a shame she hated him so.

He took a step toward her. She leaned forward as if
preparing to hiss and spit, moving into the beam of
murky light spilling through an arrow loop. With so
long a face, there'd be no one to call her a beauty, but
her hair was marvelous and her eyes, magnificent. Aye,
'twas her eyes that turned a plain girl into a striking
woman. They were almond-shaped and ringed by
thick, dark lashes, set beneath brows that were almost
straight. Their color shifted with her moods, brown
when she was calm and green when she was remembering how much she despised him.

" 'Tis time for our joining," he said quietly.

"Nay," she replied. "The abbot said the ceremony
would be delayed until Sexts."

Gilliam only shrugged. "My brother considered the

change of plan a mere suggestion on the churchman's part. He has decided 'tis time for us to wed, little girl."

"Little girl?" she retorted in anger. "Do you think to make me feel small and helpless by insulting me so? Well, two can play that game, *pretty boy*."

"I had not thought you'd noticed," he teased, impervious to her taunts. "Would you like to observe my profile? I've always thought it was my best feature." Gilliam turned his head to the side, and the guards behind him hooted with laughter.

Nicola narrowed her eyes at this preening cock's vanity. His chin and brow were perfectly proportioned, his nose neither too small nor too large and without crook or hump. Golden hair curled loosely down the strong column of his neck. High cheekbones lifted over a wide and clean-shaven jaw. Aye, she'd noticed he was a handsome man and hated herself all the more for doing so. Save for Ashby's fields and forests, a man like him would never have glanced at a horse-faced amazon like her. Angry at herself for reacting to his beauty, Nicola threw another insult.

"Your face is bare. I think this is because even at two and twenty you are incapable of growing a man's beard."

"Tomorrow's morn offers you the chance to discover the truth," he said with an amused lift of his brows.

"You are overconfident." She infected her haughty comment with scorn. "No churchman will marry us when I am betrothed to another. You are doomed to remain landless."

"I say your tale of betrothal is false. Now, why do we not go to the abbey and discover which of us will win this war of ours." He paused a moment, then shrugged his dark mantle over his shoulders. "Will you be bound this time?"

When he stepped toward her, Nicola saw how the sleeves of his blue gown strained at the bulk of his upper arms. She drew a frustrated breath. Even worse than being a murdering, home-stealing son of a rich man, the preening cock was stronger than she.

"How proud you are of your power," she said, needing to sting him, "but I think that is all there is to you. Big men are like oxen, strong and dim-witted."

A broad grin set long creases into Gilliam FitzHenry's cheeks and sparked in his bright blue eyes. "My dear Lady Ashby, sparring with you is as interesting as watching corn being ground into flour. You are like the beast, forever going 'round and 'round in the same path. Not that I mind the insults, only your lack of creativity."

Mother of God, she hated him and his taunting. Nicola turned her face to one side and closed her eyes, wishing she could shut him out of her life as easily. He was a jackanape, a buffoon, always looking to make her the butt of his jests.

"My wit has rendered you speechless, eh? Well, you're not the first to be struck so."

Nicola gasped. These soft and laughing words were spoken almost into her ear. When she opened her eyes, she found he now stood directly in front of her. His brows were raised as a smile played at the corners of his well-formed lips. She sidled right, he shifted to block her. She eased left, he followed.

"*Tsk,* Lady Ashby, how could you have been so careless?" he chided. " 'Tis a poor tactician who stages a defense in a place from which there is no escape."

He braced his hands on the wall above her shoulders, preventing any further movement. "See? Now you are trapped."

Nicola ached to push him away from her. But to fight him meant she would be bound, when Tilda might yet appear with escape thrown over her shoulder. She would simply have to endure his nearness until he was done teasing and moved. Nicola glared up at him, hoping her stare would intimidate.

He only smiled. Mary, but she wanted to slap that smug expression off his face. Instead, she lowered her gaze to his shoulders. They were massive, his chest broad. She huffed in disbelief and dismay. And folk called her a giantess? Even the heat of his body was greater than hers.

At first, the warmth that flowed from him was welcome after hours trapped in this unheated room. But with each beat of her heart, it grew warmer, until her cheeks burned with it. His nearness became unsettling; her senses all twisted and fluttered oddly within her. Nicola tensed against them. If she couldn't escape him this day, the rich man's son would take her to his bed. He had to, for until he took her maidenhead, he would not truly own Ashby.

His hands shifted on the wall behind her, his wrists now resting on her shoulders. With his touch came the reminder of how great his strength was. Here was the one man who could take from her what she would not give.

Rage at this thought roared through her. Captivity had turned her womanish. Her body was the only thing left that belonged to her, and he was the one man to whom she would never surrender it. Aye, she'd kill him before that happened. What sort of daughter laid with her father's murderer?

"Do you think to frighten me by this?" she snapped.

"Frighten you?" he asked, seeming genuinely surprised at her question. "Is that possible?"

"Nay." She raised her chin a notch, but couldn't stare down her nose at a man who was half a head taller than she. Nicola settled for a haughty look. " 'Tis just that I tire of this game of yours."

"I see. Well, then, if I cannot intimidate you, I suppose we should be on our way. We have an appointment with the abbot." FitzHenry stepped back and extended a huge hand. "I can hold your arm, or you can be bound. Which would you prefer?"

Nicola silently offered her arm. She swore her skin crawled as his strong fingers closed around her wrist.

The two guards at the door laughed. "Is this the same creature as yesterday?" one jeered. "Lord Gilliam, if all it took to master her was a ride over your shoulder, she'll be sweet as cream after this night's ride." He and his compatriot roared at the jest.

"Hey, now, mind your tongues. 'Tis my wife you discuss, lads," FitzHenry replied, his protest tainted by the amusement in his tone.

Nicola's pride writhed in humiliation; FitzHenry's touch on her was more than she could bear. She jerked her arm free. Faster than she dreamed possible, he grabbed her at the waist.

"Ride or walk?" he asked quietly. His fine features showed no sign of anger or irritation, his gaze was calm, as if he truly awaited her decision.

"Walk," she said, pride aching at having to submit to his control.

Once again, his fingers closed around her slender

arm. "Do you never eat?" he asked. "You are too thin, I think me."

"I think I do not care what you think."

The big man only laughed. "That, I already knew, little girl. Come, we have a date with a churchman."

Chapter Three

Gilliam released Nicola once they had climbed the four steps leading to the church door. Rannulf, his harsh face held tight in lines of rage, stood at the base of the stairs. The boy Jocelyn yet remained in Graistan keep, while Geoff worked himself free of his mail and into a suitable gown.

"Arnult," Rannulf said to Graistan's young castellan, who stood at the abbey's gate, "go fetch our good lord abbot. Use your sword if you must."

As the man turned to do as bid, the sub-abbot came flying from the dormer. Long and lean, the monk held his arms out in protest as he raced toward them. His habit's wide sleeves flew behind him like wings. Gilliam grinned: a stork, not an angel.

"By whose right do you come bursting in here?" the holy brother cried.

"By my right as protector of this place. I will have a word with your lord." Rannulf's voice was cold, slicing through the sub-abbot as he sought to attack the master behind him. "Warn him not to keep me waiting, else in a quarter hour's time, I will order my men to ransack your house, removing the many gifts I have given you over the years."

The monk said nothing, but his eyes widened until

they nearly leapt from their sockets. He whirled and darted back to the abbot's office.

Gilliam glanced at Nicola. The color of her gowns became her, making her eyes seem greener. Just now, she was frantically scanning the throng of people in the abbey's cobbled yard. He tried to follow her gaze, then freed a sound of wry amusement. Despite the cold and misty weather that was staining his gown, most of Graistantown's inhabitants were now crammed inside these tall stone walls.

Beggars in motley rags were pressed up against modest housewives, their hair covered in white wimples. Apprentices, stealing an hour from their masters, ducked away from the wealthy merchants, dressed in bright robes of scarlet and blue. It seemed no one could resist the promise of entertainment equal to yesterday's. Perhaps this was a good thing. Their number disguised the presence of the soldiers, drawn from Coudray, Ashby, and Graistan, who now lined the walls.

A moment more and Gilliam saw Nicola's shoulders relax as she loosed a deep sigh. So, he was right. Yesterday's tale of betrothal was nothing more than a delaying tactic. She counted on someone in the crowd to free her. Gilliam leaned toward her. "It will not work. You cannot escape me, for you are already mine."

Nicola turned on him, eyes narrowed and jaw tensed in rage. "You will never hold me, murderer."

That stung him. "I did no murder," he retorted. "Your father begged for my sword, even lifting his own in invitation. Would you rather he have burned?"

"Nay," she cried out, sounding like a small child, "I could have saved him, but you murdered him." She turned away, but was not quick enough to hide her sudden tears.

That surprised him. Gilliam hadn't thought her capable of such a feminine expression. The crowd's murmur of excitement alerted him to the newly elected abbot's appearance in the courtyard. He turned to watch.

Small and slender, his features meek, the churchman hardly looked the sort to stand down a baron. Abbot Simon was a far more traditional leader than his recently deceased predecessor. 'Twas freedom from Graistan's secular ruler he now sought, using pride as his shield and Church law as his sword.

Rannulf called to him. " 'Tis Tierce, my lord abbot. We have a wedding to celebrate."

A pinched and furious line appeared between the churchman's delicate brows. "I delayed the ceremony until Sexts, allowing more time for de Ocslade's arrival. If you think your threat of violence will alter this, you are wrong. Indeed, your attempt may only succeed in my disallowing altogether any joining between Lady Ashby and your brother."

"Praise God," Nicola muttered.

As Rannulf began to protest, Gilliam grabbed his bride's wrist. With Ashby's ownership secure in his hand, he shouted over his brother's complaint. "Churchman, you have no basis on which to disallow this contract. My dower is the village of Eilington and the cost of rebuilding Ashby. This is one third of her value, as required. Where there is no inequity, how can you refuse to wed us?"

The abbot shot him a harsh glance. "You speak with the ignorance of youth. The Church has the right to prevent forced marriage when the wedding is not in the best interest of the bride."

"I am her warden and overlord," Rannulf snarled, "therefore a better judge of what is in her best interest than an insolent churchman who reaches beyond his rights."

The abbot straightened to his tallest, hands on hips. "This discussion is pointless. She is betrothed, and you cannot marry her elsewhere, my lord. God's law supersedes even yours in this."

"Damn you, there is no betrothal," Gilliam said, his words ringing against the walls. "If there were, the man would have claimed her the day after Ashby's lord died. You called the banns. Did he come? Nay. Her tale is as false as your pride!"

"Have a care with what you say," Rannulf snapped in harsh warning.

Gilliam turned on his brother, no longer trying to suppress his anger. "Nay, I held my tongue yesterday in deference to those I saw as older and wiser, but no more. I will not put my fate into the hands of this churchman, when he is prejudiced against me."

"You have no choice in this" was Simon's scornful response. "If there is a contract between Ocslade and Ashby, you will cede those lands to their rightful owner."

"*I* am the rightful owner. By my sweat is Ashby's perimeter wall rebuilt, and by my design will I raise a new hall. 'Twas I, no other lord, who on Michaelmas delivered the hideage our king asked from us. Aye, folk who ran from me in terror this June past now gladly call me their lord and entrust in me their lives."

Outrage flamed in Gilliam's heart, and he lifted Nicola's arm to display his hold on her. "Look upon this. Ashby's ownership is in my hand, and there it will stay."

Her heart aching, Nicola wrenched hopelessly against FitzHenry's grasp. Although she didn't win free, he let her lower her arm. Could it be true that Ashby's folk called him their lord? How could they trust both life and livelihood to him, when he had killed their relatives and destroyed their homes in his seige of Ashby. Nay, he must be lying.

"Murderer," she cried, her voice harsh with hurt. "You cannot keep me, and I will never make you Ashby's lord."

"Hold your tongue, vixen," Lord Rannulf snapped. "You have no place in this discussion."

His unfairness dug deep, and she clenched her fists in indignant disbelief. "How can you speak of my best interest, then give me no voice? 'Tis my life you wrangle over, not some far-flung field." Her voice cracked in resentment. No man saw her as a being in her own right.

"Silence the bitch," the puny churchman shouted. "I will not tolerate her impertinence."

Nicola turned on the abbot in shock, then wondered why she was surprised. He, too, was a man. She should have known his concern for her was nothing more than pretense. All he wanted was a weapon to use against Lord Rannulf. Her anger at his betrayal devoured her common sense. "Damn you all," she shouted, "you will listen to me! My father's murderer will not become Ashby's lord."

In the instant of silence following her cry, the abbot turned a vicious brown gaze on her, while Lord Rannulf's eyes were steel. Nicola died a thousand deaths, all hope of escape slaughtered by her wayward

tongue. They would bind and gag her for certain.
When the pressure of her intended's hand on her arm
urged her slightly nearer to him, she did not resist. Instead, the strength of his chest at her back was almost
welcome.

"Did you think he was your champion?" FitzHenry
murmured. "More fool you. All he wants is a slice of
the power that belongs to my brother. He cares nothing
for what it costs you or me." His bitter words offered
more understanding of her helplessness than all the abbot's empty prattling of yesterday.

The courtyard behind her exploded in screams,
punctuated by the clattering of hooves against cobbles;
Nicola turned. Three knights, dressed in chain mail
with swords belted over their green surcoats, plowed
steaming mounts through the frantic crowd. Hugh de
Ocslade and his much larger nephews drew their steeds
to a heaving, dancing halt before the porch steps. She
smiled in relief and certain triumph.

"Say no more," the older nobleman called up to the
abbot. "She is my betrothed."

"This is not possible," Lord Rannulf shouted in angry disbelief.

" 'Twould appear you are mistaken," the churchman
said, his tone superior and snide.

Behind her, FitzHenry drew a ragged breath. "Nay,"
he whispered. "There is no contract."

Hugh de Ocslade dismounted, his nephews choosing
to retain their seats, and Nicola tossed a haughty look
over her shoulder at him. "Ah, but there is. As I
warned you, you will never hold me." This time when
she yanked away her arm, he released her.

"Shall I show you how wrong you are?" he breathed
into her ear.

Before she could move, the big man turned her, his arms closing tightly around her. She was jerked into his embrace, her face forced into the curve of his neck. Nicola splayed her fingers along the broad and unyielding planes of his chest, then shoved. Nothing happened.

"Leave go," Nicola managed to get out, but his collar swallowed her words. His gown had been stored in lavendar; with every breath she tasted its scent. She arched her neck against his restraining hand. His grip on her nape tightened until her head was tucked under his chin. Her cheek fitted into the curve of his throat, and she felt his pulse throbbing against her jaw.

"Lover, I am destroyed." His powerful voice carried the mocking words to every corner of the courtyard. "Did you find my caresses so lacking that you had to seek out another to take my place?" He paused a moment as the commoners recognized his game.

"How shall I convince her of her error?" he asked the crowd, his tone that of a befuddled man. Outside the cocoon of his hold, his audience responded with laughing cries for him to kiss her.

"My lord abbot," Hugh protested, "he is abusing what is mine."

"Free her this instant!" The abbot's command grew shrill as he climbed the stairs toward them, until Nicola could nigh on hear the little churchman breathing at her elbow. She waited for Gilliam's hold on her to relax. It did not.

"Shall I release her?" the big man asked the crowd, his voice congenial and easy.

The commoners' negative reply shook the porch beneath her feet. They shouted and stamped, until the

courtyard rocked with their demand that he kiss the
disputed bride into choosing him.

"Holy Jesus, do it, then, before they riot," the churchman said in irritation.

FitzHenry only called humbly to his audience, "Do
you think a kiss will do the trick? I could not bear to
lose my bride over this, not with us so nearly wed."

At their screams of encouragement, his palm cupped
her skull. The pressure of his hand on her head insisted
she tilt her face up to his. Nicola stiffened her spine,
resisting with all her might, every muscle taut. He'd
not humiliate her this way. She wouldn't allow it.

Hard fingers dug through the thick cushion of her
hair and into her scalp. Slowly, steadily, her head
leaned. When the tip of her nose met his, she glared at
him, her mouth held in a narrow line of hate.

FitzHenry was grinning, but behind that amiable
shield his jaw was so tense it created tight hollows beneath his high cheekbones. His blue eyes shone with
dangerous lights.

Nicola fought a start of fear, then despised herself
for her weakness. "Fool," she hissed, "I am no faint-
hearted female to be cowed—" Her last word disappeared in a gasp as he lay his lips on hers. The crowd
cheered in enjoyment.

His mouth was warm and soft. His lips touched hers,
lifted, then touched again. There was no offensive taste
nor any undue pressure, things Nicola had always assumed accompanied this act. Yet, somehow, this dis-
covery, that kissing was not a brutal bruising of flesh,
was more worrisome than she could have imagined.

When his mouth retreated, it was far enough so that
his lips but grazed hers. His arms were like steel
around her, holding her still when she would have

struggled. "Little girl," he breathed against her skin, "see how tightly I can hold you? If the abbot gives you to that puny strip of flesh, I'll make you his widow by the morrow's dawn and take you uncontested by the next sunset." With that said, he again pressed his mouth to hers.

Nicola was powerless to stop his lips from exploring hers. Every inch of them seemed to touch. How could there be no pain when the intensity of his caress grew? Her breath tangled in her throat, and her skin burned. Heat grew from some hidden source within her, followed by waves of terrible sensation. Frightened to the depths of her soul, Nicola gave voice to a tiny cry.

At the sound FitzHenry released her so suddenly she stumbled back in surprise, her fingers flying to her lips in a belatedly protective gesture. Her mouth felt swollen, and his male taste lingered on her lips. Nicola wiped it away with the back of her hand.

"Murdering pig!" Her voice trembled oddly. She tried again. "Dirty whoreson, I cannot bear your touch."

Her erstwhile bridegroom watched her for a moment, then slowly smiled. This time, there was only amusement in his face. "An interesting choice of words, but I would have thought it was a dirty pig and a murdering whoreson."

The commoners roared and, once again, embarrassment ate Nicola alive. She found strength in it. Aye, he had won this skirmish, but she would still take the day. Armed with new confidence, she turned her back on him.

Hugh yet stood beside his mount, but he'd removed his helmet and pushed back his mail hood, revealing black hair and beard both streaked with silver. He

opened the scrip that hung from his saddle and with-
drew a fold of parchment. 'Twas the contract that he
and her father had drawn up prior to June, the one that
she had refused when she refused Hugh. "My lord abbot, I have brought you my contract to review."

"Come, Lord Ocslade," the abbot called in friendly
invitation. "Show me your parchment."

Nicola could have laughed at the look of triumph on
the abbot's face. All she and Hugh need do was convince the abbot they had exchanged vows. In the
churchman's determination to defy Lord Rannulf,
he would surely ignore the lack of proper seals on the
document Hugh bore.

Lord Rannulf held out an arm to prevent the smaller
man from reaching the stairs. "What he carries cannot
contain my mark, since I have never seen it. Without
my approval, his contract is not valid."

"God's law supersedes man's in this," the abbot
sniffed. "If the betrothal vows have been said, they
must marry."

"You will not trespass on what is my right." Lord
Rannulf's voice held a deadly threat.

"Rannulf," Gilliam called to his brother, his tone
mild, "this has you so hot you cannot think."

Nicola stared over her shoulder at Gilliam, startled
that he was so calm when his brother was on fire. He
graced her with a brief, cool glance that said more than
words. Holy Mother, but he'd do it, he'd kill Hugh and
take her before she could petition the court for her
freedom. She'd not have a chance to prevent their marriage. Panic rose, then Nicola reminded herself to take
only one step at a time. It was useless to worry over
what had yet to happen.

To his brother, Gilliam said, "Come, let the man

show Abbot Simon his contract, whilst you read over his shoulder as my clerk. Geoff will be here at any moment to add his authority to our claims. I want no slur on my ownership of Ashby."

Lord Rannulf made a sound that was nearly a growl, and strode up the stairs to stand near the abbot.

De Ocslade glanced between the two tall men, a slight look of surprise on his face. Nicola knew he was as startled as she had been to learn that Graistan's lord could read. So few in their part of the world did so.

A moment later, Hugh came forward and found a place on the porch between Lord Rannulf and Nicola, a beech flanked by towering oaks. He handed the abbot his document. "There is nothing amiss in what lies on the page, only the lack of Ashby's seal."

"And mine," Lord Rannulf snapped.

"That is not my fault," de Ocslade retorted. "John died on your brother's blade before he had the chance to forward it to you. He meant to add his own seal after your approval. If you disbelieve, Osbert and William here, witnessed our exchange of vows."

"You exchanged vows prior to receiving approval? How very unusual, almost dishonest, one would say." Lord Rannulf's comment dripped scorn.

Nicola leapt in. She'd spent her months of imprisonment concocting answers for all the possible questions he might ask. "You are right, Lord Rannulf, 'twas unusual," she said smoothly, "but my father had been after me for months to accept Hugh. When I finally agreed, Papa insisted on immediately saying the vows, fearing I would change my mind."

The churchman fingered the single wax disk at the parchment's edge, then opened it. Lord Rannulf shifted slightly to read over the abbot's shoulder. While they

did so, Nicola looked at the smaller man who held the
properties to the south of Ashby.

Hugh's head barely topped her shoulder. He shot her
a brief glance, his sharp, sallow features hard with the
same disgust she found reflected in his black eyes.
Nicola looked away and fought a mad desire to laugh.

Of all her suitors, Hugh hated her most. At their last
meeting, she'd blackened his eye and threatened death
after he had tried to force himself upon her. He'd
called her a breastless amazon unworthy of any man's
bed, then told Papa he couldn't wait to marry her. This
was exactly why she'd chosen him for her plan to retain sole ownership of Ashby. If murder needed doing,
she would have no trouble murdering Hugh.

When the silence continued, Hugh spoke to fill the
void. "My Lord Graistan, I do not know if you recall,
but we met some years back. I hold properties along
Ashby's southern border. This makes Lady Nicola's al-
liance with me a profitable one for all concerned, even
yourself. 'Twas for this reason that John of Ashby
begged his daughter to accept me. I was grateful when
Lord Ashby's remarriage finally drove Nicola to find
her own husband in me."

Gilliam's lips brushed her ear, startling Nicola. "You
would spread your legs for this babbling dwarf? Little
girl, my estimation of you has dropped substantially in
the past moments."

Nicola wrenched away only to bump into Hugh. The
smaller man wobbled unsteadily on the edge of the
porch, before catching himself. He shot her an irritable
look, then prattled on. "I realize this comes as a surprise to you, but there is truly nothing remarkable in
either the contract or our joining."

Lord Rannulf gave a grunt of acknowledgment and

continued reading. A moment later he raised his brows in surprise, then looked up at Nicola. "On what date did you share these vows?"

Nicola hesitated, scrambling in her memory for the date that this contract had been drafted. Then she frowned as an alarm bell clanged in the recesses of her memory. He was asking more than just the exact date.

"Come, Lady Ashby," he insisted, "what was the date?"

She hedged. "I cannot recall exactly when, but 'twas at least a week before we came to Graistan for Papa's wedding."

Her overlord nodded slowly, then smiled and turned on the churchman. "My lord abbot, there were no vows spoken, and the girl proves it by her own words. On the day of Lord Ashby's marriage to my ward, Maeve, John complained before myself, my wife, and all my hall that he could get his daughter to accept no man."

Nicola suppressed her flinch. Mary, but how had she forgotten that? She sagged. 'Twas because Papa complained so often about her unmarried state, she'd long since ceased to heed him when he did.

"Now, my lord abbot," Graistan's lord bent an intimidating look onto the churchman, "about my brother's wedding."

Abbot Simon only raised his brows and turned on Gilliam. "My Lord Gilliam, you heard the girl's father say these words?"

Gilliam shook his head. "I was not at Graistan at that time."

The churchman turned back to Lord Rannulf and shrugged in dismissal. "My lord, I find in your words proof of nothing, since there is no one but you here to witness them, whereas this man has witnesses who will say that vows were spoken. I see no reason to dismiss de Ocslade's claim on her. They must be wed."

Nicola's hopes leapt even as her warden's expression froze. She was right. The churchman would uphold the contract no matter what.

Lord Rannulf released a long, slow breath. "This has gone too far. You can be assured my complaints will be forwarded to the bishop." His quiet words were more threatening than a shout. "As for this contract, you will marry my brother to Ashby's heiress as planned. If not, I will hold de Ocslade and his knights prisoner as Gilliam rides from here with the girl. My brother will keep her in secret and without marriage vows until she carries his babe in her belly, rendering moot all question of betrothal or forced marriage. You will not misuse me in this."

"Nay!" Nicola screamed as his trap snapped shut around her.

The need to win free of his control overwhelmed all else. She lunged for Hugh. The smaller man threw up his arms, expecting a facial blow. Instead, her hand curled around his sword's hilt. With a foot planted on his hip, Nicola shoved him to one side, drawing his blade from its scabbard as she moved away from him.

"I think not," Gilliam snapped, as he grabbed her upper arms from behind her.

Nicola growled in frustration and released the half-drawn weapon with a hard push. Overbalanced, Hugh tumbled down the steps, his mail rattling against the stone as he rolled. The horses danced in surprise. Braced against Gilliam's broad chest, Nicola lifted herself and landed a vicious foot in Lord Rannulf's middle. Her warden groaned as he fell into the abbot. The churchman clawed at the baron to steady himself. In doing so, he pulled the bigger man down atop him.

Before they hit the ground, Nicola had her pin out of her mantle and cradled in her palm. She smashed her heel down onto Gilliam's cloth-covered toes. He yelped, his grip relaxing just long enough for her to lurch free. Her mantle fell between them as she whirled, her makeshift weapon held at the ready. With all her might, she slammed it deep into the thick flesh of his shoulder.

"Bitch!" Gilliam roared and reared back, both hands cupped at the wound. Red showed dark against his blue gown. Nicola's stomach leapt in fear. If he caught her now, he'd kill her for sure. She whirled toward the courtyard gate and freedom.

"Come!" Tilda shouted from the courtyard floor.

Nicola sprang without thought. Even as her feet left the porch top, she knew Gilliam was grabbing for her. She felt the rush of air as he missed. Then, he was falling past her, his feet tangled in her mantle.

Yelling in a wild mix of terror and triumph, her skirts hiked well above her knees, Nicola hit the courtyard stones running. Lord Rannulf's men fought their way forward, only to be pushed back as the laughing crowd parted to let her pass. The commoners knew as well as she that a noblewoman's chance of escaping the town was nigh on impossible.

Nicola raced after Tilda, through the abbey's arched gateway, and onto High Street. A man, dressed in a deep yellow gown trimmed in cloth of gold, shouted in surprise as she and Tilda nearly barreled into him. A boy in blue and red stood beside him.

"Fetch her back," the man commanded the two soldiers behind him, but the two girls were already past him on the cloth makers lane, sprinting toward the chandlers sweet-smelling enclave. Nicola glanced behind her. The townsfolk had all tried to exit at once and clogged the gate with their mass. Those soldiers commanded to follow had not been able to do so.

Tilda pulled Nicola around a corner, then tore between a wine merchant's warehouse and a cookshop. The alleyway was so narrow, Nicola could have touched both sides with outstretched elbows. Halfway along the buildings, one of the cookshop's wall beams had curved outward until it touched the building next to it. Save for a small triangular gap near the ground, it seemed the walls met with no space left behind them. Tilda dropped her pack and shoved it through the gap, then fell to her belly and wiggled in after it.

Nicola followed suit. The damp ground reeked of slop and offal. She held her breath, then panicked at the sound of pursuit. The townsfolk were laughing and calling gleefully for the runaway bride, the soldiers were cursing, using the foulest of both French and English obscenities.

Spurred by what would happen if she were caught, Nicola thrust herself past the bend with one powerful push. Tilda yanked her to her feet. Hidden from the street by the bowed beam, they were guarded at the back by some building's rear wall, which was without window or smoke hole. Above them, the slate roof of the warehouse touched the cookshop's thatching. The gap they'd just come through was the only way in or out.

The voices of those who followed grew louder, then faded as they sped on down the lane. Nicola turned to Tilda, her fingers already loosening her gown's laces.

"Hie, open that pack. We've no time to lose. Hurry, turn me into a boy."

Gilliam curled as he fell, taking the brunt of the impact on his uninjured shoulder. He rolled to his knees and leapt up, yanking her pin free of his flesh. The fabric of both his gown and shirt ripped as it exited. Damn that vixen. His best gown was truly ruined. He started forward only to be stopped by the roiling mass of humankind fighting its way through the abbey gates.

"Alfred, hie and see the main gate shut," he shouted to the soldiers battering their way through the mob. He trusted his powerful voice to carry over the commotion. "Robert, you are for the postern."

Even if his bride reached the town's portals before they shut, the gatekeepers would not let her pass. An unescorted noblewoman was as rare as a horned horse. In that instant, Gilliam forgave her the attempt. This escape had ruined de Ocslade's plot to steal Ashby from him. Gilliam need only shut the gates and drive her from her lair. Ashby was his.

Rannulf leapt down the steps to stand beside him. A muddy footprint now marred his brother's rich attire. "Damn that idiot vixen," he snarled. "Where does she think she can go to hide from me in my own town?"

"Uncle!" cried one of de Ocslade's companions as he dismounted to aid his relative in rising. "Are you injured?"

"Nay," the small knight snarled. His horse reared suddenly, gone skittish with the excitement. De Ocslade grabbed for its reins. "Stupid bitch!" It was anyone's guess whether he meant the girl or his horse.

"Vile woman," the abbot shouted to the heavens above, then flew down the steps to de Ocslade. " 'Tis the last time I seek to intervene on behalf of the spawn of Eve. Here," he shoved the parchment at the knight. It fell between them and lay neglected on the muddy stones. "Take it to some other churchman, and get you gone from my house. Be gone, be gone all of you!" he screamed, revealing the extent to which his pride had been damaged.

Gilliam glanced at the gate. Geoffrey, now finely attired, was striding toward them. Jocelyn trotted at his heels, wearing a short blue tunic over red chausses. His cloak was clutched tightly around him against the day's chill, his nose already reddening. The boy lacked the bulk to protect him from the cold.

Rannulf turned on de Ocslade. "I want you and your kin off my lands. Leave now. Arnult, follow them," he called to his castellan. "See to it they are allowed to exit from the gate."

The small nobleman glanced from one FitzHenry to the other, then acknowledged the arrival of a third. "My lord sheriff," he said in greeting to Geoffrey, a smile tugging at the corners of his narrow mouth. "Lord Graistan, believe me when I say I leave you with all haste and joy in my heart. This event has spared me a terrible mistake. Keep the vixen," he offered to Gilliam, "and may you survive your wedding night with no more than that pinprick."

De Ocslade mounted and roweled his horse into a turn, leaving the contract yet in the mud at his feet. His nephews followed as they left the abbey far more slowly than they had entered.

Gilliam stared after them. The nobleman was too smug for either defeat or enlightenment. He looked down at the ruined parchment. Why come when he had no seals on the contract? No man was that sort of fool.

His eyes narrowed. It must be that de Ocslade not only knew Nicola would elude capture, he was positive she would run to him; he was retreating to their meeting point.

Damn, but if Gilliam could not find her first, Hugh would sweep Nicola beyond his reach. As Rannulf suggested, with a babe in her belly, no one would squabble over who her husband was. Gilliam turned to his brothers.

"Somehow, de Ocslade believes he already owns the vixen. I think this was the plot from the start. This contract was but a diversion." He kicked at the sodden parchment. "Did you see how his kin made no attempt to stop her as she ran?"

"Did they not? Well, I did." Geoff looked from one brother to the other, his eye gleaming in suppressed amusement. "Gilliam, there's blood on your shoulder. Rannulf, what happened to your gown? I seem to have missed some awesome event."

"Laugh, Geoff, and I'll take your other eye," Rannulf snarled. "Gilliam, no spoiled, devious child is going to steal from me what I have given you. Find her. If de Ocslade has her, besiege the stinking place, knowing that I will support you in your efforts. If you catch her first, take her to Ashby and close your gates until your firstborn has teeth. But no matter what occurs, I never want to see her again." He turned and stormed toward the gate.

Both Jocelyn and Geoffrey turned to watch Lord Graistan leave the abbey. When Geoff swung his gaze back toward his younger sibling, there was yet a trace of a smile on his face. "How did she manage this escape? She nearly ran me down as we were entering the gate."

"With her foot and her pin." Gilliam displayed the item in his palm. He would keep it as a reminder of how dangerous she could be. Giving his anger sharp rein, he mellowed his voice. "Come, Jocelyn," he said to the boy. "I will give you your first lesson: how to hunt runaway wives."

Geoff's hand closed over the boy's shoulder as he propelled him toward his new master. "My apologies if I cannot stay to help, but I must return to Crosswell."

"Have no fear, Jos will do fine in your stead." Gilliam laid his arm around the child's bony shoulders.

"My name is 'Jocelyn,' " he muttered.

Gilliam grinned, pleased by this show of spine. "Geoff, you may tell the boy's worried mama that I promise not to break her son whilst he is my squire."

Chapter Four

The soldiers became huntsmen, seeking to flush the hiding doe. Their search began at Graistan keep's outer walls and moved in an even line toward the town's defenses. Every building was entered, every corner explored, before they took the next step toward the walls.

In their hidey-hole, Nicola crouched, her thigh muscles burning, so Tilda could finish her hair. She listened with growing nervousness to the hue and cry. They were close, now, very close. "Hurry, Tilda, we haven't much longer," she urged quietly, her English words bearing not a breath of her Norman ancestry.

" 'Tis done," the girl replied as she handed Nicola her dagger. "Put on your hood, and I'll go check the lane."

Nicola sheathed her weapon in her belt and stood, her head feeling as if it floated far above her shoulders. Her newly bared neck prickled with sudden exposure to the cold, damp air. When she shook her head, the cropped ends of her hair danced against her jaw. As impossible as it seemed, the stuff was even curlier now that it was short. Nicola ran her fingers through it, then glanced sadly down at the thick mass around her feet.

Oh, what had she done? Her hair was her most feminine feature, the only thing to counteract her boyish figure and plain face. She dismissed her moment of weakness and pulled on her brown capuchin. This simple garment was but a hood with an extended hem that reached past her shoulders. With it pulled low over her brow, her face would be disguised. Nicola smiled wryly at that thought, dropping the hood back between her shoulder blades. With her hair gone, why should she bother hiding her face? No one would ever guess she was a woman.

Against her skin she wore a worn linen shirt, the fabric gone soft with use. On her legs were a pair of brown chausses, a combination of stockings and undergarment that served all men. If the chausses required crisscrossing strips of cloth from knee to ankle to keep from sagging down to her feet, they bound indecently around her hips and thighs. This was decidedly uncomfortable for one accustomed to the freedom of nothing beneath wide skirts.

Atop her undergarments, she wore an old tunic. Once a deep green, it had long since faded into a pale memory of its former richness. She'd had to fold back the sleeves, but its hem hit her just where it should, a hand's breadth above her knees. Finally, there was a hauberk, a sleeveless leather vest thick enough to hide what little feminine roundness Nicola could claim.

For shoes, there was a pair of short and sturdy boots. A sensible choice, save that Nicola discovered upon donning them they were a tad too small and pinched her feet. She glanced longingly at the fine slippers she'd worn beneath her gowns. Impossible. Not only were they obviously a noblewoman's footwear, they were too flimsy to survive the walk. She sighed. Seeing as she had no other option, she would have to bear the pain.

Tilda called softly under the bend of the wall, "Come now."

As Nicola squeezed back beneath the bent panel, muck smeared onto the skirt of her tunic. She came to her feet with a sharp sound of disgust, and tried to brush off the ooze. It was useless and only left her hands dirty. She gave up and joined Tilda at the end of the alley. "Have they turned the corner?"

"Not yet." Tilda shot Nicola a quick glance from over her shoulder, then caught herself to look again. She gasped and came fully around. "Colette!"

"What?" Nicola cried, and glanced over her shoulder, thinking Tilda has seen something awful, like a rat.

"You," the small girl said, more harshly this time. "Pull up that hood, then keep it as far down on your brow as you can."

"What?" This time it was a question of confusion, rather than concern.

"Do as I say, Colette, and do not argue." There was sudden steel in Tilda's voice. "If you want free of this place, you'll walk like a humpback and not move that hood off your forehead until we are a league distant. Ask me no more, we must hurry." Her friend's voice became progressively colder as she spoke.

Nicola frowned, but did as Tilda said. Even after a lifetime together, she had yet to fully understand her suckling sister's moods. They blinked on and off, like the sun on a day when the sky was full of woolly clouds.

She followed her friend around the corner. At the top of the tiny street, there was a soldier. Nicola hunched her shoulders and shuffled alongside Tilda in an appropriately servile gait. The man did no more than glance at them as they passed.

Nicola's spirits soared. This was going to work; she would be free. Once past the gates, she could make her way to Ocslade, marry and dispose of him, then . . .

Then Gilliam would marry her. Or the Church would take custody of her. Or, worse, the royal court would make her its ward and suck the life from her home to feed England's aching treasury. How could she allow any of these things to happen to her folk?

Her plans died in the face of reality. Holding Ashby as her own was nothing more than a child's fantasy, devised to fill her need for revenge and help pass her empty hours of confinement. No man would ever allow it.

Nicola stubbornly shook her head, refusing even to listen to herself. She hadn't sacrificed her precious hair only to admit defeat moments later. The plan would work, it simply had to. What sort of daughter allowed herself to be married to her father's murderer?

Beside her, Tilda laughed quietly. "He did not even raise a brow, the fool," she murmured. "How he will hate himself when he realizes we walked right beneath his nose."

"Tilda, this is no game," Nicola snapped, not so much irritated at the girl as at her own doubts. "My freedom hangs in the balance, yet all you can think of is tweaking a soldier."

Her friend shot her a harsh look. "Best be nice to me, Colette. I need only call out your name, and you are a prisoner, once more."

"Tilda!" Stunned, Nicola stopped to stare. There was nothing new in Tilda's disrespect; the commoner had never behaved as a maid toward her mistress. This was Nicola's fault for seeing Tilda as more sister than servant. It was the new hardness in the girl's tone that shook her.

"My tongue got away from me," Tilda replied with a sarcastic half bow, then rolled her eyes. "Do stop staring. You know very well I dare not do it. Stabbing a lord may mean only a beating for you, but 'twill be far worse for me if we are caught." She turned and continued on toward the gate, her hips undulating gently beneath her thick skirts.

Nicola started after her, hurt and confused by this new, harsh behavior. What could have happened to so change the girl? Any answer would have to wait until they were beyond the town wall and could talk freely. She lengthened her stride until she caught up to Tilda, but their walk to the gate was completed with an uncomfortable wall of silence between them.

The exit portal from Graistantown was only a square gap in the thick wall, framed by a small tower at either side. It was in these that the machinery of the portcullis was housed. The metal grate yet dangled aloft on its chains, but the thick wooden doors were tightly shut.

A number of people were already congregated on the wide, cobbled area that fronted the doors, muttering impatiently to each other. Nicola and Tilda found their way to the far edge of the crowd. Although some folk glanced at them, no one looked for long. There was nothing interesting to note about two young commoners.

Nicola caught a whiff of stewing mutton on the damp breeze and her stomach growled. It was useless to think of eating. Her purse, a leather pouch dangling from her belt, was just as empty as her stomach. The walk to Ocslade would not only be wet and cold, but hungry, as well.

The coarse wool of her hood prickled against her bare neck. Nicola lifted her shoulders and turned her head as she tried to ease it, but to no avail. She reached inside her capuchin to scratch her neck.

"Stop fooling with that thing. You're pushing the hood off your face," Tilda hissed in irritation, then raised herself on tiptoe to peer over the crowd. "Where is he?" she murmured to herself.

"Who?"

"The man who will take us away from Graistan, goose. Well, we are early. It did not take as long as I thought to change you." Tilda stared out at the crowd.

Nicola could only gape at her friend in sick disbelief. "You told someone about me?" Not just someone, some man.

"Aye, and glad I am I did so, Colette. 'Twill be easier if we pass through yon door as two men and a woman."

"How could you have betrayed me so?" she cried softly.

"Betrayed, is it?" Tilda turned on her, hands on hips and eyes narrowed. "Are you not free of that wedding you so despised and on the path into marriage with de Ocslade?" An errant breeze, filled with the reek of urban life, teased a tawny strand from beneath Tilda's gray hood.

"Aye, but only for the moment," Nicola retorted. "How do I know this man of yours will not give me back to Graistan?"

Tilda shot her an arch look, then shrugged confidently. "For love of me, of course. Have faith. Alan will see you safely to your destination." She paused, then made a show of shuddering.

"Oh, Colette, why did you choose that little viper when you had other, more simpleminded suitors to pick? If you think Hugh de Ocslade will stand still whilst you carve him to bits, you are wrong. He all too well remembers how you misused him." Tilda made a sharp sound of disgust, shoving her hair back beneath her capuchin. "Choose another man."

Nicola laughed harshly, the sound ringing against the stone wall behind them. "Nay, Hugh suits my purposes too well. With him bleeding his own properties dry to live beyond himself, greed drives him to me. 'Tis his lust for my lands that makes him vulnerable to my knife. If his nephews give me pause, it is only that I must plan their fates as well." She would make this work by force of her will alone.

"Well, I think you a fool to have ever contacted that little snake." The comment was thrown over Tilda's shoulder as she again scanned the crowd. "Ah, here is Alan now."

Nicola followed Tilda's gaze and groaned.

Leading a flea-bitten nag of uncertain ancestry, a helmet and undecorated shield hanging from its saddle, came a soldier. Dark hair flowed down to his shoulders, framing a bold face and thick beard. There was a good deal of pride in the set of his shoulders, but his armor was no more than a boiled leather vest, thickly sewn with iron rings until it gleamed and jingled with every step. He was either a mercenary or some small landholder's by-blow looking to make his way in the world. If there were a way to get coins for her, Nicola knew he would trade her in an instant.

"Tilda, how could you," she breathed in heartbreak.

The girl grabbed the sides of Nicola's hood and pulled her face down to whisper to her. "Listen closely. He thinks I am from the hamlet to the northwest of here for I was returning to Graistan from Ocslade when I met him on the road. You are my very shy brother, Nicolas, the cloth merchant's new apprentice or so I told him. We journey home this day to visit our dying mother. Twit, I have not revealed your identity to anyone. 'Tis only right I let you stew in thoughts of betrayal. I should be insulted."

Nicola's eyes flew wide in relief and understanding. "And I should kick you, you little brat," she said, half laughing, half angry. Then, she sighed in apology. "Imprisonment has left me overly suspicious and irritable. My pardon for doubting you."

There was a glimmer of something sad in Tilda's brown eyes, and her gay smile lay slightly crooked on her mouth. "Aye, we are friends for always, no matter what happens between us."

"Tilda, what is wrong?" Nicola asked in worry, laying a hand on her friend's shoulder.

The girl only shook free of her. "This talk must wait for later. Now, be shy, brother, very shy, and only glance at him from time to time." With that warning, she turned to greet the soldier.

Self-preservation made Nicola duck her head and hunch her shoulders, twisting her hands together as if she worried. She peered around the edge of her hood. Alan was bowing low before the petite girl.

"Ah, Tilda the beautiful, here you are waiting for me." His English was accented, but it was the accent of one who pretended to be what he was not. He turned toward Nicola. "And here is your brother. Well met, boy."

"Well met, sir," she mumbled, nodding her head in greeting. When his horse shifted toward her, she gratefully hid against its mangy neck. "Hold your steed?" she offered, making her voice gruff.

"How kind of you," the man said as if startled by the offer, "but there's no call for that."

"My brother wants to do it in thanks for escorting us from Graistantown, Alan," Tilda said sweetly. "My goodness, but even I had forgotten how shy he was. I haven't had more than ten words out him since I arrived yesterday. I do hope you'll not mistake his silence for rudeness while we journey."

Nicola stifled her urge to rear upright and scream her questions. Tilda had arrived only yesterday? If she'd not lived at Graistan these past four months, where had she been? Yet, all she dared do was peer carefully above the horse's mane.

Tilda was leaning up against the man, her hand caressing his arm. Alan's expression was glazed with his lust for the girl. Nicola's concern died away beneath bitter amusement. Men were such fools for Tilda. They never saw how the girl used them until she discarded them when they began to bore her.

"You are still traveling with us, are you not?" the little vixen purred.

"Aye, I've had no luck finding a place here," Alan replied, his voice growing husky with masculine need. "I look forward to your companionship to help ease my lonely journey."

Nicola coughed. 'Twasn't loneliness he wanted to ease. Nay, not at all.

From the lane behind them came the echoes of French words. Nicola glanced up, gasped, then caught

Alan's steed by the bridle to draw it closer and bury her head against its neck.

"My lord, I cannot thank you enough. As you well know, 'tis my sworn duty to see that commerce is not halted. Aye, the town could ill afford that."

Gilliam groaned to himself as he strode toward the gate, Jocelyn following at his heels. The headman of the town council trotted heavily alongside them. On an average day, the man's voice grated on his nerves. Today, the courvesier's prattling was too much to endure.

"While we merchants want you to know we understand what you've lost is equally as precious, I think both our needs can be served without harm to either. Aye, if the gatekeeper interviews each person who leaves, your quarry will not slip through undiscovered."

"Enough said," Gilliam snapped, "you asked, I agreed."

"Aye, aye, so you did, my—" The man fell suddenly silent as Gilliam speared him with his gaze. They crossed the small apron of cobbles to the portal.

"Alfred," Gilliam said to the soldier standing beside the gatekeeper, "be my translator. Tell him he may open one door. He must ask of those he does not know who they are and where they go. All carts and wagons must be thoroughly searched. If he doubts any answer, he should call for me. I will be atop the gate tower watching all who leave. After you've told him this, go and tell our searchers to bring their reports here to the gate."

"Aye, my lord," the man said, and began to speak to the gatekeeper in his native tongue.

Gilliam turned toward one of the towers, then

stopped. Across the yard stood an armed man. Although there was no comparison between the armor and horse Gilliam owned and that of this poor soul's, he saw in this mercenary a reflection of what could have been for himself. Without Rannulf's generosity, Gilliam would also be doomed to drift from great house to great house, looking for work.

"Jocelyn, this way," Gilliam said quietly to the lad. Drawn to the hapless knight by the potential of a shared fate, he closed the distance between them.

At the knight's side stood a petite woman. She was pretty in the way of an overblown rose, still beautiful, but doomed to fade. The girl boldly eyed him, her gaze filled with the same calculation a whore used while gauging the highest possible payment she could wring from a man. So, the knight pandered his woman to make an extra coin or two. 'Twas most likely a necessity in this case.

"Come offering to hire, have you?" Gilliam asked the tattered warrior over the creak of the gate door moving.

"Aye, my lord, but the house is closed," the man replied. His atrocious French made Gilliam take a second look. So, this was not a nobleman's extra son, but a common soldier seeking to raise himself into a higher position. That the man owned a horse spoke well of him. Keeping even the meanest steed was an expensive proposition.

"Aye, it is, and so it will remain until February. If you are traveling north, our sheriff presently visits here. He has been looking for men."

"My thanks for the suggestion, but I promised to return to my last position if I had no luck at Graistan." The man bowed briefly, neither fawning nor arrogant, then offered a smile. "By your leave, we'll be departing then, my lord."

Gilliam glanced over his shoulder at the gate. The courtyard was already empty. Those who waited to exit were all townsmen, well-known to the gatekeeper. Meaning to bid the man a good journey, Gilliam looked back at him and caught sight of the boy behind the horse.

His estimation of the soldier rose yet again. All appearances aside, this must be quite a man if he was rich enough to support a woman, horse, and a lad to act as servant. Although quite tall, the boy seemed a meek one, with a hunchback and hanging head, but his clothing reflected well upon his master. Gilliam stared a moment at the boy's gown. It was a faded green, the sort of color a garment took after it had been worn until truly comfortable. It reminded him of a tunic he'd once owned; he'd been sorry to outgrow that one.

"Good journey," Gilliam offered with a nod. "Come, Jocelyn." He set his hand on his squire's scrawny shoulder and started toward the gatehouse tower. The boy preceded him up the spiraling stairs. Gilliam rubbed the soreness from his shoulder as he climbed. Blood had clotted in his shirt, and the linen clung uncomfortably to his skin.

The tower opened up onto a narrow stone pathway atop the wall. A damp, cold wind moaned around him, crying a warning of winter's coming as it stung his face and tousled his hair. Jocelyn crouched down beneath one of the defensive upthrusts of stone that capped the wall like giant teeth and caught his cloak tightly around him. Gilliam came to lean against another.

Spreading out below him was the peaceful pattern of

civilization his brother's sword protected. The fields now alternated between the golden stubble of grain and the darker hue of plowed earth. Vineyards and orchards were nothing but horny branches, the occasional withered fruit gleaming jewel-bright against the dark wood.

Gilliam let his gaze wander along the road that snaked away from the walls, over a small hill, then into Rannulf's forest lands. Those few folks unlucky enough to have to travel on this day were moving briskly to keep warm.

"My lord?"

He glanced down at the lad. Once again, the boy sat with a most unchildlike stillness. "Aye, Jocelyn?"

"Why do you want me?" The bitter question made the boy's face twist into an expression of scornful curiosity and something more.

'Twas that unknown factor that made Gilliam check a glib answer about doing Geoff's bidding, for one more oblique and gentle. "As a knight, 'tis my duty to train the sons of my fellow noblemen to become knights as well."

"I am but your duty?" Jocelyn stared sourly away from him along the wall walk.

"That is not precisely what I said, but even if I had, duty is no horrible thing. Without it as part of our lives, how would we know what was expected of us?" Gilliam squatted down beside the boy, this conversation suddenly held great import for himself and the boy. "It is an honor to be asked to care for another man's son. When you are knighted, 'twill be my success as well as yours."

"You will have no success with me, my lord. I cannot be a knight. Lord Coudray would not heed either me or my lady mother, even when she prostrated her-

self before him, pleading for my very life." The child
lifted his gaze to stare with a martyr's eyes toward the
sky. "I am too frail for this life. Becoming your squire
will kill me."

"You have no doubt of this?" Gilliam asked quietly,
his tone reflecting neither his surprise nor his amusement at the boy's assertion.

"Aye. I will soon fall ill and death will take me. You
will see." 'Twas almost a threat.

"You do not look as if you ail, save that you are too
thin. There's color in your face."

" 'Tis but windburn on my face," Jocelyn claimed in
all seriousness. "See, look here." He stretched out his
arm and shoved up his tunic sleeve to display its bony
length. "There is naught to me but pale skin and bone."

Gilliam shook his head. "I see an arm like any other.
You do not convince me."

"Are you blind?" Jocelyn retorted in outrage.

"Jocelyn!" Gilliam's bellow shook the walls around
him as he leapt to his feet and glared down at the boy.
"Has someone forgotten to teach you manners? If you
dare to address me so rudely once again, you'll not
only hear my wrath, you'll feel it as well."

Jocelyn's eyes were great round circles in his chalky
face. His lower lip trembled. "My mother would not
like it if you beat me," he warned in a reedy whisper.

"Fie on you for standing behind your mother's
skirts," Gilliam chided, his voice as hard as his sword.
He was impressed that the boy had not dissolved to
tears. "If you choose to misbehave, be man enough to
take the punishment for your actions. What sort of
knight hides behind a woman? A coward, that's what."

For all his fear, the boy was not yet beaten. "I was
not fated to become a knight. I was meant for the

Church," he protested quietly. " 'Tis not fair that you force this upon me."

In Gilliam grew the certainty that behind the odd outward demeanor there lurked a normal lad. It was greatly reassuring; his chore would be to peel back the layers and reveal the child hiding beneath behaviors others had given him.

"You are right," Gilliam conceded, " 'tis not fair that your father and brother have died. That is a terrible thing. Nonetheless, you are now Freyne's heir and must become both knight and lord. Take heart, lad, you do not go alone into this future. 'Tis my job to help you become the man you must be."

Jocelyn blinked away his tears; the sullenness in his face dimmed a little. "My pardon for my rudeness, Lord Ashby. I hope you find your wife." It was a quiet, but gracious concession.

"Why, thank you, Jos, but we must find her together," Gilliam said, very pleased by what they had accomplished in so short a time. He again turned his attention back to the road.

The soldier and his little party were halfway between wall and forest now. Apparently, the gatekeeper had been satisfied with all their answers. The man yet led his horse, choosing to walk alongside his woman. Even from here, Gilliam knew they smiled to each other as they chatted.

Head down, the tall lad held himself apart from them, his gait stilted, as if his feet hurt. With so impoverished a master, 'twas possible the child had outgrown his shoes and there wasn't coin enough to replace them.

Gilliam stared idly at them until they entered the forest. Only after they'd disappeared behind the screen of

barren trees did jealousy rise in him. That simple soldier had what he could never own: a woman who cared
for him. He shoved that impossible wish back within
him, where it belonged.

"Who are you watching?"

Gilliam turned in surprise to find Rannulf standing
behind him, now dressed in his mail and surcoat with
spurs and sword buckled on. His musing had been so
deep, he hadn't heard his brother climb the stairs.

"A mercenary and his woman," he replied to the
man who was in truth more father than brother to him.
"Jocelyn, greet my brother, Lord Graistan. He was too
angry to meet you earlier. Lord Graistan, this is my
new squire, Jocelyn, heir to Freyne."

To Gilliam's astonishment, Jocelyn thrust out his
hand and met Rannulf's gaze. "I am pleased to make
your acquaintance, my Lord Graistan," he said politely.

"And I yours, son," Rannulf replied, gifting the lad
with a smile. "As part of my brother's family, you become part of mine. Well come. Now, I must borrow
your lord for a moment." With a nod of his head,
Rannulf released Jos's hand to walk a short distance
along the wall top. Gilliam followed. "So, Gilliam, are
you still set on keeping that ruined manor and a wife
who wishes you dead?"

"Rannulf, I have had enough of this discussion. My
heart is set on Ashby for mine own reasons. You cannot dissuade me."

"I relent then. But know I cannot bear you torturing
yourself over the past." Rannulf lay a hand upon his
shoulder and smiled, gray eyes clear of the bitterness
that had haunted their relationship until only recently.
"So, have you found yourself a wife, yet?"

"Nay." Gilliam allowed himself a wry smile. "However, you may thank me for my good works. I've found you two thieves and one poor serf escaping his rural master. As this gate is the only one open and no tall women have exited, she must yet be within these walls."

"My lord?" Walter's head appeared above the stairwell.

Both noblemen turned. Gilliam called, "What have you found?"

"This." He stepped out onto the tower roof, Nicola's gowns fluttering like pennants in his hand. Great gouts of filth marred them, leaving them utterly ruined. "And this," he opened his other hand and a long, dark coil of hair streamed out from his fingers.

Gilliam drew a sharp breath, then whirled to look past the road to the dense forest beyond it. The boy who was his bride was no longer within sight. He turned to Rannulf, unsure whether he should scream in rage or jump for joy. He had found and lost her in the same instant. "Damn her, but she's wearing my tunic," he shouted.

"What?" Rannulf cried. "No—she didn't—not even that vixen could be so brash." His face twisted at the repulsive thought of a girl dressed as a man. "You wish to wed this—creature?"

"No matter how she dresses, she is still Lady Ashby, and Ashby will be mine. Damn, but she walked out right beneath my nose, with me staring at her because her garment reminded me of one I'd had at fifteen." He grabbed his brother by the arms. "Because it *is* the same tunic.

"Jos, come with me," Gilliam called as he raced down the stairs, Rannulf and Walter on his heels. He stopped in the courtyard.

"Gatekeeper, open your gates, our bird has flown," he shouted, then waved to a man to translate for him. "Walter, gather our men and have the horses saddled. Jos and I will be ready to ride as soon as we are free of our finery."

"You will want your armor," Walter began, but Gilliam stopped him with a brusque shake of his head.

"Nay, there's not time for me to arm. Have one of the men pack my mail for me. Bring also whatever decent clothing the lady has left behind in her cell. I suspect she'll have a need for them when I find her."

"Why not let me send a man to fetch her back for you." Rannulf's tone was somewhere between a suggestion and a command.

"Nay," Gilliam gave a brief and scornful laugh. "Go, Walter," he said, signaling his man away before explaining to his brother. "Rannulf, I have had enough of your life with its politics and churchmen who reach beyond themselves. Let me collect my wife and be on my journey home. When we arrive at Ashby, the priest can wed us, doing the job just as securely as any other churchman."

"What makes you think she'll wed you at Ashby when she refused you here?" Rannulf raised a brow in question.

"The villagers accept me as their lord. I think that even if I had to bind and gag her, nodding her head at all the right places, they would aid me in seeking to make me their legal master. If they will not, I will keep her as you suggested, until she bears my child." Gilliam shrugged, but there was nothing comfortable about what he proposed. Forcing himself upon her would hardly win from Lady Ashby the cooperation he so desired.

"Now, if you are still offering favors, you could send a man to your foresters. Have him tell the woodland folk to mark the passage of a party of three: a woman, one tall boy in faded green and a man dressed in *cuir-boilli,* with a poor steed. They should not try to stop them, else she might be driven to run. At the party's present pace, 'twill be an hour or more before they reach our borders and meet up with de Ocslade."

"Easily done."

As Rannulf spoke to his man, Gilliam stared out through the open gate, wondering if he should kill or thank the soldier who led Nicola from the walls. Whether an accomplice or an innocent, if not for that man Gilliam would never have noticed the "boy" or the tunic. He smiled suddenly, impressed by the sheer audacity of Lady Ashby's attempt. No other woman would have had the daring to try it.

"Is that all you need, boy?" Rannulf asked him.

Still grinning, Gilliam patted his elder and shorter brother on the cheek. "My thanks, old man, it is. Go home to your mild, sweet wife, Rannulf, and leave me to mine. I can see I have a far way to go if I'm ever to win from her what I need."

His brother mounted and reined in his big horse as it danced beneath him, anxious to be away. "By the by, I have six marks that say she'll do worse than a pinprick in her first week."

"What! You bet against me?! I have twelve that say you are wrong," Gilliam retorted with a laugh.

"Done," his brother called back as he set spurs to his steed and galloped out the gate.

"Will she really kill you, my lord?" Jos's question had more of awe than fear in it.

"I hope not," Gilliam replied, still smiling. "Come, we must change into our riding attire. In less than an hour's time, I will have me a bride, and we'll be bound for home."

Chapter Five

Nicola's neck ached from keeping her head bowed and her feet were fair torn to bits by her shoes. Blisters were already forming on her heels and toes. The right boot had a tiny tag of leather along its upper that gouged deeper into her flesh with every step. She glanced up the road. Pain made her slow. Alan and Tilda were now far ahead of her, Tilda perched happily atop the nag.

Jealous hurt seethed in her stomach. After four months of separation from anyone the slightest bit friendly toward her, Nicola desperately needed Tilda's company. Trapped within her was a whole river of thoughts and images, all of which clamored for spilling but only to someone who understood her.

So, too, did Nicola need to hear her friend's tale. She longed to know what it was that brought on Tilda's brief sadness. Instead, Nicola's every attempt at communication had been rebuffed. From the moment they had left the gate, Tilda had kept her attention focused on Alan, as if she truly desired the soldier.

Nicola glowered impatiently at her friend's back as the couple rounded a bend in the road. Although the trees were barren, they grew so densely that the two-some completely disappeared from her view. She released a huff of anger. Friends shouldn't let a man come between them, she thought bitterly.

As Nicola neared the curve, she caught the echo of thundering hooves. A frantic leap sent her sliding across the muddy road and into a thicket. Thorny branches offered little in the way of a shield, but she crouched, rabbit-still, behind the brambles and prayed to remain unnoticed.

Lord Graistan and a few men galloped past, looking neither to the left nor right. A moment later and nothing remained of them save the deep tracks of horseshoes in the muck. Nicola came to her feet and grinned. If they were not scouring the roadside for some sign of her, they must yet believe she was within the town walls.

All thought of Tilda's foolish game with Alan was forgotten in the face of this triumph. Nicola hobbled back onto the roadbed, where she turned an exhilarated pirouette. At long last, John of Ashby's daughter was free!

The need to share her victory with someone was so strong, Nicola forgot her aching feet. She forced herself into a trot, her hood flying off her head as she ran. By the time she rounded the bend, she was panting against the pain.

Before her, the road moved away in a long, straight line, as devoid of life as the skeleton bushes that lined it. She stopped in surprise. Where were Alan and Tilda? Nicola held her place, waiting to see if the couple had also sought refuge while the nobleman passed. No one appeared from the thickets.

Concern nagged at her. With her hand on her dagger's hilt, she started slowly forward. The occasional twitter of winter birds died away into a harsh silence

broken only by the rattle of empty branches in the
wind. Her cheeks stung with the cold as the mist became an icy drizzle.

"Tilda?" she called out.

Alan stepped out of the bushes. "Ah, there you are,"
he said, his voice overly hearty in the quiet woods. He
stopped as if startled, then stared at her and laughed.
"Why, *boy,* you've just extended your life some.
Where I thought I'd caught me only a whore and a useless lad, I find instead the prettiest man I've ever met."

"Pretty? What are you prattling about and where is
my sister?" Nicola retorted, unable to make sense of
his words. Then, the cold breeze lifted her curls, reminding her that her hood had fallen.

"One such as you should not claim a relationship
with that little slut," he said, speaking in his horrible
French. "Come, Lady Ashby. Let me keep you safe
from harm until your husband pays your ransom."

Nicola stared at him, too stunned by the fact he'd
seen through her disguise to recognize his threat of
kidnap. "My pardon," she said gruffly in English, "I
do not speak your language."

"Now, now," he replied, still insisting on using her
native tongue, "do drop this ridiculous pretense. So
comely a lass as you shouldn't try to hide as a man.
Come quietly and you'll not be hurt."

Nicola's eyes narrowed as rage burned again within
her belly. This commoner thought to take from her the
freedom she had worked so hard to gain. Noblemen,
churchmen, even a commoner, they all thought they
could tell her what to do simply because they were
men and she was not.

"Peasant," she snarled in French, "you overstep
yourself if you think you can keep me where Lord

Graistan could not." She snatched her dagger from her belt and held it at the ready before her. "You'll give me my friend and let us pass unharmed, or I'll carve you like a goose."

"Ladies should not play with knives," Alan warned, his tone patronizing. He reached for her dagger and snatched back a bloody hand. "Damn you, you've sliced my palm clean through," he cried, yet too surprised by her attack to feel pain. "Cease this foolishness and give me that knife." He clumsily threw himself at her.

Nicola laughed in scorn. Did he think she'd stand still whilst he took her down? With a leg, she swept his feet out from beneath him. As he fell she brought the hilt of her dagger down on the back of his unhelmeted head. It met his skull with a satisfying thunk. He dropped, face first, into the mud.

With a foot braced on his back, Nicola threw aside her dagger and snatched his blade from his scabbard. The feel of his sword in her hands gave her a wondrous rush of confidence. She stepped back and prodded him with his own blade. "Get up, peasant, and take me to Tilda."

He came to his knees, beard full of mud, his eyes slightly glazed. "Well, do not simply watch her, you fools!" he shouted in English, spewing muck from his mouth. "We must subdue her, but be you gentle. If her bones are broken, the noblemen will kill us instead of paying for her."

Nicola drew a sharp breath as the road was suddenly alive with shouting, ragged men. Some wore bits of leather armor, the others were cloth hauberks, well stuffed to deflect blows. All of them had weapons, daggers, rusted swords, or sharpened staves. Six, there were, not counting Alan, and so filthy that Nicola could smell them as they drew nearer to her. The biggest one held a bruised and disheveled Tilda by the arm.

"Tilda!" Nicola cried out in concern.

Her friend did not even glance at her, instead the girl turned toward Alan. "Listen to what I say," she commanded. "Lord Ocslade will pay you not only for her, but for me, as well."

"Who is this Ocslade?" Alan the thief master asked, cradling his injured hand against his body. "I thought Graistan's brother was to marry her."

"Lord Ocslade is the one who came this morn to halt the wedding." Tilda's voice held a trace of desperation. "He is closer and easier to approach than Graistan, but you cannot reach him without me, for only I know where he waits."

"Waits?" Nicola cried in disbelief. How could Hugh know anything of their plans, when they'd been made only this morn? Her heart broke when Tilda shot her a bleak glance. It clearly said that Nicola's escape had been by Hugh's design. If not for this interruption, de Ocslade would have had the advantage of surprise, rendering Nicola helpless against him.

"Alan, you must listen," the girl insisted again, struggling against her captor's hold. "Lord Ocslade will pay whatever sum you ask for Lady Ashby. Let me fetch him here for you."

Alan only sneered at her. "Why, little whore, you were hot enough to share my bed only moments ago. Do I now sense you wish to escape the lovely winter we have planned for you? I have a better idea. Why do you not stay here, whilst I find this nobleman of yours? Once I have his ear, I will ask if he truly wishes to buy both a bride and a whore."

"Nay," Tilda shouted, and swung helplessly at the heavy man who held her.

"Stay still now," her captor said, his words as ponderous as he. He curled his fist and seemed to only tap Tilda's jaw. The girl reeled, then dropped quietly into the bracken.

Rage overtook Nicola as Tilda fell. No matter what the girl had done, Tilda and her kin were the closest thing to family Nicola had left. "Nay, I'll not let you have her to abuse!"

Alan signaled casually to his men. "Take that blade from her."

As they closed around her, Nicola found her first target in an old man with a toothless mouth and skin like leather. Protected by only a tattered cloth vest and armed with a sharpened stake, he cackled like a hen with each tottering step. She lunged for him, her blade coming upward beneath his staff as it aimed for the rent in his vest. Iron bit through the opening, crushing ribs and tearing deeply into softer flesh. He grimaced in pain as she kicked him off her blade, then gagged at death's rapid approach.

Her stained sword held before her in her finest defensive stance, Nicola shifted backward until she had all the men within her view. Only then did she glance at her gloved hands; they were spattered with the old man's blood. Deep within her there grew a terrible sickness.

In the space of only three breaths, she had ended a life. For all the times she'd threatened to do so and

practiced her skill with her father, she never dreamed it
would feel like this. Nicola slaughtered her cowardly
reaction. What was wrong with her? These men meant
to take at least her freedom from her, if not her life.
'Twas she against all of them.

"Who else wants a taste of what that man ate?" she
growled, manufacturing rage to protect her from her
woman's heart.

From the corner of her eye, Nicola saw Tilda strug-
gle to her feet. Relief washed over her. Surely, if the
girl took up the old man's staff, the two of them together could defeat these scummy few. When the threat
against them was finished, she and Tilda could talk. No
matter what had been done, they could resolve it between them.

"What are you waiting for, you idiots?" Alan
screamed, his face red with rage, as he stood behind
them. "Take her. She cannot kill you all."

"Take her yourself," one of his men snarled. "We
did not expect her to be dangerous."

"I cannot! She's damaged my sword hand."

"Come, try my blade, you reeking bits of ox dung,"
Nicola goaded in rising confidence as she waited for
Tilda to join her. "Aye, come for me with your ancient
blades and your wooden sticks. I'll give you a taste of
your master's better steel." She lunged at the nearest
one. As he whirled away, Nicola caught a glimpse of
Tilda. The girl led Alan's nag out of hiding.

Nicola blinked in disbelief as Tilda clambered into
its saddle, then set the sorry beast into a trot without a
backward look. Abandonment was far worse than betrayal. Swinging wildly in sudden pain, Nicola landed
a chance blow, crushing a slender man's shoulder, half

tearing his arm from his body. He rebounded off her blade with no future, save death from blood loss.

The shock of Tilda's deed woke that terrible emptiness in Nicola. She panted as she fought it. There was no controlling herself when this state came upon her. Too late. All at once, she stood amid an eerie bubble of calm. She watched in detached interest as Alan turned to spy the escaping Tilda, then saw him rotate back toward her.

"That damn bitch stole my horse! Cowards all," he bellowed at his men, " 'tis but a woman before you. Take her, then run fetch our whore. Dickon, show these curs how a true man deals with a woman."

At Alan's command, the heavy man who had battered Tilda raised his rusty weapon and started toward her. Nicola felt her face tighten into a grimace as she prepared to meet him, but no feeling lived within her. Not even fear. Dickon hesitated, staring at her, his weapon sagging in his hands.

"I like this not at all," a frail lad sniveled. " 'Tis not right that a woman be this way. Look at her, 'tis like she has no soul. She's some sort of a witch. Let her go, Alan, or she'll put a curse on us all."

"I am not afraid of her," mumbled Dickon.

He once again trundled toward her, sword raised high to strike. The wind sent his smell before him. Nicola's body needed no input from her thoughts to react to his swing. Her blade came up instinctively to block his blow. Steel grated harshly as iron met iron, then she snapped hers free.

Her body pivoted lithely away, years of training finding the movements for her. Soundlessly, Nicola buried her sword deep into his huge middle. He cried out and fell toward her. She wrenched on her hilt, but it was well and truly stuck in him. If he fell on her, she would be trapped beneath him. Nicola stumbled away from him, empty-handed.

"Take her now!" Alan shouted in triumph.

The remaining three fell on her as one, trying to drag her down beneath them. Locked in her cold, empty state, she could not tolerate their touch. She kicked and punched. The frail boy screamed and rolled away, his nose spouting blood. As he sobbed, the other two managed to pin her to the road by lying upon her arms.

"Vicious bitch," Alan snarled, and kicked her in the ribs. Nicola curled away to protect herself from another blow. "You've killed half my men, left me injured, and made me lose my horse and our whore. Perhaps I should replace her with you." He leered viciously at her.

"Me after you, Alan," said one, placing his foul lips on her cheek. "I care not for what she looks like or that I follow another man. You'll yet taste sweet enough to me, lassie." His tongue touched her neck.

Nicola felt nothing, not even revulsion. All that lived within her was the need to win free of their touch. She brought her knees to her chest as Alan grabbed her by her hair. He drew a hand to slap her, and she kicked out. Her heel caught him on the chin. Alan's head snapped back.

He screamed, spittle stained red with blood. He clumsily drew his dagger with his left hand.

As his short weapon descended, Nicola again drew her legs to her chest. His dagger's edge caught her shin, slicing through stockings and skin. There was no pain. Instead, she braced her feet against Alan's mid-section, lifting the straining man on her feet until he nearly stood upright.

Keeping one foot shoved into his stomach, Nicola drew back the other, aiming for his chest. As she kicked, he thrust hard against her bracing leg, forcing her knee to bend. Instead of his chest, her heel smashed into his throat. Alan's eyes bulged as he caught at his neck, his face going white. He dropped to writhe in agony on the ground.

"Alan!" one of her captors screamed.

Bucking wildly against their hold, Nicola managed to free one arm. The other man instantly released her and sidled away. She scrambled to her feet, grabbing up Dickon's rusty blade as she moved. The two men scurried into the brush like the mice they were.

"Wait for me," cried the lad as he wobbled unsteadily after them, hand over his dripping nose.

Nicola stared after them, her hand tight on the sword's hilt, her heart dead within her chest. The heavens breathed for her, a keening, frigid wind. Icy sleet pelted her. The empty coldness within her matched the air around her.

She drew a long breath and turned on Alan. He yet twisted on the ground, trying to drag air through his crushed throat. His dagger lay beside him. Nicola reached for it, vaguely surprised that her hand was so steady. She cut the ties on his vest so she could open it, then sheathed his knife in her belt and straightened.

With the flat of the ancient blade, she turned back the man's hauberk and rested the sword's tip against his heart. All she need do to take his life was lean on the hilt. Yet, Nicola stood frozen in place, her coward's heart incapable of allowing cold-blooded murder. The emptiness within her expanded, and she was void of all thought.

Only when Alan's movements ceased as he relaxed into death could Nicola shift her weight, her blade sliding into him. She turned without a sound and started up the road, following Tilda. For a time there was no pain in her feet or her injured leg. Slowly sensation returned and her leg began to burn, her ribs to ache, and her feet throbbed.

It was about a half mile before she found the girl and the nag at the roadside. Nicola stopped to stare at her friend. One cheek bore the red mark of a slap, a great bruise now purpled her jaw, and her nose looked swollen. The silence between them was heavy and tense. Then Tilda's expression twisted in shame and sorrow.

Nicola opened her mouth to speak and tried twice before the words actually exited. "You left me." 'Twas but a shocked whisper. The blankness receded even further.

Like a key, Nicola's words released Tilda from the trap of guilt. The pretty lines of her face resolved themselves into an uncaring expression, and she casually shrugged. "They meant you no harm. You, after all, are noble born and worth something, while I am but a commoner. I dared not stay nearby when they intended me as their winter whore, to be killed when they were finished with me."

"You left me to save yourself, not caring whether I lived or died." Nicola released her breath in a shuddering sigh. Somewhere, deep inside, anger's warmth returned. It was welcome after the awful coldness.

"You seem to have survived well enough." Her friend's attempt at a smile was horrible in its falseness. She led the nag back onto the road. "Here, you ride the horse for a time. We must keep moving."

"Why?" Nicola's harsh question echoed against the leaden sky. She let her eyes narrow as she studied Tilda. "Whatever have you been doing these last four months, my girl? I think 'tis time we share secrets."

"What I do is no business of yours," Tilda retorted.

"On the contrary. Your soul is tied to Ashby, and I am your lady. You had best tell me where you spent these last months." Nicola was startled by both the words and her commanding tones. 'Twas the first time she'd ever spoken so to Tilda.

Her friend's brows drew down. "I will answer to no one for my deeds, especially not you."

Nicola straightened to her tallest. "Then, shall I suggest a scene for you? Since the whole countryside knows Hugh keeps women, I think you have lived these last months at Ocslade as his leman. He never expected that contract to wrest me from Lord Gilliam, nor did he believe I truly meant to wed him. What Hugh needed was some tool with which to catch me. That was your role in this. You were not only supposed to steal me from Graistan, but to soothe me into his custody. Which brings us to one, final question. How much did he pay you to deliver me?"

Guilt again washed over Tilda's face, then disappeared behind a snide and superior look. "What difference does that make when you mean to go to him anyway? If he's fool enough to pay me for what he could freely have, let him pay."

"You did," Nicola breathed in aching astonishment.

She hadn't realized how deeply she'd needed to hear Tilda's denial. "You really took coins in exchange for me."

Tilda only shrugged. "Aye. 'Tis only fair. Ashby's burning cost me everything I had worked so hard to gain."

"Worked? I thought men gave you those trinkets as gifts for love's sake. Do you now say that you spread your legs for them in expectation of payment?" Nicola retorted taking no time to consider what she said. She gasped in shock, but 'twas too late to retract her words.

Tilda's face went white in hurt, then darkened in rage. "Who are you to chastise me? At least I accept what I am. Look at you. You so fear being a woman that you pretend to be a man."

"Nay," Nicola protested faintly, clasping her hands to her ears to shut out the vicious words, each one a knife's blow to her heart.

Tilda set her hands on her hips. "If you are an impossible woman that no man could love, you are even worse as a man. How clever you thought yourself, Colette. 'I'll hold the walls against Graistan's brother, Tilda,' said you to me. 'When Lord Rannulf sees how capable I am, he'll give me Ashby as my own.' Meanwhile Lord Gilliam's ballista battered our walls to dust, and you did not open our door." Her voice rose to a painful cry. "Now Ashby lies in ruins, and my mother is dead, Colette. You killed them both, my mother, your father. You killed them."

"Not my fault," Nicola pleaded quietly to herself, yet guilt ate at her. She had been so certain of her abilities, so sure of herself that she dared risk all her folk by helping her stepmother hold Lord Rannulf prisoner, even in the face of his brother's attack. From the recesses of her memory came the terrible ringing of stone crashing against stone, the roaring of the flames, the screams of her dying folk, and the sight of Gilliam's blade burying into her father's body.

Tilda stepped close and clutched at the front of Nicola's capuchin to force the tall noblewoman to look at her. "How do you bear the weight of what you've done?" she whispered cruelly, then turned her back on Nicola.

Nicola squeezed shut her eyes. The wind moaned around her, holding within its airy depths the pleas of those who had died. They had looked to her for protection, and she had betrayed them for her own selfish purpose.

"Nay." She backed unsteadily away from the girl, repeating the litany that had shielded her from her sin these last months. " 'Twas not my fault. None of this would have happened if Lord Rannulf hadn't married that witch to Papa. His meddling is the cause for this. Damn you, 'twas not my fault. Not my fault," she repeated, barely louder than a whisper.

Tilda turned to glare at her. "It is for revenge's sake that I sold you to de Ocslade. Now, I will go fetch your bridegroom for you, Colette. Know that he is disgusted by the thought of wedding you and intends to chain you like a dog. Whilst he does so, know that what he pays me will guarantee a long and rich life in freedom." She turned and mounted the sorry nag.

"Tilda, 'twas not me who killed your mother. I saw her die on FitzHenry's blade, just as my father died. You must listen to me," Nicola cried suddenly, but she no more accepted this excuse than Tilda did.

"Nay, 'twas your pride that cost her life. We are finished, you and I, but I leave you with this warning: If you do not wish to be Hugh's prisoner, go another direction." With that, she set her heels to the poor creature's sides, and the horse trotted down the road.

Nicola stared after her, the pain so deep it rooted her to the ground. The rain had ceased, but there was a curious wetness warming her face. She reached up to brush it away and was surprised to find she wept.

The need to sit reached through her hurt. She left the road for a giant oak, which sported around its huge bole a thick curtain of brush. Once hidden from any travelers, she slid down onto the damp ground, her back against the trunk.

Her trembling started as a tiny shudder, then grew until she shook like one palsied. With her head tucked against her knees, Nicola fought to regain control. Was it not enough that her folk and her father had been murdered and her home destroyed? Now, de Ocslade had turned her dearest friend against her. Soon, he would come for her. If Tilda spoke true, Hugh would hold her captive for the remainder of her life. Nicola gently rocked herself, but there was no comfort in it. This was the price she paid for betraying her folk.

Just as Tilda had betrayed de Ocslade's foul plans to her. 'Twas a tiny whisper from the farthest corner of her heart, but it made Nicola sit bolt upright in surprise. She dragged in a healing breath. Tilda must hold some love for her, else she'd not have denied herself that rich reward with her final warning,

She could not go to Hugh, and she could not return to Graistan. Ashby. A shudder shook her to her core at that thought. Home. Nicola closed her eyes as the very thought of Ashby eased all her pains. She would go home.

Heart steadied, she reached toward her sliced leg, meaning to see what damage had been done. The blood of her victims yet fouled her gloves. Her stomach turned, but she shut out her emotions. Now was not the time for this. When she was safe and beyond Hugh's reach, then would she think on what had happened. For now, she wiped her gloves as clean as she could on the grasses by her feet, then carefully and slowly pulled the torn area of her chausses away from her leg.

She eyed it with a healer's insight. 'Twas a neat slice, needful of stitching to heal smoothly. If she was to walk to Ashby, it must be bound shut. Nicola used her dagger to cut a strip from her gown's hem and wrapped it around her leg, knotting it in place. That would prevent any further damage until she was home again.

Nicola grimaced in pain that had nothing to do with her wounds. She had betrayed Ashby's folk. What sort of greeting could she expect from them? What if FitzHenry had not lied this morn when he said her peasants had given him their love?

"Nay, not my fault," she breathed to herself, her voice rising as she continued. "My folk love me still, and I am going home," she said aloud to the thick clouds above her. "When I return to them, they will rise against FitzHenry and put me in his place." The words rang as hollowly in her own ears as they did in the glade, but she pretended not to notice.

With her makeshift bandage on her leg, she came carefully onto her feet. Nicola struck out to the north through the woods. Once she was certain she'd eluded all those who chased her, she would return to the road.

"I am going home," she said to herself as she set one, aching foot in front of the other. "I am going home."

Chapter Six

Gilliam reined in his massive black steed and signaled his men to stop. In the center of the road lay the mercenary who had escorted Nicola from Graistan. No matter what the man's skill as a soldier had been, his throat was crushed and he now harbored a rusty blade in his chest. Three others, ragged commoners all, were strewn nearby. There was no sign of either the petite lass or his bride.

"Robert, keep my squire back beyond that hedge," he called behind him. "You, two"—he pointed at the men—"search the right and you, the left," he told two more. "Walter, look to these poor souls. See if any retain enough life to tell us who they are and what has become of the women."

Even as he uttered the commands, Gilliam was certain of what had happened. De Ocslade must not have withdrawn beyond Graistan's borders, but had waited here. He killed the soldier, and these unfortunates who stumbled upon him, then took the women. Damn, but he was too late.

Reacting to his master's tension, Gilliam's battle-trained mount raised himself on his hind legs in excitement. Gilliam cursed himself for riding Witasse instead of a calmer palfrey. Without his armor, he was not heavy enough to satisfy the great twit. Now, between the unfamiliar weight and the smell of blood, Gilliam would need all his strength to keep the steed from striking out at his own men.

He leaned forward and whispered gently into the horse's ear, "Cease, Witasse, or I will beat you bloody." Responding to the tone, if not the words, the dangerous beast deigned to relax, but only a little.

From either side of the road, men reported that they'd found nothing. "My lord," Walter said from beside the slain mercenary, "they are all dead, but only just so, for they yet retain some warmth."

"Jesu Christus," Gilliam swore. "Then, de Ocslade cannot be far from here. Hie, we must catch him before he leaves our lands." He set his heels to his steed, the great beast leaping into motion before his men had mounted.

Even at his fast pace there was no sign of either his bride or his neighbor. When he finally caught sight of men in the distance, there was no mistaking the green of Ocslade's surcoat, but the troop was riding toward Graistan, not away. Relief warred with irritation. While this meant de Ocslade did not have Lady Ashby, where on God's earth was she and who had killed those men? Gilliam raised a hand to stop his men.

"We stand here, our swords loose," he commanded, "but we avoid conflict. Ashby cannot afford to war with our neighbor just now." At Walter's sign, the men brought their mounts into a line across the road.

Gilliam glanced behind him, searching for Jos on his sturdy pony. The boy was yet pasty-faced with the death he had witnessed. "Jocelyn, draw your steed behind Walter's and keep you close to the woods. If this comes to battle, you must guide your mount into the trees and wait quietly for the outcome."

"Aye, my lord," the boy managed in a shaky voice, then set his pony into motion.

Gilliam almost smiled. The lad's education was moving far more quickly than intended, but Jos was taking it better than his lord expected. "That's my lad."

When de Ocslade halted, it was no more than a lance's length from Gilliam, which sent Witasse into yet another frenzied attempt to free himself of his rider. By the time Gilliam had regained control, his neighbor's men were clustered untidily behind the small landholder.

Gilliam scanned them for any sign of Nicola. There was a girl riding pillion behind one of his neighbor's soldiers. He looked more closely and recognized the woman he'd seen at Graistantown's gate. Her face was battered, but he was certain it was she. So, here was the one de Ocslade had used in his attempt to steal the heiress from Gilliam.

"My apologies for trespassing," the smaller knight offered evenly, "but I seem to have lost something during my travels."

De Ocslade boldly surveyed Gilliam's men, and a smile tugged at the corners of his narrow lips. "I see you have not found it, either. How reassuring. This means I can withdraw and wait until it comes to me." His meaning was as clear as the insult in his words.

Although Gilliam knew full well he was being goaded, anger still flared in him. "We both know you have no lawful claim on her. She is mine. Lay a hand on her, and you do so at your own peril."

His rival raised a sardonic brow. "How careless the young are these days. When I was your age, I'd have thought twice about antagonizing a warrior of some twenty years experience."

Gilliam's anger solidified into cold fury. His grip on the reins tightened and Witasse pranced in worry. This time, the distraction was welcome, for it prevented him from drawing his sword. As he fought the horse into submission, he also subdued his own emotions. Calmness brought with it the realization that two could play at de Ocslade's game.

He forced himself to smile. "I would suggest to you that 'tis equally foolish to judge a man's skill by his age. Perhaps I should warn you that I won my spurs in the Holy Lands killing the Infidel. Our king, himself, delivered my *colee,* wishing to honor me for my prowess in battle. Now, have we finished taunting each other? If so, 'tis time you returned to Ocslade."

Hugh shrugged nonchalantly. "I think I will set my camp where the road turns north toward Ocslade and Ashby, then start my journey afresh in the morning. Aye, 'tis an excellent site, for I do so enjoy watching the travelers."

Once again, there was no mistaking de Ocslade's implication. If Gilliam found Nicola and tried to ride for Ashby with her in his custody, Hugh would be there to challenge him. Well, the solution to that was simple enough as there was more than one way to reach Ashby.

Gilliam paused in surprise. Why would the man be so open with his plan when it cheated him of the very opportunity he sought? Understanding turned his smile into one of genuine amusement. Like Lady Ashby, it seemed his neighbor had also taken Gilliam's great size to indicate a lack of intelligence.

"As you will," he said pleasantly. "I shall wish you

good journey back to Ocslade and be on about my business. Once all this is settled, 'tis my hope we'll be able to put our animosity aside and know peace as neighbors should." He held up a hand as if a thought had just occurred to him. "Ah, I have just the thing. Perhaps you will agree to stand as godfather to my firstborn?" The goad struck home.

De Ocslade's eyes narrowed, and rage darkened his sallow skin. Without another word, he signaled his men into a turn, then roweled his horse around on the roadbed. As he started away, he called over his shoulder, "Boy, I'll have Ashby, one way or another."

"I shall await your attempt," Gilliam retorted to de Ocslade's receding back.

"My lord," Walter said a moment later, "I think that man intends you harm."

Gilliam laughed. "Nay, Walter, he intends me dead should I wed Lady Ashby. Come, since he doesn't have her, 'tis sensible to assume she remains within these woods and at the mercy of whomever killed those men." He turned his nervous steed and started back toward the battle site.

Although Walter suggested they wait at the road for Rannulf's foresters to come, Gilliam could not bear to be idle. He had a groom bring him a calmer steed from Graistan, leaving the big warhorse in the man's capable hands. With Jos lingering at the campfire, he and the soldiers scoured the road for some clue to his bride's passage. They quickly found their first sign beneath a huge oak.

Gilliam stared at the crushed and bloodied grasses. The thought of his bride's death should mean nothing to him save his freedom. With her demise, ownership of her lands returned to Rannulf, and Gilliam's brother would still install Ashby upon him.

Unbidden came the memory of the tall girl caught tightly against him while they stood atop the church porch. Their fine garments proved no barrier to sensation; he had been intimately aware of her body touching his and how well they fit. 'Twas as if they'd been made for each other.

Having more than learned his lesson by his sin with Rannulf's former wife, Isotte, Gilliam had used only whores since then. These women always charged him extra for his unusual weight, and never let him lay atop them. Until today and his talk with Geoff, he'd not dared to even consider the possibility of lying with Nicola as a man lay with his wife. Aye, there would be a brief communion to break her maidenhead and stain the sheets, but he expected no more than that.

Now, the memory of her lips, pliant and warm on his, made Gilliam's breath catch in his chest and his blood heat. Their kiss had deepened far beyond any intention of his. Had she not cried out he'd be kissing her still. Nay, they'd be doing far more than that. He swallowed and closed his eyes as a fiery desire rushed through him. Why had she kissed him that way, if she hated him so? By God, who cared why? She had.

"My lord?"

Gilliam started and opened his eyes to see Walter standing before him. Concern was written in the soldier's plain features.

"We have found a trail leading toward the north." The man paused, then continued hesitantly. "Are you ill? You look as one fevered."

'Twas a fever, true enough, but not one of sickness. Gilliam nearly choked on his own foolishness. Nicola would never join him in love play. It was more likely they would have naught but a single rape between them.

"I am fine," he said. "Come now, let us find that bride of mine."

Leaving Jos at their makeshift camp, along with two men who would also run messages and meet the foresters, Gilliam sent two others to scour the road all the way to Rannulf's borders. Meanwhile, he and Walter followed the meager trail north.

The weather chose not to cooperate, rain turning to sleet, then back to rain again. Even walking behind the shield of his mount, the wind penetrated his layers of clothing to sting his skin. Their passage was achingly slow to keep from missing any sign. The morning slipped into midday, hour after long hour without success. Impatience gave way to worry.

They had nearly reached the end of Rannulf's holdings when the sound of someone walking through the brush caught Gilliam's attention. He strode swiftly in the direction of the noise, Walter trotting behind him. Coming toward him was Hobbe atte Lea, one of his brother's huntsmen. Caught in Hobbe's fist was the bony arm of a starving lad.

"What have you found there, Hobbe?" Gilliam called out.

The slight man dressed in a forester's green garb raised a hand in greeting. "My lord, I had no idea you were so far afield. You've saved us quite a walk back to camp and fortunate that is. I think I may have found a clue to your missing woman."

As they skirted brush and bush to close the gap, Gilliam saw that one of the boy's eyes bore a dark ring and blood stained his peaked face. He arched a brow in surprise. "Hobbe, was there truly a need to beat him? He hardly looks capable of putting up a fight."

The woodsman's smile was a weasel's snarl. "'Twasn't I who abused him. The lad claims he got the eye from a beautiful witch woman, who lay a curse upon him and his fellows, leaving four of them dead. He is so afraid of her, he leapt from hiding to beg me lead him to the nearest church for protection."

"A witch who killed four?" Gilliam asked in wary disbelief. Unwanted within him awoke a new and shocking explanation for the dead bodies on the road. Nicola could wield a sword. Had she not attacked him with her father's weapon after John's death? True, she did not have his strength, but she was skilled enough to thrash poorly armed commoners. Nay, it could not be. Not four men by herself. "Ask him to describe his witch."

As Hobbe translated the question, Gilliam once again found himself wishing he spoke the peasants' language. Even though he trusted Ashby's reeve and priest enough to depend on them, he felt crippled by his lack of knowledge. 'Twould be far better if he understood what was being said around him.

When the boy fell silent, Hobbe turned to his lord, a grimace of disappointment on his face. "My pardon, Lord Gilliam. I was wrong. The lad's tale is so far-fetched, I fear it could only have been brought about by hunger."

Gilliam shook his head. The empty branches clattered and rustled in the wind. He drew his cloak more tightly around him against a brief spate of icy rain. "Tell me everything."

"He says the witch was dressed as a man and wore her hair also like a man's. Not only that, but in the boy's fevered dream, she fought better than any soldier. As I said, 'tis beyond belief." The forester shrugged in apology for wasting his lord's time.

The corners of Gilliam's mouth lifted in sudden respect, and he touched the pin at his shoulder. "She did it all alone," he said quietly.

"My lord?" the forester asked.

"Hobbe, this is no dream. The boy has, indeed, seen my bride."

Hobbe blinked and said, "Condolences, my lord."

While his better judgment screamed warnings of his own future, Gilliam dared to grin. "Hobbe, taming this woman will be a feat worthy of legend, and even better than that, Lord Graistan will lose his wager. Walter, best you tell those men who have bet against me that they should rethink their positions."

"Aye, my lord," the soldier replied, but the look on his face said he believed his lord to be mad.

Turning to Hobbe, Gilliam asked, "Does the boy know where Lady Ashby is now?"

A moment later, the man translated. "His two remaining companions have been following the witch— your pardon, Lady Ashby—in hopes of capturing her for ransom. While the boy is terrified of confronting her again, he fears being alone even more. Thus, he trailed them. My lord, they can be no more than a half mile distant, for I have only just now found the lad."

"I have her!" Gilliam called out in triumph, then paused. With Ashby again secure in his hand, plots and plans swam through his head. He grinned.

"Now, Hobbe, here's a terrible wicked thought. Since the boy wants the security of a church, you must take the poor creature into Graistantown, to Abbot Simon. The child should tell his tale of witches in our forest, but make you no explanations. This should keep the monks in an uproar for months."

The forester laughed under his breath, and nodded.

Gilliam turned on Walter. "As for you, bring our men and my squire, along with a horse for my lady to that hamlet north of here. Do you know the place?" At the man's nod, he continued. "Do not come by the road, but cut directly through the chase. We'll ride from there to Ashby."

In a futile attempt to judge the time, Gilliam glanced up at the overcast sky. 'Twas his stomach's emptiness that suggested it was well past midday. This meant they'd yet be on the road well after dark. He frowned. Dark or no, he needed to be home with her safe behind his walls and married to him, all before this day became the next. But how to get there without facing the possibility of de Ocslade's ambush at every turn?

"Hobbe, will you carry a message to Graistan's castellan for me?"

"Aye, my lord," the forester said, then closed his eyes to absorb the words as those who could not read or write were wont to do.

"If de Ocslade thinks we haven't yet found the missing bride, he'll not be looking toward Ashby as I make my way there. Arnult must keep men moving up and down the road, as if we yet searched. At twilight, the tallest among them must don armor whilst another, dark-haired man must wear a leather vest over a green tunic and brown chausses. These two will ride that devil of mine. Have a care. Armed, I am nigh on twenty-one stone. If they are not to end up beneath Witasse's hooves, they will need to approach that weight."

Walter interrupted in confusion. "Where are they to ride him, my lord?"

"Why, right past de Ocslade's camp at a full gallop, of course," Gilliam said with a casual lift of his shoulders and a wicked smile. "Once they have him on their tail, they can scatter and return to Graistan. Arnult should send Witasse to me in a day or two. Take heed, Hobbe. I'll be right disappointed in Arnult if any of Graistan's men are caught. The quality of de Ocslade's horseflesh and his men does not approach Graistan's."

The man's expression blossomed in amused understanding, and he again took hold of the boy's arm and started off to the west, lad in tow. "Good traveling, my lord, and may you survive your wedding night."

"My thanks, Hobbe. Your confidence in me is awe inspiring," Gilliam called after him. Walter had mounted. "Hie, now, Walter. The sooner you arrive at the hamlet, the greater the head start we have on de Ocslade and the sooner we are home."

"No longer than an hour, my lord," the man assured him as he started back toward their gathering place.

Gilliam also mounted, but did not urge his palfrey to any speed. A thick carpet of leaves and grasses hid many a digging creature's burrow. To lame his palfrey now would only further delay him.

His stomach again reminded him of the time and he reached behind him for a leather packet. Inside were meat pasties, dried fruits, bread and cheese. He ate swiftly as he rode, leaving the bread and cheese for later, then smiled. Rannulf would have scolded him for his lack of manners. Ashby's relative insignificance was one of the nicer aspects of the place. Gilliam would never need worry over aping Graistan's grand lifestyle, with all the bits of etiquette and diplomacy that it required.

As the beast picked its way at an easy walk in the direction Hobbe indicated, Gilliam scanned the landscape for some sign of Nicola or her pursuers. Here the land began to roll, rising into a series of small knolls and hills, peppered with the occasional stony outcrop. Holly grew thick and green, startling in a world now trapped in shades of brown. Moments passed without sight of any soul. When he finally caught a glimpse of movement, Gilliam lifted himself in his stirrups to better see.

Hood pulled up against the rain and leaning heavily on a thick branch, the boy who was not a boy hobbled painfully through a clearing. Gilliam watched her slender form for a brief moment, waiting to feel repulsed now that he knew 'twas a girl beneath that old gown of his. Instead, he found only an ever-growing respect for her boldness and determination. Even shearing her hair had taken courage. There were only two reasons a woman's hair was cut, either to relieve fever or in punishment for lewdness.

He peered through the general dimness for some sign of those who followed her. There was no movement to indicate their presence. Easing back down into the saddle, he urged the horse to a faster walk and started in her direction. As he rounded a thick copse of trees, he again caught sight of his bride.

She stopped, then slowly turned her head to look over her shoulder. Gilliam stared in surprise as he saw her face. Where Nicola of Ashby had been almost plain as a woman, she was beautiful as a boy.

Wild and tangled curls framed her face, a dark brown halo of hair, softening and shortening her features. Her jawline was round and feminine and he now found cheekbones, where before it had seemed she had none. As he watched, she chewed thoughtfully on a thumbnail, then turned her back to him once more.

Gilliam clenched his teeth to stop his shout of protest. He wanted to stare at her until he could reconcile this pretty, soft woman with the angry plain bride he'd been offered. In the next instant, she stumbled and fell. He went rigid with concern. If her ankles were as slender as her wrists, she must surely have broken something in that fall. Once again, he set the horse into motion, his gaze yet trapped on her.

She drew up a knee and lay her head upon it as if exhausted. In the scrabble of brush between him and her, he caught signs of movement. 'Twas two men, crouching and creeping closer.

The need to keep her safe roared through him. He urged his mount into a faster pace. They would die before they touched her.

Chapter Seven

Nicola slowly eased herself into a sitting position, then drew her knee up to pillow her head upon it in defeat. She was too exhausted even to groan against the pain. Her side ached, her leg wound burned, and her feet were naught but bloody ribbons. Empty since last even, her stomach took this moment to register its protest. She tried to rub the pain from her twisted ankle. It was useless.

Whatever it was that had been following her now came closer. In her mind's eye, she saw the wolves of last winter, huge and gray, their yellow eyes shining with hunger. Without raising her head, one hand reached for her stick, the other went to her belt and the dagger sheathed there. She'd not easily give them her life.

A shiver wracked her from head to toe, and she cursed her addlepated dislike of being dirty. Like a fool, she'd stopped at a small stream to cleanse the blood from her clothing and the muck from her hair. In removing the grime, she had also given herself an unexpected dunking when she'd slipped down the bank. Her gloves had gone floating away on the current and her sodden garments turned icy cold in the chill day.

Nicola freed a sound that mingled a laugh and a sob.

Perhaps this was God's justice, her punishment for trying to escape a woman's life. She smiled in bitter amusement. At least she could blame only herself for what happened now.

"We can take her, Ott." Although the words were no more than a low utterance, they rang clear among the silent trees.

Nicola kept her head on her knee. 'Twas one of the three remaining thieves she heard speaking. Damn her, but she should have brought that sword with her, instead of leaving it in Alan. She rolled her eyes at that thought. What good would it have done her? Not only was she too tired to lift the heavy weapon, her feet would never support her as she struck.

The rustling of their approach grew steadily louder, then ceased. "Wait. What if she is not hurt, only resting?" This was a sibilant hiss, borne to her on the frigid wind.

Her spirits lifted a little. Their uncertainty gave her an edge, however slight. Without raising her head, she slowly drew her dagger and tightened her grip on the stout stick in preparation for their attack.

"She's not moving. Together."

Branches snapped and saplings cracked as they rushed her. Nicola reared back, raising her stick. There were only two men, not three, coming at her. Her edge grew a little larger.

Grinning, the one who had dared touch his tongue to her cheek wrenched away her staff, without seeing the dagger in her other hand. Nicola lunged upward, shoving the blade deep into his belly. He screamed and thrust her away, then staggered to one side.

Nicola toppled backward, rapping her head against a stone as she met the ground. Stars popped into being before her eyes, her vision of them framed in a soft, warm darkness. She gasped for air; her lungs refused to work. Shouting, the other man threw himself atop her. She barely felt his impact before he was scrambling back onto his feet and was racing away from her. As from a great distance, she heard his scream. The sound was cut off, mid-cry.

Breath rushed back into her. With air, her whirling thoughts steadied. She struggled into an upright position, her head now pounding in tune to the pulsing of her feet, and immediately wished she hadn't.

Coming toward her was a horse. In its saddle sat Gilliam FitzHenry, his thick golden hair curling charmingly against his perfect brow and cheekbones. He was cleaning his sword on his cloak hem and had not yet looked at her. She stared at him in dismay.

The rich man's son was the picture of comfort. Beneath a leather vest much like hers, he wore hunting garments dyed a deep chestnut color. His knee-high boots, no doubt well-fitted and wondrously comfortable, were bound to his legs with cross garters. As he returned the huge blade to its scabbard at his side, he looked toward her. His blue eyes came to life as he smiled. Between his sword and his smile, she thought his broad grin by far the sharper weapon.

Nicola clenched her teeth. Mary, but she hated FitzHenry and his sick wit. Why couldn't de Ocslade have found her? Hugh might have bound her, beaten her, or killed her, but she was absolutely certain he wouldn't have laughed at her. This murdering whoreson would start by jeering at her for dressing as a man. He would continue by poking at her inept escape attempt. But his crowning moments would come while he taunted her over her hair. Her pride would never survive his battering.

Jamming her hood farther down onto her brow, Nicola threw herself to her feet. Her ankle screamed in protest, her toes burned as blisters tore, but her need to be free of him was by far the stronger impulse. Hobbling as swiftly as she could, Nicola made her escape.

The jingle of iron and creak of leather behind her suggested he was dismounting. She drove herself harder. After no more than fifteen yards, she heard him right behind her. Nicola released a small cry, but it had more to do with anger than pain. Damn him, he wasn't even running.

She felt him reach for her. With her fists clenched, Nicola whirled, ready to battle him to the end. Her ankle gave as she turned. Instead of striking out, she yelped and fell into his surprised grasp, then slid out of it and down his legs into a crumpled heap at his feet.

Defeat was absolute. She was finished. Nicola stared at the knee above the top of his soft leather boot and gulped back a sorry sob. "Not a word," she warned his leg. "I'll not tolerate a word from you."

He made a deep, rumbling noise that sounded suspiciously like a muted laugh. She leaned back to glare up at him. "If you tease me, I vow I will tear out your heart."

The murderer raised his finely arched brows over his beautiful blue eyes as if weighing the value of her threat. "I thought you intended that fate for me, no matter what I do or say. Are we parlaying here? If so, then I agree not to tease you, if you agree to wed me without complaint."

From her seat on the cold ground, his height and breadth were indeed intimidating. Nicola scooped together the shattered bits of her pride, and swiftly sewed them back into some sort of protection. "Murderer, I will never wed with you, nor will you ever own me."

He considered her in silence for a moment, then squatted down beside her to look her eye to eye. "Too late, my girl, for it seems I own you already."

"Nay!" She scooted back from him. As he reached for her, there was fiery glint on his shoulder. "My pin," Nicola cried, grabbing for that precious reminder of her previous life.

" 'Tis yours no longer," Gilliam warned, catching her hand.

"But you cannot keep it," she protested, wrenching her wrist from his grasp. Regret, sharp and sudden, rushed through her. She should have understood that when she struck with it, it would be lost to her. As with everything else she'd done this day, she hadn't thought far enough ahead to consider the outcome of her actions.

"What are you willing to trade for it?" he asked quietly. "For the right price, you can have it back."

She instantly blinked away her hurt. If he thought the item meant enough to her, he would use it against her. She shrugged. "Nothing. Keep it, if you want it. I always thought it a gaudy piece, anyway."

Gilliam nodded slowly, the curve of his mouth touched with consideration. "As you will. Are you hurt?" Ignoring her yelp of protest, he grasped her leg to examine her twisted ankle. "*Jesu Christus,* what have you done to your foot?"

His harsh question made Nicola start. "The boots were too small," she answered weakly.

"Fool," he snapped. He tugged on the shoe, but her

foot had swollen and it was stuck fast. From his belt he
took a small dagger.

"What are you doing?" She tried to kick free of his
hold.

He shot her a look of disbelieving irritation. "Sawing off your foot, what do you think I'm doing? Hold
still."

Using only his knife's tip, he tore at the shoe's
seams. With an unexpected gentleness, he peeled away
the leather shoe, then cut away her stocking. Instead of
being thankful at this release from torture, her foot
throbbed with thrice the intensity. Nicola leaned back
on her elbows, clenching her eyes shut to keep tears
from falling. The pain ebbed to a tolerable level.

"Give me your capuchin to use as a wrapping." His
voice was now soft with what might have been pity.

Hating that he had seen her momentary weakness,
Nicola sat up, harsh words on her lips. But Gilliam
paid her no heed, only worked to loosen the sodden
knot in her cross garter. She watched in fascination.
How could hands so big be so nimble?

When the narrow cloth band was loose, he looked up
in expectation. "Come now, give me your hood."

Nicola reached for her capuchin, then stopped. The
thought of his disgust when he saw her hair was daunt-
ing. Her jaw tightened in anger. What did she care
what he thought?

Drawing herself up with as much dignity as possible
while sitting on the damp ground with her foot in his
lap, Nicola yanked the garment off over her head. With
it still clutched in her hand, she made a show of running her fingers through her short curls, then held it toward him. She boldly met his gaze, brows lifted as she
dared him to say a word.

Gilliam studied her face for a long moment. His gaze touched her brow and her cheeks, then softened as he stared at her mouth. His look awoke in her the oddest need to touch him. Nicola's breath caught in her chest. What sort of spell was he trying to weave over her? Seeking to distract him, she shook the hood before his face.

"Take it, then." She shoved it at him. "But you best save half of it for the other foot. 'Tis worse than this one."

There was a flicker of hurt in his eyes as he took the hood from her and tore it down its center seam. "Is your hatred so deep that you would rather cripple yourself than marry me?"

Nicola shrugged and looked off into the distance. "You murdered my father. I cannot marry you."

"I did no murder," he protested as he used one portion to cover her bared foot, binding it in place with her cross garter.

"I was there," she retorted. "I saw what you did. Yours is a useless argument."

"That's true enough," he replied, and fell silent as he started on the other boot.

This time, when he peeled away the sodden leather, Nicola was already leaning back on her elbows, steeled for pain. The throbbing tore through her far worse than the other foot. With a quiet moan, she collapsed against the earth and concentrated on giving him no further sign of weakness. The hurt ebbed only as he encased her foot in cloth.

"What is this?" he asked a moment later, tugging gently on the strip of gown wrapped around her calf. The fabric of her chausses had clotted to her sliced leg.

As he moved the bandage, the scab reopened. Blood trickled around her calf, warm against her icy skin.

" 'Tis a knife wound. Leave it be." It was a tired request. Nicola lay on her back, staring up through bony branch fingers at the glowering sky above her. "I'm trying to keep it flat so it can be stitched shut. I'd not have it heal all warped."

"You want stitching?" There was genuine horror in Gilliam's voice. She could fair hear him shudder. "Have you ever had a wound stitched?"

His reaction did much to restore her and ease the sting of her defeat at his hands. Nicola levered herself up on her elbows to look at him. There was a decidedly greenish tinge to his fair skin. The thought that a man as powerful as he could be afeared of needle and thread made her smile. She pushed herself into a sitting position, folding her legs, tailor fashion. "Nay, but I've done it enough times to others."

"That explains it," he said weakly, then continued in a stronger voice. "Were you wounded anywhere else in that battle of yours?"

His question brought the event of this morn rushing back to her with sickening intensity. Nicola gagged, remembering the feel of her blade entering living flesh, the spray of warm blood over her hands and arms, and the ease with which life departed a body. Trying to control her womanish reaction, she swallowed and stared at her lap. Her hands lay there, palms up and still stained with her last victim's blood. Her stomach rolled and heaved within her.

"Holy Mother, I killed them," she moaned softly, staring with horror at her fingers. Her stomach tried to empty what was already barren.

Nicola twisted around to hide her reaction from

Gilliam. What a fool she was, becoming sick after killing in her own defense! She chided herself for being naught but a weak-kneed woman, but it did nothing to stop her stomach from heaving again. Fists clenched and back stiff, she demanded it cease. It paid her no heed. She leaned forward, her arms crossed tightly about her middle.

Gilliam grabbed her by the shoulders. She tried to pull away, but he was stronger than she. He dragged her back into his embrace, his arms forcing her to lean against his chest. When he spoke, his voice was low and soothing. " 'Twas your first time to kill, eh? Your illness will pass. Breathe."

"I cannot," she gasped in humiliation.

He pushed her head back against his shoulder and tilted her chin upward, then held it there. "Breathe," he commanded.

Nicola drew one shuddering breath, then another. Still, the image of killing clung in her mind. Her stomach bucked again. She gagged against it.

"That was quite a deed you did, four of them by yourself. Nay, 'tis five now, and you only half trained," he said, his voice even and calm. "My brother owes you a debt, I think me. Those thieves could have cost him dearly had they remained to live in his chase."

With his soothing words, her gasping eased slowly until her breathing returned to normal. A moment later, he released his hold on her chin. Nicola let her head turn to one side, her cheek resting against the fullness of his shoulder. When a long, shuddering sigh tore from her, he began to rock her gently in his arms. Nicola relaxed.

Some time later, he leaned his cheek against her bare

neck. "Are you steady now?" 'Twas but a velvet whisper against her throat.

She shivered as his warmth flowed through her, driving away all other thoughts. Another deep sigh of relief made her shudder. "Aye, 'tis better."

"Good." The word was a husky breath as he pressed his lips to the same spot touched by that filthy creature's mouth.

"What are you doing?" Nicola screamed, catapulting out of his hold. She was crippled, exhausted, and weaponless now. Where the thieves had failed to wrench control of her body, he could succeed.

She scrambled farther from him, then cried in pain as her feet reminded her she was shoeless, as well. Seated flat upon the ground, Nicola turned toward him, her fists held up in defense. He would not find this, her final defeat, so easy to come by. "You'll not take me," she snarled.

Although he sat within arm's reach of her, Gilliam only watched her impassively, his blue eyes unreadable. The moment stretched. "Can I help it if you tempt me beyond control?"

"Tempt you?" she cried out. This taunt was worse than any she had expected. She was an ugly woman with cropped hair and dressed as a boy. He was mocking her. Nicola's eyes narrowed in hurt, and she flailed out in attack. "Oh, so that's the way of it, is it? 'Tis that I am dressed as a lad. I've heard there were men like you."

Her insult only made him laugh. "Aye, perhaps I have been a soldier too long. Come now, little *boy,* we must be on our way."

"I would rather stay here and die than go with you." She crossed her arms in finality.

"Now that is a strange thing to offer me when your father has no other heirs," Gilliam replied calmly. There was no anger or irritation in his expression. "If you die, Ashby becomes Rannulf's once more. He will yet give it to me, despite your death."

Nicola stared at him in shock. If what he said was true, why did he not kill her in this secluded spot? None would be the wiser. So would Hugh have done, she realized, given the same circumstances.

He seemed to guess her thought process, his responding grin slow. " 'Tis fortunate you have misjudged me, no? 'Twould appear I am no murderer."

She cursed her relief at his words. "I will go with you," she muttered.

He gave a small nod and stood. When he reached for her, Nicola thought he intended only to raise her to her feet. Instead, he lifted her into his arms as if she were but a child. She tensed, ready to be uncomfortable, but he was so blessedly warm. And her feet hurt like the devil's lash.

Nicola curled into his embrace, her teeth chattering loudly. When he shifted her to better carry her, she wrapped her arms around his neck to steady herself. He started as her hand touched his bare nape.

"You are as cold as ice." There was concern in his tone.

" 'Tis what comes from walking all the day long in the frigid rain without a cloak," she retorted sharply, her shivering taking much of the sting from her words. Her life would end before she told him about falling in the stream.

"And you called me dim-witted?" he said with a brief laugh as he carried her.

With each step, his hair grazed softly against her ex-

posed wrists. The feeling was a pleasant distraction
from her aches and bruises. When they were beside the
horse, Gilliam loosed her legs, but did not remove his
arm from around her back. Ever so briefly, she was
again pinned against him, nose to nose. A smile flitted
swiftly over his mouth and was gone.

Slowly, carefully, he lowered her until her feet
touched the ground. Nicola caught back her gasp. How
quickly the pain had receded, and how quickly it returned. She turned to put her foot into the stirrup. Only
then did she realize her injured ankle would have to
bear all her weight. Well, there was no help for it. Bit-
ing back her scream, Nicola thrust herself up and into
the saddle.

Before she realized what he meant to do, Gilliam
freed her foot from the stirrup and was seated behind
her. She slid back against him. He wrapped his arm
around her and drew her closer still. His nearness was
suffocating. "I thought you would lead the horse."
Nicola pried vainly at his arm around her waist.

He made a sharp sound of irritation. "Stop that. Unlike some fools I know, I have no intention of walking
when I can ride. Now, be done with that or I will know
you have decided you'd rather dangle over the saddle."
She dropped her hands from his arm. "Good. You may
rest your feet on my legs so your calves will not
cramp." With a touch of his heels, he set the horse into
motion.

Common sense suggested that further resistance was
pointless and she was wasting energy better saved for
their next battle. Pride chafed against this rationale, but
she was simply too tired to worry over it. With a quiet
huff, she relaxed against him. Her stomach, fully re-

stored from its earlier sickness, took this moment to rumble hopefully.

"Are you hungry?" he asked in response to the sound. "I have bread and cheese."

"You do?" All other concerns disappeared as her stomach sang in expectation. He handed her a leather packet, which she fair snatched open. Inside lay a good-sized chunk of dark brown bread, slightly dry, and an oily wedge of cheese.

Mouth watering, Nicola gnawed on the bread. It was heavy, but rich with flavor. She chewed in a happy silence. Gilliam handed her a flask of watered wine. Although she was hardly full when she was finished, her stomach was thankful for what little it had been given.

Gilliam laughed when she returned his empty packet and the flask. "My, that was quick. Glad I am that I had it to give you."

Cringing slightly at this criticism for her lack of refinement, Nicola opened her mouth to explain that she'd not eaten since the prior day. She caught back her words in a rush of anger. Who cared that she'd insulted the rich man's son with her rustic manners? Certainly not she.

Still, she'd not want him to think she had no manners at all. Even enemies could be civil. No matter how she felt about him, Gilliam's kindnesses deserved recognition. She cleared her throat. "My thanks for sharing your meal and your help with my feet." The words came out forced and stiff, hardly grateful.

"You are most welcome." Even though she could not see his face, she knew she had surprised him by managing even this much.

"Now, do not mistake my words as a change in my

feelings for you," she added in swift amendment. "I only thought your aid deserved acknowledgment."

"So noted." There was subtle pleasure in his voice.

The silence between them lengthened, punctuated by the soft whispering of the wind in the trees and the horse's snorting breath. When Nicola shivered in the cold, Gilliam pulled his cloak around them both, offering another layer of protection. She had to lean against his chest to hold it shut.

With the cloak's hem tips tucked beneath her legs, she was surrounded in a cocoon of his warmth. Her muscles relaxed into limpness as exhaustion nibbled at her. Although she swore she would not do it, a moment later her head rested on his shoulder. She could not lift it. She sighed and shifted slightly to find her ease. His arm around her waist tightened, and she heard him draw a quick breath.

"Are you settled now?" he asked, his voice husky. With her head pillowed on his shoulder, his words fair brushed her cheek. This woke a strange sensation in the core of her being, but she was so tired, she spared no energy wondering over it.

"Aye," she breathed. "Be warned that I will fight you once again, after I am rested."

"I know that." It was a gentle reply. "This is but a suspension in our hostilities, no?"

"Just so." She yawned. "How did you recognize me?" Nicola didn't realize she'd spoken her thought aloud until he answered her.

"You are wearing my gown." There was amusement in his voice, but it was harmless.

Nicola closed her eyes in resignation. No wonder she'd had to fold back the sleeves. "Are we returning to Graistan?"

"Nay." He moved his head, rubbing his jaw softly against her hair. It was soothing.

"Then where?" she insisted tiredly.

"Home" was all he said.

Chapter Eight

Within the hour, they arrived at a hamlet. Twenty cottages there were, all tucked into one corner of a wide field. The persistent wind lifted smoke from thatch roofs long since gone moldy. A wall of interwoven branches surrounded this tiny spot, this poor defense missing more than a few sections. Children, clothing naught but undyed homespun and faces permanently stained with dirt, giggled at the new arrivals through these openings. The adults knew better than to interfere with what happened outside their boundary; they stared from a distance.

They stopped here to wait for Gilliam's men. Nicola dozed against her captor's shoulder until the soldiers appeared. Within their ranks was a horse with an empty saddle and a sullen lad on a sturdy pony. Her heart flinched for the child; he was the picture of misery, his nose reddened from the cold and his cheeks burned raw.

"My lord," one soldier called, "there was none who saw us coming."

"Good work, Walter. Surround us, so my bride is not tempted to run before I mount the other horse," Gilliam called. The power of his voice made her ears complain. He leaned his head down to say more softly,

"We must be parted now. I cannot tell you how this makes me ache." His jibe reawoke her anger.

"So you would say," she snapped.

"So I do," he replied, his tone filled with amusement. When his men encircled them, he dismounted, bringing the reins over the horse's head.

Nicola glared at him. He was not going to let her guide her own horse. She was well and truly caught; all that wanted doing was for him to lash her to the saddle as Lord Rannult had done when they traveled from Upwood to Graistan. Her need to be free rose to frantic proportions, and she stiffened automatically, ready to fight.

One of his men handed him her mantle, and Gilliam offered it to her, a teasing glint in his eye. "Since you no longer own a pin, you must knot it around your shoulders." When she did not immediately take the garment, Gilliam cocked a brow as he studied her face. "I will not tie you," he said softly. "I only seek to insure we travel in the same direction."

Gratitude rushed through her before she could stop it. She stomped on the emotion to keep from spilling thanks over being made only half his prisoner. She snatched her mantle from his hand, then remembered it had no hood.

At that moment, Nicola would have given her life to cover her head. Why had she sacrificed her precious hair? Even as Tilda cut the first strand, she had known full well there was no possible outcome to her escape attempt, save recapture. She would wear proof of her foolishness atop her head for years to come.

"Jos," FitzHenry called over his shoulder, "ride you alongside my lady and bear her company."

"I am not your lady," she warned in a harsh voice.

"You will be. When we arrive at Ashby, we will wed." It was a flat statement.

"You cannot force me where I will not go," she retorted, but a kernel of fear awoke in her heart. She had betrayed her folk. They had no reason to support her against him.

"We shall see."

'Twas the boy who responded to Gilliam's call, drawing his pony beside her taller palfrey. He stared at her, the expression in his brown eyes far older than his youthful features.

" 'Tis rude to stare," she snapped.

"My pardon, Lady Ashby, but I have never seen a woman dressed as a man." It was a considered response, not at all a child's impulsive blurt. "Walter said you killed those thieves. Did you?"

"Aye." Once again, her sickness returned. She thanked God that it lacked its original intensity, when she should have thanked Gilliam.

Ahead of her, her captor called his men into motion. The boy's short steed trotted alongside hers, making the child bounce in the saddle. "Will you kill Lord Ashby?"

"He is not Ashby's lord." She shot him an angry look, but behind it lurked the knowledge that killing was not as easy as she once believed. "Who are you, anyway, and why do you ask these questions?"

"I am Jocelyn of Freyne, squire to Lord Ashby." He made this sound like a fate worse than death.

"You do not wish to be a squire?"

He lifted his scrawny shoulders in a dejected shrug. "It does not matter what I want. Maman says that I am too weak and small to tolerate the life of a squire. I will soon die." He sighed deeply, his brows peaked in a hopeless look.

Nicola again studied him, this time with her healer's eye. His skin was pale beneath the chafed spots on his cheeks, but this was his natural coloring. There was no sign of the dark rings under his eyes that sometimes indicated a consumptive illness. "You appear hale enough," she said after a moment.

"What do you know of it," he shot back in indignation. "I have been forced here against my will, and now I will die."

"So, we are captives together, are we?" she asked as the boy reflected her own emotions back to her. "Well, then, if I win free of this trap, you can come with me."

"Where would we go?" he asked, a trace of interest in his brown eyes.

Where would she go? No matter what direction she fled, there was some man waiting at journey's end to capture her. Nicola grimaced, then shrugged. "It was but a wishful thought."

"At least we have each other," the boy offered, some of the sullenness leaving his expression.

"Aye, at least we have that," she agreed. "You are a strange boy, Jocelyn of Freyne, but I like you."

Her statement seemed to please him, for his mouth lifted into a small smile. Gilliam called for a faster pace, and there was no possibility for further conversation. They rode, long and hard, continuing even after night settled around them.

The sun's setting brought an end to the rain, but the wind only rose to take its place. Its icy breath battered them in their steady northward journey, while it swept the sky free of clouds to reveal a moonless night.

Jocelyn had given way to exhaustion and now rode

with his lord, much as Nicola had earlier done. For
herself, she couldn't remember ever being so tired or
so cold. Her mantle did little to protect her from the
sharp wind. She shivered, wishing 'twas she who rode
with Gilliam.

This wayward thought brought her bolt upright in
her saddle. What sort of daughter desired comfort in
her father's killer's arms? Damn him, but Gilliam was
using kindness to lure her into complacency. Aye, here
was the explanation for why he kept asking after her
well-being and stopping when she requested it.

Clutching the pommel, she glared at the plain saddle
until her hate was fully restored. Let him think he had
succeeded. They were but a stone's throw from Ashby.
Her folk would rescue her from him. She hoped.

Nicola scrambled to reassure herself. Surely her villagers would never allow her to be forced into a union
with their lord's murderer. Despite Papa's lazy ways
and slipshod management, they had loved her father.
They would deny Gilliam if only to honor Papa's
memory.

As they rounded the last bend separating her from
her homeland, excitement drove away all other worries
and concerns. She peered about her, eager to catch every nuance. Starlight showed her only glimmers and
shadows of landmarks; still she heard the tumble of the
river alongside her road and the rush of the wind
through her thick forest. With every breath she found
familiar scents, the smell of fires on hearths, the richness of turned earth and resting meadows.

They rattled across the bridge, the toll taker long
since gone to bed, and entered the village compound to
a chorus of dogs and geese. Nicola gaped in surprise as
they passed cottage after cottage, the gentle roundness

of their thatched roofs outlined against the dark sky. In June past, Gilliam had burned every one of them to the ground before laying seige to Ashby itself, and November was too soon to expect the village to be rebuilt. How had her folk managed to so swiftly restore their homes?

Instead of riding for Ashby's gateway, Gilliam led them to the right and halted before the church used by both noble and commoner. Caught into a corner of Ashby manor's defensive wall, the church's stone tower was a solid square of black against the airy darkness. The barnlike extension of the church proper was lost against the wall behind it.

Nicola grinned in smug confidence. How foolish of him to think he could marry her this very night. The villagers would resent being awakened from a sound sleep, and Father Reynard cherished his quiet evening hours. Then, again, let him try; it could only work to her advantage.

"All of you, save Alfred, leave the horses and go to the reeve's house," the tall knight called out. "Walter, tell Thomas what I intend this night, then help him rouse the village. I want every man here to witness in no less than a quarter hour. If you must, use your blades to spur them on to speed."

"Aye, my lord," his man replied. Saddle leather protested, iron rattled, and steeds stamped and blew. Five men dismounted, their stride stiff-legged as they moved off toward Tilda's father's house. In a moment, they were only shadows in the night.

"Jocelyn, you must mount your pony once more," he said to his squire as he set Jocelyn's feet onto the ground. The boy staggered to his mount, failing twice to insert his foot into the stirrup before rising into the saddle.

Gilliam dismounted and turned to the remaining man. "Alfred, ride with Jos into yon walls and rouse the serving folk. Take these." He handed the man his cloak and sword. Nicola stared at his belt. Gone, too, was his dagger. She grimaced, then shrugged. Aye, he offered her no opportunity to take his weapons, but in doing so he also left himself disarmed against her.

"Send two grooms to come fetch the horses," Gilliam was saying. "Only they and the guards at the gate may linger within the manor walls. Everyone else will stand as witnesses, even the pig herd. Bring with you fodder for fires and torches. I'll have a blaze at either side of the church door and torches held all around. I want it as near to day's light as we can achieve. All must clearly see what is done here this night."

"Aye, my lord," the man replied. He and the boy rode for the gate, some hundred yards distant.

Gilliam came to her side and set his hands at her waist. When he tugged slightly, Nicola clung to her saddle. 'Twas time to make her stand, and she would make it with every ounce of her being.

"So our peace is at an end," he said without emotion. "As you will, but take heed, my lady. I am already tired and hungry—do not make me angry as well."

"If you wish to rest and eat, go within yon walls and do not let me stop you." Her voice was hoarse with cold. "Why persist at this? I have already said I will not marry you, and you cannot force me where I do not wish to go."

"Free your feet from the stirrups or pay the price in

pain when I pull you off the saddle." Again, there was no anger or irritation in his voice.

Resisting was fine, but not at the expense of her poor feet. Suddenly empty, the stirrups swung free at the horse's sides. Gilliam slid her into the cradle of his arms, then carried her around the church to the cottage behind it. 'Twas a squat, square house with thatch for a roof, just like the other cottages. Father Reynard's few sheep murmured sleepily in their pen near a dormant garden.

Gilliam made his way up the well-worn path to the wooden door. When he shifted her weight into a single arm to pound upon the panel, Nicola teetered unsteadily in his grasp. Her arms came rushing up to latch around his neck. Beneath her fingers his shoulder muscles were corded and tight. He pounded a second time. "Father Reynard," he shouted, "come, open up to your lord."

The wind swirled around her, tangling in her hair before it reached down her bare neck. With her mantle only knotted around her shoulders, it gapped to allow the cold air to enter into her clothing. She shivered, turning her head into his shoulder. Just as he raised his fist for yet another knock, she caught the priest's reedy call.

"I come!" Two simple words, yet the very sound of Father Reynard's voice as familiar to her as her own, woke within her a wondrous sense of safety and security.

Nicola caught back a sudden and happy cry. Home! She was home. Here, folk cared for her and loved her; they would never let her be misused.

The bar lifted, and the door swung open with a soft sigh of oiled leather. "Come in," the priest called as he turned back into the cottage's single room. Wooden-soled sabots thudded dully on the beaten earth floor. "Give me a moment to fetch a lamp, then tell me what it is that brings you here so late."

Nicola followed the sound of his shoes to find the man. Reynard glanced over his shoulder. Caught in the starlight from the open door, his face floated out of the darkness, round as the moon and equally as pale. Her memory gladly supplied his features.

There was a great beak of a nose above a wide mouth and a dense beard streaked with gray. Beneath thick brows, his brown eyes were trapped in a web of creases along his cheeks. Nature gave him his tonsure, removing fine dark hair in an ever-expanding circle atop his head.

"Father!" she cried out, incapable of containing her joy at homecoming any longer, " 'tis I, Nicola."

"My lady," the priest crowed in excitement, "God be praised. Oh, damn my fingers, I cannot get hold of the fire cover." There was shuffling, the clink of an iron hook against clayware, then glowing embers appeared as the pottery shield that protected the house from its own heat source was lifted. He touched a frayed rush to a coal until it glowed, then lay the burning stalk against the lamp's wick. A tiny flame appeared and grew, fed by the rancid fat in the bowl. "My lord, 'twas good of you to bring her here to show me she is well and whole."

Now encircled in a yellow bubble of light, Father Reynard turned. The glow turned his pale skin an ivory color, and made dark hollows of his eyes. Silver glinted in his beard where the shadow of his nose did not obscure it. He wore a farmer's rough tunic, no doubt hastily donned, its worn collar loose around his scrawny throat.

"That was not my purpose in coming," Gilliam said. "Although I am glad it pleases you to see her once again. Father, you must wed us this very moment."

Nicola looked up at the man who held her. The lamplight showed her his profile, even and strong. His calmness worried her. She found herself wishing he would rage, as another man might have done, so she could know how to battle him.

"What?" The churchman's brow rolled up into thick creases. "But, I thought you were married yesterday, my lord."

"There were complications—" Gilliam hedged.

"I refused," Nicola's voice overrode his. "And I will do so again."

"Whatever made you refuse him?" the priest cried in astonishment.

Nicola's heart sank. Of all her folk Father Reynard should understand. "There is more to it than a simple refusal," Gilliam replied, "but your explanation must wait. Come now, grab up your mantle and hie you to the church to gather what you need for the ceremony." Still holding Nicola, he turned, preventing any further conversation, and strode swiftly out of the cottage. Left with no option but to follow, the priest clip-clopped along beside him, two paces to every one of Gilliam's.

As they rounded the church's corner, Nicola saw no one standing before the door. She grinned in relief. They would not come after all.

Father Reynard opened the door to the holy chamber, then hurried in, his heels rapping sharply on the tile floor. Gilliam entered behind him, stopping just beyond the open doorway. Only then did he lower Nicola's feet to the floor.

Her knees shook at the sudden requirement of bearing her own weight, the wound on her shin stretching painfully. When she faltered on her complaining feet, she grasped at his arm to keep herself upright. He let her cling, then moved his arm around her to brace her.

The priest's lamp flame weaved and hopped in the draft as he crossed the room's length. Setting the burning bowl on the altar, he pulled a robe on over his tunic, then took up his great cross. Once again, the lamp came flickering through the dark toward her. Reynard stopped directly before them. Nicola watched his eyes widen in reaction to what he saw. "My God, what have they done to you?"

"What you see she did to herself in trying to escape me," Gilliam said. "Lower your lamp and look at what she wears."

Reynard did as suggested, and his expression sagged. With a thick finger he touched her hauberk, then caught one of the short curls that lay soft against her cheek. "Jesus God and all His saints, she's made herself a boy this time," he said with a gusty sigh of strained patience.

"This time?" Gilliam laughed. "Do tell me what else she has done. I cannot wait to hear."

Nicola cringed in the face of his amusement, then rage washed over her, taking with it her common sense. "Do not laugh at me!"

She swung at him, her fist rebounding off his arm. An instant later, she hung over his shoulder, bottom up, head and feet dangling. She tried to lift herself, but the bruise on her side came to life, taking her breath with its pain. "Damn you, put me down." It was barely a gasp.

"My lady, cease. You must not do so to your husband," Father Reynard pleaded, stunned by her assault on the nobleman.

"This dirty pig is not my husband, nor will he ever be," she cried. "Leave me go, you great oaf." She slammed a fist into Gilliam's back.

"I have had enough of your abuse," the big man shouted, the power of his voice shaking the rafters above him. "Hit me once more and pay the price."

Awed and not a little frightened by the strength of his anger, Nicola went instantly still. Blood throbbed into her head. "Aye, and what will that be?" Although she made of her question a dare, she waited warily for his answer.

"Hit me and you'll know," he said, his voice tense and hard.

His open-ended threat was worse than any specific promise, since she could not guess what he had in mind. Her imagination insisted on offering her image after possible image, all of them unpleasant. Trapped between fuming anger and very real worry, she was utterly helpless. Once agin, the potential of defeat loomed before her.

"My lord, put her down," the priest begged on her behalf.

Nicola sighed in relief. There would be no need to submit. Reynard would convince Gilliam to release her.

The priest continued in a placating tone. "Come now, my lord, be at ease. 'Tis late and we are all tired. Go you to bed and rest. Everything will seem better in the morning. You can marry her then."

"Father, I will not tolerate your interference here." Gilliam's words were hard as stone. "This is no child to be protected, but a woman full grown. She must learn that if she abuses me, she will pay the price. I think she has been too long indulged in her rages and misbehavior."

Nicola's eyes flew wide. "Misbehavior?" she cried out, her voice muffled by her undignified position. "I have been kept a prisoner for months, my home has been given to the man who killed my father, and when I resist, you call it misbehavior?" She blinked away angry tears. "I hate you!"

"You may hate me all you wish, but you will not hit me," Gilliam snapped. "Vow you will strike me no more, and I will let you down. Do not swear to this lightly, for I will hold you to your word. Break it at your own peril."

"Father Reynard, make him put me down," she cried to the priest, not willing to give Gilliam control over her fists.

" 'Tis wrong that a woman strikes a man," the priest said softly.

"I hate all men." It was a private snarl of rage, said under her breath. "I am sorry I struck you," she managed louder, through gritted teeth. 'Twas not what Gilliam wanted from her, so he said nothing. Her head was pounding now. "Brute! You take this battle by simple virtue of your size and my injuries. I vow before God in this holy place to strike you no more. There. I have sworn, now I hope you choke on your victory."

Gilliam still said nothing and made no move to release her. Nicola knew what he wanted, but she waited until she could absolutely no longer bear her aching head.

"Please put me down." It was but a soft whisper.

She was immediately lifted off his shoulder. Her vision swam, and she swayed against him when he set her feet on the floor. He caught her close, holding her tightly to his side.

By God, but she hated him. Nicola wanted desperately to push him away, but knew if she did 'twas she who'd fall. Nor did she wish to look at him, knowing he would be smiling now that he'd dealt her yet another defeat.

When she was again steady in herself, she managed a huff of rage. "Leave go. I cannot bear your touch."

"What a shame that is." There was, indeed, a smile in his voice. "I have discovered I find you enormously attractive, if a mite wild."

His taunt sliced through her, sharper than Alan's knife. No man found her attractive. "Liar! Now, leave me go. I can stand on my own," she said, keeping her eyes averted from him. "Leave me go."

"I think I cannot do so until we are well and truly wed. De Ocslade may be breathing hot and heavy on my heels. I'll not cede him Ashby for want of exchanging simple vows."

"De Ocslade? What do you mean?" The priest's nervous question brought Nicola's attention back to him. The man's eyes shifted from her to the taller man at her side.

"Your lady claims to be betrothed to Ashby's neighbor—" Gilliam got no further in his explanation.

"What!" Reynard yelped. He started at her, his brows fair leaping from his face in stunned disbelief. "How dare you lie about so holy a thing!"

"Do you think I would have done so if I'd had any other option?" Nicola retorted in irritation. Through the open door she saw a parade of light as Ashby's serving folk came bearing burning torches. If she did not win the priest's support, her cause would be finished. In desperation, she clutched at the churchman's sleeve.

"You must understand," she begged, "I never meant to stay married to that little ferret for long. Once de Ocslade was in his grave, Ashby would be where it belongs, in my hands."

Father Reynard's mouth dropped open, and his face grew icy still.

Gilliam stood so close, she both felt and heard his chuckle as it rumbled from him. "Oh, my girl, here I was thinking you preferred that man to me. If my heart quails that you intend that same fate for me, at least my self-worth is restored."

"Murder!" the priest finally managed to gasp out, tearing free of her grasp to back away. "You meant to do murder? Holy Mother, come this night and save this poor woman from herself," he prayed aloud, then abandoned heavenly intervention for a more earthly solution. He grabbed Gilliam's free hand and knelt before him.

"My lord, I beg you, if you can tolerate the union, let me marry you this moment. Truly, she is not as insane as she sounds. Lady Nicola is a fine healer, she keeps a clean house and a savory kitchen. Her cheeses are renowned, and that's God's own truth. 'Twas her father who spoiled her by refusing to curb her headstrong ways. Please, my lord, I see how desperately she needs your controlling hand. Perhaps what her father ruined, you can restore."

"Nay, Father Reynard!" 'Twas a cry of frustration and outrage as she staved off panic with a loud voice.

Gilliam's laugh was warm and deep as he drew her closer to him. "Have no fear, I want her, mad or no. Gather your wits for the doing of this deed, Father. As you can see, she will fight us to the end."

Nicola tried to wrench free of him, but there was no escaping his powerful embrace. When he lifted her into his arms, she strained against his hold and he played as though to drop her. With a gasp, she caught him around his neck, then angrily brought a fist before her in threat. He arched a brow.

"Is your word worth nothing?"

"You took my vow unfairly from me," she retorted, yet let her hand open and drop to her side. Unable to strike out but still needing to vent her rising anger, she grabbed him by the collar of his hauberk. "None of this is fair."

He looked at her. Caught between the glow of the priest's lamp and the growing brightness outside the church door, Gilliam's hair glinted like spun gold. Shadows played along the contours of his face, outlining his finely molded lips. It must have been a trick of the light that made his expression seem gentle and almost sad.

"I know," he agreed quietly, "but screaming over it solves nothing. We will be wed, and you must find what good you can in this."

"What sort of daughter does that make me?" she protested, heart aching. Against her will, a single tear traced its way to her jaw. He opened his mouth to protest, but Nicola put her hand over his lips to silence him. "I cannot bear to hear you say again you did not do what you did, when I was there and saw it all."

His eyes closed briefly, then his lips touched her palm. She jerked her hand away in surprise. When he spoke, it was more sigh than comment. "You have turned my blow into what it was not. Would that I could retract it, for I see now it will cost me more dearly than I imagined."

"Nay," she said, her voice strengthening as she fought to hide her weakness behind anger. "Nay, I do not accept your apology, and I will not marry you. The villagers will support me against you."

"I pray not," he replied. Where his face had shown sympathy a moment before, there was now only amusement. "Those cheeses of yours have me positively intrigued."

She turned her face away from him as he carried her out of the church. When he set her down before the door, her hauberk was caught firmly in his fist. Nicola blinked against the artificial brightness, then scanned the growing crowd huddled around the doorway. Wrapped in cloaks, mantles, or blankets, flickering light gleamed off their brows and noses, but left their identities disguised by the night.

The wind toyed with the fires, sending great tongues of flame leaping high into the sky. Showers of sparks were teased away from their mother source and into whirling dances of death. In a sudden gust, the torch flames all bent to one side, their stinking black smoke so dense it was even visible against the darkness.

The reeve pushed his way through the crowd. 'Twas his rolling gait, caused by rheumy hips, that identified him as Thomas. Tilda's father wore only a short tunic beneath his mantle. Outlined by the fire's glow, she saw the thick hair covering his legs; he'd not even taken time to don his chausses. At his present age, it was hard to tell if Thomas had ever resembled his beautiful daughter. He was all wild tawny hair and heavy beard with eyes so deeply set they disappeared into the leather of his face.

Nicola let her mouth lift slightly as the stocky man stared at her. The creases of his face drooped in disappointment as he took in her attire and shortened hair. After a moment, he shook his head and backed into the crowd. Thomas would not support her. Her betrayal of Ashby had cost her his love. Once again, a tear dared slip free of her control. She angrily wiped it away.

"My friends," Father Reynard called to the assembled folk in their native tongue, "our new lord asks you here to witness his wedding to Lady Nicola. Our lady has refused to wed with him once before, and will attempt to do so again. You must decide if it is in our best interest to ignore her cries of forced marriage and see the deed done."

"This you cannot do," Nicola protested in that same tongue. "If you choose to support him, you dishonor my father's memory. Do not allow Ashby's new lord to be the same man who killed your loved ones and destroyed your homes."

"With respect, my lady, who among us can afford to worry over honoring or dishonoring a memory." This was Alexander atte Lane, the village carpenter. "Besides, no killing would have happened if your sire had not taken Lord Graistan prisoner. Lord Gilliam cannot be blamed for coming to free his kin."

"How can you excuse him?" she cried in disbelief. "Is this how you feel about it, John over Brook?" She turned to confront a grim-faced man of middle years. "Your daughter was among those who perished that day." The girl had been one of Nicola's dairymaids.

She had picked the man because he usually loved to scream over the injustices done him. Tonight, he betrayed her.

"My daughter is just as dead no matter who did what. 'Tis my home and farm that must concern me now. Over the last months I have found Lord Gilliam attentive to those issues first in my heart. Look around you. What he destroyed to rescue his brother, he has spent his sweat to rebuild. By the strength of his arm did we have trees to hold up our new walls. Aye, 'tis by his decree and his assistance that we have both house and harvest to save us from the winter's cold."

"Hah!" It was a scornful sound to mask her ever deepening despair. "Do you not see that he has done so only to buy your loyalty? Once he has it from you, you will no doubt find a different sort of man hiding behind that ploy."

"What she says could be true, but after five months of dealing with this lord, I think it unlikely." William Smith, Ashby's blacksmith, crossed his hefty arms over his chest. "What does the reeve say to this?"

Thomas threw back his shaggy head. "I will say nothing. You all know the noblewoman is closely bound to my family. My opinions will remain my own."

There was a subtle easing in Nicola's heart. If he would not support her, neither would he participate in her downfall.

"My lady, there are worse husbands to have than this one." 'Twas a woman's sultry voice, its owner hidden by the crowd. "A great hulking man like him will keep you warm these long winter nights." The folk erupted in laughter.

"He's a right good swimmer, too, my lady." The

child's piping voice was filled with the confidence that this was the ultimate criterium in husbands.

"Enough of this foolishness!" Ralph by Wood shouted, his gravelly voice echoing off the church walls. As holder of the greatest portion of land in the village, his opinion carried a weight equal to his acreage. The crowd fell silent as Nicola caught her breath, awaiting his words.

" 'Tis cold out here, and there's threshing to be done come dawn's light. 'Twas she that closed the drawbridge upon Lord Gilliam when he came calling, seeking to free his brother. Thus, she bears the blame for our past trouble. This lord is a better one that her sire, that much is certain. I say we ignore her cries of forced marriage to protect our homes and farms."

Nicola swayed as her heart fell into pieces onto the ground. They would not support her because they blamed her for Ashby's fall. It was more than she could bear.

Chapter Nine

Gilliam caught Nicola closer to him as she moaned softly and faltered. He signaled to Walter. "What did that man say?"

"My lord, Ralph by Wood asks the villagers to ignore your lady's protests of forced marriage and see the two of you joined. The rest are following where he leads."

Gilliam's eyes closed in a brief prayer of thanks. Here was the test of what he had labored so to build. The same folk who had petitioned for their lady's return had ignored her pleas in his favor. This boded well for his plans for Ashby's future.

At his side, his bride found her feet and her tongue once more. It was odd to hear her voice curl around the peasants guttural language. He had no need of a translator to tell him she begged her folk not to give her to him. The priest shook his head and stepped forward.

Once again, Gilliam breathed deeply in relief. Ashby would be his. And, so would she.

By God, his wanting for her had become like a fire in his belly. Their short ride together this day had nigh on killed him. Her clothing had gapped as she leaned against him. Every glance downward had revealed the sweet curve of her breast. Between the motion of the horse, her body caught tightly to his, and the bare stretch of her neck just begging to be kissed; he'd been drunk with longing by the ride's end.

But she wanted him not at all. He shook his head in pained amusement. Was it because she hated him so that his desire to have her grew by leaps and bounds? There was perverse logic in that thought.

The priest turned to him. "My lord, the villagers have all agreed that their lady is suffering from a temporary madness, which causes her to refuse you. In this unbalanced state, no heed can be given to her cries of forced marriage. The folk hope you will yet agree to wed her despite her mental deficiencies."

Gilliam glanced down at the woman beside him. Where Geoff's wife had truly suffered madness, Nicola had no insanity in her. All that plagued her was a desire to be something other than what was expected of her. "I will have her to wife."

"Nay." Her complaint was but a quiet breath.

He reached for the tall girl's other arm, turning her so they stood face-to-face. When she looked up at him, he saw how deeply the villagers' decision had cut. She was clearly stunned. Her eyes, brown for the moment, were filled with unshed tears. The firelight sparked, jewel bright, on this sheen of moisture as her mouth softened and trembled.

Gilliam's breath caught. Mary, but she was lovely when she was not angry. He longed to run his fingers along the velvet curve of her cheek and the long, slender line of her throat. Aye, and then he'd touch his lips to hers once more and feel her melt against him. Only to have her wipe his kiss off her mouth. After this defeat, surely no caress would be strong enough to destroy her hate.

Standing behind them, Father Reynard cleared his throat. "My lord, I am no great churchman. I can give you no pretty speech, only the vows."

He glanced at the priest. "'Tis all that matters, is it not?"

"Just so." With a nod, the churchman began, simply ignoring the question of willingness. "I have heard the recitation of their heritages, and know there is no obstacle to their joining. So, too, have I heard the contract for their union. Lord Gilliam's dower is suitable, it being the village of Eilington. Their banns have been read. Your vow, my lord?"

Gilliam's hands tightened over hers, and Nicola turned her head to the side, refusing to look upon him as he spoke. "I, Gilliam FitzHenry, holder of Eilington, take thee, Nicola, heiress of Ashby, to my wedded wife, to have and to hold, from this day forward, for better or worse, for richer, for poorer, in sickness and in health, till death us depart. To thee do I plight my troth."

The priest turned on Nicola. "My lady?"

She yet stared into the flames. "I will say no vows. To do so would dishonor my father." Her words would have been hard and cold, save that they were interrupted by a soft sob.

Reynard looked out at the villages. "This madness of hers has rendered our lady mute. Who will speak for her?"

"I will," Thomas the reeve replied.

"Nay," Nicola cried out as if mortally wounded. "Not you, Thomas."

"Let me speak for her." A woman, great with child, waddled from the crowd, her hair a bright coppery red. "I know the nobleman's language well enough."

"Alice!"

Before Gilliam realized her intent, Nicola wrenched her hands from his grasp to throw her arms around the woman. As he grasped her by the back of her hauberk, the tall girl stepped away from the villager to run her hands in a knowing way over the woman's huge belly. Alice only smiled serenely, content to let her lady do so. Nicola began to speak again in English, her tone low and urgent.

"Lady Nicola, the decision had been made. You will do your duty by us," the reeve said in French. Gilliam thought he sounded very much like Rannulf, when his brother had made a decision and would tolerate no more argument. "If you cannot, the folk will no longer welcome you in their homes. I will say so as well."

Nicola stared at the burly man, her eyes wide in panic at this threat. Gilliam shook his head in disbelief. What was this hold the commoners had on her? She acted as though she'd rather die than be disowned by them.

Reynard held up his hand. "We have all seen her designate Alice as the one to speak for her." He turned to the fecund woman. "Alice, if you wish to speak, do so. We would all be abed once more."

Again, Gilliam turned the tall girl toward him. "I would hear your voice saying these words," he told her, catching her hands in his. Like the rest of her, her fingers were long and slender, and cold as ice. He folded his hands around hers. She only shook her head and looked away again.

"I, Nicola, Lady Ashby, do take thee, Lord Gilliam FitzHenry now of Ashby, to my wedded husband," Alice's voice rang out as clear as a bell, her words lilting with her accent. "To have and to hold, from this day forward, for better, for worse, for richer, for poorer, in sickness and in health, till death us depart, if it be ordained, and to thee do I plight my troth."

Reynard nodded once in satisfaction. "Have you a ring, my lord?"

"I do," Gilliam replied, releasing one of Nicola's hands to open the purse at his belt. He offered the priest the golden band, its surface etched with a geometric design. Reynard blessed it, then returned the band to him.

Nicola's hand had disappeared behind her back. "I will not take it," she warned him.

"Do not make me do this," Gilliam said quietly. "I have no wish to hurt you."

"Do as you must," she said in an equally low voice. "I cannot take your ring."

He caught her arm and wrenched it out from behind her, knowing how he must be hurting her. When he glanced at her, her eyes were squeezed shut in the effort it took to resist him. Her hand now lay in his, but her fingers were tightly fisted to prevent him from placing the ring on her fingers as the rite required. He pried open her hand. As quickly as possible, he touched the golden circle atop each of her fingers, then settled it on the one that led to her heart. "With this ring I thee wed, and with my body I thee honor."

"Nay!" She flung away the ring and lurched free of him. Gilliam leapt after her. His hands caught her around the waist, but her vest was smooth and she slithered from his grasp. Limping heavily, she dodged the priest and tried to enter the crowd.

They offered her no escape. Instead, they raised their voices, chiding and shouting, as they encircled her. The few women in their ranks separated from husbands and brothers to gather around her. Nicola frantically shook her head at whatever it was they said. Gilliam stood tense and alert, waiting for her to shove through them and make her escape. To his astonishment, the village matrons led the now-unprotesting girl toward Ashby's gates.

" 'Tis done!" Father Reynard shouted for all to hear. "I say this marriage is complete. We have all witnessed this." He turned to his new lord. "The women go to prepare her for the bedding. We should be after them, my lord. I would like to be back at my own rest."

The bedding. Gilliam again lifted his gaze to Nicola, watching until her tall, slim form disappeared into the darkness. Consummation of this marriage was the final link in his hold over Ashby, but she wanted him not at all. Rape was not how any marriage should begin.

Trapped in a sudden and bitter disappointment, Gilliam looked down on the priest and hid his emotions behind a smile. "My thanks, Father Reynard. To all of you as well," he called to the villagers. "Go, now, and find your peace. The priest and those women will witness our bedding. Know that I am grateful to all of you for sharing with me this most memorable joining."

When his words were translated for the benefit of those who did not speak his tongue, there was a rumble of laughter. As they departed for their own beds, they sent him calls of congratulations and hopes for fertility.

Gilliam turned to Walter. "Find that ring," he said in a tired voice. "It was my mother's and precious to me. When you have it, hurry all the servants back within the walls and close the gates. Although I think it improbable, 'tis not impossible that de Ocslade may arrive this night searching for me and my wife."

With that, Gilliam and Father Reynard started toward the manor's gate. Where the river fronted his property at the east and north, here his defense was a water-filled ditch whose embankment was studded with sharpened stakes. They followed the moat along the recently restored south wall to the arched opening. At this late hour the gates were usually closed, the drawbridge nestled tightly between its two small towers. Just now, the long tongue of wood spanned the ditch, and Ashby's gates were thrown wide with two men alert within the opening.

The narrow bridge rattled on its supporting chains as he and the priest crossed into the manor's home farm. As they passed, the guards stood aside and offered their congratulations. Gilliam managed a nod in acceptance, then strode swiftly into the bailey with Reynard tapping along beside him.

Unlike Graistan, which held little land within its walls, the wide expanse here supplied his table with honey, fowl, fruits, and vegetables. Even the fish he ate on holy days came from the mill pond. They crossed over the well-worn path that led to the two tall mills used by his villagers to grind their corn.

His villagers. Gilliam stopped suddenly. Pride of ownership rushed through him. For the first time in his life, he was well and truly home. This did much to ease his hurt over a sour wedding.

"My lord?" the priest asked at this unexpected pause.

"Give me a moment, Father," he said as a clutch of serving folk walked past, calling their good wishes. They moved off toward what had once been the manor's main barn. Gilliam glanced at the long narrow building, his hall for the winter's duration.

While this barn was a big enough structure to house and table all those to whom he owed food and shelter, it had but wooden walls and the same thatch roofing his peasants used. There was only beaten earth for a floor. For a man raised within the security of stone walls thicker than he was tall, it seemed both indefensible and uncivilized.

Gilliam looked to Ashby's keep tower. Designed to serve only as a last, desperate refuge during war, the square stone building was tiny and could never be used as a residence. Ashby's hall had once clung to its side, but when the flames of the siege had died away, all that remained was the tower and a gaping stone cellar. 'Twas a testimony to the fragility of building with wood.

Aye, he'd set his heart upon a hall of stone. Come spring, new walls would rise, incorporating the tower into a far stronger residence. In anticipation of that day, Gilliam had claimed the keep's upper room, turning the chamber that had once imprisoned Rannulf into his own private refuge. It was in that room Nicola awaited him.

He turned away from the keep and walked toward his makeshift hall. "Come, Father, I'd have a bite to eat and take a moment to wash before I rejoin my bride. Perhaps I can offer you a cup of something?"

He was stalling, and he knew it. Somehow, he would find the strength to do what he knew he must.

"Uncle, I think we are too late."

Hugh de Ocslade shot William an impatient look, before returning his gaze to the brightly lit church. His younger nephew ever found it necessary to speak the obvious. Hugh, William, and fifteen of their men had drawn their horses to a halt atop the southernmost field in Ashby's farmland. At their backs was a meadow and the welcome concealment of thick woodland just beyond the lea. His other nephew, Osbert, had remained at the crossroads to serve as a decoy while Hugh returned to Ocslade. Hugh had been pleasantly surprised to discover Graistan's arrogant brother had not been so easily led. This surprising show of intelligence added spice to the challenge of removing the big man from that stupid bitch's bed. He gave thanks to God that he had nephews to marry her. Who in their right would want her?

"Aye, William, but only barely so." Hugh watched the bonfires being doused. "Would that Watt hadn't lamed his horse."

His nephew snickered. "'Tisn't an error he'll repeat twice." Watt's mistake had cost his life.

"There is never an excuse for failure, lad," Hugh agreed, "and dead men rarely fail me. Well now, poor Osbert will be sorely disappointed to learn he no longer has a bride. Do you think he'd care to have a widow in her stead?" The corner of Hugh's mouth curved into a sardonic smile.

"What will you do?"

"I think me we shall give the man a day or two to enjoy his bride, then thieves will infest Ashby's woods. They are much the same as those who stole Lady Ashby from my whore, only a more vicious sort and very careful to leave no trace of who they are. That lordling will have his hands full trying to locate these imaginary thieves, while he protects his new lands."

His nephew's brow creased as he puzzled over this. "I cannot see how this will turn a bride into a widow."

Hugh shook his head in dismay at his kin's slow

wits. "If I saw nothing else this day, I saw the pride
and arrogance in Ashby's new lord. He thinks himself
right powerful and capable, does he not? Otherwise,
why the claims of royal acknowledgment for deeds
done in the Holy Lands? When the harassment starts, I
think he'll come racing to my gate, saying that 'tis me,
not thieves, doing the damage. His insult will cause me
to wage war on him. When he dies in combat, there's
not a man who can blame me for it."

"Aye, but killing him will hardly make Lord
Graistan want to give Osbert Ashby if you kill his
brother," the young knight said.

Hugh laughed. " 'Twas Graistan, himself, who offered me the heiress by his words. He's right, with a
babe in her arms, no one will quibble over who her
husband is. Come, 'tis time to be home before a warm
fire." He turned his mount and started through the
meadow.

"Uncle, your whore's all beaten. Might I have her
tonight?"

"Nay, not yet. If her face heals just as it once was,
I'll keep her for a while longer. She does such marvelous tricks if you dangle coins before her, especially if
she thinks she's stealing them from you."

Chapter Ten

"Nay!" Nicola's heated refusal clouded the air before her. With no hearth or a brazier to warm the confines, 'twas nigh on as cold in here as it was outside.

The village women stood in a circle before her, some holding tallow lamps. The gentle light revealed a fine bed, four posts jutting almost to the wooden ceiling above her. Except for that huge piece of furniture, the room held only a tall night candle and a stool. The light also showed her the pale color of the door's new wood and the floor beneath their feet, the previous, age-darkened wood having been consumed in the fire.

"You had better do as duty requires you." That was Emotte, Ralph by Wood's wife. Sour-tempered and heavy, the woman had no patience. "Dressing like a man does not make you one. You'll bear your husband's weight just as we all must."

"Oh, hush, Emotte. Can you not see the poor girl is afeared?" said coppery-haired Margery, Alice's compassionate sister.

"I am not afraid," Nicola insisted. "Why can you not understand this? That man owns everything I once called mine; I will not give him my body."

"Bah! You all hear her. She's not afeared, she's a

stubborn, spoiled bitch and has always been so. You stay here and coddle her, then. Make way," Emotte snapped at those crowded behind her, "I am going home to bed."

"Come now, my lady, let us remove these things you wear," Athelina, the village ale taster said. A lifetime spent selling ale had taught her to keep a low and soothing voice, what with her long custom of easing tempers made sore by too much drink. "You must be ready when your husband comes."

"'Tis obscene, what you did to your hair," chittered Anne, the toll taker's wife, as she took Emotte's place.

"Enough, you silly bitch," said Maida, the oldest woman in the village. Her grandsons now farmed what her husband had once held. "Her hair will grow. Now, as for those clothes, the sooner you are out of them, the better you will feel." She nodded in agreement to her own words, the rapid movement of her head mouse-like.

Nicola glared at them all, arms crossed tightly before her. "If you no longer want me in your homes, so be it. Be gone with you."

Margery lay a hand on her shoulder. "You cannot mean this, not with your own heart still aching over your father's death. Think of Alice. She was so hoping you would return before the babe's coming. Look, here comes Berthilde with warm water for washing." The group shifted to let a portly woman enter with a bucket and cloth. She made her way to the stool and set her things upon it.

"Come now," Athelina cajoled, her rough hand comforting as she took Nicola's fingers. "Come now, lass. We're so glad you've come home to us. 'Tis but a little thing you need do to be one with us again."

Beaten by her own need for them, Nicola was drawn from the corner. She stood silent and still as the women fell to their work. They stripped away her hauberk and ruined tunic, then lifted off the shirt. There were soft cries and gentle clucks at the great bruise made by Alan's kick.

When it came time to remove her chausses, the bucket was set aside and Nicola given the stool. After the warm, wet cloth had loosened the material from her wounded leg, she looked at the knife wound. It was angry and swollen.

Margery took a wide blanket from the bed to wrap around her as someone ran to find bandaging for her leg and a salve for her torn feet. Fully washed and her hair combed into some semblance of order around her face, Nicola sat shivering beneath the blanket. Berthilde had gone to fetch the priest.

Nicola's eyes closed. She was exhausted and injured, incapable of preventing Gilliam from taking what she would not give him. The door opened. She peered up from her crouched position on the stool. Gilliam ducked to enter the room. His head nearly touched the ceiling, his shoulders made the chamber seem impossibly small.

Murmuring softly and looking like a flock of doves in homespun gowns made dull by the dim light, the women circled around the tall man to remove his clothing. Father Reynard went to bless the bed, and Nicola latched her gaze onto the priest, refusing to look at what went forward only three feet from her nose.

The bed was an expensive piece, what with its embroidered curtains. Even in this low light the yellow and green stitching was vibrant against the blue background. The priest pushed back the bed curtain to reveal a thick mattress, covered with blankets and furs. Bolsters promised lush softness for her aching head. In all her life, Nicola had never slept in such a bed; her body ached to be at rest within it. Were she but alone, 'twould be a wondrous experience.

"Come now, my lady," said Margery, her voice sweet. "'Tis time."

There was a woman at each elbow to lift her whilst the ale wife pulled the blanket from her grasping fingers. Those at her side put their arms behind her back to support her on her injured feet. The cold air made her skin prickle as Nicola closed her eyes in abject shame. She knew all too well she lacked the roundness of a true woman's body, and Gilliam already thought her too thin, having said as much. His scorn would come at any moment.

"I see no defect." Gilliam's deep voice seemed oddly breathless.

He had not laughed. Relief and gratitude washed over her, and Nicola hated herself for it.

"'Tis your turn, my lady." Berthilde whispered in her ear. "You must say if you see any defect in his form."

Nicola opened her eyes. He was watching her, the gleam of the low light against his blue eyes disguising any emotion she might have recognized in them. Mother of God, but he was beautiful. Golden light lay shadows on the gentle curve of his brows, the fine rise of his cheekbones, and the strong column of his neck. He had washed, for his hair was now the color of dark honey and yet heavy with moisture.

His shoulders were nigh on twice the width of hers, one of them bearing an almost round bruise. She grimaced in the sudden realization; 'twas where she'd stabbed him with her pin. Force of habit made her consider the wound with a healer's eye. She'd done only a little damage, there was no need for even a bandage now that the wound had formed a scab.

'Twas in this same, safe dispassion that she finished her inspection. The wet strands that clung to his neck were yet dripping water onto his shoulders. Nicola followed a single, shining bead as it traced its way over the smooth, masculine swell of his chest to the flat plane of his stomach. Here the droplet crossed a scar.

The old injury gleamed ruddy where it marked him waist to hip. No wonder he disliked the needle. It had taken many a stitch to close him. 'Twas a miracle he'd survived at all, much less regained his health and strength. Her gaze descended past his hips. Jesu, if he was massive, there was no excess weight clinging to him. His legs were long, each thigh thicker than her own waist. Even his feet were big.

She looked at her own slender and torn feet. Although she was the tallest woman she knew, never had she felt so small or helpless. She would lose, even if she fought him with all her strength. "I see no defect," she mumbled to her toes.

"There, see this was not so difficult," Berthilde murmured. She and Athelina led Nicola to the bed. "Go beneath the blankets so you do not freeze. Remember now, there must be blood on the sheets in the morning." The women helped her into the bed and under the bedclothes, then backed away from her. "Do as you are told and on the morrow you will be a woman. You will see, all will be well." They were drifting to the door.

Nicola slid across the mattress to where the bed met the wall. Only when they were gone, taking Father

Reynard and the light, did she cry after them, "When have I ever done as I was told?"

The night candle flickered just outside the head of the bed, its meager illumination barely penetrating the thick darkness. She watched as Gilliam moved to shut the door, his form but an uncertain shadow. At the heavy clank of the lock, Nicola's heart exploded in panic. The new door had been fitted with the previous panel's lock. Once again, this chamber became a prison, only this time, 'twas Ashby's lady, not its overlord, who was its occupant. Oh, sweet Mary, but he was locking her in to assure his success.

Rage came roaring in after panic. Damn him, but she'd not let him take all she had left. If those godforsaken betrayers in the village wanted to turn their backs on her, they should do it. 'Twas better to lose them than herself.

The mattress dipped as he sat on its edge, the ropes supporting it straining against his weight. Nicola eased back until she felt the cold wall against her shoulders. Drawing new strength from the stones of her home, she tensed in preparation for the coming battle.

Gilliam sat on the bed's edge. He had no experience with unwilling women. Bedding Isotte had been a spontaneous event, goaded into being by both his youthful lust and his desire to prove the injury had not damaged his manhood. He used only whores since then, paid to feign desire. He glanced across the mattress at his wife. She was clutched into the bed's far corner, hidden from him in the dimness. He didn't care to see her face.

A few moments before, when she had looked at him in the required perusal, he had expected to see hatred,

pain, or even disgust in her expression as she faced
what was for her the ultimate defeat. Instead, there had
been only a worrisome blankness. Gilliam knew many
a man who sought just that sort of emotionless state
prior to battle. If she fought him, how in God's name
was he supposed to do what needed doing without
hurting her?

Turning so his back was braced against the head of
the bed, he eased his legs beneath the cold bedclothes
and shut the curtains. There was an instant darkness
within the bed. It shielded him from what he could not
bear to face. Gilliam closed his eyes with a sigh.

Her image rose before his inner eye, stripped of her
masculine attire. Even with her cropped hair, there was
nothing boyish about her. She was sleek as a cat and
as fragile-looking as a reed, with skin smooth and
white, except where her side was marked with blue
and green. He opened his eyes in recognition of a neutral subject.

"That's a right awful bruise you've got. How came
you by it?" He kept his voice quiet and calm.

"I was kicked whilst defending myself from rapists,"
she replied, making it clear that she considered him
one in the same.

Gilliam squeezed his eyes shut in a disappointment
so terrible he wanted to howl against it. "Do not do
this," he begged softly.

"What choice have I?" she retorted. "I have sworn
not to make you Ashby's lord. Now, since you seem to
put such stock in my vows, you'd hardly want me to
break this one, would you?" It was the gauntlet
thrown, pure and simple.

Gilliam rubbed his hand against his brow, fighting
an errant surge of anger. He eased down onto the mat-

tress and tried to stretch the stiffness from his legs, but
his knees remained bent to an uncomfortable degree.
God's blood, but he was cold·and tired to the bone.
Ashby could be attacked at any moment, his wife
would fight him, and he could not relax because the
damn bed was too short.

He turned to her, attempting reason before anger
completely overtook him. "You have stabbed me, run
from me, made an enemy of my neighbor, and tried to
use the villagers against me. These things I can understand and forgive because of what you say I did to
your father. Now, the battle is done; you fought honor-
ably and well in defending his memory, but you are
beaten. Accept your defeat with grace. You are no
longer his daughter, but my wife. You must cede to me
in this."

"I will not."

"Do you beg me to force you?"

"Try it, if you dare." It was a viper's hiss.

Her arrogance sent rage roaring through him, all
hope of control destroyed by her threat. "You go too
far, madam. Whether you like it or not, you are married to me and you'll not tell me nay on our wedding
night!"

With that, he reached into the shadows to catch hold
of her. The little fool lashed out, and he immediately
grasped her arm. She pried futilely at his restraining
hand as he slowly and steadily dragged her toward
him.

She braced a foot on his thigh to throw herself back
at the wall. Although she did not get far, he could
move her no more. The tension in her body told him
she had wrapped her free hand around the bed's far

post. Unless he chose to dislocate her shoulder, she was impervious to his pulling.

"Come to me," he demanded. Every irritation and inconvience of this day was fuel to his anger. Yet holding her wrist, he reached into the darkness of the corner and gripped her opposite shoulder. She tried to sink her teeth into his forearm. "Damn you!" It was a deafening bellow as he snatched back his arm.

Her feet scrabbled against the mattress, shoving the bedclothes onto the far end. She thrashed and twisted as she struggled to free her trapped arm.

Gilliam tugged hard, then released her. She fell back into the corner with a cry, too surprised to fend him off as he lunged forward and grabbed her at the waist. His hands did indeed span her middle, but beneath the silk of her skin he felt the hard strength of her muscles. He yanked, but she now had both hands fastened to the pole behind her.

"Nay," she cried as he wrapped an arm around her. She was gasping and panting for breath. Within him flickered the beginnings of triumph. If she were already winded, she'd not last much longer.

Again, her foot slammed into his thigh with bruising impact. He grunted in pain and caught her leg to prevent her next kick. She yelped, and he realized he gripped her knife wound. Gilliam freed her calf, but not before he felt the warmth of blood on the binding. The thought of her pain rode him hard. He'd have done better by her if he'd simply ripped her from the corner, rather than trying to ease her out.

"I am done with this," he warned her, anger hardening into determination. "I'll not allow either of us to be wounded in this foolishness of yours."

Rising to his knees, he reached over her back and

into the corner. His hands closed over the delicate bones of her wrists, and she gasped at his bruising grip. With his thumbs, he forced her fingers to open, then tore her hands free of the post. With both of her wrists caught in one hand, he wrapped his free arm around her waist.

She writhed and kicked, but he threw her down onto the mattress, then pinned both her legs to it beneath a thigh. He eased atop her until his wife lay trapped beneath him. He drew a deep breath against the effort it took to hold her down while trying not to crush her with his bulk at the same time.

"What if you did win free of me, where would you run?" he asked sharply. "The door's locked."

She cried out, a desperate sound of frustration and something else. Against his chest, he felt the rapid pounding of her heart. Her breath came in short, shuddering gasps. Then, she bucked beneath him, trying to dislodge him. It was a horrible parody of the lovemaking they should be doing.

Gilliam's stomach twisted in him, and he knew he could not force her, not even for Ashby's sake. He wanted to scream, then shake her into understanding the hurt she was doing to them both. "Yield," he demanded hoarsely. "You must yield."

When she again writhed beneath him, he could bear it no longer. Better to crush her than make himself sick. He relaxed atop her, letting her bear his full weight, certain that not even she could lift him. Her breath came whooshing from her in what almost sounded like a sob.

"Do not force me," she cried as if her heart were breaking. "Please, please, do not force me." There was no longer any trace of hatred or anger in her voice.

Gilliam lay his cheek against her and felt the warmth of her tears on his own skin. "You should have told me you were afraid." In his relief, the words were no louder than a whisper. "I do not mean to hurt you. What happens between us cannot be worse than tearing that wound of yours afresh."

"I am not afraid," she insisted, then shuddered in a wracking sob.

He could feel her cries as they tore through her. Lowering her arms, but not releasing his hold on her wrists, Gilliam eased to one side, then drew her back against his chest. Her hair was soft against his throat, her skin warm on his.

"If not fear, then what?"

Another sob shattered her before she could continue. "Is it not enough for you that you now own my home and my folk? Take me then, but know that you destroy me in doing so, leaving me nothing to call mine own, not even my body."

Gilliam raised his brows in surprise at the true nature of her resistance. "Why did you not say this to me when I first came to bed? This is something I can understand."

"Why should you, of all people, listen to me when no one else does?" Her words were broken by her weeping. "Not Lord Rannulf, not the abbot, not even my folk."

Encouraged by her honesty, he took a moment to consider his options. He already knew he could not force her, and she was telling him a willing joining was impossible for her. At least for now. Whether their marriage was consummated this night or not, their futures were forever intertwined. The importance of that long line of tomorrows far exceeded his need for bloodstained sheets tonight.

He smiled slowly. She was offering him the tool he needed to gain from her what he most craved. "Will you parlay with me now?" he asked, keeping his voice low.

"Parlay? Why should you wish to do so, when I lay in utter defeat beside you? You can take what you want." Her fading sobs came as soft hiccups.

"How do you know that this is what I want?" he asked gently. "What I need is for you to prepare this house for winter. I am told you can do it, but I need to know you will do so honestly, not trying to hurt me by cheating Ashby and its folk. Give me this and I will be content."

"You need me?" The surprise in her voice was colored with the slightest trace of pleasure.

"Aye," he replied, startled by her surprise. "There is much here that I do not know and more to do than I can ever accomplish alone. Did Rannulf not tell you that 'twas I who asked him to move forward our wedding date? He wished to wait until the hall was rebuilt."

"You need me." Her words were barely audible.

Gilliam freed a confused breath. "Of course I do. Are you not Ashby's lady, the one on whom we rely for our daily meat and bread? What is your answer? If I leave you as the owner of yourself; will you give me what I need?"

"I must think a moment." She lay still and soft against him. Gilliam bowed his head to rest his brow on her shoulder. Her skin smelled clean and fresh. His knees fit nicely into the bend of hers, and her back was warm against his chest. Lord, the curve of her buttocks against his groin was tantalizing. He freed her wrists to lay his hand against her hip. It was necessary to put a bit of distance between her and that part of him not willing to trade lust for cooperation.

"I cannot comprehend how you dare to offer me this," she said, as if his movement had stirred her to speech. "Without our union, you are not truly Ashby's lord."

"Who is to say there was no union, save you and I? I will say you were virgin when I took you but left no blood. If you call me husband and share my bed each night, why should anyone question our marriage?"

She peered over her shoulder at him. Even in the dimness, he could see the wary lift of her brows. "'Tis not good enough and you know it. You must take me, and there must be blood on the sheets to prove it."

He shrugged. "Since I will not force you and you cannot give yourself to me, what choice have we? My little falsehood will have to do."

A slight movement of her head sent a thick curl tumbling over her brow. By God, but he wanted to run his fingers through her hair, if only to see whether it was as springy as it looked. The corner of his mouth lifted in a small, bitter sneer. Should he do so, she would only scream and leap away, just as she had done when he had kissed her cheek in the woods. She wanted him not at all.

"What have you decided?"

"That you are mad," she said, wariness yet lingering in her voice.

"'Tis a possibility," he agreed with a humorless laugh. It was sheer madness to think he could lay abed with her night after night and not touch her.

The tiniest of smiles glimmered on her lips. "Who

am I to argue with a madman. I agree to do as I have
always done here at Ashby, and make my home ready
for the winter."

"Good," he said, then continued in a matter-of-fact
tone. "Now, we should speak of how we will present
ourselves to Ashby's folk. I would keep our differences
private. If you wish to discuss a thing with me, take
me aside. I'd not have our folk see us wrangle and argue over every little deed and word between us."

Looking over her shoulder at him, Nicola drew a
deep calming breath, then gave a swift nod. "As what
you say is sensible and for Ashby's good, I will agree,
but only if you vow to truly heed what I say whilst we
are private."

"Have I not just shown you I intend to do so?"

"Aye, that you have."

She rolled onto her back to lay next to him. Even
through the dimness, he could see her expression was
now quiet, her mouth soft. With no bedclothes to conceal her form from him, his gaze drifted down to the
gentle curve of her breasts. Catching a quick breath,
Gilliam lifted himself on an elbow to keep himself
from reaching for her.

She yawned. "I am tired beyond tired," she murmured. "If I am to do as you wish, I must sleep. Pull
up the bedclothes, will you?"

"I think your feet will keep you at a slow pace for
a day or two," he said as he did her bidding. "They
will take time to heal."

"If you want me to succeed, you had better hope
not. 'Tis already the first week of November, and God
alone knows what yet needs doing. Now, hush and let
me sleep."

The command in her voice made Gilliam smile. It

said she was glad to be home and even more pleased to be needed. Aye, she would do as she said, at least for a time. He'd be a fool to think her resistance finished.

Gilliam eased down onto the mattress beside her, wondering what avenues of escape he had left open to her. She could still run to Ocslade, but having avoided the man in Graistan's woods, he doubted that possibility. Her folk had thrown their lot with him, ending the chance of supporting her in rebellion.

Look as he might, he could find nothing left for her, save his own murder. In that case, 'twas a good thing he had installed the main barn's lock onto the armory's door. His men had searched all of the home farm, bringing every weapon and sharpened tool to be locked within that shed. The cook was vowed to count his knives and relinquish none to his lady, save for the task at hand. He smiled. They had found weapons scattered all over Ashby, sheds, barns, even the little chamber built off the dairy apparently used to store herbs and cures. He only hoped they'd found them all.

When he was sure she slept, Gilliam dared what he could not do while she was awake and combed his fingers through her hair. It was heavy and soft, curling around his fingers in a wondrously silky web. 'Twas truly a shame she liked him so little. He lay back into the bolsters and let sleep overtake him.

Chapter Eleven

Nicola started at the wet touch on her cheek and opened her eyes. Pushed into her face was the great, square muzzle of a huge, spotted dog. As the beast snuffled and nosed her, its breath clouded, warm and moist, around her in the cold air.

"*Jesu,*" she whispered, too startled to move. Her word made the dog's eyes narrow. Its lip lifted into a trembling, soundless snarl. Nicola's eyes widened at the sight of huge teeth.

The bed curtains were thrown wide, and the tiny chamber was bathed in hazy light, entering through the east wall's single narrow slit. At the edge of her vision were legs clad in dark chausses above familiar boot tops. She rolled slowly onto her back, and the dog freed a deep and threatening rumble.

"Nay, Roia," Gilliam said. The noise instantly stopped.

Fully dressed, with her pin catching his mantle around his shoulders, her husband watched her. "I can hold them off no longer, my sweet."

As if to prove his words, there was a sudden sharp knock on the door. The dog turned and charged the thick panel, its bark vicious as the hair on the back of its neck rose.

"Holy Jesus," she gasped, coming bolt upright and shifting deep into the bed's interior, the sheets pulled up to her neck as if linen were somehow a defense against sharp canine teeth.

"Enough," Gilliam said quietly. The dog looked at him, gave the door a final husky bark, then returned to the bedside. It leapt into the space Nicola had occupied with an ease that spoke of ownership.

"Get down, you twit," Gilliam told the creature with a laugh. His pet leapt down, and he sat beside Nicola on the bed's edge.

"My lord?" came a woman's fearful cry from outside the door. The huge creature growled again.

"Give us a few more moments," Gilliam called in return.

"Is this your dog?" Nicola asked him in an angry whisper.

"Aye, she is Roia, so called because she is the spawn of our own king's alaunts." Upon hearing her name, Roia placed her head on her master's thigh, eyes suddenly soft with pleading. He scratched her ear, and she grinned, her massive jaws agape. "You are a great hunter of boar, are you not, sweetling? She has also decided this chamber is hers and mine, alone. We must convince her that you and Jos are not intruders, but family. Until she is accustomed to you, 'tis best you make no sudden movements toward me; she's a jealous bitch." He quirked his brows at her, a smile playing at the corners of mouth.

"Now I know you are truly mad. No one in their right mind would keep such a pet." It should have been a stronger retort, but Nicola kept it gentle, not wishing to antagonize the dog.

"Nay"—Gilliam laughed—"you have it wrong. 'Tis I who am her pet. So are you ready to face them?"

"Nay," Nicola looked at the door in dismay. Beyond that thick barrier were the women who came to witness her removal from a yet pristine marriage bed. "This explanation of yours will not work."

He lifted a single, finely arched brow, and deep creases appeared along his cheeks as he smiled. "Ah, my wife, what need have we for explanations when there is blood on the sheets?" He seemed very pleased with himself.

"What!"

Roia lunged for Nicola, snapping and snarling. Gilliam grabbed her studded collar. "Down."

Much more carefully, Nicola pulled back the bedclothes. There was, indeed, a small smear of red staining the middle of the bed. Damn him!

"You lied to me," she cried as quietly as she could. She dragged the bedclothes back around her to guard against both him and the cold. "You took me while I lay unconscious in exhaustion."

Gilliam's eyes flew wide in shock. "I swear to you now, on my honor and all I hold holy, that when we lay upon this mattress in lovemaking, you will not sleep through it." Although laughter tainted his protest, she could tell her accusation had truly stung him.

So the peacock thought himself a great lover, did he? She supposed it went along with his pretty face. Still, 'twas nice to have tweaked him, however blindly she'd managed it. "Have I insulted you?" she asked in feigned innocence.

His mouth lifted in a crooked smile. "Deeply. Look at your leg, then, perhaps I should tell you how I found that spot." His good humor was back.

"I do not wish to know," she replied in her haughtiest voice. He was as bad as a little lad, needling and prodding, his teasing endless and his barbs as sharp as Roia's teeth. Nevertheless, she extended her wounded leg out from beneath the blankets. Blood had soaked the bandage, then overflowed. Aye, here was the source of the mark. Once again, she looked at the stained linen.

Understanding and triumph rose in her. Through this little bit of blood, she gained all she wanted: her home, her folk, and control over her own body.

"Here," her husband said to her, reaching for last night's cloth, yet hanging over the bucket's edge. It was stiff from cold. He shoved it into the icy water, then handed it to her. "Wash that leg to conceal the source before I let our witnesses enter, then you must be up and about your day. I'll not have it said my wife is a lazy slugabed."

"I have nothing to wear," she said, suddenly impatient to reclaim her place as Ashby's lady. More than anything, she wanted to peer into every nook and corner of her home to refamiliarize herself with what was hers. "My gowns were left behind at Graistan."

"Your wedding gowns were ruined," he said, the muted laughter in his tone warning her that some sort of dig was on its way. "You would hardly want those any longer."

"That much is for certain," she retorted warily as she scrubbed away the blood. Nicola didn't dare glance up for fear she'd only feed his game. " 'Tis the other set of gowns I meant, my everyday wear."

"Well, if you had truly wanted them, you'd have stayed at the abbey and wed me, rather than running. Ah, well, there's naught to be done about it now, but I have an idea. Since you are already accustomed to male attire and we know you can wear my clothing, I will lend you a tunic."

This brought her head snapping up, and Nicola glared at him. Although there was no smile on Gilliam's lips, his eyes gleamed wickedly. Here was his barb. Just as she suspected, his taunts over yesterday's events would be endless.

"I think not," she managed as she lowered her gaze to glare at her clean leg. She wouldn't give him any further fodder for his sick wit.

"A pity, that," he murmured, rising. "I rather liked seeing your legs exposed beneath a tunic's hem. Come, Roia."

Nicola watched from the corner of her eye as he and the dog moved to the door. Once he had a hold on his beast's collar, he opened the panel. The alaunt growled and tried to lunge at those who waited outside, but Gilliam's grip on the dog was as inescapable as his hold on Nicola had been. " 'Tis safe. Come you within."

Margery, a chamber pot tucked under her arm, and Emotte, bearing a steaming bucket, eased cautiously around the dog and into the chamber. They had their backs toward their lady as they warily eyed the huge animal.

Only then did Nicola realize she yet held the bloody cloth. It would hardly do to have the women find it and make unfortunate guesses. She shot Gilliam a swift and worried look, holding it up for him to see. He raised his hand, suggesting she should toss it to him. The damp ball sailed over the villagers' heads and disappeared into his palm. His mouth curved, and he winked to compliment her accuracy.

"I will wait for you in the bailey below," he said to her, then he and the dog were gone down the stairs.

"Thank the Lord above," Emotte said with a sigh as big as she when they were gone. She set her bucket of warm water on the floor. "That creature looks half wolf if you ask me."

"I'm told 'tis but a hunting dog, an alaunt with royal lineage, no less," Nicola said, making conversation to steady her nerves. "I can only hope that he does not wish to keep it in here, since it clearly dislikes me." She boldly threw aside the bedclothes to reveal the red mark.

"My lady," Margery cried in pleasure, setting down the pot she carried. Even Emotte managed a fair imitation of a smile.

Nicola slid from the bed, her sly sense of triumph growing. "Margery, I've nothing to wear, not even shoes for my feet. Can you help me find something suitable?"

"Your clothing is here, my lady." The peasant woman unwound Nicola's gowns from around her arm. "Your lord brought these with him."

Nicola's eyes widened in dismay as her shoes clattered out from beneath Emotte's arm. He'd offered her men's clothing, knowing full well where her gowns were. "Ooh, that horrible jackanape," she muttered beneath her breath.

As the women set to stripping the stained linen from the bed, folding it carefully for preservation, Nicola washed in the water Emotte had brought. The bone-chilling cold of the air urged her on to swiftness. She donned the fine linen chemise, then grabbed up her undergown. The high neck garment was made of a fine woolen fabric and dyed a pale green. When Margery had laced the narrow sleeves from forearm to wrist, they fit like a second skin.

The overgown was a contrasting green and made of a warmer fabric than its companion gown. Wide, bell-shaped sleeves were trimmed with a silken braid. Its hemline rose in the front, but the back trailed out behind her.

These gowns had been made for her at Graistan, where a fashionable cut and much lacing were mandatory. Here, at Ashby, the dragging hems would be a nuisance and the long sleeves a fire hazard. Still, since everything else she owned was naught but cinders, she was grateful for them. Given time, she could make others.

Once Margery had salved and bandaged her feet, Nicola carefully drew on stockings and eased into her shoes, loosely tying the laces. Nicola knotted her belt around her waist; the eating knife was still missing. She pulled her mantle around her shoulders, tying it in place. There was no pin. Nicola turned toward the door.

"Wait," Emotte said. "You are a married woman now, where is you wimple? 'Tis not fitting that you go out without a head covering."

Nicola shot her an irritated look. "Would you like to loan me yours, since I have none? Give me time to make one."

"Do not wait too long," the woman warned as she opened the door. " 'Tis bad enough your hair is short, but if you go about bareheaded as well, folk truly will begin to think you an immoral woman." Emotte opened the door and was gone.

"Well, folk already think you are a sour old woman," Nicola muttered after her, then turned to Margery.

"My thanks to you for coming with Emotte this morn. Your company makes hers bearable."

"She has her moments, my lady," Margery said with a laugh. "Alice would like to know when you might come to her."

"As soon as these feet of mine will bear the walk," Nicola said, then smiled in true enjoyment. "I could not believe it last night when I saw her, all full with a babe. 'Twas like an omen."

Margery looked at her as if Nicola had just grown another nose. "How is that?"

"Here is Alice with a history of losing babe after babe, yet despite the terror of June past, she held this one. Surely this pregnancy of hers is a promise that things will return to what they once were." Nicola shrugged against her sudden and silly belief that delivering a healthy child for Alice would somehow remove the burden of Ashby's destruction from her heart.

Margery laughed. "Alice would think you daft for putting such a sign to her babe." The commoner's soft brown eyes gleamed in amusement. "My lady, 'tis right fine to have you home. We have all sorely missed you and your care for us." With that, the woman left the chamber, her shoes tapping briskly down the stone stairs.

Nicola stared after her, hope growing steadily. She was needed and missed. If Gilliam thought building cottages were enough to steal her folk's loyality from her, he was wrong. No matter how hard she needed to work, she would restore the trust she had destroyed until they loved her as they once had.

She followed Margery to the open door, then stopped on the short landing just beyond the threshold. Before June's fire, her view would have been of the hall's back wall. Now, she saw only open sky. It was well into the middle of a cold, but sunny day, with just a wee breeze to play around the hems of her skirts.

The chill air brought with it myriad familiar sounds: the cry of wild geese on the wing, the song of men hard at threshing, and the soprano voice of the river against the steady drone of the mill wheels it powered. The yeasty aroma of bread baking in the public ovens wafted to her.

Her gaze drifted right, to the thick forest of oak and ash, which gave Ashby its name, then to the south. Here, outlined by more distant woodlands, the hills rolled gently away from her walls. Those nearest to Ashby were covered with furrowed fields, their crazy pattern speaking more to the needs of drainage than order.

Nicola knew by heart which strips were hers and which belonged to the villagers. The fields already rested, although the season was not yet done. Some showed the dark, rich hue of turned earth, having been plowed and sown with winter wheat, while others were yet ankle-deep in stubble. The harvest remains were presently being consumed by both cattle and sheep.

Clutched between these fields and her walls, was the village. Newly thatched and whitewashed, cottages were scattered haphazardly along the riverbanks, their fresh gold and white colors startling in a rapidly fading autumn world. Chickens and pigs wandered freely along the rutted paths between the dwellings. In the village green, children screamed and raced, tossing a ball between them. It was all so familiar and right, Nicola was filled with joy. She was home.

"Do you intend to stand up there all the day?"

Gilliam leaned against the raised stone cellar wall,

Roia sitting at his heels. Just above his head, where her hall floor had once been, there was now only wooden planks to keep out the elements. Suddenly, she saw him as she had that day in June, his mail stained with blood, his sword swinging as he cleaved his way through her folk in the burning hall.

What an arrogant child she'd been, foolishly thinking she could hold the walls against this man. How arrogant she still was to think things could ever return to what had been. Every day for the rest of her life, she must face how she had hurt those she loved most. Nicola covered her face with her hands, refusing the burden of what she'd done. She heard Gilliam climb the stairs.

"Nicola?" It was the first time he'd used her Christian name. His deep voice turned its syllables into soft silk.

"This is very hard," she breathed into her palms. "Seeing you standing there made me think of that day."

"Would that I could retreat into the past and change what was done, but I cannot." His voice was filled with regret.

Oh, Lord God, so did she wish she could change the past. Nicola dropped the shield of her hands from her eyes. Gilliam stood on the step just below this short landing, bringing them eye to eye. He watched her with such intensity that she drew a sudden breath. His gaze touched her brow, then her lips, down the exposed line of her throat. An odd pressure woke just under her heart.

"That color suits you," he murmured a moment later, lifting his hand as if he meant to touch her face. He caught back the motion, his hand dropping to his side. "It seems you found your clothing, Lady Ashby." His brows lifted in tune to his smile.

His words destroyed the disturbing sensation of the previous moment and reminded her she was angry with him. "What would you have done if I agreed to wear your tunic?"

His eyes glinted in pleasure. "You are very predictable. Your pride would never allow you to take my clothing."

"Predictable, am I?" She drew herself up to her tallest. "Good, then you'll soon become bored and go torture some other unfortunate soul."

He only shook his head, untouched by her scorn. "Boredom is the one thing I cannot imagine existing between we two."

"More's the pity," she snapped. "Oh, and by the by, while you continue to wear my pin, you seem to have forgotten to give me one. Or a knife with which to cut my meat." There was no longer any banter in her words.

"God's truth, madam? Now, why ever would I have forgotten to give you these things?" he asked, his expression innocent and surprised. His fingers touched her pin on his mantle.

Nicola narrowed her eyes at his possessive gesture. Another taunt on his part. "I am at a loss. Why?"

His hand moved from the pin to his wounded shoulder as he grinned. "No doubt 'tis this ache of mine that has caused my absentmindedness."

"I thought we agreed that the house would be peaceful. Do you not trust me?" It was a neutral question.

He arched a brow. "I do, indeed. I trust you to be strong, capable, and deadly with even the smallest of blades in your hands. Give me time to know you better before I arm you again. 'Twas only your need to argue with me over every word between us that I meant to curb last night. Now, do you need help down the stairs or can you manage them?" It was a swift and smooth change of subject.

Nicola opened her mouth to argue, but he laid a finger against her lips. "Say no more."

Her breath hissed from her, and she jerked her head away from his touch. So he believed he could keep her disarmed, did he? Fool. If God still smiled on her as He had last night, her weapons would yet be stored in her stillroom, hidden behind the equipment she used to create her herbal cures. Aye, between the dog and her husband, she would feel much safer with a dagger in her purse and a sword where she could reach it.

"I can walk. Go you before me. This way, if I fall, I will knock you down as well," she retorted.

"Just for you, my sweet," he replied with a laugh. "Shut the door and we'll be off."

Chapter Twelve

By the time she reached the base of the stairs, her feet were hurting. Gilliam offered his arm, but when she took it, Roia thrust herself between them. The dog need only a brief growl to make Nicola put a goodly space between herself and Gilliam.

"Roia, cease." As with his other commands, Gilliam did not raise his voice to utter them. The massive beast hunched her shoulders in protest. "Here." He pointed to his other side. When Roia was in place, he again offered Nicola his arm.

She accepted carefully. "Would she truly do me harm?"

"Until she knows you better, I would not cross her were I you," he said with a laugh. "Take heart. Since she chooses to spend her time with me, there's not much chance I won't be present to stop her, should she attack."

"Thank you ever so kindly," she said with a wry glance at him. "Have you anything in those cellars?" she asked about the storage rooms that had once lain beneath the hall.

"Aye, casks of tar, cart wheels, and the like," Gilliam replied. "Any supplies that are of no interest to rats."

Nicola nodded. That was wise. She glanced at her pear and apple orchard, now plucked clean. "What was the yield on the orchard?"

He shot her a sidelong look and shrugged. "I know not."

As they passed the garden, which supplied her kitchen with peas, beans, onions, garlic, and both healing and cooking herbs, she asked, "Have the latrines been cleaned and the muck spread on the garden?"

"I think so" came his reply. "I did notice they no longer smelled quite as strongly."

Beehives, woven from willow withes and shaped like small mounds, stood between orchard and garden. The two ovens, shaped much the same as the beehives only far grander in size, were nearby. Village women gathered at the nearby bake house, seeing to their loaves.

"Has the honey been harvested and the new hive fed? Was the chimney in the far oven repaired?"

"Am I supposed to know that?" he asked, now sounding a little irritable.

"Only if you like your cakes sweetened," she retorted. "Ach, 'tis pointless asking you questions. I shall have to look into everything for myself."

If there was no edge to her words, it was because her confidence was restored. So, her husband had no real interest in the day-to-day running of Ashby. Then Gilliam would be no different than her father. As long as he could hunt and hawk and was only asked to sit in judgment at the hallmote, Gilliam would leave her to run Ashby as she pleased. The very thought of telling him what he could and could not have from Ashby's treasury made her smile.

They were crossing the wide expanse of the bailey,

this area long since beaten into only hard earth. "So where have you put the temporary hall?"

"Here," he said, pointing to the main barn. The long structure was made of wood with thatch for roofing and had bays at either end. The big door, which had once sported a lock to prevent thieves from taking the precious grains stored within it, now stood ajar.

Nicola stared. Smoke curled up from one end of the building. "You cannot use this barn," she protested. "Where will I put our barley and wheat?"

He shrugged. "You will have to use the other barns."

"Nay, I must have this one." How could she prepare for winter if he crippled her by taking her main storeroom? Oh, Lord, but if this was evidence of what had happened in her absence, she could not imagine what other damage he'd done here.

"Come now, you know this is the only place within the walls that's big enough to be used as a hall. I trust you to find room for all our supples."

"I do not know how I can," she said with a breath of scorn. "You should have raised a hall, instead of seeking to buy favors from the villagers by making them houses."

"Ah, but look how I purchased myself a wife with that boon," he teased, leading her into Ashby's temporary hall.

A fire burned brightly at one end, its light doing little to lift the dimness of the windowless enclosure. Smoke drifted and clung to the thatching, despite the hole above the hearth stone that was supposed to serve as an exit portal. Near the fire there were three tables, all made from lengths of wood atop braces with benches for seats. Two were set lengthwise away from the fire, the other crosswise just above the hearth where it most benefited from the fire's heat and light.

Roia set her nose into the layer of rushes on the beaten earth floor, sniffing her way toward the nearest table. Two dairymaids sat there, chatting as they plucked stubble-fed geese for the morrow's meal. Nicola glanced at the other table. Thomas was there, watching her. She looked away; he was waiting for her, and she did not wish to speak with him.

"Jos, where are you?" Gilliam's call rang in the exposed rafters above him. The boy appeared from the shadows at the room's far end. "Have you eaten?"

The reluctant squire merely shrugged. "I am not hungry."

Gilliam frowned. "How can you expect to do a day's work on an empty stomach? Take one of the loaves from our table and come with me."

Shoulders slumped, the boy took a single roll from a basket at the end of the farthest table. As he made his loose-jointed way across the room, Gilliam murmured to her, "I think me he is accustomed to eating like a churchman, fasting morn and night, with but a moderate midday meal. His mother was preparing him for a religious life."

"Who would allow a child to have such a diet?" Nicola asked. "Such a thing is not healthy for a growing boy."

"Glad I am to hear you say so, when you seem to lack appetite, as well," he said with a tiny laugh. "His mama set some odd ideas in his head. 'Tis up to us to shake them out his ears."

Nicola couldn't help but laugh. "Shake them out his ears?"

He lifted a brow, his eyes gleaming. "Aye, if I must hold him by his heels to do so, I will."

As Jocelyn joined them, Gilliam lay his hand on the boy's shoulder. "Come now, my lad. We have a goodly walk before us."

"Do you hunt this day?" Nicola asked, her tone as friendly as could be.

"Hunt? Nay, there'll not be much time for that this season. We have until the midday meal to walk the assart. After that, we'll be searching out the shepherd."

Nicola stared at him in stark surprise. "For what purpose?"

Gilliam grinned at her. "Why my lady wife, that shepherd has ideas on improving the strength of our flock, and now's the time to do so. My eldest half brother has kin in the wool trade who say the value of English wool grows by the day. Therefore, I think it in Ashby's best interest if I listen to our man. Come, Roia."

The alaunt appeared from beneath one table and trotted toward them.

"Aaiye!" Jocelyn screamed, stumbling back from his lord. His face went chalky with fear, his eyes full round. Interested in this newcomer who was as tall as she, Roia followed. "I hate dogs!"

"A shame, since she seems to like you," Gilliam replied calmly. He caught the lad's scrawny shoulder to keep him from running. Jocelyn froze as the dog pressed her nose to his clothing, her narrow tail waving like a pennant in a lazy wind.

Nicola fought her laugh. "Aye, Jocelyn, you must take heart. She's let you live, when she only growls and snaps at me. Take pity on him, my lord. Your pet is an awesome creature."

"What? This wee beastie? She is but a lapdog. Roia, here." Gilliam pointed to his side, and the bitch immediately complied. He started out of the hall, the boy at one side, the dog at the other. "Steady yourself, Jos. She likes boys."

"My name is Jocelyn, not Jos," the boy managed in a trembling voice, then they were gone.

Nicola shook her head at their backs, then started toward the table where food awaited her. Each step was slow as she sought to keep her feet beneath her without pain. She was only a third of the way across the room before yesterday's ache was more than a memory.

"Take my arm."

Nicola glanced sharply at Thomas, who was suddenly at her side. "I can do this on my own. Besides, I am not speaking to you."

"Take my arm, Colette," he repeated harshly.

"I'll take no aid from the man who threatens to cut me from his life and the lives of those I love."

"Fall, then." The stocky man drew back, hefty arms crossed over his burly chest and an angry glare in his deeply set eyes.

Nicola tried another step, but it was pure agony. "Oh, give your arm," she snarled.

Thomas led her to the table, then sat across from her. He squinted, forcing his weak eyes to focus on her. After a long moment, he reached out to finger a strand of her cropped hair. The leathery lines of his face drooped sadly. "Ah, Colette, how could you have done this to yourself?" he asked quietly. "Would that I could not guess."

Nicola turned her head to the side, pretending to study the basket of fresh rolls and the two wheels of cheese that yet remained at the table's end. She took a bread. "I did what I had to do to honor my father's memory," she replied stiffly. "You of all folk should understand why I refused to marry that man. Agnes died on his blade, just as Papa did."

Thomas drew ragged brows down over eyes that glowed with sudden grief. "Aye, Lord Gilliam swung the blade that finished my wife, but I think me you have more to bear in this. And do not lie to me by saying your stepmother was solely at fault. If you had truly wanted to honor your father, you would have opened that gate when Lord Gilliam came atapping. Lord John might yet live, our houses might not have burned, nor would your hall be missing, if you had surrendered."

"Nay." Nicola bowed her head in pain, wishing she could run from the burden he would set on her.

"Father Reynard said you also involved Lord Ocslade. Is this true?" His tone was stern.

"I meant to shield you from Hugh—" she began, but he cut her off.

"Colette, headstrong you always were, but you never before lacked sense. Prove to me you are not silly enough to do what I am thinking. What happens to you if you rid yourself of this new husband, my lady?" It was a father's chastisement. Silence grew between them as he waited for her to answer.

"I become someone else's captive," she finally said. "Thomas, I know this. Ach, I knew it before I ran yesterday, but Ashby is mine by right of birth. 'Tis not fair that another can take it from me simply because I am female and he, male."

Breath hissed from Thomas in angry surprise. "You little fool, you are still believing you can hold Ashby as your own! I told your father 'twas wrong to indulge you in this sort of thinking. That noble idiot was too amused by your mimicry of a soldier to see what harm he did you."

Nicola's anger met and matched his. "What right do you have to speak to me of fathers and daughters when Tilda has become de Ocslade's leman?"

The reeve's shaggy head snapped back as if she'd struck him. Deep lines of pain set in his face, then disappeared beneath an uncaring expression. "I'll take no blame for that little whore. For every attempt I made to correct her sinfulness, there you were telling her I had no right to control her. Finally, she came to believe herself free of any responsibility."

"I did not tell her to be a whore," Nicola protested, truly stung.

Thomas dragged his fingers through his wild hair, then held up his hand in a gesture of peace. "My pardon, I should not have said that. 'Tis just that you and Tilda together are like sparks flying into dry tinder. Colette, I came not to scold, but to plead. You have already cost us too much, and I fear your intentions. Do you understand that without a husband, you make of Ashby and its folk naught but a tasty bit of flesh to be consumed by any man's son who passes our way?"

She began to protest that she could protect them as well as any man, then caught back her words. That was but a child's dream, and she had already hurt enough folk by pursuing it. "Aye, I do."

He reached out to take her had. "Colette, hurt us no more. Agnes thought of you as if you were her own blood—make Aggie proud of what she taught you to be, heal us. Let Lord Gilliam become Ashby's lord as he should be. If you cannot accept him, tolerate him for our sake."

"You would have me give him free rein here?" she said in sudden outrage. "What does this man know of Ashby? Nay, I will not stand aside and let him run my home into the ground the way de Ocslade has done to his own properties. If that rich man's son had any understanding of what it means to be Ashby's lord, he'd have raised a hall instead of building new cottages."

Thomas's grin was sudden and startlingly similar to Tilda's pretty smile. "Oh, understanding he has plenty. That man has himself a head full of plans. Colette, your sire was willing to let the years plod by, each one the same as the last because that was the way it had always been. Lord Gilliam has his eye on the future and needs our cooperation to achieve this design of his. Giving us homes was a means to an end for him. That, and I think he regretted being so hasty in setting the village afire. 'Twas also his attempt at atonement."

" 'Struth?" she asked in surprise, having only thought Gilliam meant to steal her villagers from her.

The reeve made a sound that mingled amusement and scorn. "Do you think your sire would ever have bestirred himself to clear us an assart with his own ax, then give us the wood so we could build homes?"

That made Nicola smile. "Thomas, you know well enough that my father would never have cleared an assart because you'd expect him to do it for you the next time you wanted a field. I think you have taken grave advantage of this poor newcomer and his lack of knowledge over our traditions. I am onto this game of yours, forever trying to cheat the manor of the fees and boons owed to it by the village. Be warned, I am home, never to leave again. You'll have no more chances to pull the hood over that poor man's eyes."

Thomas laughed, his normal deep rumble of pleasure. "Lass, I like this game of ours. I think I will teach it to Young Thom in preparation for next year."

"What happens then?" she asked.

" 'Tis these aching hips of mine. I'm thinking by next year I'll be a cripple and naught but a burden to my family. The choice for reeve will be my boy and Ralph by Wood. With Ralph such an ox's ass, Young Thom is sure to be elected. Now, break your fast. I've better things to do than sit and jaw with you." He left the table, his rolling gait evidence of his coming handicap.

Nicola stared after him, gnawing on the roll's hard crust. She knew better than to take all Thomas had said at face value. 'Twas his duty to protect the villagers' interests, even if they conflicted with what was Ashby's good.

So her husband had a head full of plans, did he? Gilliam's comments on the wool market leapt to her mind. Ashby's folk had always been farmers first, their sheep raised more for their milk and meat than for their wool. Nicola paused. The western edge of Ashby's lands was a wide expanse of grassland, suitable for sheep. Why had she not thought of this before now?

She made a soft sound of disgust at herself. 'Twasn't just her father that had let the years plod by unchanged, 'twas herself as well. It had never occurred to her to do anything differently.

Nay, she would not step aside and give Gilliam control of Ashby. This was her home, not his. The petulance of that thought brought her up short. Whose good was at stake here, hers or Ashby's? Even to her own ears, it sounded more like she did not wish to share what she named hers, no matter the cost. Nicola did not like the way that thought fit, nay, not at all.

Chapter Thirteen

B y day's end, Nicola knew two things: she would not regain her ability to work until her feet healed and her stillroom was empty of weapons. Since there was naught she could do about the weapons, she stretched her feet a little closer to the hearth stone, hoping the heat would speed healing. Not being able to walk was worse than being a prisoner. Here she was trapped in her hall, when all her home waited for her inspection.

Night had seeped beneath the hall door and through the smoke hole to enfold the big room in a quiet darkness, the loudest sound now the fire's crackling hiss. Through the dancing flames, Ashby's servants and soldiers were but gentle mounds, draped in blankets as they found their ease on their pallets.

Trapped by her feet, Nicola had turned to sewing to pass the time. She jabbed her needle into the side seam of what would soon be an undergown for herself. In the basket by her feet lay the pieces that would become the overgown. Both were cut from the sturdy brown fabric meant for soldiers' tunics. They would hardly be fashionable, but they would suit her needs. All she lacked now was a proper piece of linen from which to make a wimple.

If her feet took too long in healing, there was retted flax and clean fleece laid by in the cellar, just waiting for her distaff and loom. These chores were usually left to winter's depth, when the cold trapped every man within doors. Still, better weaving, than boredom.

The door opened and she glanced up, already knowing it was Gilliam and Jocelyn. The boy yawned, tired rings beneath his eyes. Trotting behind his new lord all the day had left its mark on him.

"Did you see an owl?" she asked when they joined her near the fire. She caught the needle into the material, then folded away her handwork, storing it in the basket.

"Nay, my lady," Jos replied in what almost sounded like disappointment. When Gilliam had suggested they search for the night hunting birds, the child had sneered, saying that he had no interest in such things. "Lord Gilliam thinks we might have heard one."

Nicola nodded, slipping her shoes back onto her feet. The heat had helped; the blisters were drying. She banked the fire, laying the cover atop it, then stood. She handed Jocelyn the lamp from the table's edge. "Carry this for me. I can manage the bucket." The morrow's washing water stood at the opposite end of the table.

"Nay, I'll carry the water," Gilliam said, grabbing the bucket's handle. "You've trouble enough staying upright and walking, much less trying to carry anything."

"What do I look like, some weak woman," Nicola shot back. She needed no help, especially from him. "You were gone all day, and I managed well enough without you. I can do so now."

He smiled at her. "Of that I have no doubt. However, since I have the bucket and you'll need to fight me to retrieve it, humor me in this. Come, now, poor Jos is struggling to keep his eyes open." He started toward the door.

Nicola glanced at the boy, awaiting his reaction to the shortening of his name. Jocelyn only rolled his eyes in defeat, then followed Gilliam. Still shaking her head in amusement, Nicola brought up the rear, her steps far less stilted than this morn.

They waited for her at the door. "Jocelyn," she said, "I've laid you a pallet in the keep chamber, but that room's too crowded even with just the bed in it. Your lord will have to have a care for where he steps."

"I would never step on Jos," Gilliam protested with mock hurt, his foot suddenly resting atop the boy's toes. Jos sidled out of his way, something akin to a giggle escaping him. When Gilliam tried it again, the lad slid out the hall door ahead of them. With his hand cupped around the lamp to protect the flame from the wind, his passage across the bailey was ghostly.

Drawing her mantle tightly around her against the frigid wind that spattered her with icy moisture, Nicola stared after the boy. "Gilliam, he should be sleeping in the hall, where there's fire and warmth. So should we."

She turned to look at her husband. It was so dark between them, he was hardly more than a shadow. As always, she felt his heat reach out to her.

"Nay, 'tis my chamber, and he must sleep with me. Come spring, the hall will rise. I've planned for an antechamber where Jos can keep his pallet. Until then, we will have to survive in those cramped quarters." His hand slipped beneath her elbow and led her into the bailey. "Come now, with the three of us in that small room, we'll be warm enough."

The sky was heavy, the wind whistling around them as they crossed the open area. Leaves rattled past them, and the oxen lowed from their byre. There was a movement from behind them. Roia followed.

"She's not sleeping with us, too, is she?" There was a touch of panic in Nicola's voice.

His laugh was low and quiet. "What can I do? She'll stay nowhere else. I chained her in the stable last night, and the grooms say she howled the whole night long."

"But Jocelyn hates dogs," she protested, then started up the steps. She was less intent on defending the boy, than on protecting herself. Gilliam kept his hand at the small of her back against the possibility of ice on the steps.

"Not so much after today. He and Roia have come to an understanding. Do not worry, I will keep you safe from her."

"Even if she doesn't eat me alive, she will give us all fleas," Nicola said, recognizing a hopeless cause.

Jocelyn had left the door ajar for them, lighting the thick night candle from his lamp. He'd left the little bowl, now dark and solemn, beneath the big iron candleholder. With but a single flame to shed its light in the room, the bright bed curtains were naught but gray shrouds, the bed's interior a dark cave.

The boy had already stripped away his tunic, but kept his chausses and shirt on against the chill. When Nicola knelt beside the thick straw mattress that lay against one wall to shove aside the blankets and furs, the boy leapt within them. He settled, his back toward the wall, and she swiftly tucked the many layers around him. She smiled at him to bid him to sleep.

"Good night, my lad," Gilliam said from beside the

bed's head. "Sleep deeply, we have much to do on the morrow."

"Aye, my lord," he managed, his eyes already closing.

As Nicola stood, Roia moved past her, this time offering no comment on her dislike for Ashby's lady. Seeing the pallet for its potential warmth and comfort, the big dog circled several times over the half Jos left empty, then settled with a groan.

Nicola turned, meaning to ask Gilliam for help with her laces. Her husband had his back to her, his tunic and shirt already stripped off. The candle's golden light gleamed against his bared shoulders and back. She held back, once again in awe of the very size of him. If she touched him, would he feel hard like a wall or would there be the normal softness of skin? The desire to know grew until she lifted a hand.

Startled by this ridiculous urge, she brought her errant fingers back to her side and cleared her throat. He looked over his shoulder at her, the light flowing over the handsome lines of his face. This was the man who would share her bed for the rest of her life.

"Would you mind loosening my gowns?" It was a shy question.

"Not at all," he replied with a quick laugh, turning toward her. His hair shone like gold as he moved.

Nicola offered her wrists first. "By the morrow's end, those gowns I'm sewing should be done, or so I hope." The words came out in a hurried stream as she watched him work at the thin string. It still surprised her that his fingers could be both so nimble and so large.

"That brown color does not suit you at all," he said, glancing up at her.

She shrugged. " 'Tisn't the color that matters, but the practicality of the gown," she said, keeping her voice low so as not to disturb Jocelyn. "I can hardly do the slaughtering in these, that much is for certain. The other I can stain without worry. Besides, you cannot much like having to do this chore like some fine lady's maid."

He smiled. "You are wrong. I am a man who thought never to marry, therefore, so domestic a task as this gives me great pleasure." There was something more than simple pleasure in his voice, and it set her pulse to a new beat.

Nicola was very happy to turn her back to him and let him work on the overgown's string. "Why would you think never to marry?" She released her belt's knot and hung it from a hook on the bedpost, then glanced over her shoulder at him. The masculine planes of his chest glowed in the weak light, outlined by night's shadow. "Your brother is a powerful lord who holds many properties. Surely he would give you your own fief."

His hands stilled suddenly, resting against her spine. "Who can say? My father left me nothing but his name, and that was all I ever expected."

The pain in his voice surprised her. More than that, it told her he had never expected more because he did not feel he deserved it. Something terrible must have happened between the brothers. Again, she glanced over her shoulder at him. There was a bitter cast to his mouth. "Why?"

"Here, this one is done," he said, ignoring her question.

She slipped the loosened gown off her shoulders and stepped out of it. The undergown had a single tie at mid back. He worked at the knot. In the silence of the room, the material's rasp seemed overly loud.

"You'll not say?" she prodded quietly.

As he freed the tie, he said, "Perhaps another time." His voice was tight and low. He turned swiftly away from her to finish disrobing.

Nicola slipped out of her undergown, leaving on her chemise. This she did not do for modesty's sake, since all men and women slept without clothing, but as one more layer against the room's deep chill. She gathered up both their clothing and hung them over the bedpost, then retreated to the bed. Gilliam already lay near the wall, hidden in the dimness.

Only when she slipped beneath the bedclothes, did she realize her husband's back was toward her. Nevertheless, he was blessedly warm. She closed the curtains, creating an instant and complete darkness. When she lay down, it was just close enough to him to borrow his warmth. She drifted to sleep, wondering what he could have done that was horrible enough to banish his humor.

Smoke curled up and over her shoulder. Nicola turned to look behind her and saw tiny tongues of flame hop, one above the other, up a wall. Men and women she'd known all her life raced soundlessly past her, mouths wide in horror. She looked to where they ran and saw the hole carved in the wall. There was safety for her there.

Nicola started to follow them, but something held her trapped. When she looked behind her, she saw the fire now had her by the skirt. The flames swiftly consumed the fabric as it sought to reach her. She thrashed and kicked, desperate to be free of the burn-

ing cloth. A huge dog ran toward her, growling and
snapping. She cried out, no more capable of escaping
the terrible creature than she could the fire ...

"Roia, nay. Hey now."

Startled by an unexpected voice and a touch upon
her arm, Nicola cried out and fought her way upright.
She was trapped in complete darkness. Panic exploded
within her. Which prison was this?

There was movement behind her, a rustling and
creaking, then arms came around her. By their strength
and bulk, she recognized Gilliam. "Are you awake?"

"Aye," she murmured, waiting to feel trapped by his
hold. Instead, she found only comfort. On the morrow,
she would warn him against such intimacy. They had
agreed her body was her own. But just now, she was
too tired to talk about it.

Nicola relaxed against him, and he leaned his cheek
against her bare neck. His skin was rough with the
day's growth of beard. A tiny spark of amusement
filled her. Was he so vain he kept himself barefaced
apurpose? She yawned, already drifting back to sleep.

"What did you dream?" His voice was low and so
deep, it rumbled around the confines of the bed. He
lowered her back into the bolsters, his huge hand moving to ease the tension from her back.

She murmured and leaned forward, giving him access to more of her aching spine. He worked at the
kinks in her muscles. " 'Tis the same each time. I am
trying to escape the fire, but no matter how I run the
flames are eating me up."

"Hmm. 'Twas a frightening thing, that."

"What?" she managed, more asleep than awake.

"The fire. Me in my armor and gambeson, I kept
expecting to drop with the heat, but I couldn't allow

myself to do so. When none of you inside Ashby answered my calls, I was certain Rannulf was dead. I had set my heart on avenging him, even if it cost me my life. I owed him that much."

"Why?" she asked, more to hear his voice than in any need to know the answer and forgetting she'd asked him this earlier.

"A few days before he came to Ashby and was taken captive, we fought, he and I. I said things"—he paused—"things of which I am not proud." His hand receded, and he eased back down beneath the bedclothes.

She smiled just a little into the bolsters. "I see he has not yet forgiven you your harsh words," she murmured.

"How so?" It was a surprised question.

"He gave you me, did he not?" 'Twould serve Gilliam rightly to be served a little of his own humor.

"You made a jest," he breathed in astonishment.

"Did you think I could not?" she retorted in sleepy irritation. "Now, leave me to my rest. 'Tis the middle of the night." As she drifted off, she was sure she heard his laugh, low and soft.

Chapter Fourteen

Nicola carefully picked her way through the muck in the bailey, her mantle drawn over her head to protect her from the steady rain. Her steps were cautious for safety's sake, not because her feet hurt. 'Twas her third morning home, but her first to be pain free. It was also her first morning to wear her new gowns.

What a joy it was to dress herself. The brown garments fit comfortably, needing nothing save a belt to hold them in place. The undergown had long sleeves loose enough to be rolled up to her elbows when necessary, while the overgown was sleeveless.

She entered the hall, expecting to see Gilliam and Jos. They'd left the bedchamber over an hour ago, just before dawn. She stopped in surprise only a few feet into the hall. Not only was her husband and his squire gone, but so too was most of Ashby's soldiery. The dairymaids looked lonely sitting at a table by themselves. Thomas, whose right it was to take his meals at Lord Ashby's expense, was also missing.

Curiosity, tinged with the slightest bit of worry, woke in her. She should have roused herself to ask Gilliam why and where they went. Now, she cursed herself for not being more aware. As its mistress, she wished to know all of Ashby's comings and goings. Where was everyone?

Nicola held her mantle before her and snapped it in midair. Water droplets flew. Roia leapt out of nowhere, rising into the air, her jaws snapping shut with a sharp click. Nicola cried out in surprise and not a little fear. With Gilliam gone, who knew what the dog would do to her.

Instead of attacking, the big dog settled on her haunches and watched Ashby's lady. There was a pleading look in her eyes, and her tail thudded dully against the earthen floor. It was not hatred that drove the beast this morn. Nicola hesitated a moment, then snapped her mantle again. The dog leapt for the scattering bits of moisture.

"Why, you are playing a game," she breathed in surprise. The alaunt grinned at her, begging for another chance to chase the water.

She shrugged in apology. " 'Tis dry already. I was not outside long enough." Nicola moved carefully past the dog, stopping at the hearth to see what the cauldron suspended over it contained. Beans and barley simmered in a rich broth. Just as she seated herself at the table, she heard the party ride up to the hall door.

A piercing whistle called the stable lads. Leather groaned, harnesses rattled, and men shouted. Gilliam strode into the hall, his faithful shadow, Jos, at his heels.

Although Ashby's new lord had not donned his mail, he wore a steel sewn hauberk over his usual tunic and his sword was belted into place. He'd thrown back his cloak hood before entering the hall, moisture clung to his hair, making the fair strands gleam even more brightly.

Like Gilliam, Jos wore a leather vest over his tunic, but he was a sorry sight. His hands were tucked beneath his arms to warm them. The hair that had escaped his hood was plastered to his forehead, the tip of his nose red with cold. Roia came to walk beside them, her tail moving in greeting.

"Where did you go so early this morn?" she asked as they stopped at the fire to remove their sodden garments. Ashby's soldiery began to file into the hall, all of them as soggy as their master. The noise of their voices was reassuring after the previous, unnerving silence.

"We chased thieves." Jos stood shivering beside his lord, his fingers trembling so badly he could not loosen the tie on his hood.

"What thieves?" Nicola came to do it for him.

"The shepherd found a stranger who had his throat cut and everything of value missing from him," Gilliam said, as if this not unusual event plagued him. "The man had been dead a few days. Also, two ewes were missing. Jos, lad, spread your wet cloak before the fire, then go to the table. 'Tis well past time to break our fast, as we'll need to be getting on with our day."

When Nicola moved to stand beside Gilliam, he said, "You are moving right well this morn." There was a quick lift of his brows as he removed his cloak. He went to his big armor chest at the wall.

"God be praised for that much," she replied stiffly as she watched him lock his sword into the chest, then lay his cloak atop it to dry. He was managing to keep all the weapons out of her reach. Not that she wanted them any longer. For Ashby's good she would tolerate him.

"We've had trouble with thieves in the past," she said. "Ashby's forest is thick, offering many a hiding spot. Did you ask the villagers if they knew the man?"

He returned to stand beside her. "Aye, neither the reeve nor any of the hundred recognized him, and no one goes missing from the village."

Nicola watched him for another moment. "Why does this bother you so, if no one knew the man?"

"What makes you think so?" he asked her, a faint air of surprise in his manner.

"Because you are not smiling. You always smile."

He smiled. "God help me, you have learned my secret now. You are right, the whole idea that this murder was done by thieves bothers me. The body had been dragged from the woods so it lay in the open. Most men of that ilk seek to concealment, not revelation. I shall have to ponder this a time." He fell silent, still looking at her. A moment later, he said, "I knew that color would not suit you." His voice was touched with disappointment.

Nicola shot him a sharp look as she turned to go to the table. "I do not care if the color suits me or not."

"I do."

The softness of his words made her nervous. She slid onto her bench. A moment later, Gilliam sat beside her. His thigh was pressed tightly to hers, and his nearness was overpowering. Mary, but she hated the way he made her feel small and helpless simply by being himself. No doubt he knew this about her, and used it as another form of intimidation. Since Nicola dared not push him off the bench, she moved, slipping onto the seat next to her.

"Coward," he whispered with a laugh.

Nicola lifted her chin. "You are too big to share a

seat," she retorted in an equally hushed voice as she tried to keep their conversation private from Jos. "I'll not be able to move my arm to eat."

The cook's woman set before Nicola a thick slab of yesterday's bread, a goodly portion of its middle removed to create a bowl. 'Twas into this that the woman ladled a helping of the pottage. Nicola picked up her spoon and set to filling her stomach.

"Might I have some of that as well?" Jocelyn asked, his tone almost shamed.

"Jos," Gilliam cried in astonishment. "You are asking for food. I'm proud of you, my boy."

" 'Tis not that I am hungry, only that I am very cold and it looks warm," the boy said, crossing his arms before him, his jaw stiff.

Nicola looked at him in surprise. Again, she saw in the lad her own reflection, stubbornly refusing change because others asked it of her. Jos wasn't going to admit he was done with his fasting and his ideas of life in the Church. More importantly, the tilt of his head and his outthrust jaw said he did not wish to be teased about this decision.

Gilliam's mouth was already forming another comment, the lilt of his lips promising some barb. She lay her hand upon his and squeezed slightly. He shot her a startled glance, but managed to catch back whatever it was he meant to say.

"Eat it just this once, then. On the morrow, if you are not so cold, there's no need to do so again. 'Wyna, bring Jos a trencher and serve him some pottage to warm his stomach."

"Aye, my lady," the woman said.

Jos shot his lady a grateful look, then set eagerly to eating the stew.

"Well-done," Gilliam breathed to her. "How did you know?"

"Some folk do not tolerate your humor well," she retorted in a whisper. "We are both tired of being your pincushions."

He only laughed and started on his own meal. Ashby's new lord took six boiled eggs, three small loaves of bread, and a quarter wheel of mild cheese. To wash it all down, he helped himself to a cup of sweetened barley water. He had begun again, with more eggs and bread, by the time Nicola had finished her own meal.

The cook's woman was passing behind her with an empty pot. "I swear, my lady, 'tis as if he carries a great hollow space within him and cannot fill it."

"That's God's own truth," Nicola said in English, then switched back to her native tongue. "Gilliam, I have decided the rest of us will starve this winter whilst we try to keep you fed."

Gilliam only smiled. "Have more faith in yourself, my lady wife. So what will you do now that you have your feet under you once more?"

Excitement made her smile, and she chewed on her thumbnail as she ordered her thoughts. More than any other time of the year, the harvest season showed the only difference between Nicola and the village women was the honorific "lady" placed before her name. Their chores were hers. Animals, culled from the herds and flocks to spare consumption of fodder over the winter months, would be slaughtered. The meat was salted, cured, or turned into sausages. Grapes would become wine, barley turned to ale, and apples to cider and vinegar, all in quantities enough to see Ashby's family of servants through the winter months.

"I think I will start in one corner of the home farm, and look at every byre and barn as I make my way across it. When I know what we have, I will better know what we need. If I have a few extra minutes, I will visit the village." Aye, she'd see to Alice.

"Come find me before you do," Gilliam said, brushing the crumbs from the table, collecting the bigger ones for Roia. "If I cannot come myself, I'll see to it you have an escort."

"An escort?" she said with a disbelieving laugh. "To walk Ashby's lanes?" Then, it struck her. He meant to keep her under guard. "My lord, may I speak with you in private?" It was an icy request.

"But, of course, my lady." There was a touch of confusion in his voice. "Where do you suggest?"

"The far corner, there"—she pointed to the room's back wall—"will suffice."

Nicola stalked into the dimness, her arms crossed before her. Gilliam followed more slowly.

"After all that prattle over parlaying and agreement, you still betray me." She kept her voice low, not willing to give him the opportunity to say she'd broken their pact. "You intend to keep me as a prisoner in my own home." The pain was so deep, she turned her back to him to hide how he had hurt her.

He put a hand on her shoulder, but she shook it off. "Do not touch me." It was no more than a whisper.

"If you do not wish me to touch you, turn around and face me."

She drew a ragged breath and considered refusing, then decided it was pointless. When she turned, she glared up at him. He watched her, his eyes filled with disappointment. "Think, Nicola. Why can I not allow you to leave the manor walls without an escort?"

"Because you believe I will try to run from Ashby," she snapped.

"Run? Where?" He lay a gentle hand on her arm. She did not bother trying to dislodge it. "I can see how your love for this place consumes you. I think you would never leave again, if that choice were given to you. Try again. 'Twas not I who invited de Ocslade to take you."

Nicola gasped, then chided herself for her own stupidity. Hugh's greed for Ashby was what had drawn her to him in the first place. Then, she shook away her worry. "Nay, what hope has Hugh now? To all the world we are well and truly wed."

Gilliam drew his fine brows down in a touch of impatience, crossing his arms over his chest. "He cares naught for our vows, only that we have no heir—" He fell silent so quickly, his final word was nearly lost. Suddenly, his face lightened.

"I am understanding these thieves far better now. Here is how our neighbor intends to allay winter's boredom: he works to render you a young widow. Now, would I not be a fool to offer him the opportunity to steal you from me? If he took you, he would need only hold you close, certain I would come to fetch you back. Two birds, one stone."

"What have I done?" Nicola cried. Vicious and capable, Hugh would surely try to fetch what she had offered him; she knew him well enough to be certain of that. Her blind determination to hold Ashby as her own had opened the gate and let the wolf into the fold. By spurring Hugh's greed, she would be the cause of her home's hurt, once more.

"Do not mourn for me yet, wife," Gilliam chided

with a laugh. "I have no intention of dying. I only seek to keep the damage you have done to a minimum."

"I have been such a fool," she muttered angrily to herself. So deep was her chagrin, she forgot he yet listened.

"Aye, but you are my fool, and I'll be damned before I let anyone take you from me." His laughter cut through her, like a whip's slash.

"Stop laughing at me," she snarled, grabbing the front of his hauberk and giving it a yank. "Is it not enough that I hate myself for my shortsighted stupidity? Must you make it worse?"

She turned, meaning to flee both him and his horrible humor, but her intentions were more agile than her feet could follow. Her soft shoes slid on the rushes, and she stumbled. If he had not grabbed her, she would have fallen on her face.

Gilliam easily lifted her back onto her feet, then brought her into his embrace, all before she'd caught her breath. She stiffened, trying to push away from him, but, as before, her attempt was useless. Once again, her head was forced into the curve of his throat.

"Hey, now, I was not laughing at you." His voice was low and soothing. " 'Twas never my intent."

"Leave go," she groaned, trying to lever herself out of his grasp. "Leave me go. I cannot bear the way you maul me any time you wish." It was not Gilliam who angered her, it was herself. She was sick to death of this blind stubbornness of hers.

When Gilliam still did not free her, she relaxed against him in defeat and lay her head on his shoulder. "Please," she breathed, "please release me. I have just seen with crystal clarity what I have done, and I like it not at all. If I cannot find me something to occupy my hands just now, I fear I will sob until my eyes can no longer see. I promise, I will come find you before I leave the walls."

"You are too hard on yourself," he said softly, and brushed his lips across the top of her brow, then released her. Nicola hurried as fast as she dared out of the hall.

By day's end, Nicola had made herself too tired to worry over anything. As with the last nights, this one found her sewing. She dropped her square of linen in her lap and leaned back, stretching and rubbing at her stiff neck muscles.

There had been no chance to leave the walls this day, so the question of her needing an escort to the village was moot. The dairy had been in desperate need of cleaning, and her hives were, indeed, overflowing. These two chores had taken her well past the midday meal, after which she'd walked the farm.

It wasn't that Thomas truly meant to cheat the manor, 'twas only that little game of memory commoners everywhere played against their noble masters. Because Ashby's new lord lacked an in-depth knowledge of the boon work owed to the manor, minor chores had been ignored. Harvesting the grapes growing along the far wall was but one example. Just a few clusters had survived the onslaught of the birds and rot. This meant that she and Gilliam would be drinking ale with their servants all winter.

Only her kitchen garden seemed to have fared well. Mayhap, this was because the cook depended on it to keep Gilliam fed. The ground had, indeed, been enriched and worked into a healthy softness. Come St.

Edmund's Day, she'd be planting their beans and garlic.

Other things, exclusively hers to do, had also gone wanting. Her store of herbs had not been replenished. With autumn almost gone, there'd be no chance to replace those that grew only in lea or woodland until summer next. What little she had left in the stillroom were nigh on too old to be of use.

Nicola once again picked up the linen square, drawing needle through cloth in another stitch. If she could finish the edge, she'd have a head cloth for the morrow.

Gilliam came to stand behind her and rested his hand on her shoulder. She lifted her hand, meaning to push away his fingers, but his thumb began to move on her nape, seeking to ease the tension in her muscles there. Nicola gave a soft murmur of reluctant acceptance as his caress eased the terrible stiffness caused by her hard work.

"How goes it?" he asked.

"I am almost done." She bent her head farther forward so he could continue to massage her neck. It felt wondrous. When he finally drew his hand away, she leaned back against him, her head resting on his belly so she could look up at him.

If his lips didn't smile at her, his eyes did. "Jos fell asleep helping me eat my meat pies." This was Gilliam's sixth and final meal of the day. "'Tis time we were abed."

"Not yet," she protested quietly. "I'll not go bareheaded another day, and have the village women point and laugh at me." Every married woman in the world covered her hair; whether Nicola's marriage was valid or not, she had no desire to be a laughingstock.

"A shame," he said softly, touching a curl. The feeling of her hair sliding through his fingers sent a chill down her spine. "Your hair is beautiful."

She was too tired to wonder why he would think that the mop atop her head was anything but a disgrace. He seemed to take her lack of response as an invitation to continue toying with her hair, for he combed his fingers through it. The tenderness of his big hand caused an instant and uncomfortable pressure beneath her heart. Nicola caught his wrist.

"No more," she said quietly. "You are right. 'Tis time for bed."

As she stood, Roia came from beneath the table to join them. Nicola found their lamp, then covered the hall fire and took up the bucket of clean water. Gilliam lifted his sleeping squire in his arms. She matched him stride for stride as they crossed the bailey for the keep tower.

In their chamber, Gilliam laid Jos on his pallet, leaving Nicola to cover the boy. Roia waited patiently, then found her own spot next to Jos. Nicola dared to lay a soft touch on Roia's shoulder. The dog squinted at her and moved her tail, just once. From deep in his sleep, Jos edged closer to the alaunt, then threw his arm around her.

"Did I not tell you he decided he liked dogs," Gilliam said with a laugh as he stripped off his shirt and tunic.

"So you did," Nicola replied, coming to kneel before him to loosen the cross garters holding his boots and chausses to his lower legs. When she was done, she stood back, waiting for him to free himself from the garments so she could hang them and put the boots beside the door. "This squire of yours is a strange one."

"He grows better by the day," Gilliam said, sliding beneath the bedclothes. "Are you still planning to slaughter the pigs on the morrow?"

"Aye, first thing. Why?" She hurriedly stripped off her gowns and hung them atop Gilliam's clothing, then leapt into the bed. Even before she'd pulled the blankets to her chin, she was shivering.

"Save a bladder for him, will you?" An inflated pig's bladder was every boy's necessity, especially during this season.

"What a good idea," she said, yanking the bed curtains shut. "He'll like that." She rolled onto her side and was asleep in moments.

Chapter Fifteen

She was late for the next day's midday meal because it had taken her longer than she'd thought to craft her gift for Jocelyn. By the time she entered the hall, Gilliam and the boy were nearly finished with their meal. 'Twas a fish stew, it being the day for it.

"I was wasting away to a mere shadow of myself," Gilliam called to her as she and 'Wyna entered. "My pardon, but we started without you." He served himself another portion of the stew.

"How can I complain over you when I am the one who's late?" Nicola stopped in the doorway to stomp the mud from her shoes and loosen the knot at the mantle's shoulder. Roia appeared suddenly, sitting alert in the open area before Ashby's lady, great jaws agape and tongue lolling.

"Hold this 'Wyna," Nicola said softly, handing the inflated bladder to the woman as she took her mantle by the corners. Today's rain was a far gentler sort than yesterday's, but she had been outside much longer. She snapped the mantle in the air, over and over, until it was free of the clinging droplets, and Roia was panting against her efforts to catch them.

"Silly beast," she told the big dog, tying her mantle

back around her shoulders. The alaunt widened her grin as if to agree.

Retrieving the bladder from 'Wyna, Nicola hid it behind her back and started through the big room toward the back table. Thomas sat as he always did, at the head of the right table, placed above the soldiers that guarded Ashby's walls. Instead of acknowledging him as she used to do, guilt kept Nicola's gaze fixed ahead of her. Did Thomas also believe Hugh was behind the murder? If so, she was certain the reeve would never forgive her, not after what her earlier meddling had cost him. She moved around the table and took the bench next to Gilliam's, it having become her accustomed seat.

"Does the reeve's presence bother you? I can tell him to eat with us no longer," her husband offered in a whisper.

Nicola shot him a startled look. "Nay, you cannot," she said sharply. "Tradition says Ashby's reeve takes his morning and midday meal at your expense. You cannot bar him from our hall." To escape this conversation, she turned to face the boy across the table from her. "Jocelyn, I have something for you." She produced the inflated pig's bladder and rattled it for the lad, to show it contained beans.

"What is it?" he asked, staring at the toy, but not taking it from her. Nicola looked at him in surprise and set the ball in the middle of the table.

"Jos, 'tis a bladder, for tossing or kicking," Gilliam said, sounding shocked. "Now, boy, do not tell me you've never before had a ball. Why, this is the necessary plaything for all lads during autumn."

Jocelyn looked up at his lord with an adult expression of disdain. "The tossing and kicking of balls is for commoners. My lady mother does not approve of such things."

Nicola laughed as Gilliam rocked back on his bench. He was truly mortified by Jos's claim. "Then call me common," he cried. "What sort of mother keeps her son from the joys of boyhood?"

"I find my joy in the quill and scroll, my lord," the boy replied.

"You scribe and read?" Nicola asked in surprise. Outside of churchmen, the only folk whom she knew could read and write were Lord Rannulf and his wife. Everyone else, at least in her corner of the world, left that chore to hired clerks or monks.

"Aye, 'tis all I am fit for." What should have been a self-deprecating comment was uttered with great pride.

"Not true," Gilliam retorted swiftly. "Here"—he took the bladder from the tabletop and bounced it in his hand—"take it."

"What's the use?" Jocelyn asked with a deep sigh. "I cannot throw it, and I cannot catch."

Nicola eyed him in skepticism. "You just said you'd never been allowed to have one. How do you know you cannot throw or catch?"

"I know," the boy replied with absolute certainty. He mournfully lifted another spoonful of stew off his bread trencher and into his mouth. "What other boys can do, I cannot." Nicola thought he was taking his helpless role a bit far, having gotten a rise out of them.

"Try it," Gilliam said, his voice empty of any emotion. "Come, lad, hold up your hand."

"I cannot do it," Jocelyn insisted with a sad shake of his head.

"Hold up your hand," his lord said again. His voice was quiet, and Nicola looked at him. Gilliam was angry. He had not drawn down his brows, nor was there any black look in his eyes, only a humorless tone of voice.

"Jocelyn, you should try," she said softly, then wondered why she attempted to intervene.

"I mean no disrespect, my lady, but I do not want the thing." 'Twas nothing less than a stone wall he set between himself and what he had decided he could not do.

The bladder bounced off the top of the boy's head, then rebounded toward Nicola. As Jocelyn blinked in surprise, she grabbed the ball out of the air. Gilliam said nothing, only made a motion with his fingers indicating she should return it to him. When she did, the ball again flew across the table and struck Jocelyn atop his head. Gilliam snatched it back.

"What are you doing," Jocelyn asked in irritation, then remembered to add, "my lord."

"Hold up your hands, boy," Gilliam said, calmly and quietly.

Jocelyn eyed his lord, his jaw firmed in refusal. The ball rattled as it struck his head, then struck him again. Jos made a small sound of anger, the growl of a just-weaned pup. When Gilliam tossed it at his head yet one more time, he snatched it out of the air with no difficulty.

"Will you look at that, my lady? Our Jos has just caught himself a ball," Gilliam said with a laugh. "What do you think, Jos? You have just done what you cannot do."

Jos clutched the ball to his chest in surprise, his eyes wide. "I caught it," he breathed to himself, then stared down at the bladder held tightly in his arms. "I caught it."

"So you did," Nicola said with a wide smile. "Here, toss it to me, and let us see if you can do it again."

Jos rolled the thing across the table, not daring to throw it. Nicola sent it back to him, careful to aim the bladder so it would fall into his arms, whether he caught it or not. It wasn't necessary. Jos snatched it out of the air with ease.

If Jos had not lied about this being his first time to play with a ball, the way his eye and hand worked together spoke well of his coordination. A man with this ability had archer's hands, or so her father had always said. If Jos were longsighted as well, he might do well with a bow.

Gilliam set aside his stew. "My turn," he said taking the bladder from Jos, bouncing the thing in his hand. He sent it high above the table. Jos frowned as he watched it, but caught it nonetheless.

"I did it," the boy breathed in complete astonishment. "I can do this."

His lord reached over to tap him on the cheek. "Jos, take a moment to consider this. If you can do as other boys do and catch the ball, might your lady mother be mistaken about your capabilities as a squire?"

The boy clutched the ball to him, a pinched look on his face. " 'Tis possible." It was a quiet statement. As if he had startled himself by this admission, he hurried on. "This is but a single thing. What if I cannot do the others?"

"Jos, you can if you let yourself try. All I ask is that you do not fight so hard to prove yourself incapable." Gilliam laughed and came to his feet. "Grab up your cloak, boy, and let's go see if you can toss the thing as well as catch it."

A horse's high-pitched and frightened complaint

echoed in from the bailey. The sound of men screaming exploded in its wake, shattering the gray silence of
a rainy day. There was the splintering crash of wood.

"My lord!" came a frantic shout from outside the
door. "That devil horse of yours has arrived and hurt
Alfred!"

Nicola leapt to her feet, but not as quickly as
Gilliam was on his. He ran for the door, shouting behind him, "Roia stay! The rest of you as well."

Nicola interpreted his command to mean the servants, not her, and raced after him. If a man was hurt,
she was needed. She stopped just outside the door.

At the center of the bailey was a huge, black monster of a horse. Men peered out from behind a nearby
shed. Two soldiers were trapped behind Ashby's broken and fallen cart. Lying still in the muck was Alfred.
Hooves flashed above him; mercifully the horse did
not land his blows.

"Hold still, all of you," Gilliam bellowed. "I must
bring him to me." Putting his fingers to his mouth, his
piercing whistle echoed against the tall stone walls. The
horse responded with another high-pitched cry, then settled onto all four feet, grunting and groaning. Great
clouds of steam appeared before the horse as he snorted,
skin twitching.

Nicola stared, torn between fear and appreciation.
Rain made the beast's ebony coat gleam. When
Gilliam took two steps toward his horse, the creature
swung his head toward his master. The big horse was
pretty for his breed. As massive and vicious as the
warhorse was, Nicola could imagine Gilliam sitting on
no other steed; they matched each other in their beauty.
Another of Gilliam's whistles shrieked against the

cloud-cast skies, and the horse shifted toward his owner.

Alfred made a small noise and moved, just a little. As Nicola gave thanks to God for sparing the soldier's life, she willed him to crawl out of range of those iron-shod hooves. Alfred drew his knees up as if preparing to do so.

The horse sidled, startled by the movement, then tensed to rise again. Alfred instantly relaxed into limpness.

"Witasse, my little lad," Gilliam crooned in a sing-song voice, "come to me, my child. Come, now." The great horse shuddered and shivered, seeming almost to shake his head in refusal. He turned to face his master, putting his back to his victim, but did not move out of kicking distance.

"Witasse, lad, come now, come to me." Gilliam took a step toward his warhorse. He repeated the words, again and again, until he was nigh on singing the steed a lull-aby, taking tiny steps toward him. Witasse held his ground, drawing sharp breaths as if testing the air for some enemy scent.

Nicola glanced around the circle. If she came at Alfred from behind the shed, the horse would not see her. She might be able to drag the man out of range. Nicola slipped away, now set on saving Alfred's life.

When she reached the shed's corner, she peered out from behind it. Gilliam was closer to his steed, but the horse had not yet moved. Willing Alfred to lie still and soundless, she crouched down and eased out from behind the corner. Every move she made was fluid and slow, to keep from startling the horse.

"Nicola," Gilliam said in the same soothing tone,

"he is disturbed by the smell of the man's blood. You must come away from him."

Nicola gave her head a small shake. His words only added to her urgent need to rescue Alfred. She eased into a squat beside the man's shoulder, forcing herself to ignore the massive hooves with their sharp iron shoes. Alfred's head was toward her, covered in blood. His eyes were closed, but the tenseness of his form said he was not unconscious.

Slowly and carefully, Nicola extended a hand and laid it on Alfred's shoulder. "I can only drag you," she breathed in English, her words barely above a whisper.

The warhorse gave a startled whinny, ears shifting as he caught the unfamiliar sound of her voice. Gilliam's soothing tones had the stronger influence. Witasse's attention remained on the big man.

Gathering a handful of Alfred's tunic, she slowly tugged him toward her. Inch by painful inch, she eased the soldier out of range of Witasse's massive hooves. The man's head struck a stone, and he groaned in instinctive reaction. Instantly, Nicola thrust backward, yanking the man toward her, certain the warhorse would strike.

Hooves flashed toward her face, only a foot from her nose. Nicola bit her tongue. A scream of fear could only make matters worse. She wrestled Alfred to the edge of the cart, thinking only to get him out of the creature's sight. The two men behind it helped her pull the injured man into its protection.

She glanced over the broken cart as Gilliam grasped his steed by the bridle. "Once they've taken the horse to the stable, we'll get you into the hall, Alfred," she panted, sitting down hard into the mud. "Mary, but I think my stomach is still out there in the mire."

"Mine as well, my lady," Alfred managed in a hoarse grunt of pain. "You have my unending gratitude."

Nicola gave his shoulder a squeeze while on the other side of the splintered cart, Gilliam called to the grooms. "Come fix his leads. I will help you take him to his paddock. Nay, nay, my lad," he said as the horse snorted again. "You are home now. You are home."

"Stupid man," Nicola cursed him quietly. "Only you would turn a beast like that into a pet." She checked Alfred's eyes, looking for a sign of damage to his brain, then smiled when she found none. The blood came from a nasty cut at his hairline.

"Arm's broken," he said. "Held it up to take the blow."

Nicola smiled at him. "I can fix that," she said soothingly. The sound of the grooms and her husband speaking to the horse grew faint.

"Right, then," she said to the two men, "let us get our Alfred into the hall."

Once the injured man lay on a table, his head pillowed on Nicola's mantle, she sent a dairymaid for bandages from the stillroom, while 'Wyna went to find two pieces of wood of the shape and size she needed. Safety allowed Alfred to release his hold on consciousness and drift to a place beyond pain.

She lifted his arm. It was crooked, but the broken bones had not cut cut through his skin. That was a blessing. She felt along his arm, checking for the right spot to place her hands so she could force the two pieces of bone into one. A firm thrust, and it was done. Now all that was needed was to bind it into stillness and let time mend it. She lay his arm gently at his side.

"We need to talk." Gilliam's words were cold and

hard as he grabbed her arm, then yanked her along behind him, nearly knocking off her feet.

"What are you doing?" she cried as he forced her
around the hearth. She tugged on her trapped arm as
her feet slid in the rushes. "Stop it, I say. I have work
that must be done. Leave go this instant."

Once at the room's far end, he swung her around
him, shoved her up against the wall, pinning her to it
by her shoulders. His eyes were alive with rage, his
mouth narrowed and hard. "I commanded everyone to
stay in the hall," he said, the words barely managing to
exit past his gritted teeth. "You disobeyed me. I told
you to leave the man. You disobeyed me, again. You
went behind Witasse, you idiot."

"I could not leave Alfred to be killed," she said,
struggling against his hold on her. "I knew I was quick
enough to escape your brute's kick. Now, let me get
back to that poor man."

"Why you are not dead is beyond me!" If one could
scream in a whisper, he had just done it. "I should kill
you for this."

Nicola relaxed against the wall to stare up at him in
scornful confusion. His reaction made no sense. "You
would kill me for not dying?"

Gilliam drew a deep and shuddering breath, then
leaned his brow against hers. "By God and all his
saints," he whispered. "I have never been so frightened
in all my life as when I saw Witasse kick at you. I was
sure you were dead. Do not ever, ever do that to me
again." With that Gilliam released her and strode
swiftly away.

Nicola stared after him in amazement. Now, what
was eating him?

"Jos," Gilliam called to his squire, who hung a shy

distance away from the injured man as if he wanted a better look, but dared to come no nearer.

"Aye, my lord?" The boy had his ball tucked beneath his arm.

"Come, let us find a dry spot and see how far you can toss that ball of yours." There was no sign of his previous emotion in his voice. Nicola shook her head in bemusement over her husband's odd behavior, then returned to tend poor Alfred.

Chapter Sixteen

")Tis you who wants to sleep in this unheated chamber, so you must be the one to break the ice on the water. I'll do it no more," Nicola said sleepily. It was the end of her second week home, and in only two weeks, she'd come to be right sick of this awful room.

"Living at Graistan has made you soft," Gilliam said, by way of a "good morrow."

"If being locked in a storeroom for months on end can make one soft, then soft I am," she retorted.

The day's chores called to her, but it felt so good to lie here, surrounded by warmth and comfort. She reached out to crack the curtains. Dawn's rosy glow had begun to fill the room.

"We'll see the sun this day," she said, letting the curtain fall closed and pulling her arm back beneath the blankets.

"Thank God. I am tired of riding in the rain. More to the point, I am tired of riding between here and Eilington." He tuned his back to her and yanked the covers up over his shoulder.

Nicola stared at what she could see of him above the blankets. He lay with his back to her, his hair tousled from sleep. The fair strands were longer than most men wore and lay in fine curls along his strong neck.

"I heard you went yesterday." She hadn't seen him since yestermorn, when they broke their fast together. From that time on, her day had been occupied by processing apples. Some had been sliced for drying, others would become cider and vinegar, stored in casks. The task had been finished by torchlight, long after Gilliam and Jos had retired. Nicola looked at her hands. The fruit had left a dark stain on her skin. 'Twas a sign of work well-done. "What sent you there?"

"One of the farthest-flung houses had its wall broken. Everything of the slightest value was taken, the rest laid waste."

He told this to the wall, his voice holding a tone of frustration. This was the third incident since the stranger's murder. A field had been trampled at the beginning of this week, and another ewe had gone missing.

"Oh," was all she said, understanding his distress. She knew all too well how hard it was to sit idly by while others suffered. It must be harder still, when one possessed the size and strength Gilliam did. "Thieves, again."

The linens rustled as he turned to lie on his back beside her. "De Ocslade," he said.

She stared at the perfection of his profile. "You are wrong. As I said, we've had this sort of problem before. What happens now is no different." He had to be wrong, else she could not bear it.

"Well, one way or the other, I am tired of riding between here and Eilington. I think I will set our men into a patrol."

Nicola stared up at the cloth ceiling above her. "My father tried that in times past. The thieves waited until they knew when the soldiers came and attacked in between."

"That's easy enough to cure. Our patrol must not be regular. We'll do it by coin toss. If we see our beloved monarch, we go to Eilington, if we see the cross, we stay home." He tried to stretch, but the bed was too short for him. His hands hit the wall behind him and his knees stayed bent. "I am getting up. Go you first, so I do not have to crawl over you."

"Crawl over me," she said. "I am not yet ready to rise."

"I will break the ice for you," he offered with a laugh.

"My thanks," Nicola grumbled as she arched her back to ease the kinks, then sat up, clutching the bedclothes to her against the frigid air. She pushed back the curtains and reached blindly along the post for their clothing. Tossing them into her lap, she found her undergown and tugged it on before separating what was hers from his. She turned, putting her legs over the bed's edge, lifting and pulling until the warm gown reached her ankles.

He eased across the mattress to sit beside her. They both looked at the sleeping boy and dog. "What would he do without her to keep him warm, or she without him?" Gilliam mused.

Jos had taken Roia beneath his blankets with him, the two of them sharing the bolster. The dog acknowledged her master's rising by opening her eyes and twitching her ears, then retreated into sleep.

"Far less scratching. She has fleas," Nicola said, thrusting Gilliam's chausses at him. "Dogs should stay in a kennel. They are dirty creatures."

"She is not a dirty creature. Roia is very well behaved; she never uses the hall as a latrine."

Neither of their voices contained any rancor. This
discussion had become part of their morning routine.
She tied his cross garters, and they argued over Roia.
Gilliam eased off the bed to don his chausses. Dawn's
light fell across him, revealing the scar on his abdo-
men.

"What caused that scar of yours? It looks like it
must have been horrible." Nicola untangled her overgown from his shirt.

"It was."

While waiting for him to expound, she tugged on her
final gown, then tied her mantle around her shoulders.
The cold air was once again at bay. As Nicola took up
her stockings and shoes, she looked up at Gilliam. He
had tied the drawstring to his chausses and was reaching for his boots, leaving his shirt and tunic for last as
he always did. The cold never seemed to affect him.

"Well?" she asked after another moment.

"Well, what?" he asked blankly.

"How did you get that scar? Do not pretend you
misunderstand me, for I know very well you do not."
If the last two weeks had taught her anything about the
man to whom she was married, it was that he was
hardly dim-witted. 'Twas his placid manner that had
fooled her into thinking it of him. Nicola eyed her feet
as she pulled on her stockings. There was only a trace
of a mark left on one, all else had healed. "Come now,
tell," she insisted, donning her shoes.

He had one boot on, the other yet in hand. " 'Tis embarrassing." He actually flushed.

Nicola smiled at his discomfort. "What? You, embarrassed? Now, that's a hard thing to picture. Put on

your other boot, and I will come tie your cross garters. You can tell me the tale while I do it." He shoved his foot into the boot, and Nicola knelt before him, leather bindings in hand.

"Why are you so curious about it?"

"I am not curious," she scoffed, "I am amazed. The thing has the look of a death wound. I would know what caused it."

"If you must, then," he said reluctantly. "I was but ten and six and yet residing with my foster father. He had five of us squired to him, and we were a daring bunch, each always trying to outdo the other in acts of what we thought were bravery. One day, we were hunting boar and"—he paused to lift a shoulder just a little—"I said I could ride it before we killed it."

Nicola sat flat on the ground and stared up at him in shock and disbelief. "You didn't."

"Aye, I did. Ride it, that is. Not for long, mind you. He nigh on took my insides out in repayment." Gilliam smiled a sheepish smile. "I told you 'twas embarrassing, a boy's stupid trick. Enough of that." When he offered her his hand to aid her in rising, she let him draw her to her feet.

"I cannot believe you were such a fool," she whispered, still unable to comprehend his story. "Ride a boar? And, here I'd come to think you more clever than that."

"Do not make me sorry I told you," he warned. Again, she shook her head in disbelief. "Taunt me over it, and I will get my revenge."

"Do you think me afeared of you, big man? Hah! I think I shall cherish this bit of knowledge forever, oh great boar hunter." She smiled in smug satisfaction.

"Now you've gone too far," he growled, and jerked

her into his embrace. Before she could resist, he had
tossed her onto the bed, then dropped atop her. "I will
squash you like a bug."

"Nay!" she squealed, trapped beneath his weight.
"Cease, you, or you will damage me. Get off, you
great oaf," she managed, "or I'll box your ears."

Laughing, she braced her hands against his chest,
pushing and shoving to make him rise. His skin was
warm and smooth, his heartbeat strong beneath her fingers. The heat of him flowed through her palms. Suddenly, her fingers were alive with the feel of him. As
if by their own will, her hands crept up his chest to his
shoulders, then his neck. His hair was soft against her
fingers. An incredible and new warmth awoke inside
her, so strong it made her sigh.

Her hips were pressed to his. Even through the layers of their clothing, she was aware of his desire. For
her; he wanted her. Impossible. No man wanted her.

Deep within Nicola, something shuddered and shivered. She gasped against it, her gaze flying to his face.
Gilliam's eyes were closed. He bowed his head to
press his lips against the place where her neck met her
shoulders, then he moved his mouth up the column of
her neck to her ear. Where his lips touched, her skin
tingled, sending impossible sensations careening down
her spine.

"Nay," Nicola whispered even as she turned her
head to offer him more to touch. He was weaving that
spell again. Oh, but what he was doing to her felt wondrous. Her insides were alive in a way she'd never
known before. His hand slipped up from her waist, his
fingers splaying around the small curve of her breast.

"What are you doing," she breathed in hoarse protest when her breast responded to his touch. She should

be fighting him, not lying here like a spider's victim, bound tight in a web of sensation.

"Driving myself mad with wanting you," he whispered in her ear, then rolled onto his back to stare at the cloth ceiling above them. His eyes closed after a moment, and he drew a long unsteady breath. "You said me nay. Hurry, Nicola, else I'll reach for you again. I cannot promise I will listen to your nays if you stay."

With a sharp cry of dismay, Nicola threw herself off the bed. What was wrong with her? Roia leapt to her feet with a deep bark, and Jos cried out in startled awakening. She snatched all the bits of her attire, then threw open the door to race blindly down the stairs.

Nicola stopped at the cellar's tall wall, yet trembling in reaction. Jesus God, what had happened to her need to keep her body as her own? Closing her eyes, she realized that now even her body would betray her. Aye, a goodly portion of her was still eager to know more of him, begging her to let him touch her once again. She leaned her forehead against the cold stones and fought to find her anger.

What sort of daughter panted after the man who had ended her father's life? The harsh chastisement had no effect. Her body still pulsed and throbbed in a most disturbing way.

Never before had any man ever looked at her the way men did Tilda. Those who came to sue for her hand had only wanted Ashby, but Gilliam already had Ashby. Not only that, he was a man who could have any woman he desired. Yet, he said he was driving himself mad for want of her. Her!

Pride scolded her for this foolish thought. This could only be another of his terrible games. No man wanted the ugly giantess of Ashby. The anger she sought returned, destroying this silly weakness she was developing over him.

She cinched her belt around her waist. Let this morn's event stand as a lesson to never again try to repay his taunts with one of her own. Nicola found her comb in her purse before tying on her head cloth. She would have to be constantly on her guard if she was to keep herself from becoming vulnerable to him.

Striding swiftly to the hall, she let the morn's deep chill drive away what remained of the heat he awoke in her. At the door, she called, " 'Wyna, bring me a bit of bread and cheese and come with me. We have sausages to make. Bring a cloth as well, for I need to do my washing in the kitchen shed." She did not wait, instead retreated to the kitchen and began rebuilding her defenses.

Chapter Seventeen

"Alice," Nicola said, "your time is too close. The babe already sits right atop the doorway. See how low you carry him?" She touched the top of Alice's great bulge, which had lowered substantially in the last days. "If the babe has not come before tomorrow midday, you should stay at home."

Ashby's manor and its lord hosted an ale, a dinner for the villagers, three times a year. In spring it was to celebrate planting, and there was one to mark midsummer, but what with this year's tangle of events, the summer feast had been forgotten. The final ale was usually held on Martinmas in honor of the plowmen. It, too, had been disregarded because Ashby could not provide the meal just then, but Nicola did not wish to miss the celebration altogether. Thus, she had reset the date for December's first day.

"My lady, every other soul in the village will be in your hall tomorrow," the commoner protested, brushing the remains of the bread and stew they'd shared onto the floor for the chickens. "What if this wee child of mine decides to come after the meal has started? I would have to trundle to the hall by myself, shouting for you to come." Alice laughed gently at that image and handed her lady the rinsed cups.

Nicola stepped around the fire and set them on the hearth wall's shelf. As tall as she was, she had to duck beneath the hams and slabs of bacon hanging from the cross beam. "The music and dancing may serve you ill."

"I am hardly going to dance," Alice said with another laugh, then paused and caught her lady by the arm. "Now, why is it you worry so over me? 'Tis not birthing that has given me difficulty, only keeping the babes until that time. Why, when Edwin was born, it took me but a few hours to produce him. I remember Agnes remarking on how easy his coming was." In her first pregnancy, the one that secured her marriage, Alice had brought forth a boy-child. The lad had died of illness the year after his birth.

Nicola gave a small shrug. She yet clung to the delivery of Alice's child as the event that would release her from the burden of Ashby's destruction. " 'Tis only a little foolishness on my part. When I left, Ashby was naught but a ruin. I returned to find it half rebuilt and you at long last successful in carrying a child past the first months."

"Aye, Margery said that you called it an omen," the woman said with a smile. "That's a heavy responsibility for one so simple as me to bear. Still, I will do my best to give you your sign." Alice settled onto the stool before her own hearth, knees spread wide to accommodate her heavy belly. She reached for a partially woven basket and set it upon her knee, her swollen fingers already finding the familiar rhythm of plaiting. "The babe and I will be fine. Until the morrow, my lady."

"Until the morrow, then," Nicola offered with a smile, but her worry refused to be eased. Birthing could be dangerous and she so desperately needed this child's arrival to go well.

As Gilliam had been called to Eilington when the carpenter's daughter had gone missing, 'twas Walter who guarded her this day. She signalled to the soldier that they were ready to leave. The man, his plain face caught in lines of boredom, preceded her out of the cottage for safety's sake. She followed, shutting the panel behind her.

This day found the world trapped beneath a deep and silent blanket of clouds. The air stung her nose, promising sleet or, possibly, an early snow. Nicola had traded her coarse wimple for a scarf of thick wool to protect her from the day's deep chill.

"So, you drew the short straw this day, eh, Walter?" Nicola hid her laugh at his startled look. It was a source of great amusement to her to know she was the bane of these soldiers. They complained to Gilliam that she worked them too hard and made them participate in menial chores.

"Pardon, my lady. You shouldn't know about that," he said in embarrassment.

"You can ease the sting by talking to me of these thieves as we walk to the reeve's house," she offered. "Tell me why my husband is so convinced that 'tis our neighbor who does these deeds." She crossed her arms tightly beneath her mantle, starting down the lane toward the outskirts of the village and her last stop of the day.

"I think me 'tis the carefulness with which things happen. Thieves count on their speed and their ability to elude their pursuers, not taking the time to obliterate their tracks as these do."

Nicola made a face, accepting the logic of his words

against her desire to do otherwise. "Still, it might be thieves, just a different sort."

"Aye, it might be," Walter agreed. "That is just the issue. There is never a sign left that says it is or is not Lord Ocslade who does these things."

They stopped before the wooden door in the long house. The low of oxen came from the ell at the building's far end, the warmth these animals provided almost as valuable as the beasts, themselves. It had taken all her strength to work up the nerve to make this call.

Nicola had not been able to face the reeve since that first attack, but Thomas's absence from the table this day, coupled with the cold weather, told her that his hips must be aching so badly he could not walk. She reached into her pack to touch the wax-sealed jar of rub and found herself praying the stuff could do more than ease physical pain. If Thomas did blame her for the village's latest troubles, perhaps the balm could soothe his anger. She lifted her arm, hesitated, than rapped sharply on the panel.

'Twas Thomas's daughter by marriage who opened it, rather than their serving girl. "My lady, what a surprise." Johanna was a fresh-faced lass with bright eyes, no more than a year Nicola's senior. She'd done well in her marriage to Young Thom, turning a middling farmer's daughter into a leading village wife. Her son, delivered just before their wedding two years ago, clung to his mother's skirts. So, too, had she benefited from Agnes's death, becoming the mistress of the house years before she might otherwise have held that position.

"Is Old Thomas in?" Nicola asked shyly.

"Aye, he's been laid low by this cold. Come in, my lady, come in."

Nicola shook as much mud from her shoes as she could before stepping inside. Several chickens darted within doors as she entered. "My thanks, Johanna. Can my man here sit by your fire whilst I visit?"

"Of course, my lady." To Walter, Johanna said, "Take a seat by the fire. Would you care for a cup of ale and a bite of bread?"

"Aye, I would. Thank you, goodwife," Walter replied with a smile for the pretty girl. He shut the door softly behind him and the room retreated into deep shadows, save where the fire's light reached. The air inside was heavy with the smell of animals and smoke, flavored with the scent of curing meats and of beans stewing in the large iron pot hanging over the fire.

Johanna set her son on a stool, then took a lamp bowl from a shelf at the back wall. With a burning twig from the fire, she lit the wick. Grabbing up a stool from a corner, she started toward the back of the room. Nicola followed, looking around her with interest.

Thomas had rebuilt his house without much change from its original design. As with every other cottage, the hearth wall was filled with shelves. Some of these held cups and spoons, others bore small pots and knifes. Precious iron-bladed tools hung on pegs, wooden handles shining with a recent oiling. Bags of grains, nuts, and dried fruit were stacked alongside barrels of cider and ale. Johanna had left her spindle and distaff leaning against one such stack when she answered Nicola's knock. The housewife was turning hemp nettle into thread.

A new loft now reached out from the back wall, held up by thick posts, the only access a ladder. Since Old Thomas could never have climbed the rungs, Nicola assumed the upper floor was where Johanna slept with her Thomas.

"Father," the girl called out, "our lady has come to visit with you." Johanna set the stool down just beneath the loft's edge. Her lamp went onto the room's only chest. The meager light illuminated a thick pallet covered deep in blankets.

Thomas gave a startled grunt, as if awakening. The straw in his pallet rustled as he moved. "Has she now?" His tone was surprised. With a groan and much shifting, the burly man brought himself into a sitting position. The lamp's light revealed little more than the curve of his cheeks and the redness in his beard before it threw flickering shadows onto his thick, bare chest.

Johanna handed him his tunic from a hook on one post. As Thomas shrugged into his garment, Nicola sat upon the stool and Johanna retreated to the fire. The silence between the noblewoman and the reeve lengthened into discomfort.

"My lady, 'tis good of you to come visit an old man." It was a formal and polite statement, not at all his usual manner with her.

"My lady, is it now, Thomas," Nicola chided softly. "What happened to Colette?"

A slow smile spread across the man's mouth, his remaining teeth gleaming in the low light. "Then you've forgiven me for trespassing into your life, have you? I had no right to scold you that day. I thought you were avoiding me for hatred's sake."

"Oh, Thomas," her cry was low, but full of pain, "I've been avoiding you because of my shame, not your words. My lord thinks that 'tis de Ocslade behind these incidents of thievery we have suffered. If it is true, I will have betrayed you and Ashby twice. 'Tis bad enough I caused Agnes's death, now this. How can you ever forgive me?"

"Ah, lass, have you been tormenting yourself, then?" The man rubbed a weary hand over his face. "Let us begin at the beginning, with my Aggie's death. If I had listened to my wise wife that June morn, we'd have stayed home and dined at our own fire. She warned me you meant to snap the gates shut to try your skill, but I would not heed her. Nay, I was stubbornly set on preserving my own status, and a reeve always eats in his lord's hall. Now, tell me, who holds his wife's death in his hands?" He tried for a light tone, but there was sadness in Thomas's voice.

Nicola looked up in surprise. "You blame yourself?"

"Blame? Nay, but I hold myself accountable to God for my foolish pride. I do my penance and pray for forgiveness. Where's the point in blaming when Agnes remains just as dead no matter who did what? As for Lord Ocslade, how long has that nobleman been after Ashby, Colette?"

Nicola straightened on her stool. "Since my brother's death, when I became heiress." Even at twelve, she had been taller than Ashby's neighbor.

"Aye, he has been set on owning Ashby for years. How, then, does it become your fault now? If it is he who does these things, then I think it more likely he seeks to discover what sort of man lurks beneath the youthful exterior of our new lord. Were Lord Ashby easily intimidated, Lord Ocslade would have gobbled us up already."

"Would that this were true," Nicola said, hearing but not certain if she believed.

"Who can say? I do not much care to waste my time on trying to fathom the thought processes of noblemen.

Taken as a whole, I find they make no sense." His eyes gleamed from their deep sockets, then dimmed. "I can only hope that little whore of mine is not helping Lord Ocsalde to hurt us." He reached out to lay his rough palm against Nicola's cheek. "Where you can only hurt me, Colette, my Tilda's betrayal could kill me."

"Nay," Nicola said instantly. "She would never betray her home." She paused. Why not? Tilda had meant to betray her to Hugh.

"This is where her heart is," Nicola said with more confidence than she felt. "When Tilda has had enough of de Ocslade, she will come home." Oddly, she found herself wishing Tilda would never return. How could they ever mend what they had destroyed between them?

"Would that she does not." If Thomas's words were hard, his tone was broken.

"You would turn your back on your own daughter? Thomas, you cannot." Her cry was as much a plea for herself as for Tilda.

"Ah, Colette, I cannot look at my daughter without spewing harsh and hateful words. She is my shame. Although she has dowry aplenty, there's not a decent lad within the village who would have her. Those she's wounded want her naught, and those she's not yet touched will not go where others have been."

He freed a scornful laugh. "Save Muriel's son. The boy's a good enough farmer even at sixteen, but 'twould gall me to pay merchet to wed my daughter where there was no dower."

"Nor would Tilda like living with Mad Muriel in that hovel," Nicola murmured. The woman was the poorest in the village, her young son barely keeping life and limb together from their garden and few strips of land, coupled with what he earned when he hired out. "Mayhap, this would be her penance for using so many men," she added softly.

"Mayhap." Thomas's wide mouth lifting into a bitter smile. "You do your penance, too, do you not?"

"Aye, prayer after tedious prayer," Nicola said with a small smile. "Just when I think I've come to the end, Father Reynard finds me another sin to bow over."

"Nay, I meant by this marriage of yours. It must gall you right smartly to be wed to the man who took down your walls and ravaged your hall."

"Do you know, I've been so busy doing a whole season's worth of work in one month, I haven't had time to even think about this?" Nicola leaned back on the stool, her hands laced over her knees. "Aye, with days that stretch from dawn to well past the midnight hour, I am too exhausted to care who shares my bed at night." Save that Gilliam was wondrously warm and never failed to use his hands to ease her stiff and aching back.

"Is that so?" The low light found Thomas's deeply set eyes and made them glimmer oddly. His strange tone made Nicola nervous. She opened her pack to find the jar.

"Thomas, I came not only to speak with you, but to bring you a rub. When I did not see you in the hall this day, I guessed the cold had made your pain worse."

"Ah, you are a saint, Colette," the man said with a broad grin. "These hips are so bad, I could not join the folk gathering osiers, and reeds, for you this day."

"Augh!" Nicola exclaimed, heels of her hands pressed against her forehead. "More things to be sorted, and me with no place to put them nor time to shift things. Do you know, I yet have bags of shelled

nuts atop a shed roof, covered with a greased cloth for lack of another spot? I need that barn!"

"Poor babe," Thomas crooned. "Best you be dashing home, then. The bundles will be in your yard come nightfall."

"My thanks for your pity," Nicola said with mock sarcasm, then leaned forward to press her lips against the man's leathery cheek. "Be well enough to come to the ale, Thomas. I would see you dance and laugh. Until the morrow."

"Until the morrow, Colette," he said in fond farewell.

With her heart easier than it had been in a month's time, Nicola left the reeve's house with a spring in her step. She and Walter made their way back along the deeply rutted lane that led to Ashby's gate.

From behind them came the pounding of hooves. "Make way!" Jos's voice rang against house and sky. Nicola and Walter leapt out of the track. His chunky pony tore past them, mouth open and hooves flying as if the devil were after it. Nicola looked back along the lane to the road. Because it was.

Witasse's dark coat was visible against the faded brown of the hills through which the road cut. Ashby's lord turned his mount off the road and onto the lane. Nicola and Walter moved well aside to watch. 'Twas an awesome sight.

The huge black beast came galloping toward them, head straining forward and mane flying. Fully armed with a maroon surcoat atop his mail, Gilliam's cloak flew out behind him in careless disregard for the cold. His mail shone like silver, even in the day's gray light. When her husband saw her, he raised an arm in greeting, then set his knees to Witasse's sides. The horse's gait changed and slowed.

"Walter, I'm coming for her. Do not let her run." Gilliam's shout echoed in the clouds.

The soldier looked at his lady with a grin. "He'll lift you. Hold still or you could be hurt by mistake." He eyed the lane, as if gauging, then moved Nicola into position. His hand on her shoulder kept her in place.

"What!" Nicola protested in disbelief at this fool-hardy game her husband played. She could think of no worse death than being trampled beneath Witasse's iron-shod hooves. If fear filled her, pride would not let her run. Be damned if she'd let Gilliam or his man see her fear.

Gilliam extended an arm. Nicola squinted in her determination to survive this event. He leaned a little to the side and caught her around the waist. As her feet swung free of the earth, she dug her fingers into the links of his armor, clinging to his arm as if her life depended on it. Even beneath his mail and padding, she could feel his muscles harden as he bore all her weight. An instant later, she sat sideways on his saddle. She latched her arms around his middle.

"Are you mad?" she hissed. "This beast of yours could have killed me." All she could see of his face beneath his helmet and chain mail hood was his mouth. As always, his lips curved in a smile.

"As long as you did not move, you were in no danger," he said with a brief shake of his head. "To Witasse, this was just another jousting exercise. Besides, I have decided you live a charmed life. You should have died in the fire, on my blade, in battle with those thieves, in the woods, and under Witasse's hooves. Since none of this happened, I am convinced you are indestructible."

She huffed in disbelief. "Well, do not do it again. I did not much care for the experience. How is it in Eilington? Did you find the girl?"

Gilliam's smile dimmed, and he slowed Witasse to a walk. The big steed protested with a momentary sidelong dance, then submitted. "We found her," he said quietly. "They were brutal, doing torture to her for the pure joy of hurting."

"She was dead?"

His jaw clenched. "She is now. Damn," he said quietly, then buried his reaction behind a smile. "So, how was your day, my lady? More pleasant than mine, I hope."

Nicola looked at him, then understood that his hurt over the girl's death went too deep to bear discussion just now. In an effort to protect him from his pain, she threw herself into her complaint. "Not yet finished," she said. "Thomas is sending me bundles of willow withes, reeds, and rushes, all of which we need and all of which I have no place to put. Gilliam, I need that barn. You should have raised a hall, instead of cottages."

He tilted his head back a bit to peer down at her from beneath the arch of metal over his eyes. "There wasn't time to finish the hall before it grew too cold to lay mortar. Come spring, we'll build ourselves a hall." The weight of knight and steed made the drawbridge spanning Ashby's ditch groan as they rode into the bailey.

"Mortar?" she replied in surprise. "You want a stone hall?"

"Aye, think on it, my sweet. With slate for a roof

and stone all around us, we'll never again worry over fire eating up what is ours. Nor will we worry over an enemy trying to drive all of us to starve in that cramped keep tower. We'll sit, safe and secure, in our own house atop our own cellar."

As he reined in Witasse near the hall, Nicola looked up at him, stunned at his words. As Thomas said, here was a man with plans for the future. Building a stone house would bite into years of income, even with what they now earned from Eilington, but it was more than that. *Our* house, he had said, *our* cellar. How easily Gilliam included her into his own path, creating theirs out of his.

"I won!" Jos screamed from atop his palfrey in the yard's center. He lifted his arms in triumph. Beneath a steel sewn leather hauberk, recently sent by Lord Coudray, the boy wore a thick woolen tunic and chausses equally as warm. Somewhere in the past month, he had forgotten to be sickly, so his cloak hood had fallen back during his ride. If his ears and nose were red with cold, his dark eyes were alive with delight.

"Do not let it go to your head, lad," Gilliam responded with a laugh. "I gave you nigh on a half-mile head start."

The grooms came running from the stable, armed with heavy leads and their best courage. Witasse only allowed his favorites to attach the leather straps and his affection could be fickle, save for the love he gave his master.

With Gilliam's arm to brace her, Nicola slid to the ground. She flew out of range of the beasts's hooves. As her husband dismounted, the huge steed turned his head toward the tall knight, his whickering nod a plea. Gilliam drew off his knitted steel gloves and fondled

the horse's ears, whispering and talking to the massive
beast as if it were a babe.

"You coddle him worse than you do Roia," Nicola
called to her husband as the grooms led the horse to his
paddock.

Gilliam wrenched off his helmet, pushing back his
mail coif, then removing the leather cap he wore beneath it. "Aye," he replied as he ran a hand through his
hair, "my heart is taken. I'm sorry that it could not
have been you who won it. Alas, you have been
usurped in my affections by a horse." His blue eyes
gleamed as he gave his head a sad shake.

Nicola could have groaned. Why was she forever
trying to match wits with him? All she ever ended up
doing was feeding his ceaseless need to play. She made
a face at him, then turned to enter the hall.

In the bailey, Gilliam said, "Come, Jos, since we're
dressed for it, let's be off for the practice yard."

Even from inside the hall, she could hear the boy's
groan. "My lord, you know how poor I am with a
sword—" Jos caught himself. "I will try, my lord."
There was grim, if hopeless, determination in the lad's
voice. Nicola shook her head at the steady change in
the boy. Jos had never had a chance against Gilliam's
persistence. Each day he behaved more like a respect-
able boy.

Chapter Eighteen

Nicola paused to push an errant strand of hair out of her face with the back of a hand, then straightened. With these sacks moved out of the cellar's corner, there was just enough room to stack the bundles of osier branches. The reeds wanted drying before they could be stored.

She stepped back to see what she had accomplished. There was a slender bit of dark wood curving out from behind the sacks, its color startling against the whitewashed wall. Nicola shoved her way back into the newly emptied corner to look, then cried out in pleased surprise.

Trapped between barrels and the wall was her father's crossbow, which had once been stored in her stillroom. She pushed and shoved the sacks far enough away from the wall to begin easing the bow out, and something else clattered to the floor. It was her practice sword, the one her father had given her when she was but eight. He had promised she would grow into it, and so she had.

Nicola stared in astonishment. How in God's name had these come to be here? Then, again, with the chaos that was Ashby before her return, she wondered why their presence here surprised her. Nothing had been where it should.

She picked up the sword. The grip felt good in her hand, the blade's balance familiar. She and her father had sparred from time to time, and he had been proud of her ability to use the weapon. Eventually, he had grown too heavy and slow to be a challenge for her. She smiled a little at the memories and set the sword by the cellar's ladder, then came back to extract the bow.

When it was free, she ran her hands over its shining length, checking the bindings for rot. It took a special craftsman to fix a bow such as this. Only the string was loose. 'Twas a two-footed bow, meaning a man braced both feet into the bow to draw its string into the catch. Although its range was limited, its accuracy was a thing to be reckoned with.

She had toyed with it only long enough to learn to shoot and hit a target, then set it aside. With all her other duties, there had been a limit to the amount of time she could dedicate to weapons, and the sword was her favorite. Her sword in one hand and the bow in the other, Nicola clambered up the ladder, meaning to restore the items to her stillroom where they belonged.

The day had grown into an unseasonable cold, making each breath sting her lungs. As she crossed the demesne, nearing the practice yard, she heard Jos's whine.

"Please, my lord, you can see this is hopeless. I will never be able to strike with a sword, and 'tis awful cold out here."

"Boy, do not complain. If you work hard enough, you'll be warm. Try again." Gilliam's voice was patient and calm.

" 'Tis hopeless."

"You have only begun to learn. You cannot expect perfection when you've just started. No more excuses. Come, Jos, lift that blade," Gilliam urged.

Nicola detoured to watch for a moment. The two stood in the center of a beaten square of earth. Jos now had his hood tucked tight around his ears. His cloak was buckled into his belt, and his nose was bright red. He clutched a short practice sword in one gloved hand and a round leather shield in the other.

Armed with an identical weapon and shield, Gilliam was bareheaded, having discarded his cloak along with his own sword and scabbard. With the thickness of his padded gambeson and his heavy woolen chausses, donned to protect his skin from the metal coat and stockings he wore, 'twas hardly surprising he had no concept of the chill.

Her husband extended his blade out before him. Jos squinted in concentration, lifted his sword for a sideways blow, and swung. Gilliam twisted his wrist to give the boy an extra sting as their weapons connected. There was a tiny clash of metal, and Jos fell back with a cry of dismay.

"My lord, it shivers in my hand when I hit your blade," Jos complained. "How am I to hold it when it leaps and bounces in my hand? It hurts."

"Nay, it cannot hurt you when you wear gloves, you twit. Besides, this is what you seek to learn. You must find the grip that allows the blade to vibrate as it will without causing you to loose your hold. Come, boy. Try again."

Jos once again prepared himself to strike. As he swung, Gilliam lifted his blade just enough so the boy missed. "You are supposed to strike my blade, not turn in circles," he chided with a laugh. "Keep your eyes open."

"My eyes were open. You moved your blade before I struck." Jos was panting, his breath misting before him. "Now, hold it still." He swung. Again, Gilliam shifted the blade just a little, so Jos's blade took its edge in a tooth-jarring impact. The boy fell back in surprise.

Nicola grinned. "For shame, my lord," she called to Gilliam, "you are cheating."

Her husband instantly turned toward her, the strong planes of his face revealing a subtle pleasure. Where his gaze touched her face, her skin warmed. Thank the Lord she had hours filled with reasons to keep her distance from him. "I did not know you were watching us," he said with a quick laugh. "What are you carrying there?"

He set down his weapons and came striding to her, his eyes on the crossbow. Nicola damned herself. Too late to hide the one, but she swiftly moved her practice sword behind her back. Why had she even stopped to watch? "I found this old bow in the cellar while I was making room for the willow branches. I was taking it to be stored with the rest of the weapons," she lied.

"Hey now, this is a pretty thing." Gilliam took the crossbow, testing the trigger.

"It belonged to my father, given to him by the old king. I am glad it did not burn in the fire. 'Tis good to have something to remember him by," she said, ready to sacrifice the bow in order to keep the sword.

"Aye, that it is," he agreed, and pulled off a glove to run his hands over the wooden bow, then lifted the stock beneath his eye to check its aim. With his eye still sighted in the distance, he asked, "So, what story clings to the sword?"

His question startled her, since she hadn't realized he'd seen it. "None that I know."

"God's truth, madam?" he asked with a lift of his brow. "Since the armory is in the opposite direction from where your toes point, your answer has me wondering."

Nicola shrugged in defeat, then was surprised. The thought of Gilliam taking her weapon awoke no anger at all within her. " 'Tis mine. My father gave it to me."

"So, you have no further use for it, do you?" There was laughing skepticism in his voice. Only when he was done speaking did he lower the bow and glance at her. There was nothing for her to see in his expression save amusement.

" 'Tis but an old practice sword. What use has a meek and mild housewife for such a thing?"

"Meek and mild?" he threw back. "You dare not call yourself that when I have seen the fruits of your skill."

"My lord, I am so cold," Jos said, his teeth chattering. "Are we finished yet?"

Grateful for Jos's interruption, Nicola sought to return the favor. "You should let him go within, my lord. He has not your capacity to generate heat, and 'tis an icy day."

"Now, why should we quit when we're having such fun?" He dropped his arm around the lad's shoulder. Jos stumbled under the weight of it.

"Fun? Only you would think standing in a chill wind swinging a sword would be fun," Nicola scoffed. "Poor Jos is miserable. Let him go to the kitchen and get himself a cup of warm broth." The prospect of food always seemed to move Gilliam.

Jos gazed hopefully up at Gilliam, his thin brows raised in question. Ashby's lord looked from the boy to Nicola. A slow grin spread across his face and woke in his eyes. "Since you plead for him, I'll let him go, but only if you bring that sword of yours and come spar with me."

"What?" Nicola cried in disbelief. "You must be mad to suggest such a thing. You are a knight and fully armed, whilst I have only wool to protect me from your blows. I am not even wearing gloves."

"What is this? Excuses? These I hear from Jos, I do not expect them from you. Since you have no gloves, neither shall I. What's a few blisters between friends, eh?" Gilliam tore off his other glove and tossed the pair aside, then retrieved his practice sword and shield.

The wind tossed Nicola's skirts and lifted her head scarf. Even as the desire to meet him, sword to sword grew in her, she realized how idiotic the notion was. All she would earn was his disgust and scorn. "Why?"

Gilliam shrugged. "I would know how you did those men." There was nothing in his tone to indicate some other motive.

"Oh, well, if that is all, I will tell you. 'Twas naught but sheer good fortune coupled with my strong desire to live. Besides, they were but starving thieves, while you are a knight, fully trained. There can be no comparison."

"Since you are so afraid of me, I promise you I will only defend myself against you, not strike out." There was amusement in his voice.

"Afraid of you, big man?" Her words dripped scorn, "I think not."

The memory of how easily he had disarmed her after her father's death rose within her. She had been overwrought by smoke and grief, else he'd not have done it so quickly. Now, her sword seemed to quiver in her hand as if it had a life of its own. The need to meet him and show him she was not as inept as he thought her overwhelmed her sense.

"Come, Nicola," he goaded, his deep voice filled with teasing challenge, "show me what you know. Unless you wish me to think you incapable. We both know that is an untruth, do we not?"

Nicola rolled her eyes at this ridiculous prod. It would serve him right to taste her skill. Aye, she could repay him just a little for all his taunts. She gazed at Gilliam. His eyes were alive with interest as he juggled the sword before him in what she presumed was invitation.

"My lady, please," Jos begged, "do what he asks. I am nigh on frozen, through and through. Please?" The boy wrapped his arms around himself and shivered, a little too violently to be credible.

"For you, then, Jos," she said, trying to hide her growing excitement over the match behind a casual voice.

Gilliam smiled broadly. "Jos, give Lady Nicola your shield and take yourself to the kitchen. Be swift in returning, as this is but a pause in your lesson."

Nicola's brows rose, almost insulted by this. Did he truly think she would be so easily beaten? The urge to show him differently grew to tantalizing proportions.

Jos dropped his sword without a second thought and thrust the shield into her hand. "Thank you, my lady," he said in gratitude, then dashed for the kitchen. His relief was so deep, he hadn't considered the oddity of what was happening.

She waited until he was out of sight, then loosened

her mantle and threw it aside. Reaching for her skirt hems at either side of her, she tucked them into her belt.

"Cheat! I shall be distracted by the sight of your bared legs." He laughed.

"Does that mean you will change your mind about this match?" she retorted. "This is how it must be, for I cannot spar with you if my skirts keep tangling around my ankles."

"I will suffer the distraction," he said, a brave hand over his heart. "Come now."

Nicola strode forward to meet him. When she stopped in front of him, he lifted his blade. "Ready?" he asked.

In response, she swiftly brought the sword up from her hips. Had he been a second slower, he'd have felt its blunt edge against his ribs. Gilliam's eyes widened in appreciation, and he grinned, then gave his blade a casual twist. The motion sent her stumbling back, but even before she'd caught her balance, her sword was moving.

Their blades met again and again, in a rapid fire staccato. As he vowed, he played only a defensive game, working to simply deflect her attacks. That he so easily anticipated her movements spoke both to his speed and her own lack of practice. After a few moments, her muscles began to warm, making her motions more fluid. Of a sudden, her body began to remember what she'd spent years teaching it.

Now Gilliam was striving to block her attacks. Dressed as he was in his heavy armor, she held the advantage in both speed and agility. She pinned him with four upward strikes using all her power, driving him back step by step.

Through her concentration Nicola watched him; his smile never dimmed, although sweat beaded on his brow. When he caught her look, he lifted his brows to encourage her. She grinned broadly, dropped an overhand attack on him, then used his all-too-predictable backward thrust to turn her. She whirled, blade dropping, then coming up at him in an arc.

Gilliam stumbled back, having barely fended off the attack. *"Jesu,"* he breathed in surprise. "I just saw my life pass before me."

She opened her mouth to retort, but he had discarded defense and was coming for her, sword raised for an overhand blow. Armed with the power of his shoulders, 'twas the only blow of his against which she had no defense. Nicola dropped, rolled to the side, then leapt out of his reach even as her husband's sword cleaved through open air.

"Big men are so slow," she snorted in disgust, hands on hips.

Gilliam laughed and tossed aside his weapons. "Slow am I?" he yelled, and started toward her.

"Nay, we are dueling," she cried in protest, backing swiftly away from his steady advance. "Now, who is cheating? I cannot strike an unarmed man. Back off, you."

He snatched her into his embrace. Her sword and shield clattered to the ground as he lifted her into his arms and turned a wild circle. "You are an incredible woman," he bellowed in pleasure. "And I thought you only half trained. Hardly so. I will have you and only you as my sparring partner for the rest of my days!"

"You are mad, stark, raving mad," Nicola protested with a laugh. "Put me down before your mail cuts me to ribbons."

"Not until you tell me why you hold your blade so low," he retorted.

"Fool." She filled the word with amused scorn and locked her hands behind his neck to hold herself in place. "Look at yourself, then at me. Where you are all shoulders and back strength, I have only my hips. 'Tis my only source of power, and the first thing I learned at my father's knee."

"I am looking at you," he said, his blue eyes suddenly intense, the laughter gone from his face. "I am amazed by what I see. How is it I am so fortunate to be married to you?"

Nicola drew a swift breath, for the magic came rushing back with three times the strength of a few weeks ago. She sought desperately for some defense. "Fortunate to be tied to the giantess of Ashby, with her cropped hair? The same ugly amazon who dresses as a man and wields a sword?" Her pulse steadied with these words.

Gilliam lifted his brows in an expression of disbelief. "You are no giant to me," he said softly, "nor are you an amazon. Most likely you heard that from some jealous man who lacks the strength you own. As for ugly, that you most certainly are not. Your eyes are beautiful beyond any woman I have ever seen, and your hair full of marvelous life. I find myself so tempted by your form that I'm fair drowning in my desire for you."

With that, he set her feet back on the earth, but did not release his arm around her back. Nicola found herself caught tightly to him. She released her hold on his neck and let her hands rest against his chest. His surcoat was soft beneath her fingers. Although she knew she shouldn't, she looked into his face.

There was no laughter in his blue eyes, only desire. For her. She saw it in the softness of his mouth and the tight line of his jaw. Nicola shook her head in disbelief. No man wanted her. "Now, I know you are mad, truly mad." It was supposed to be a hard retort, but it left her lips as a breathless whisper. "You must let me go."

The icy breeze curled around her, sneaking beneath her skirts to chill the bare skin of her legs. As had happened on the church step, his hold tightened, forcing her to rise to her toes. Still, she looked into his eyes. He wanted her, only her. It said so in his expression. He thought her beautiful. Nicola gasped at the wondrous pressure that filled her heart. Her eyes closed as he turned his mouth to meet hers.

Their joining was warm and soft, no more than the passionless kiss exchanged in formal ceremonies. Yet deep inside her something throbbed. Her mouth clung to his, her hands sliding up along his surcoat to clasp behind his neck. When his lips moved slightly on hers, her breath caught in her throat. She sighed to release it.

There was a tiny tug as he pulled off her head scarf, then his arm freed her. His hands came to either side of her face. His fingers threaded through her hair, his calloused palms rough against her cheeks. Nicola eased back onto her heels, letting him hold her so as he took her mouth in kiss after light kiss, teasing and taunting until her blood was nigh on fire.

Within her grew a terrible, gnawing need to catch his mouth with hers and not let go. Her arms tightened around his neck, and she pulled herself hard against him, ignoring the bite of his metal coat. When her mouth took his, it was with the demand that he cease his play and kiss her in earnest.

He gasped against her lips, one hand coming to cup the back of her head, his other arm catching her in an unbreakable hold. His mouth slashed across hers, communicating a need so deep she felt dizzy with it. Her answer to him came roaring through her, blazing with heat and desire. She tore her mouth from his to kiss the line of his jaw, then to nip at the lobe of his ear. His shudder was followed by a low moan that sounded almost like pain.

'Twas Nicola's turn to gasp. She was shocked by what she was doing, yet she could not cease. The sensations they made between them so goaded her, she was powerless against them. Her lips touched his throat, her fingers tangled in his hair, forcing him to lower his head so she could taste his lips once again. He groaned softly, his hand sliding between them to cup her breast. As a bolt of raw feeling exploded within her, she arched away in pleasure and surprise.

Then his hand was gone, and his arms closed around her again. She was held tightly to him, his brow leaning on hers. "Dear God, but this is sweet torture." He breathed the words. "If you do not intend to lay with me, you must cease."

Nicola frowned in disappointment. She did not wish to cease, not when his every touch fed what now lived within her. "But I—" she started, then could find no more words to speak beyond these.

Gilliam released her and caught her hands in his. When he stepped back, Nicola freed a tiny cry of desolation. With all her heart, she wanted his arms around her again. He closed his eyes, then pressed a kiss into her palm.

Her knees quivered in response. Nicola drew a sharp breath to steady herself. What was this magic he did to her? Again, need rose with her, yet, Gilliam still backed away until he was standing just beyond her reach. Her arms returned to her side, her hands yet begging for his touch.

"Will you lay with me?" Gilliam's question was hoarse and deep.

Nicola shivered as the cold wind swept away the heat their bodies had made. Its icy fingers drove the intoxicating sensations from her brain as it chilled her to the bone. She felt frozen and alone, but sane again.

She stared at him, her gaze marking the rise of his fine cheekbones and the way the wind tossed his golden hair against them, the line of his jaw and the gentle curve of his mouth. His eyes were deep blue with his need for her. Oh, but he was a beautiful man. Not only that, but he thought himself fortunate to have her. Gilliam was not disgusted by what she knew. Nay, he wanted her as his sparring partner.

From the depths of her memory came the image of him standing before her father. She saw again the arc of his great sword as it came around, then buried itself into her father's neck. Nicola's heart broke and her eyes filled. " 'Tis not fair," she whispered in pain as a tear traced its way down her cheek. "Why is the only man who values me for who I am, also the man who ended my father's life?"

Gilliam turned his head to the side. "Damn me," he muttered. "He was nearly dead already. Why did I have to strike? I thought only to give him a quicker death than burning."

Nicola caught back a gasp. Without considering what she did, she came to stand before him and pressed trembling fingers to his mouth. "I cannot let you blame yourself."

She snatched back her hand, stunned at what she'd said. "What is happening to me?" she cried, torn to pieces in her confusion. With that she turned and ran, not caring where she went.

Chapter Nineteen

G illiam awoke the next morning, his head aching. He had not seen Nicola since she'd run from him yesterday. He knew she had gone to see the priest; Walter had escorted her. So, too, did he know that she had worked in the kitchen for a time. She had been within Ashby's walls when the gate closed at dark.

Over this past month, each time he had cracked her defenses, even slightly, she retreated. She hid from him in her hours of labors, in her trips to the villagers, in the care she gave Ashby's servants and men. He had wondered how much farther she could run. Now he knew. She had not come to sleep with him last night.

He closed his eyes and remembered the stark confusion in her remarkable eyes. She had not expected to forgive him for her father's death. That had come purely from her heart before she'd even known it was there. He had breached her last defense and left her walls a shamble.

Moving to the bed's side, he opened the curtains and sat up. The room beyond the fabric was filled with dreary light, and the atmosphere was as icy as yesterday. Jos had retreated completely beneath his many layers of blankets. Roia lay curled tightly beside him.

The dog pricked her ears at her master's movements, but stayed where she lay.

"I should be insulted by your fickle affection," he said to her. "I think you are liking that boy better than you do me."

His voice brought her to her feet, stretching and groaning. She lay her head in his lap, eyes beseeching. He scratched her ears for her, then gave her sides a good drubbing. When he drew back his hands, Roia returned to Jos.

Gilliam let his lips twist in a wry grin. "I suppose I cannot complain when I have given my heart elsewhere, too."

He reached for his clothing. Perhaps it was a good thing Nicola had not come to him last night. Mary, but he was eating himself alive for want of her. The touch of her mouth on his neck, the fiery way she kissed him, it had all served to drive his desire almost beyond his control.

After donning his chausses and shirt, he pulled on his boots. Standing at the beside with garters in hand, he looked down at his legs. Nicola had taken to tying his cross garters as her own task. What if she chose not to share his chamber any longer?

Gilliam shook his head. If she thought to leave his bed, he would drag her, kicking and screaming, back into this room. He would not allow her to escape him now.

That thought made him sit down again. In one month, he had made no progress at all. Instead, they had come full circle. Here he was, once more contemplating forcing her where she did not wish to go. This time, he had not the patience to start the process over again. He wanted his wife.

What if he forced her and it drove her away from him for all time? Gilliam groaned and fell back on the mattress to stare at the cloth stretched above him to make the bed's ceiling. It was more than desire he harbored within him for Nicola. He liked her; she made him laugh. If she grew to hate him, life would be unbearably lonely.

Gilliam struggled into a sitting position, his back yet bowed in pain. "Jos," he called loudly enough to awaken the boy, his voice tired. " 'Tis time to be about our day."

The boy gave a squeaky groan and stretched. "It's the ale, today," he said around a yawn. "I cannot wait. Lady Nicola said she made a fruit compote with stewed pears. 'Tis my favorite."

Gilliam smiled. Over this last month, Jos had found a boy's appetite, if he did not yet own a lad's daring. "Aye, and since the hours will be taken up in feasting from midday on, there's no sense in attempting doing anything much. Why don't we do us a bit of hunting? Roia would like the run." It was not the dog that wanted to run, but himself. He could not tolerate the thought of meeting Nicola somewhere within these walls, only to find the rejection he feared reflected in her eyes.

Jos sat up in surprise. "You would take me hunting?"

"Is there a reason I should not?" Gilliam leaned down to wrap a garter around one leg.

"My father said I was useless at hunting," the boy replied, his voice quiet and humble.

That brought Gilliam upright in a hurry. So, 'twasn't just a mother at work here; both sire and dam had their hands in destroying their child's spirit. "Well, my lad,

I've yet to find you useless. Untrained mayhap, but hardly useless. I cannot think you'd begin to disappoint me at this late date." He was careful to keep his voice matter-of-fact.

"Nay, my lord, I will not." It was a stout reply.

Gilliam leaned down, not only to tie his other boot into place, but to hide his smile. Even if he and Jos returned empty-handed, the very fact they went would help the boy regain a bit of what had been stolen from him. The day would not be a total loss.

This helped to raise his own spirits. Aye, at midday the villagers would come. He and Nicola would be trapped together until late in the evening. Somehow, he would find the way to make things right between them.

Gilliam found his place at the high table as the last of the villagers rapidly filled the room. His folk all wore their finest attire, their gowns and tunics brightly dyed in hues of green, blue, and red. Not only did people come with their own cups and bread, but a goodly number carried with them stools or benches. It had taken almost every piece of wood Ashby owned to make tables for them, leaving the hall short of seating.

Gilliam frowned. There was still no sign of his missing wife. She and Walter had departed some time this morn, but he knew not where they had gone.

Ashby's lord leaned to the side to let Jos set a water bowl onto the table, then held his hands above it. Gilliam tried not to look at the child, but was too late to stop himself. Jos had already managed to slosh water over the front of his pale blue tunic.

As the boy tilted the ewer, the tip of his tongue exited from the corner of his mouth and a tiny line of concentration appeared between his brows. Slowly and carefully, he dribbled water over his lord's fingers and into the bowl, then offered a towel.

In an effort to stop his smile, Gilliam glanced toward the floor. Worse and worse. Clad in red chausses, the boy's thin legs looked like a mummer's painted stilts. He cleared his throat and regained control.

"Well-done, Joscelyn," he said to his squire.

"It is my duty to serve," the boy responded, then ruined the formality by smiling. Gilliam knew his pleasure came from the fact he'd not spilled the water in his lord's lap as feared.

Jos might be pleased thus far, but Gilliam counted on wearing a goodly portion of this meal. He looked down in regret at his only other formal gown, a scarlet affair emblazoned with lozenges of blue. From its place in his belt, the gem in the handle of his finest dagger glinted at him. Aye, he looked the part of a lord, but for how long? When he returned his gaze to the room, the cook was standing before him, nervously trying to get his attention.

"Aye?" Gilliam asked to encourage the man.

The cook frowned as if concentrating deeply. "Alice Atte Green. Lady Nicola . . ." The man made a frustrated sound and grabbed the reeve as that man made his painful way past them to the table's end. Thomas looked a step up from his usual, what with his tawny hair neatly combed and wearing a bright blue tunic over brown chausses. There was an exchange of English.

The village's highest-ranking official turned to his lord. "Seger, here, says the meal's ready to begin service, but your lady has gone to the village to tend to Alice atte Green, who is giving birth. Lady Nicola sends her apologies and says you will have to begin the meal without her, my lord. She will return as soon as the child is delivered."

Gilliam nodded to the burly commoner, hiding his reaction. Not only had his wife abandoned him, but her desertion left him helpless. This celebration was an Ashby tradition and had been her idea. He had no notion of the protocol expected of him in such an affair.

The reeve pulled out a bench and seated himself to his lord's far right, leaving space for the missing noblewoman. Gilliam's table not only hosted the reeve, but that pompous ass who owned almost as many fields as he did. That man Ralph by Wood, and the battle ax who was his wife, Emotte, were seated at Gilliam's left, between himself and Father Reynard at the table's opposite end.

When Gilliam picked up his cup, one of the village girls who served this night came running to fill it with ale. She was a pretty thing, all pink cheeks and glowing eyes. He smiled at her, and she dissolved into giggles, then shot him a coy look over her shoulder with just the hint of invitation in it. He raised his brows in response, and she smiled a sultry grin, then turned to walk away, her hips moving suggestively beneath her gown. Well, if his wife did not want him, there were other women who did.

But he did not want them. He wanted Nicola.

"There are others competent to deliver babes, Nicola," he said to his cup as he brought it to his lips. "You should not have left me."

"Ah, but your lady's a hardheaded one who trusts only herself to rightly do what's needed. 'Tis a failing of hers."

Gilliam looked sharply at Thomas. With the noise level in the room nigh on deafening, he hadn't expected to be overheard. Nor was he certain he wished to share his marital troubles with a stranger.

The commoner cocked his head to one side and sighed, the sound filled with masculine commiseration. "Learned that from my Agnes, your lady did. Not only did my Aggie suckle Lady Nicola, but 'twas at my wife's knee that yours learned her healing skills. Aye, my lord, I know well how you feel. I cannot tell you how often my Aggie turned her back on me and my commands to do for others. Women," he said with a shrug, a friendly glint in his deep-set eyes, "what can you do?"

"I wish I knew," Gilliam muttered to himself. Still, there was some consolation in knowing that Nicola would have gone to the village woman whether she was running from him or not. "Thomas, I have no knowledge of this sort of gathering. What is expected of me?"

The reeve again set his head to one side, as if doing so was what made his lips work. "We're a simple bunch, my lord. First, have Father bless the food, then say a few words in welcome to us and comment on the harvest past. I'll translate for you. After that, we eat. When the eating's done, the drinking begins in earnest. 'Twill be the night's goal to see who can hold the most ale without sickness or sleeping."

Having said this, Thomas leaned a little closer and offered in a low voice. "The boy should sit and eat, rather than serving you, my lord. There's no need on our account to wear your meal, the way the child's already wearing the water."

Gilliam looked at the commoner for a long moment, unsure whether he should be insulted or complimented by such familiarity. He decided to be complimented,

mainly because it made his life much more comfortable. With a smile, he said, "I like this place more and
more, Thomas. Here I was thinking I had to be on my
best behavior."

Turning to the left, he leaned forward to speak to the
priest at the table's opposite end. "Father, it appears
that most everyone is seated. Any time you wish to deliver the blessing, you may do so. I am ready to eat."

And eat they did. By Nicola's design, they dined on
roasted beef and mutton, the last of the stubble fed
geese and doves from the cot, stewed with onions.
There were tench and eels from the millpond and two
types of stewed fruit. One was a compote, the other
just stewed pears, for Jos.

As the reeve suggested, the drinking was done as a
competition. After four hours of participating, Gilliam
was ready to cede victory to Ralph by Wood. The man
had a hollow leg. Unlike the reeve who was struggling
to fend off unconsciousness, the only mark of Ralph's
prodigious consumption was the change in his temper-
ament.

Gilliam glanced beyond Ralph, pitying the priest
who had to endure the farmer's crude guffaws of
laughter. Where Father Reynard had been was now an
empty bench. He raised his brows in surprise, not having seen the churchman leave.

With the remains of the meal confined to two tables
for a later distribution to the poorest cottars, the other
tables had been dismantled and set at the walls. Those
villagers who owned musical instruments had brought
them. Tambours thrummed, pipes twined their discor-
dant sound into the sawing draw of bows against
string. Those who danced did so in twisting, swirling
circles of flying skirts and fleet feet. Those yet seated

stomped in tune to the melodies. The air grew heavy and warm with so many folk in so small a space.

Gilliam looked for Jos. With Roia confined to the stables for the night, the boy lacked a companion. Jos had drifted to a clutch of village lads and was peering shyly over their shoulders as the boys threw dice, gambling for the odd treasures precious to these youths.

As he looked away, he caught a glimpse of motion from the room's far corner. 'Twas a couple doing what he wished he could do with his wife. Filled with jealousy, he turned his attention back to the room's center as the door opened and shut.

It was Walter, but where was Nicola? He started to lift his hand to signal his soldier, but Walter was already pushing and shoving through the crowd toward him. The man's frantic motions brought Gilliam to his feet. He swayed, noting he was just a might giddier with drink than he'd thought.

"What is it?" he called.

Walter was shaking his head, his face caught in worried lines. "I ran ahead to warn you. It went badly, and something's wrong with our lady, terrible wrong. She tore her clothing, then went blank. Come, my lord, come with me."

Before Gilliam could rise, there was a sharp cry from near the barn's door, then those nearest to it scattered from the opening. 'Twas like watching a wave on the ocean. Folk rolled and parted, stumbling and crying out as they squeezed against the walls. A stool shattered against the beaten earth floor. The music screeched to a halt, dancers fell aside, giving their lady ample room to pass.

Nicola entered the now-open space at the room's center and stood staring at the fire. She was without mantle or head cloth, her skirts stained with blood and covered in straw. Her overgown was rent from neckline to near her waist. But, 'twas the pallor and stillness of her face that most worried Gilliam. She was gone, hiding deep within herself. When he turned to move to her, the reeve caught his arm.

"She'll strike if you touch her," Thomas said to him, struggling to speak clearly as he rocked on his bench. "She's deadly, you know."

"Aye, that I do," Gilliam said, removing the man's hand from his arm. He started through the crowd now clustered behind his table, his gaze never leaving Nicola. She turned slowly, looking around her with eyes that did not seem to see, then moved toward the food-laden table. Gilliam knew without doubt that she meant to tip it.

"Move aside," he said, yet hampered by the crush of villagers. He broke free and strode swiftly for her as she took hold of the table's edge. "Cease, Nicola." He made his voice hard with command, hoping to rouse her.

The reeve laughed. "Her name's not Nicola, 'tis Colette, my lord."

The tabletop tilted. "Cease this instant, Colette," Gilliam bellowed from behind her, his hands gently on her arms, ready to stop her if she did not comply.

The tabletop clattered back onto its braces, stews sloshing and trays rattling. Nicola turned so swiftly, he stepped back in reaction, losing his grip on her arms. The folk in the room gasped as one.

She struck out, but he caught her fist. She raised the other, his hand closed around it. Gilliam forced her arms down at her sides. With her hands contained, the blankness in her eyes receded just enough to show him what she hid beneath it. "Ah, Colette, does it hurt you so much?"

She drew a deep and trembling breath. Her face was yet pale, but his Nicola returned. Gilliam released her hands. His wife kept her gaze locked on him. Just now, her eyes were a deep green. He combed his fingers through her hair, then moved his thumbs on her temples in a gentle caress. Nicola leaned her head into one of his palms.

"Spill your grief on me, my sweet," he offered quietly. "I will carry what you cannot bear."

She blinked. Her mouth trembled as she spoke. "Gilliam." It was a breath of a whisper. She took a step toward him and rested her brow against his neck, her arms coming around his waist.

Gilliam embraced her. "You need to sleep. Let me put you to bed." When she nodded, he leaned down and caught her beneath her knees, lifting her into his arms. He started toward the door, silent folk easing back out of his path. At the door, he called to the room, "Please continue your celebration without me."

The reeve's voice rang in the rafters. "That we will, my lord." His words were followed by a loud hiccup, a belch, and a sudden thunk. Ralph by Wood shouted in triumph. With Nicola still and soft in his arms, Gilliam smiled and exited into the bailey.

The same icy wind that soughed and sighed around him had finally driven away the clouds. With the solstice so near, the sun was already settling into the gentle bosom of Ashby's rolling hills, leaving a sky stained in grays and purples. The frigid breeze caught in Nicola's curls, setting them to dancing around her cheeks.

Gilliam turned her a little in his arms, trying to

shield her from the chill, then wondered why he bothered. Their chamber would be just as cold. Besides being too small, the room lacked the draft for a brazier; there would be no hearth for them until the hall rose. If these last days were any indication of the coming winter's temper, they would soon be forced to retreat to the hall and fire.

He climbed the stairs, then fumbled with the latch a moment until he managed the door. The movement seemed to rouse Nicola from whatever place she was in. She made a tiny sound, as if she were just awakening.

Lowering her to sit on the mattress at the bed's foot, he turned back the bedclothes. When he sat beside her, it was to draw her close for warmth's sake. Now, he needed to prod her into spilling what festered in her. When she'd done so, he would put her to bed.

He stared out into the small chamber, waiting for her to speak. Twilight was just beginning, but the room was already dim and gray. Shadows marked the unevenly hewn stones in the walls and dulled the bed's brightly colored curtains to a gleaming pewter tone. Even with the window shuttered, a breath of the wind entered, just enough to set the heavy curtains shifting softly on the wooden floor. Still, she said nothing.

Gilliam crooked a finger beneath her chin and tilted her head so he could look at her. He still had trouble reconciling this pretty girl with the angry virago who had attacked him at the abbey. She was watching him, her eyes still deep green. The blankness that clung to her expression reflected her battle to subdue whatever it was that hurt her so. He ran his thumb over the soft curve of her cheek.

"Will you tell me what happened?"

Nicola shook her head nay, but her arms came around his waist and her head leaned on his shoulder. He rocked her gently. When she shifted slightly, it was to touch her lips against his neck. He started. She moved her mouth from just above his collar to below his ear.

He shuddered in reaction. "Nay, Colette. 'Tis tears you need, not this."

Her hand came up his back to his nape, her fingers toying with his hair. "I cannot." It was a whispered cry. "Make me feel what only you can."

Gilliam caught his breath, then clenched his teeth against his own need. He released her and eased away. Her hand came to rest on his thigh. Even through his clothing, his flesh burned where it lay. "Nay. You do not know what you are asking."

She only slid her fingers across the thick, smooth material of his gown until her hand lay atop that part of him that most wanted her. Gilliam groaned and grabbed her hand, his fingers lacing through hers. "Nay," he said, shaking his head. Dear God, but he wanted to run his fingers through her hair and bring her mouth to his.

Her free hand came to touch his face. She traced the line of his brow, the tip of her finger leaving a trail of heat in its wake as her hand descended over his cheek. A breath shuddered from him. There was not enough strength in him to stop her.

"Cease," he breathed against her hand when her finger outlined his lips.

She again shook her head to refuse his command, then leaned toward him to place her mouth on his. 'Twas the reflection of how he had kissed her yesterday. She teased and plied his mouth with small touches of flesh to flesh.

He caught her about the waist and willed his hands to force her from him. Instead, as she struggled to draw her knees up onto the bed, he helped her. Somewhere deep inside him a hunger started. His hands trembled with it.

She knelt on the bed, bracing her hands on his chest. It took only her gentle push, and he eased back into the bolsters. With his hands yet clasped to her waist, he drew her down beside him. She lay, half atop him, her leg between his. His body reacted to the thought of what it would be like if there were not so many layers of cloth separating them.

Still, her mouth toyed with his. His need for her made him ache so badly, he had trouble catching his breath. Gilliam willed his hands not to leave her waist, just as one drifted down to the curve of her hip, his fingers burying into the softness of her flesh.

Her teeth nipped gently at his lower lip. *"Jesu,"* he breathed against her mouth. "You will regret this, Colette."

"I need you," she murmured as she kissed his ear. Each word was torment, and his spine melted.

She touched her tongue into the cup of his ear, and he was done for. His hands went to his belt, his fingers trembling as he tried to work the tongue from its clasp. Between drink and desire, he was hopelessly clumsy. When he groaned softly in frustration, his wife's hands came over his, strong and sure.

Gilliam let his hands fall to his sides as she opened his belt. He was gasping like a fish out of water, unable to catch his breath. The best he could do was lift his hips when she eased his belt from beneath him. It hit the floor with a rattling clunk.

She eased from the bed, then stood at its side. Her belt followed his an instant later, her gowns the moment after. The waning light touched her pale skin, showing him the gentle curve of her hips and the small roundness of her breasts, their nipples as hard with need as he was.

The sight of her slaughtered what little sense remained in him. Gilliam groaned and stood to tear off both gown and shirt as one, rending seams. He tossed them carelessly aside. Her hands were already at the tie of his chausses. He growled and pushed her away, falling back onto the bed to rip off both stockings and shoes. They had barely hit the floor before he caught her to him and fell back onto the bed with her beside him.

Gilliam jerked the bedclothes over the both of them and rolled onto his back, gathering her atop him. His mouth took hers, and she matched his need with her own. He could feel the pounding of her heart against his chest. There was a fire where her breasts touched him, but there was an inferno where her hip lay against his shaft.

He smoothed his hands down the long line of her waist, then caught her hips and moved her until 'twas the soft curls covering her woman's flesh he felt against him. She shifted slightly in reaction to this new sensation, her mouth slashing across his as she buried her fingers in his hair. Gilliam could not bring enough air into his lungs.

Leaving one hand to hold her hips to his, the other crept between them to cover her breast. She lifted slightly to let him touch her. He brushed his thumb across its tip until she tore her mouth from his, panting against what he did to her. 'Twas the sign he wanted. He released her breast, letting his hand slide down between them until he felt her nether lips.

She cried out, arching and lifting above him to let him ease a finger into her. Gilliam shuddered at the warmth and wetness he felt. When she moved against his hand, he groaned in reaction.

Suddenly, she was rolling off of him, her grasp on his shoulders begging him to come atop her. Somewhere, deep inside, he knew he should not do this, but 'twas she who owned him now. He did as she wished and settled atop her, his thighs between hers, his shaft at the entrance to her womb.

She took his mouth, kissing him with the same desire he knew for her. He eased himself into her, just a tiny bit, and felt the barricade of her maidenhead. His hands caught her at the waist as he fought to move carefully, rather than with the brutal thrust his shaft demanded.

She wrapped her hands around his neck, her fingers combing through his hair. When she drew a soft line down his nape, a great shudder wracked him. He tore his mouth from hers to kiss her cheek, her brow, then her ear. Once again, she caressed his nape, this time using her nails. Gilliam cried out as a shock of pure feeling shot through him, demanding that he enter her, right this instant.

"Cease, Colette." 'Twas a breathless whisper. Again, her nails drew lines on his sensitive nape. "Oh, *Jesu,* I cannot—*Jesu.*"

'Twas too late to stop himself. He drove past the constriction until he filled her. Her body closed so tightly around him he moaned against it, incapable of the gentleness he intended. He thrust, and she lifted her hips in reaction, urging him to move again. As if he could have stopped.

Gilliam lost himself to the incredible sensations she stirred in him. Her hands left his nape to clutch him around the back, her legs twined over his. He reached back to lift one of her legs until her calf lay across his hips. She brought the other to join it, her heels goading him into driving even deeper into her. When he did, she cried out, arching beneath him.

He thought he heard himself moaning, but pleasure rendered him deaf and blind. Somewhere, in a deep corner of his mind, he worried that he was hurting her, but she made him feel impossibly good. Again, she arched beneath him. He grabbed her by the hips to hold her still, then drove himself into her as he filled her with a life's time of passion.

The release was so great he was beyond feeling. When it finally ebbed, he lay trembling atop her, every muscle spent. With satisfaction came the return of sanity. Gilliam flinched at the sort of damage, either physical or emotional, he'd done to her.

He lifted himself onto his elbows, meaning to gauge her mood, and Nicola shoved angrily at him. When he rolled onto his back, she leapt from the bed with a cry that was pure rage. His heart breaking, Gilliam stared at the bed's ceiling. May the devil take his soul, but he'd killed all hope for their future.

Chapter Twenty

With a scream of rage at herself, Nicola threw herself off the bed. The room's frigid air drove all heat from her. She turned to look at Gilliam. Her husband lay still in the bed's center, staring up at the cloth ceiling above him.

What had she done? Used him to ease her horror of Alice's death and the demise of her hope to be free of Ashby's destruction, that's what. Nay, that was only the excuse she'd made, so she could lay with him. *Christus!* Damn her betraying body!

She stared at the fine line of his profile, working desperately to create some defense against the softness he made in her. Instead, she found herself cherishing the way the corner of his mouth always lifted, as if preparing to smile. Her gaze drifted downward to the powerful lines of his chest.

Dear God, but it had felt wondrous to hold him atop her. Her gaze drifted even lower. It had felt even better to hold him inside her. With every move he made into her, pleasure flowed through her. Even remembering caused the embers of her lust to explode into sudden and potent life. She wanted him again.

"Nay," she whispered, turning her back to him.

She would not desire the man who had murdered her

father. Closing her eyes tightly, Nicola retrieved her memory of that moment, seeking strength in it. The image came to her with greater clarity than ever before. She heard again the fire's roaring breath as the stink of burning thatch and wood filled her lungs. Gilliam's demand that her father lift his weapon rang in her.

As if she once again lay on the floor watching, Nicola saw the way Papa had strained to raise the heavy blade's tip. This time, she saw how her father had worked to expose his neck to Gilliam's sword, begging for Gilliam's blade to end his life. Her husband had spared her father a far worse death with that single stroke.

"Nay." She abandoned that avenue for another attempt. Gilliam was the man who had destroyed, then stolen her home. Aye, only to return it to her, promising to rebuild it into a much finer place than it had been. He was the man who had forced her to wed him—then honored her needs. Worse than that, Gilliam thought her beautiful. He desired her for what she knew and who she was, not what she owned. Yet, despite his craving for her, he had begged her not to lay with him, fearing how she might be hurt.

Nicola bowed her head. She wanted to be Gilliam's wife, but how long would it be before this desire of hers turned her into the sort of simpering idiot her father had been? The thought of Papa's foolish fawning over his second wife turned her stomach.

"I won't allow it," she whispered harshly. But how was she to prevent this when she already yearned for him?

Her gaze fell on his belt at her feet. The fool had left his dagger in its sheathe. Quick as a cat, she leaned down and grabbed it out, her hand curling around its awkward hilt. Two steps took her to the bed's side. She glared down at him.

He glanced from her face to the knife she held, then to her face again. There was nothing in his eyes but sadness. Her heart ached at his pain. She crushed her reaction. Slowly, she raised the dagger for the thrust that would finish him.

Gilliam watched the blade rise above him. He fisted his hands into the bedclothes, leaving his chest open to her attack. Nicola's arms would lift no higher. A quirk of worry sapped her strength. He was not going to fight for his life.

"I mean to kill you," she said hoarsely.

"I know," he said quietly. The defeat in his voice tore through her.

"You must fight me!" she cried.

"Why? You hate me. I do not wish to live with your hate." The flatness of his tone pierced her the way she meant his dagger to do to his heart.

"You must fight, then you must make me stop hating you." Nicola gasped in shock at what she'd said. This was all too confusing to be tolerated. She lowered her arms.

"Can I do that?" The hope in Gilliam's eyes made her heart's ache ease, but panic swiftly followed. She wanted to soothe his hurt and feel his arms around her once again. Life without him would be dull and empty.

"Nay, you cannot! I hate you!" She threw the dagger away from her as she turned and fled into a corner. She pressed her cheek against the hard, cold stone as tears filled her eyes. He owned her body and soul, and she loved him for it.

The ropes bearing the mattress creaked and groaned

as Gilliam left the bed. A moment later he put his arms around her, drawing her against his chest. He touched his mouth to her shoulder. The warmth of his body flowed through her, mingling with the heat that his kiss awoke.

"I love you, too, my sweet," he murmured.

"I do not love you," she lied through trembling lips. "I tell you, I will not do it. 'Tis bad enough that you are a terrible jackanape, always goading me. Now, you want to leash me like one of your pets."

His laugh was soft and deep. "Would that it were true. Perhaps then I would be able to train you to sit and stay as Roia does." He laid his cheek against her head. The silence lengthened between them. "You were wrong, you know. 'Tis you who holds my leads."

There was enough sadness in his voice to make her turn in his arms to face him. Pain lingered in his eyes. Needing to soothe him, Nicola lay a hand against his cheek. He gave a breath of a laugh, then turned his face to kiss her palm. The caress sent a quiver shooting through her, and she took back her hand.

"You have me on my knees, Colette. I cannot bear your hate. I need you to care for me the way you do for this place and those folk." He gestured toward the hall. The muted sounds of revelry floated into the room on the icy breeze. His voice dropped to a whisper. "If you cannot say you love me this day, promise that you will, sometime in the future."

Nicola stared at him, then her eyes narrowed in mock disgust. "How dare you put the choice in my hands. You leave me with no option but to declare my love for you."

Gilliam's eyes came to life as he smiled. "God's

truth, madam? I shall commit the maneuver to memory, then."

She made a face at him. "I can only pray that this love of mine does not turn me into a weak and foolish woman, all simpers and smiles."

Gilliam's smile widened. "I would hate that. Vow you will never change, Colette."

"Who told you, you could call me Colette?" she said with a scornful lift of her brows. " 'Tis a private name." He looked startled until she laughed, and added another barb, "Oh, great boar hunter."

He grabbed her to him in an embrace that set her ribs to complaining. "You are teasing me," he bellowed in pleasure.

A moment later, she found herself on the mattress, once more trapped beneath him. "Leave go, you great oaf before you hurt me."

He instantly moved to the side, lifting himself on an elbow to look down at her. There was an expression of deep regret in his face. "I have done enough of that for one day, I think," he said quietly.

"What are you talking about?" Nicola asked.

"You," Gilliam replied with a shrug of embarrassment. "I meant to be gentle in our joining, but you kept moving until I could not think."

"What is this? An excuse?" she demanded, fighting to control her laugh. "I would expect as much from Jos, but not you, big man."

He stared in her in surprise.

She grinned in triumph. "What do you know? I've tweaked you twice in less than a quarter hour. I want you to know I am deeply insulted. What do I look like, some weak-kneed woman to cry over a pinch?"

"A pinch?" he retorted, then pushed at her. "Move aside, I would see if you left a mark on the sheets."

Curious herself, she did as he bid. The linens bore no sign of her maidenhead's demise. Nicola stared in shock, then worry. Now he would think she had not come a virgin to his bed. She grabbed the bedclothes, tearing them back to the bed's foot. Nothing. When she looked at him, 'twas in panic. "I vow to you, I gave to you what I would give no other man."

Gilliam raked her with a long and scornful look. "Do you expect me to believe that?" he said in a harsh voice, then he lifted his brows in amusement. "I know you did. Have a care, little girl. If you want to play at taunts and teases, you'd best be willing to take the blows."

"You!" Nicola shouted, and threw herself at him. He caught her in his arms, his mouth claiming hers. They fell back upon the mattress.

When she shivered, 'twas not against the cold. It was the way her skin slid across his. Where her breasts touched his chest there was a new and wonderful tingling. She could feel his heart beating, almost against her own. Her hands moved over his shoulders and down, the contours of Gilliam's chest smooth and hairless. Her palms were alive with the feel of him. He moaned and lifted his body to offer her more to touch. There was a quickening deep in her womb.

"Mother of God," she breathed. "I did not know touching a man would feel like this."

Gilliam looked at her, his eyes a clear blue and filled with pleading. "Not any man, just me. I vow I will kill you if you touch any other man." His threat lacked teeth, being broken by a gasp as her hands lowered past his waist.

"Aye, just you, only you," she vowed. "Only you want me. Only you look at me and make heat in me." She leaned forward to run her mouth along his collarbone, then kiss a line up his neck. He shivered, then turned his head to offer her more to touch and groaned when she did so.

Nicola smiled against his throat. To make so powerful a man shiver with a mere touch was a heady thing. The taste of him intoxicated her. Nicola lifted her mouth from beneath his ear and found his lips.

Her husband caught her to him, his kiss ablaze with his need for her. As before, her answer to his desire came roaring through her, and there was room in her for nothing else. She moved her leg slightly and felt proof of his readiness against her thigh. Nicola smiled suddenly. Tilda had always said that if you held a man by his cock, you owned him.

She reached down, curling her hand around Gilliam's shaft. He tore his mouth from hers to groan. She moved her hand, feeling skin soft as silk against her palm. He shifted beneath her, his thigh rising between her legs.

The touch of his leg against her woman's flesh sent a shiver up her spine. His hand enclosed her breast, his thumb toying with its peak as his mouth returned to hers. The quickening in her belly became a low throbbing. With it came an awesome pressure that drove her to move to ease it.

As she shifted on his thigh, pleasure as sharp as a dagger pierced her womb. Nicola cried softly in surprise, then shifted again, her hand moving on his shaft as she did so. It was better this time. Gilliam echoed her cry, his own deep voice full of the same wonder she felt.

Knowing she pleased him made it even better. She moved her hand slowly to the base of his shaft, then up again. He arched beneath her, then tangled his free hand into her hair, pulling her near to him. When he kissed the spot just behind her ear, her womb softened. The feeling was so intense, she released his shaft and sat up on her knees, his leg yet trapped between hers.

Gilliam freed her breast to push himself upright as well. Her hands came to rest against his shoulders. The heat of him drew her forward until her nipples grazed his chest, sending waves of feeling washing through her.

Sitting as she did made her slightly taller than him. Nicola looked down into his face. Even in this low light, his hair gleamed like gold. His eyes were dark with desire, his lips full and soft. She owned him; his expression said so. And, he owned her. Nicola sighed, liking both.

She caught the gleam of his sudden smile before he touched his lips to her collarbone, then lay his mouth against her breast. Nicola struggled to breathe as his lips closed over her nipple, his teeth gently catching the tip of it. Her nether lips grew flushed and swollen at what he did.

"You are making me melt," she cried softly, her voice unsteady with the passion he woke in her. Nicola did not know which she wanted more, to push him away or to draw him close. His laughter rumbled through her.

"Good," he whispered against her sensitive skin, "I am already a puddle at your feet." Once again, his mouth closed over her breast, this time to suckle like a babe.

Nicola gasped in sheer delight. She combed her fingers into his hair, forcing his mouth to stay where it was when he would have drawn away. When he sucked again, she leaned down to kiss the place where his shoulder met his neck. As she had the last time, she drew her nails gently along his nape, up, then down.

He shuddered beneath her, his shaft moving against her leg. When he tore his mouth from her breast, it was to lay his brow against her collarbone. He was shivering. Nicola felt his panting breath against her nipple. Again, she drew her nails along his nape, then smiled when he cried out.

"*Jesu,*" he managed, "stop that. You are destroying me."

When she did it once again, his hand came between her legs, his fingers seeking the place his shaft would soon fill. Even knowing what it would feel like did not stop her moan. Nicola leaned back on her arms, letting him touch her in this most private place. Feelings exploded in her. This was wanting, and she wanted him. 'Twas her turn to tremble.

"Colette," he begged softly.

What he needed, so did she. She straightened, then rested her hands on his shoulders so she could straddle his thighs. Gilliam caught her around her waist, holding her above the part of him her womb now craved.

"I am on fire for you," he breathed, looking up at her. So he was, she could see it in the way color stained his cheeks. "But you must not let me hurt you."

Nicola looked down at him in disdain, then she laughed, almost insulted by his statement. "What am I, some sort of weakling? You cannot hurt me." She lowered herself onto his shaft, once again enjoying the fullness of holding him within her.

"Oh, *Jesu,* but you feel good," he sighed, easing down onto the mattress. Nicola lay atop him, and Gilliam drew the bedclothes over them. She turned her head, then touched her lips to his neck.

His hand rubbed her back, the movement soothing and not at all what she wanted. Nicola smiled, now knowing how to wring from him what she desired. She raised her hand to caress his nape, then touched her lips to his ear and freed a gentle breath. At the same time, she moved atop him.

He made a sound deep in his throat, his hands coming to grasp her hips. "You are impossible," he said, his voice filled with both laughter and desire.

"Do you not like what you feel?" She breathed her question into his ear and reveled in how he shivered in reaction.

"Very much," he managed in a hoarse voice.

"If that is true, why do you keep stopping me?"

He laughed and released his hold on her. When Nicola moved this time, she gasped at the pleasure that shot through her. She caught his mouth with hers and tested herself atop him. Each movement was joy, but the wanting for more only grew apace.

Suddenly, 'twas he who gasped. His arms came around her, and Nicola found herself lying beneath him. With that, he began to move within her, steady and slow. She arched beneath him, her fingers digging into his back. His mouth was again on hers, his kiss fiery in its urgency.

Wanting grew greater still. She cried out against his kiss, her hands coming to hold him at the hips to urge him to satisfy what ached in her. He tore his mouth from hers, breathing raggedly with his need. His motions grew faster. With each thrust pleasure roared through her, wave after wonderful wave. Her body demanded that she move. She met his next thrust with her own. As if from a distance, she heard him begging her to match his rhythm.

Nicola lifted beneath him, meeting him thrust for thrust. Still, he spoke to her, his voice deep and soft, telling her how much she was pleasing him. Knowing she did so only increased her own enjoyment. There was more, with each thrust, there was more.

When she thought she could bear it no longer, he groaned, driving himself into her with all the passion he had for her. She swore she felt his seed entering her. Her hands left his hips to hold him tightly to her once more. The pressure in her eased as he filled her, and her body sighed. From within her came a deep knowing. What she felt could be bettered with practice.

He lowered himself to lay atop her, gasping and panting. All her muscles softened in reaction as her body accepted his weight atop it. Nicola kissed his jaw, then caught his mouth with hers.

His lips moved in a tender caress, and he tried to slide to the side to spare her his weight. When she would not let him move, he rolled onto his side, taking her with him. Nicola gave a small sigh of disappointment. "But, I like you atop me." She whispered her complaint against his lips.

Gilliam shuddered and groaned, his kiss deepening. The desperation in his caress startled her, for it had naught to do with heat or pleasure. She caught his face in her hands, then eased back to study him. There was fear, longing, and joy all tangled together in his eyes. No smile touched his mouth.

"Did I do wrong?" she asked quietly.

He shook his head, his eyes suddenly full. "Colette, my heart is aching. All I can think is that I have made a child in you, and you will die."

All the joy she had just experienced dimmed. Nicola bowed her head as Alice's death came rushing back. "You mean as Alice did," she said flatly. "At least she set a fine, healthy son in her husband's arms before she went. That pleased her so. 'Twas the afterbirth that did it, tearing her womb as it exited. She bled."

In the speaking of it, her grief over Alice separated itself from the symbolism she'd placed on the commoner's child. "Oh, Gilliam, it was all my fault," she cried, then fell silent in surprise. She hadn't meant to tell him about how she had betrayed Ashby.

"It cannot be your fault that her womb tore," he replied, his voice soothing, but his tone confused.

The urge to spill her pain for him to hear became undeniable. "Nay, 'tis not that," Nicola said, staring at his chest to avoid meeting his gaze. "It is Ashby's fall that is plaguing me. Ever since June, I have been trying to run away from what I did, even turning the birth of Alice's babe into a silly hope that I would not have to accept responsibility for it. 'Twas my fault. Aye, my stepmother took your brother prisoner, but it was I who closed the gates against you, Gilliam. I thought if I could prove to Lord Rannulf how competent I was, he would allow me to keep Ashby as my own. Because of me, the hall burned and the village was destroyed."

"You give yourself a greater role to play in that than is yours," Gilliam said softly. "I, my brother, your father, and his wife, also contributed to what happened here."

Nicola kept her gaze focused on his chest. " 'Tis kind of you to forgive me, but even your words cannot change what I did. By my actions have beloved folk been killed, and those I should have protected, hurt. I am trying, but I cannot find a way to bear the weight of what I have done." Her eyes filled against the pain in her heart.

Gilliam eased far enough from her so he could catch her face in his palms. He tilted her face up until he could see her. "Ah, but you will," he said gently. "If the weight of your betrayal never leaves you, your shame becomes tolerable." There was just enough light left in the room to show her that his eyes were filled with sadness and understanding.

"How is it you know what I feel?" she breathed in astonishment.

His mouth tightened. "I have also betrayed one whose love I treasured. Oh, *Jesu,*" Gilliam closed his eyes. "Now I have said too much, and my stomach will not let me tell the tale." He freed her, then lay on his back, eyes yet tightly shut.

Pain radiated from him. Stunned, Nicola could only stare at him, unable to believe that this man who constantly smiled and jested could carry such an ache within him. All at once understanding flowed over her. Just as his placid nature had led her to believe he lacked intelligence, his ever-present smile hid what ate him.

When she said nothing, he opened his eyes, but still did not look at her. "I fear your newfound love for me will be killed should you hear my tale."

Nicola shook her head at that. "There is nothing that you could ever have done that would change what I feel for you. You are the only man in all this world who understands and accepts me, making you precious beyond anything else I own."

Gilliam turned his head toward her, his gaze filled with pleading as he struggled to believe her. "Not even adultery and incest with my brother's wife?" The words were barely audible. "She died, bearing my son."

What he had done was terrible, indeed. In that instant, Nicola knew she held his life in her hands. She need only show disgust or horror, and he would be destroyed. "Nay, not even that." Even to press him for details or explanations now would seem she demanded justification, and that she did not. Her love needed no more than she already knew.

His breath left him in a slow stream, his expression relaxing against his relief. Somehow, his reaction was hers. Within her the burden of her betrayal shifted until the weight no longer overwhelmed her.

"Stride for stride, my love," he said softly. "Let us go forward into this life together, sharing between us our sins. I will help you rebuild what you have destroyed, and you will love me despite what I have done."

"With the greatest of pleasure," Nicola said, slowly smiling.

He smiled in return. "Best you beware. Now that you have given your heart to me, I will want children as well. I will kill you if you die doing it." Gilliam laid on his side so they were once again face-to-face.

"Me, die?" Nicola said with a breath of scorn. "You should know by now that 'tis not luck that keeps me alive, but my ill temper. Both God and the devil are afraid of me."

She ran her hand down the solid curve of his shoulder and upper arm. His skin felt wondrous beneath her palm. "I missed you last night. I have decided I would rather be cold with you, than alone and warm in the hall."

"Thank the Lord for small favors," he retorted as he toyed with a strand of her hair. His little game sent a shiver through her. "Speaking of favors, will you do me one?"

"What is it?" The heat in her woke again. Nicola decided she liked marriage very much.

"Will you teach me to speak English? I am tired of never know what is said around me."

She looked up at him, making her expression skeptical. "I do not know if I can."

"It is a difficult tongue?"

"Nay," she replied, "at least not to me. 'Tis just that the last thing I wish to do with you is talk. Especially not now." She touched her mouth to his chest, running her lips over his skin and using the tip of her tongue to taste him.

"*Jesu,* Colette," he breathed, "I should go back to the hall."

"Why?" she murmured against him. "Ashby's folk know how to drink without you to guide them along. Stay with me. I think I am finally beginning to understand how this joining thing works. With a little more practice, I might get it right."

He caught his fingers in her hair and lifted her head to look at her. "There is only so much I can do," he warned with a laugh.

"Shall we see how much?" she asked with a smile.

"I know, I will turn this into your first lesson. Pay careful heed as I describe for you all the parts of the body."

Gilliam groaned. "I am a dead man."

Chapter Twenty-one

"Just one more, Jos," Nicola urged in a quiet voice, then turned her back to the target. She did not want to watch in the fear that her attention would somehow affect his aim.

'Twas a typical day for Epiphany, combining bitter cold with an icy wind and low slung clouds. There was a skin of ice over the surface of the millpond, and a patchy layer of snow covered the ground. Shivering, she waited for Jos to shoot, pulling her mantle shut over her new gowns. They were a gift from Gilliam, combining the functional cut her lifestyle demanded with fine fabric dyed the color of emeralds.

"I can do this," the boy whispered to himself. He drew a deep breath. She watched him steady the short hunting bow that had been her first gift to him over this Christmas holiday. There was a sharp twang as the arrow left the weapon. Nicola clenched her eyes shut until she heard Jos release his breath with a hiss of satisfaction.

She whirled. "Did you?"

"Aye!" the boy crowed, dancing in excitement. "That's all six in the center. *This* I can do!" The Jos of two months ago was gone. In his place stood a robust lad who had begun to look his years, and who had added almost two fingers of height in just this last month.

"Did I not tell you that you had the eyes and hands of an archer?" she cried, as pleased as he by his victory. " 'Tis a rare talent for sure. Think on it! If you can do this in only a few days practice, you'll soon be a master." She started toward the target to retrieve the boy's bolts.

"Please, my lady, leave them. I want Lord Gilliam to see when he returns. Mayhap he'll not be so quick to leave me here when he patrols. He'll trust me at his side, just as he would any other squire."

While Ashby's commoners enjoyed their last day of leisure in the Christmas holiday, Gilliam and Ashby's soldiers were still riding their borders. Over the past twelve days, three pregnant ewes had gone missing, hurdles had been destroyed, and an ox shot.

"Jos, he leaves you here not because of lack of trust, but you have not progressed far enough with your sword."

"I am working on it," he protested.

"Aye, but remember that you got a late start on your lessons. Where other lads have had their swords since their earliest years, you've had yours but two months. 'Tis a hard-earned skill, crafted by much practice. Give yourself time."

"I will work harder," Jos said, his jaw tensed. "If it comes to battle, I wish to be at my lord's back."

Nicola made a wry face at him. "Do not be in such a rush to kill men. 'Tis a terrible thing. Makes you ill, it does. Now, as I am frozen through and through, I say you are done for the day." Gilliam's absence during the short daylight hours had turned Nicola into Jos's tutor.

"Can I not wait out here for him?" the boy asked, a hopeful look on his face. He glanced beyond Nicola, and his face blossomed with a smile. Raising his bow and waving wildly, he shouted, "Lord Gilliam, come and see what I have done!"

Nicola turned. Dressed in his mail, her husband came striding across the bailey toward them, cloak swirling around his knees. As always, Gilliam was bareheaded and bare-handed, his mail hood dangling down his back with his cloak hood and his gloves tucked into the belt over his surcoat. Even from a distance her body acknowledged his presence with a sudden warmth. When he stopped beside her, she reached for him, laying a possessive arm around his waist, her fingers hooking into his mail.

"And what have you done?" Gilliam asked with an expectant smile. Although he kept his attention on Jos, his arm came around Nicola to bring her closer still.

"The target, my lord," Jos insisted impatiently. "Look at the target."

"What target? That's no target, 'tis a hedgehog." Then he gasped with every bit as much emotion as a mummer. "My God, 'tis a target, and you have killed it!"

"Aye. Six times in the center." The boy beamed. "Now, you must do as you vowed and let me try that crossbow."

"You promised him my father's bow?" Nicola asked in surprise.

Gilliam shot her a quick look. "My pardon, I forgot

to ask you. Our Jos has his heart set on drawing that bow. You do not mind, do you?"

His words startled her. "Why should I?"

"It is by rights your bow, having come to you through your father."

"It is our bow, and you may lend it where it pleases you," she said with a shrug. " 'Tis just that he's barely strong enough to draw the bow he has, much less bend that monster."

"I can do it," Jos insisted. "I know I can."

"Not this day," Gilliam warned him. "It will be dark soon, and I am hungry. Gather your arrows, lad, and we'll be withdrawing to a warm fire."

The boy did as commanded, and Nicola turned to catch Gilliam's mouth with hers. He made a soft sound of longing, tugging off her head scarf to bury his fingers in her hair. Their passion for each other again exploded to life between them. In one month, her wanting had only increased.

"I thought we were going within doors. If you are going to stand here and do that, I am going to shoot again." Jos's voice was filled with disgust.

Gilliam smiled against her mouth. "I think he is tired of us, my love."

"What more can I do?" she whispered, leaning against him. "I put his pallet in the hall to spare him your caterwauling."

"Me?" He drew away, his eyes laughing at her even as he lifted his head in insult. " 'Tis not I who shakes the rafters with my screams."

Nicola fixed him with a narrow look. "You make me do it."

"I know," he replied with a satisfied smile, tucking

her head scarf into her belt as a reminder that he preferred her bareheaded. "Come, take me within doors
and put something in my stomach."

Jos had to hurry his stride to keep pace with his foster parents. " 'Tis the twelfth night, this one." It was a
blatant prod.

Gilliam smiled. "So it is. I have your gift, but what
have you got for me? You'll not have yours until I see
mine."

"Should we show him?" Nicola glanced at Jos,
knowing that the boy was frantic to reveal what they
had for Gilliam.

"Can we?" he begged breathlessly. At her nod, he
grabbed his lord's hand and tried to turn the big knight.
"We have saved the best for last, my lord. Come now."

"But I am so hungry, I may faint." Gilliam made a
show of staggering. "Catch me before I fall."

"I will let you fall, then leave you where you lay,"
Nicola retorted. "You can wait a moment for your bath
and meal."

"I get no sympathy," he complained, allowing Jos to
lead him to a far shed. Soft yips could be heard from
within the woven reed walls. Gilliam's brows rose in
response. "What is this?"

Jos threw open the door to reveal the pups, some
just weaned, others almost grown. "They are kennets,
all," he informed his lord. "Now, we can hunt fox." To
prove his point, one of the smaller, flop-eared hounds
lifted its tiny mouth and bayed bravely in its infant
voice.

The boy could not refuse its call. He squatted amid
the pups, letting them crowd around him, laughing as
they licked and nuzzled. Gilliam reached down to pick

up a half-grown bitch. The dog yelped in surprise, then sighed as he scratched its ear.

"Twelve of them when I expected one or two," he said, offering Nicola a pleased smile. "Here I was thinking you did not notice my hints."

Nicola laughed. "You were not very subtle. Six come from Coudray and six from Graistan's kennels."

Gilliam shot her a disbelieving look. "Rannulf sent you dogs? Last I saw him, he was none too pleased with you."

" 'Twas the strangest thing," she said, struggling to look befuddled. "Not only did he send dogs, but he returned the coins Jos and I sent to pay for them, saying you bought them from your winnings."

Her husband had the grace to look sheepish. "I had forgot about that. My pardon, Colette. I should not have wagered over you."

She patted his cheek. "Do not fret. I used the coins I did not spend on dogs to buy myself a lovely new knife."

He raised a hand to his mouth in mock fright. "You have me cowering in fear, but please, could you hold off gutting me until Jos and I have blooded the older dogs?"

"I suppose I can," she sighed, as if doing so was a terrible burden. "Now, set her down and I'll feed you." She waited for him to do so, but he only picked up another pup. "Gilliam, I thought you were fainting for lack of food."

"So are these wee pups," he said, a soft look in his eyes. "We must bring them into the hall so they can eat and stay warm."

"Only for now," she warned. "After the plow race,

Thomas is sending the men to raise us hurdles to make a kennel. Gilliam, are you listening to me? A kennel, where they will stay."

Even before he looked at her, she knew it was a lost cause. He would have the dogs in the hall for the winter. He and Jos were already herding the bigger pups out the door. Gilliam gave her three of the younger kennets to bear.

"You are hopeless," she muttered, then buried her nose against one and breathed in its sweet scent. Mayhap, it would not be so bad, if they could be trained to leave their droppings elsewhere, the way Roia did.

Like all the cottages in their village and Father Reynard's church, their hall was bedecked in holly and ivy. The long braided strands hung as a reminder that, although the earth lay dead and barren, spring would come to restore them all. Where the first night had been feasting with the villagers and the second full of gift-giving to the servants, the holiday was now at a close. Epiphany's mass was already said, making this but a quiet evening home, a last day of rest before the new year's work began.

The servantry and soldiers who made up their family were gathered in the hall. While the men had gathered in one corner to throw dice, the women were clutched in another, laughing and chatting, their fingers busy with handwork. The cook's children left a simple game of tag to admire the pups.

"What of Roia?" Nicola asked. "Will she not eat these wee ones?"

Gilliam shook his head. "Nay, she has been a mother a few times over. Not only that, she is accustomed to dwelling with more than one dog. Jos"—he tapped the boy on the shoulder—"you cannot share your pallet with the pups and Roia. That she will not tolerate."

"Aye, my lord." Jos stayed to watch over the dogs while Gilliam and Nicola made their way through the hall to the far end. There, with Gilliam's armor chest nearby, Nicola had set the great tub reserved for bathing. It was already filled with cold water, wanting only what now simmered in the iron cauldron hanging over the hearth stone to make it bearable.

After she had wrestled Gilliam out of his chain mail coat, Jos came to take it from her. Gasping under its weight, he bore it to his corner. It was his job to check the iron circles, looking for broken or weakened links. He returned to fetch the mail leggings as she helped her husband remove the padded gambeson and chausses. These were set atop Gilliam's armor chest to air.

Once the hot water had been added to the cold, Nicola pushed her husband toward the tub. "Hie, fool, 'twill be cold soon." He sank into its depths, and water surged over the tub's edge. "Ack, why can I never get this right? Now, the floor will be muddy again. How heavy are you, anyway?"

"Between fifteen and sixteen stone," Gilliam murmured as he dipped beneath the surface to wet his hair, then rose, his eyes closed in contentment. "Do you know I have become accustomed to this bathing routine of yours. Until I was married, I never realized how enjoyable it could be. I like your hands on me." He opened one eye to gauge her reaction.

"You just like me," she said with a smile, offering him a tray full of cheeses, breads, and smoked fish.

"That I do," he agreed, eating while she washed his hair and his back. The tray was empty before she was ready to rinse him. That done, she handed him the cloth so he could wash the rest of him. He said it was torture when she did it.

She sat beside the tub on a stool, knife in hand as she waited to shave him. "Gilliam, why do you not let your beard grow? You'd be far less dangerous to kiss, were you to do so."

That made him smile, and he handed her the cloth. "You were right."

"About what?" She leaned his head to the side, but waited for his answer before beginning.

"I cannot grow a man's beard. 'Tis sparse and not at all attractive." He grinned at her. "I think me 'tis the fair hair, for my brother Geoffrey has the same problem. You will have to bide your time for a goodly while before you'll see me bearded, as he is seven years my senior and struggling still."

Nicola grinned broadly. " 'Struth? You cannot? Hah! I tweaked you and did not even know it, pretty man."

"Aye, now do not gloat so and be done with this. The water is cooling."

With his bath finished, he dressed in his tunic and chausses, then the two of them retreated to the fire. Nicola had planned to spend her evening sewing, as one of her gifts had been a length of fine linen to be used for making a proper wimple. When they seated themselves, backs to the table, feet stretched toward the fire, Jos came to stand before them, a pup in each hand.

"So?" He drew the word out in expectation. "I have given you your gifts. Now you must give me mine."

"Cheeky lad, this one." Gilliam laughed. "Well, then, I suppose I must. Walter?" His voice carried easily across the long room.

From the dicing group, Walter rose and retrieved something from the darkened corner. When he neared them, Nicola saw he bore a leather container filled with quarrels, long lengths of wood, iron-tipped on one end and feathered at the other, along with her father's crossbow.

"Is this what you seek, little lad?" the soldier asked as he waited for the boy to discard the dogs and take what he carried.

Jos took the bow and quarrels from the man, looking up in astonishment at Gilliam. "You knew I could do it, even before I did."

"Lad, when my lady wife tells me you have the eyes and hands of an archer, who am I to disbelieve her? However, you had me right concerned this morn. Here it was the dawn of the twelfth and final day, and you'd not yet accomplished your goal. 'Tis a good thing you managed it, else you'd have had no gift for the night."

"Thank you, my lord," Jos breathed in awe, as much affected by his lord's confidence in him as by the gift.

Gilliam laid a hand on the boy's shoulder. "Take heed. Those are fresh quarrels with iron tips, not just sharpened sticks. For God's sake and mine, never point the bow at anything you do not wish to hit. I've seen a good archer send a quarrel through the gap in his enemy's mail to pierce the man with deadly effect."

"I will treat it like the weapon it is, I vow. Thank you, my lord." Stars shining in his eyes, Jos clutched the crossbow to him as he made his way to the corner where his pallet lay.

"It seems you forgot to do more than simply ask me if Jos could use it." As pleased as Nicola was at Jos's success, Gilliam should have at least discussed it with her before giving away the bow.

" 'Tis not your bow," he said quietly, watching the boy with a smile on his face. "Your weapon was made for a man, full grown, who had great strength of arm. Jos could never draw the string. This is but a one-foot bow, scaled to our Jos's size and made to resemble the other."

Gilliam turned on her, still smiling. "I've stored your father's bow far from his sight. It can do him no harm to believe he draws a man's weapon."

Nicola stared at him for a long moment, her heart full of love for him. " 'Tis a fine thing you're doing with Jos. Lord Coudray was right to send him to you."

"Aye"—Gilliam nodded slowly, trying to twist his mouth into a sad line—"without Jos, I would be bored senseless. You will not throw snowballs or try skating and, although you have a marvelous arm, you'll not even play quoits with me. All you ever do is work. Aye, and when you do not work, you wish only to lie abed. Girls are boring. Ask Jos, he'll tell you."

"Well, since you seem to prefer Jos's company, I shall return Jos to our chamber, whilst I take his pallet. 'Tis far more pleasant sleeping in here than in that awful room." She turned her back to him, and lifted a shoulder in dismissal.

"But if you do not come this night, you will not receive your final present." He whispered the comment in her ear.

"That's no present. I can have that any night."

"Nay, not that, although I harbor hopes." He murmured the words against her neck. "I put your final presents in our room in the fear you might be embarrassed by them, were I to give them to you in the hall."

Nicola turned to look at him. That he was extremely

pleased with himself, there was no doubting. His eyes fair danced with excitement. Her interest piqued, she hesitated, then set aside her handwork. "As you will, my lord. Let us see what you think might embarrass me."

They donned their cloaks, Nicola taking up a lamp, and started from the hall. The men in the corner burst into great bellows of laughter.

"My lord," Walter called as they passed the gamblers, "Seger, here, wants you to know that the first year of marriage is but a process of ringing. Whilst you give your ring to your wife, she fixes one in your nose. Once a woman is sure her ring's in place, your nights become all sleep and no joy. Seger says you must enjoy this now for it will not last."

Gilliam grinned wickedly. "I am, Walter. I am."

Nicola lifted her head. In English, she said, "The only reason I can imagine our nights to be all sleep is that my lord lacks staying power." That sent the men rolling on the floor. Cupping the lamp's flame against the wind, she preceded her husband out the door. "Now, what did I say to them?"

"You spoke too quickly for me to catch it all, but I recognized the words reason, night, sleep, and power."

"Well done," she complimented him, choking on her laughter.

"You'll pay later, trust me," he warned. "They'll tell me in the morn, and you'll pay."

He climbed the keep stairs and pushed open the door. Nicola stepped inside. Although the sun had made no appearance this day, the growing dimness in the room said it was descending. She looked about, but saw nothing within the walls save the usual: the night candle and the bed, curtains tightly shut. She went to light the candle with her lamp, then turned on him.

"Well, where is this gift of mine?" she asked.

"In the bed." He grinned again.

"Gilliam!" She gave a frustrated breath at his game and threw open the curtains, then stared.

Gilliam came to stand behind her and look over her shoulder. "This is so we can spar in earnest, my love. I am tired of using those wee playthings."

Lying atop their bedclothes was a pair of armed gloves and a steel sewn hauberk. Folded beside it was a quilted tunic to wear between it and her skin. The conical helmet worn by ordinary soldiers lay to one side along with the cap that went beneath it. Curled at the other side was a belt, a leather scabbard, and a plain shield. And there was a sword.

Nicola breathed in surprise and reached for the weapon. "It is my father's sword," she cried softly. "Oh, Gilliam!" She lifted the blade in her hands, testing its familiar balance. The grip had been wrapped with new leather that wanted forming to its owner's hand.

"It survived the fire. I set it aside thinking we might someday have a son who would wish to carry his grandsire's blade." He put his arm around her and drew her back against his chest. "If it is too heavy or too long, I will have another made for you."

Tears filled her eyes as she laid the weapon back on the bed to turn in his embrace. "Until last month I was screaming over how I hated you. How could you plan for our children against my hatred?"

" 'Tis because I am an extra son, the youngest of four brothers, who never dared dream of marriage or home or family." Gilliam shrugged slightly and smiled.

"When I agreed to marry you, I allowed myself to hope that, having achieved one impossible thing, you might someday accept me and we might make a family. Keeping the sword for a future son was like a promise that it would happen."

Her tears spilled over. "I cannot believe how fortunate I am to be wed to you. Thank you for honoring my sire this way," she managed. "In doing so, you honor me in all ways." She touched her mouth to his, the kiss soft and full of her love for him.

He let her lips cling to his for a moment, his arms tightening briefly. Then he stepped back. "Ah, but you have not counted your gifts."

Nicola wiped away her tears, then turned. There were ten items on the bed. "Are you saying there are two more?" she asked with a shaky breath.

"Aye." He reached over her shoulder and fastened her pin to her mantle. The garnet-encrusted surface gleamed in the candlelight. "You have been nagging me over a pin for so long, I have decided 'tis time to relent and give it back."

Nicola closed her eyes. She was dying, overwhelmed by the strength of her love for this man. The tears spilled again. When he turned her in his arms, she lay her head against his shoulder, incapable of speech. He held her for a long moment, the movement of his hand on her back soothing.

"The last one I must beg you to take, as you have refused it once before." He caught her hand, then set a golden band on the finger leading to her heart. "This was my mother's ring, the one my father gave her upon their wedding day. Although I never knew my mother and cannot remember my father, Rannulf tells me theirs was a great and enduring love. It would honor me if you would wear it."

Nicola threw her arms around his neck. "For all my life," she whispered, and sobbed like a babe.

Chapter Twenty-two

Low Sunday's mass had just finished. Nicola and Gilliam were standing before Father Reynard's church as all their folk dispersed, Gilliam's expression trapped in worried thoughtfulness. April's newborn breath lifted his hair. Even on an overcast day, the heavy strands shone like gold.

That gay breeze swirled around Nicola, tangling in her wide sleeves. It brought with it the sweet songs of mating birds and the joyous fragrance of a pregnant earth. Proof of this fertility showed in the fairy green leaves appearing on barren branches and was scattered in happy abandon along Ashby's ditch. Daffodils nodded at her, their yellow flowers vibrant against new grass.

It had become their habit to dress well for Sunday services. Gilliam wore his new blue gown, the one she made to replace what she'd ruined, while she wore her fine green set with its trailing hems. Her head was covered in but a simple cloth, her yet-short locks escaping confinement to curl around her face. This she did to please Gilliam, who disliked any attempt to cover her hair. She'd agreed to wear this skimpy head covering to church after she understood how much the informality of bared locks annoyed Ralph and Emotte by Wood.

Jos dashed up, also wearing his better gown, with red chausses on his legs. "My lord, the lads would like to come watch me shoot at the target. 'Tis Sunday, and there'll be naught else for them to do. Might they come within and see?" Jos's sudden grin was full of mischief. "I've wagered them I can hit the target's center at two hundred yards."

Gilliam bestirred himself from his heavy thoughts to respond. "You did? That is your bow's limit, I think me. What do you stand to win?"

"Alexander knows where a hawk nests, and he'll show me. Dickon has four stones that gleam red. John has a carved stick. The rest come only to watch."

"Ah. Treasures, indeed," Gilliam said with a smile. "And, what will you lose if you cannot do the deed?"

Jos only laughed. "I will not lose. I've done this a dozen times."

"Boy, what did you promise?" Gilliam's tone demanded an answer.

"Only to let them pet the pups," he hesitated, "and they may have one of my arrows, the ones Lady Nicola gave me. My lady, I will not lose it. I vow, I will not."

Gilliam laughed. "There is no guaranteed outcome to anything, Jos. You must never wager what you are not willing to lose. Now, go, but change into your everyday tunic first."

"I will, my lord," he cried out, racing toward Ashby. The three boys he planned to hoodwink joined him at the lift of his arm, the others following eagerly behind them. If Jos's English was yet as halting as Gilliam's, he seemed to have no difficulty in making his meaning clear to the village lads.

"He has grown again," Nicola said, watching him dash away. "That gown of his is now too short."

"Aye," Gilliam said. With Jos's departure, the worried tone returned to his voice. "Give him another half year and he'll be the size he should. So does his voice deepen. Soon, girls will no longer be so boring. 'Twill be your job to tell him why he must continue to keep his distance from them."

"Why mine? Is this not a man's province?" Nicola laced her fingers with his, catching her other hand in the bend of his elbow. She leaned her arm against his.

" 'Tis yours because I would not lie about pleasure," her husband said with a quick smile. He would have started forward once more, but Nicola held him where he stood.

"Gilliam, talk to me. Two weeks without a violent incident says to me that the damage was caused by nothing more sinister than thieves in the forest. We have peace now because they had moved on to some other area." Holy Week had been the first week to pass without some incident since November. So, too, had the week after Easter now passed without an assault against folk or property.

He shot her a glance filled with frustration. "More likely, our neighbor gave up taunting us to celebrate Easter like the righteous man he is. May God damn his persistence. I was praying he would have admitted defeat by now. The stone cutters and masons come at May's start; I cannot be chasing de Ocslade and protecting our quarry at the same time."

"How is it you are so sure 'tis de Ocslade. Convince me."

Gilliam shrugged as if he were surprised at her. " 'Tis because he is doing exactly what I would do, if I wanted to destroy a man and take that man's wife and home."

She frowned at him. "If you are so certain, why not go to Ocslade and call him out? We have been helpless long enough."

He laid a finger to her temple. "My sweet wife, you are thinking in straight lines. Let me show you. Say that I was de Ocslade and your father yet lived. Say also that your father and I met on the road one day to exchange heated words. I then warned your father I intended to steal Ashby from him. Several days later, a few sheep disappeared. Later, more sheep were taken, fields were trampled, houses broken, and the rest. Now, I left you no sign that 'twas me who did these deeds, but you remembered my words and believed I was but fulfilling them. Tell me now, since de Ocslade assumes I am like your father, what would John's reaction have been?"

This question had a simple answer. "Papa would arm and ride for Ocslade, shouting for you to come out and meet him as honest men should," Nicola said, then exhaled a soft "Oh," of understanding.

"Aye, you have it now. See how if I go to Ocslade, our neighbor can openly attack me, goaded to it by what he calls my insult. As you say there is no proof that he has a hand in what is happening here. With de Ocslade's greater number of men, it is not impossible that I might fall beneath his blade. In that case, I seem naught but a hotheaded youth who overstretched himself. At Graistan, our neighbor hinted to my brother that he no longer wanted you or Ashby. Because he can blame the confrontation on me, de Ocslade believes he can avoid Rannulf's animosity. Thus, he will keep you and your lands after my death."

"If this is so, why has he now ceased his attacks? I am your wife still." And would be for all her life.

"I think 'tis the growing season that has him stymied. If there is no need, he'll not harm fields he already calls his own. Nay, he has retreated to find some new strategy that will drive me to my death without appearing to stain him." He gazed off into the distance, but his focus was inward as he wrestled with his thoughts.

Nicola looked up at him, her heart quaking. The briefest imagining of life without Gilliam made her ache. Her hand tightened possessively on his arm.

"I should be insulted that you worry over me as if I were but a child," he said without looking at her, a touch of laughter in his voice. "This is womanish thinking, my sweet."

She made a face, no longer surprised that he knew her so well. "I cannot help it. De Ocslade has more men than we and a better stocked armory."

"Ah"—he laughed—"but Ashby has me." His eyes gleamed as he looked at her. "And after me, there is you." His amusement died in the face of his frustration. "Would that I could afford the patience to let him continue his games until he decides 'tis hopeless, but building begins in three weeks." He fell silent as if what he said to her should be perfectly clear.

Nicola waited, then finally prodded, "Aye, and so?"

"When de Ocslade learns of this, he will fly between attacking the workers at the quarry, both villages and the fields, knowing I cannot protect all of them. I must confront him to stop him. If I do not, we will starve this coming winter."

"Then we must delay building until another time." Nicola leaned up against him.

"Nicola, we need a hall. You, better than any, know that."

"We could put up another wooden building like the last." It was a hopeful suggestion.

He only shook his head. "My neighbor is nipping at my heels the way the kennets nip at Roia. I have set aside the coins to pay the workmen. If I send the masons away and de Ocslade continues his harassment, what I have set aside for our stone hall will be eaten up by replacing our losses. I cannot let this man destroy what I have planned."

"I suppose this also means we cannot borrow soldiers from your brothers to guard the workmen and prevent a confrontation?"

"Aye, we could borrow them, but what would they eat?" he asked in helplessness. "Between last June's fire and this past winter, our larder holds barely enough to feed the workmen and see us through until the harvest."

"Can we not buy food?" It was a plea, without much hope.

"If we do, we cannot afford to build the hall; and do not ask if we can borrow to feed them. To do so means de Ocslade drives us into penury so deep, I fear we'll not recover. With what we yet owe for our king's ransom, the new hideage, our marriage fees and the costs of rebuilding, we have already exceeded our income for years to come. None of this is insurmountable, except that our neighbor continually destroys what we work so hard to build. I must find a way to free us."

She rested her head against his shoulder. "Forgive me, Gilliam. I wish I had never offered myself to Hugh." He opened his mouth to reply, but she held up her hand to forestall him. "I know. I take more responsibility for this than belongs to me. Nonetheless, I participated, and I am heartily sorry I did so."

Gilliam smiled at her. "Just so. Now, instead of blaming yourself, help me answer the question that now plagues me. If you could get no reaction from your enemy, what would your next step be?"

"I would quit and go home to spend all my time with my husband," she said quietly. He only smiled and turned as they started for their own gate.

Even at this slow pace, they matched each other, stride for stride. Nicola stared at her toes as they kicked out her long hems before her with each step. Her husband stopped suddenly.

"Now, here is someone I have seen before, and I liked not the company she kept. I think me you know this girl. Tell me why de Ocslade has sent her here."

Nicola followed his gaze to the short plain, marking the distance from the forest's edge to Ashby's walls. "Tilda," she breathed in astonishment.

The reeve's daughter was coming over the green grass, her cloak flying behind her with each step, hood thrown back to reveal her wealth of tawny hair. Beneath her outer garment she wore a rich blue-gray gown. If distance made it impossible to read an expression on the girl's pretty features, there was no mistaking the sultry way she moved.

Rage roared through Nicola. Tilda had thrown over de Ocslade and now came to fetch herself another lord with whom to toy. She whirled on Gilliam. " 'Tis Tilda, Thomas's daughter and my suckling sister, and I will kill her if she touches you."

Her husband laughed at that. " 'Tis not likely I'd give her the chance, my sweet. I would have to be a mindless idiot to jeopardize what we share between us. Besides, you have ruined me. Were I to now lay with a smaller woman, I'd break her for certain." There was still laughter in his eyes.

Despite Gilliam's assurances, anger seethed in Nicola. He did not understand how vulnerable men were to Tilda. "Thomas will be none too pleased to have her home. He says she is his shame."

Gilliam wasn't listening. His eyes narrowed in thought, then his face lightened. "Hah!" It was a soft sound of triumph. "I would send one capable of penetrating my enemy's defenses to seek the possibility of betrayal from within. De Ocslade has erred now, thinking things have not changed here." He caught her arms. "See how he, himself, delivers us from purgatory?"

"What? By sending us Tilda? Nay, I'd not let you recruit her to aid us. We could never trust her." She tried to push away from him, but he did not release her. "Gilliam, the last time I trusted her, it was to learn she had been promised coins to deliver me to de Ocslade."

"Better and better," he said mysteriously, his smile broadening. "You must run and greet her. 'Tis for you that she comes."

"Nay," Nicola said firmly. "Why should I welcome her into my home, when she may only want to sell me to de Ocslade, once more? Besides, I would not know what to say."

"Let me tell you, then," Gilliam replied with a quick lift of his brows. "First, you must take her to her father's house and find some way to twist Thomas into keeping her. If he fights you, send him to me. Once you have your friend's ear in private, tell her you have only escaped my prison for a few moments and must hie on home soon. Cry over how I have beaten and abused you, then beg her to help you escape me as she has done once before. Say whatever tale will make her think ill of me."

Rage died in astonishment. This time, when Nicola pushed against his hold, he released her. She stared at Gilliam in confusion. "I would not defame our love with lies. Why would you ask this of me?"

"Because she will relate to de Ocslade how little care I have for you. This guarantees that, should the worse happen and I be killed, he will not seek to harm you to spite me." He lay a hand against her cheek, his thumb smoothing over her brow.

Nicola stared at him for a long moment, then slowly smiled. "This cannot work. You are not subtle in your affections for me, nor me for you. She will know 'tis a lie if she speaks to anyone about us. Oh, Lord, but if she asks Emotte, she'll get an earful of our brazen displays."

His amusement matched her own, then he shrugged. "Ah, but this is not just any woman. You look at her and see one who does not think any man capable of resisting her. Her arrogance will make her believe she can turn me away from you. Am I right?"

From Nicola's memory came Tilda's words, telling her she was a hopeless woman that no man could love. "Aye, that is so."

"After you have convinced her of my hatred for you, you must beg her to give you to de Ocslade. By offering de Ocslade what he most wants, control of you, we draw him into the open. He will try to set the trap that finishes me."

Nicola shook her head. "Gilliam, Hugh is no fool. Did you not say he wished to avoid your brother's animosity? If trying to steal me might not move Lord Rannulf to tears, your death most certainly will. Do

you think your brother will let Hugh keep me or Ashby
when I say what he has done?"

"Why would you say so?" Gilliam shrugged. "You
are telling his woman that you hate me and wish to escape. Did you not do the same in this November past
when you sought his aid in avoiding marriage to me?
Unless you tell our neighbor differently, he has no reason to believe you have changed in these last months.
Indeed, I would expect him to be kind and gentle to
you as he works to bind you to him against me. At
least, that is what I would do, where I he." He managed a meager smile.

"You are mad!" Nicola stepped back to stare at him
in shock.

"Possibly," he said, his face once again drawn in
worry, "but this is an immediate way to free us of our
dilemma. It buys us both house and peace. If Hugh has
sent the reeve's daughter, she will offer you a chance
to meet with him. De Ocslade will come, thinking to
secure your support against me. There is no reason to
even cross swords. I need only observe the meeting
from hiding. Once I have, my hands will no longer be
tied; then can I borrow soldiers and attack him as the
man who sought to kidnap my wife."

Nicola closed her eyes in defeat. He was right. This
lie coupled with her past behavior would bring Hugh
racing here, thinking he could finally finish Gilliam.
She leaned against him in a terrible fear. "What if you
do cross swords, and he kills you?"

He rested his cheek against her head. "You will send
to my brothers. They will come, all three, and lay
waste to Ocslade in revenge."

Suddenly, his arms closed around her in a bone-crushing embrace. "*Jesu,* stop me. Tell me you will not do this. I am gambling what I cannot afford to lose."

"How can I?" she said softly. "I want you and Ashby, whole and well. What you plan can give us both our hearts desire, but if he hurts you, even the slightest bit, I will not wait for your brothers. I will carve him into pieces too small for the crows to eat." 'Twas a vicious snarl.

Gilliam laughed, stepping away from her. "I am counting on it. Now, I will retreat into the church until I see you take the reeve's daughter into the village with you. Run, set your seeds in her brain. Say to her that de Ocslade should come five days hence, as I am expected to be gone from Ashby that day. When you are done, hie yourself home. I will not breathe easily until you are safe in my arms once more."

Chapter Twenty-three

Nicola turned her back to Gilliam and started toward Ashby's gate, resolved to do as she must. She glanced only once over her shoulder, but her husband was no longer in sight. Ahead of her, Tilda now stood on the drawbridge as the guards called for her to identify herself. The petite commoner tilted her head to the side, her smile a beautiful thing.

" 'Tis just I, Tilda, daughter of Thomas the reeve, come to call on Lady Ashby," she replied. "I have been gone from Ashby for a time, and now I am returned."

"See her, yourself," the man said, pointing toward Ashby's lady.

Tilda turned, her bright expression dimming. Although Nicola stopped within arm's reach of the girl, the gap between them felt like a chasm.

"Colette," the commoner breathed in English. "Oh, but look at you. I am hardly recognizing you." There was sadness and a touch of dismay in her voice. "You are so changed, I will have to come to know you all over again."

Nicola stared at this woman before her. Her face was a fine oval, her brows lifting in a gentle arch over luminous brown eyes. Lush, full lips, usually held in a tempting pout now trembled. Without the sensual mask

Tilda usually wore, every beautiful plane of the girl's face was achingly familiar. Why must it be this woman who betrayed her, once again?

Despite her pain, memory after memory filled Nicola, some happy, some sad. One stood out and would not be denied. "Oh, Tilda, of a sudden I am remembering how I hid you in Ashby's cellar to keep your mother from giving you a beating. She'd caught you with someone, I cannot remember who. I lied for you, saying you had run from home, never to return. After three days in the dark, me feeding you on the sly, you emerged."

Tilda's face resolved into the carefree expression of the girl she'd once been. Her laugh was simple, clean of anything save the fondness they had once shared. "Oh, I cannot believe you thought of that! Do you remember how happy Mama was when she learned I wasn't dead? She forgot all about beating me. I never thanked you for that, Colette." Her mouth twisted into a wry grin, and her eyes gleamed in pleasure. "Thank you for saving me then, and all the other times you spared me what was no doubt deserved punishment."

"It was what I wished to do for you," Ashby's lady replied softly. So it had always been between them, Nicola having long since formed the habit of shielding Tilda from herself. Silence opened up between them, and she swallowed the tears that filled her throat. "Oh, Tilda, how did we ever arrive at this moment?"

"Things happened," Tilda said in a sad whisper. "I know we cannot go back to repair what we destroyed between us, but mayhap, we can begin anew?" Her expression altered into one of rue. "Colette, I have come to beg your forgiveness for what I have done. These last months have been naught but a horrible mistake."

Nicola hesitated in replying. What if Gilliam were

wrong and Tilda had thrown over de Ocslade? She might have come home to heal, not to hurt. The tiniest flicker of hope woke in her. "I can only keep reminding myself that even as you tried to lure me to Hugh, you were warning me against him."

"Do you know he yet believes that 'twas the thieves who took you from me?" Tilda struggled to smile at how she had succeeded in fooling the nobleman. "Oh, Colette, this whole mess lies in your lap. Why did you send me to him, knowing he was the way he was and I, who I am?" She looked up to the sky, blinking away tears. "You should have chosen a simpler man to use."

Nicola watched Tilda in silence, stunned at how easily the commoner shifted the blame. Where others sought to ease Nicola's sense of wrongdoing, her erstwhile friend tried to heap more upon her.

When she said nothing, Tilda continued. "He wooed me, Colette, speaking words of love and promising a life I could never have at Ashby. It was a lie; all he truly wanted was you. Can you imagine my hurt when he wanted me to help him wed you? Oh, he vowed you would never mean anything to him, but I could not bear sharing him, even with you. I made certain you would not come to him." It was a hushed confession.

"You want him no longer?" Nicola waited to be convinced by Tilda's response.

"Oh, Colette," she breathed, "he wants me no more." She threw herself against the taller girl and sobbed. "I cannot believe how I hurt over this. 'Tis repayment for my cruel rejection of others and a terrible lesson."

Nicola gathered Tilda into her embrace, feeling her friend's pain. So, too, would it destroy her if Gilliam were to no longer care for her. "Oh, my poor girl, you have come home to heal. Johanna is with child and sick as she can be. She'll be right glad to have your help in the house."

"Nay, I cannot go there. Papa will only scream and call me whore. Might I not stay with you?" Tilda pushed away, wiping away her sorrow. The quickness with which her sobs ended was startling.

Nicola searched the girl's expression and found the same sort of desperation she'd seen when Tilda had bartered with Alan. Aye, de Ocslade was done with Tilda, but the reeve's daughter was not yet finished with him. Whatever it was she yet needed from Ashby's neighbor, Tilda meant to use her noble companion to get it. Would it be coins, again?

Only then did Nicola understand that their course had been firmly set on that day in November past, and it was far too late to change now. Nicola had no choice but to play her part and see this dance to its end. Sweet Mary, but she did not want it to happen this way, with Tilda betraying her once again.

"I cannot keep you with me. My lord husband would never allow it." It was a flat statement.

"Please, Colette, I cannot bear Papa's hatred for me. You must need a maid; your lord would not deny you that. I need you, Colette, you and no other."

The pain and pleading in the girl's voice washed over Nicola like a wave, waking her old habit of soothing the reeve's daughter. It did not matter to her heart that Tilda meant to hurt her. Only with great effort did Nicola manage to look away. She turned it into a fearful glance.

"Dear God, what have I been thinking? We have been standing here where all can see us. Come, we must hie, praying all the while no one tells my lord that I have been speaking with you." She took the smaller girl's arm and began to lead her away from Ashby's gate at a quick pace.

Tilda hurried her steps to keep up. "Colette, I do not understand this. What is it you fear?"

" 'Tis my lord husband. If he knew I had an ally in you, he would soon see you gone. He's not much different than his brother, Lord Graistan. A true brute. *Jesu,* I can only hope we find some way to convince your father to let you stay. Tilda, no matter what Thomas asks of you, agree to it. If you cannot stay with him, you will have to leave Ashby. Now, say no more. I cannot tell you this tale unless we are private."

In silence, they strode past the green and down the narrow lanes. When they reached the village outskirts and Thomas's house, Tilda gasped. "Look, 'tis all re-made, just as it once was. I never thought to see it this way."

She stood back to look at her father's cottage. The door stood half-open against the day's mild chill. The shutters on the two small windows facing the path were thrown wide.

Over the winter months, the thatch had darkened into brown while the whitewash on the exterior dulled to a less brilliant hue. The front garden was thick with leeks, onions, and cabbages, all three of which were much farther along in growth than the herbs Johanna had just planted. Chickens wandered before the door, while a sow suckled her newborn piglets in the small pen at the cottage's side.

"Look at you, you old thing." Tilda went to scratch the swine's ear. The pig grunted in recognition of a former household member. "Another year, another litter to feed us."

Johanna thrust her head out of the door in surprise, her face pale against the sickness she suffered. "Tilda!" she cried in disbelief. It was not a happy greeting.

"Johanna," the girl said coldly. "You look awful."

Thomas pushed past his daughter by marriage, his gait even more painful than ever, despite spring's warmth. He halted before the door, arms braced on his hips, feet widespread. His brows were drawn sharply over his eyes, his mouth but a harsh line. 'Twas obvious he had no intention of letting Tilda enter his house.

"Johanna, go inside and close the door." He waited until he heard the panel shut. "So you have dragged yourself home at last, have you? Be glad Young Thom's not at home just this moment to meet you; he'd kill you for sure. And you," this venom was aimed at Nicola. "What are you thinking bringing her here. I've told you I'll have no whore in my house."

In response, Nicola meekly bowed her head. "Thomas, I have already told Tilda how my lord would never allow her for my maid. Since she cannot stay with me, you must—" she let her voice linger on the word as she eyed a message to him, "keep her here. You know the sort of man my lord husband is." Nicola hoped that between her fearful woman's stance and her words, she could drive Thomas to understand her meaning. If only he could be led to play along until she could explain it to him later.

Thomas brought his full attention onto her. After a long moment he said, "Aye, that I do. This means I had best hie myself to him, I think. He'll not much like it when he learns my daughter has just arrived, after I had told him she was dead."

Nicola's head snapped out her meek pose. That old

cheat! But, his message was clear; he was reminding
her of their game over the fees and boon work owed to
Ashby manor by its villagers. It was the same day
they'd spoken of Gilliam and his plans. She fought a
start of amusement.

"You told my lord Tilda was dead? Oh, Thomas, my
lord husband will think you lied to avoid paying the
fee you owed him for letting her live outside the village. I fear for you and your family at what my lord's
reaction may be." Better that he fear what *her* reaction
would be, as keeper of the accounts.

Still struggling with what she was trying to convey
to him, Thomas stared a moment longer, then turned
on Tilda. "Look on how much you continue to cost me.
How many fees for adultery and lewdness have I already paid, and now this? Go within and confine yourself to my hearth. I do not wish the neighbors to see
the whore who is my daughter."

"Aye, Papa," Tilda said, staring at her toes. "I will
do as you say."

Thomas glanced at his lady. "I will go see how I can
soothe this situation. Do you know where your lord is
just now?"

"Nay, I left without gaining his leave." It was a
humble statement.

"And without his escort," the reeve pointed out.
"What will he think when he hears of this? Best you
return with me." He knew not the reason she was always escorted, only that Gilliam wished to keep her
protected.

"Oh, Thomas, I would stay with Tilda just a few
moments. I pray you, please, do not tell him you have
seen me." Her voice quivered in anxiety.

Nicola could see Thomas worry mightily over her

behavior. At last, he shrugged. "Do as you will, but I think your lord would not be happy to hear that you comport with whores. Do not stay overlong. If you must visit, do it within doors so no one sees you."

As Thomas left, Nicola and Tilda entered the long house. With the shutters open to let light enter, the fire was banked to a low glow. It emitted just enough heat to make the vegetable stew simmer in its iron cauldron. Most of the bags and barrels that had occupied the far wall were gone now, leaving the emptiness that only next autumn would fill. This made Thomas's great chest, used to store the village tally sticks, seem all the larger. So, too, was the cross beam above them empty, all the meat having been consumed over winter; Johanna's pottage was nothing but a bland mix of beans, cabbage, and leeks, filling but without the spice of herbs or the brawn of meat.

"Everything looks just as it once did," Tilda said in amazement, then leaned close to Nicola. "Watch how easily I drive Johanna out the door," she whispered, and continued in a louder voice. "Aye, all is the same save that loft, there," Tilda pointed. "Makes me think that my brother no longer cares to perform with his wife before the whole room." She sent Johanna an arch look.

Johanna stepped back, her face tight with dislike. "I think I will go tend to my garden and see if the chickens have left me any eggs." With a huff, she swept from the room, catching her son by his hand as she went.

Tilda made a face at her back. "She's made herself right high and mighty taking my mother's place, has she not?" She kicked out a stool and fell onto it. "Who do they think they are, judging me? They're nothing but peasants, who'll live and die in this place, not knowing or caring that something better exists." It was a muttered comment, not meant for a response.

When Ashby's lady sat beside her on another stool, Tilda turned to her. "Colette, best you tell me all now. What has happened to my fiery girl? I take hope in hearing he keeps you under guard. This must mean some of you yet exists."

Nicola stared into the shifting flames as she spoke. "Oh, Tilda, FitzHenry hunted me down, then brought me here as his captive. He had purchased the folks' loyalty by building them new houses. Everyone ignored my cries of forced marriage when he made Father Reynard wed us." She had not lied yet. "Did you not see the harsh way your father now speaks to me? I think all the villagers yet hate me for June's destruction. And, look you upon this bit of cloth atop my head. My lord husband insists I expose my cropped hair for all to see."

Tilda grabbed her hand, patting it as if she meant to console. "No doubt he seeks to humiliate you by this." Even the cottage's dimness did not hide the tiny flare of satisfaction in the girl's eyes.

Nicola bowed her head in hurt. Why should it please Tilda to think that she was being humiliated? Because Tilda could use this emotion as a tool to soothe her into Hugh's custody. Nicola wanted to leave, unable to bear this. "I fear to stay any longer. If your father reveals that I have left Ashby's walls, I cannot say what will happen to me."

"Your husband beats you, as well? Oh, Colette, my heart aches for you. This is impossible. Here I thought I would come home to find you once again owning Ashby."

"Were you blind in November, Tilda? Did you not see FitzHenry? He is a giant." Nicola shot the petite commoner a disbelieving look. "I told you I could not control him. Thus, my desperate need to escape before we wed. Oh, Tilda, he owns me." She hung her head as if this were the sorriest state she could imagine.

"My poor Colette," the girl soothed. "Once you were alive and free; now you are but a caged bird at Ashby. Poor me as well. If I stay, I think I will suffer your fate. Damn my father. He wants to control me when I am sick to death of men not only telling me what to do, but forcing it on me."

She freed a sharp sound of irritation, then turned on her stool and laced her hands over her knees. The firelight gleamed against her flawless skin and lay beautiful shadows along the gentle planes of her face. "What a fool I was to think I could come home again."

" 'Tis true, you're not now welcome," Nicola said, "but if you work hard and show your father you are different, this can change." It was what Nicola had done, and the success she'd garnered from her efforts had been spectacular.

"Ah, but, Colette, what if I am no different?" Tilda shot her lady a brief, but glowing smile. "Do you know, there were times in my absence I actually considered marrying one of the lads here? Of course, each time the thought crossed my mind, I would realize the impossibility of it."

Nicola watched her a moment. "Why is it impossible? Are the lads here different from those in any other village?"

Tilda laughed. " 'Tis not the lads, but the village. I quail at the thought of falling into the dreary routine of life at Ashby. Toil through spring and summer. Toil harder through autumn, then tighten your belt for winter's duration. When winter closes, the process starts again. It is not like a wrestling match or a dice game, where someone wins and others lose. Nay, this is but a trap that locks a body into never-ending drudgery."

Where Tilda saw drudgery, Nicola saw the chores and duties that gave her her stability and purpose. Each year at Christmastide, she celebrated the triumph of life and health, of home and family. Last year's celebration had been better than any other, as she also celebrated the love she'd discovered in her husband. She glanced down at her hand and the golden ring it bore, then back to Tilda. "If you did not want to come home, why did you return?"

"Unfortunately, when I left Ocslade, I could think of nowhere else to go." It was a wry comment. "Now that I am here, do you know what I see?"

"Nay, what?" Nicola peered into the dim room. It was not so different than the barn that she and Gilliam used as their hall, only smaller. There was the same layer of rushes covering on the floor, the same plastered and painted walls. Even the cauldrons over the hearth stones were similar.

"Dirty straw, muddy floors, and poverty. Being leman to a lord has spoiled me. While at Ocslade, I was never asked to lift a finger, save to please my keeper. Pleasing him seemed a small price to pay in order to live a good life."

Tilda kicked a chicken away from her feet, then glanced at Nicola. "I must think again over staying here. Papa's harsh words suggest to my heart that were I to stay, he would see to it I wed the meanest of all the lads."

"Robert son of Robert," Nicola murmured.

"You jest!" It was a shocked cry. Tilda had imagined it, but never believed her father would truly do it. "Mad Muriel's son!"

Nicola gave a helpless shrug. "That's what Thomas said to me. He thinks Robert a good farmer, suitable to work your dowry fields. Thomas said none of the other lads here would have you. You hurt too many of them, Tilda."

The commoner's beautiful face formed into a hard mask of hate. "He lies. This is Papa's way of humiliating me, as your lord does to you. If I wanted any one of those filthy, lice-infested boys, I could bring them crawling to me, even over their mamas' objections. Ach, but why would I want them? This is a hard and dirty life, Colette, and I will not submit to it. Nor should you."

"What choice have I?" Nicola let her voice ooze hopelessness.

Tilda leaned close. Once again, danger's spice came to life in her dark eyes. "I say we run as we have done before."

Nicola's heart ached. Tilda would do again what she had in November; she would sell her friend to Hugh. What price had she wrung from the nobleman this time? More than anything, Nicola did not want this to happen.

"Do not be foolish, Tilda. If I run, my lord will only hunt me down. This does not mean you must join me in my prison. Run now, Tilda. Live free for me." She willed Tilda to go this instant, before the girl uttered her words of betrayal.

"That I will do, but I'll not leave you trapped here. Hugh wants you still, Colette."

Nicola squeezed her eyes shut against the pain, then

looked at her friend. "Do you hate me so? Did you not say he meant to chain me like a dog?"

" 'Twas only a lie to drive you from him, Colette. Aye, if he sees the humble woman I do, he'll be right pleased."

Tilda turned on her stool and took Nicola by the shoulders, her face alive in practiced excitement. "Colette! Here is your answer. With your husband finished, you can become your old self once more. Aye, and after Hugh has made you a widow, you can turn on him and finish him. To all the world you've done no more than avenge your dead husband. Then, you will hold Ashby as your own, just as you've always dreamed."

"Tilda, I thought you loved Hugh. How can you speak of his death?" Nicola's voice grew quiet against the thought of Gilliam dead. How could Tilda wish this fate for the man of her heart?

The smaller girl waved away the words, but hurt flickered in her eyes. "Hugh's done with me, so why should I care what happens to him?" Tilda rested her hand against Nicola's cheek. "Now, tell me if you wish me to arrange a meeting between you and Hugh."

"Aye, I think you must do so. Set it for five days hence, for on that day does my lord depart Ashby on some private business," she said, straining to force the words from her tongue.

"Hah, but watch me tweak my father as well," Tilda said with a scornful laugh. "Let Mad Muriel's son earn himself a few coins carrying a message in lieu of the wife Papa would give him. Does your lord let you tend to the village ills as you were wont to do?" At Nicola's nod, she continued, "Good, when I have the response, I will fall ill and Papa will send for you."

"I am dying here," Nicola said, her soul begging Tilda not to do this thing. "I must escape." She stood swiftly, not daring to sit an instant longer, else she'd be crying.

"I can see this weighs like a millstone on your back," replied the commoner. "Take yourself to your hall before someone notices you are missing. Let thoughts of freedom be your soul's ease for these next days." She grabbed the taller girl's hand.

"I love you, Colette," Tilda said gently.

Tears filled Nicola's eyes. "And I, you, Tilda."

God help her, but it was still true. With that, she raced from Thomas's house to her own hall, seeking Gilliam. He would let her spill her grief on his shoulder.

Although it was the depths of night, Gilliam was only dozing. He came instantly alert at the sound of footsteps on the stair and turned onto his side. The bed curtains were open, pushed to the side, and the glow of the night candle was the room's only illumination.

The door opened to admit a cold breath of air, thick with the perfume of apple and pear trees in bloom. The candle's flame flickered wildly, setting jagged shadows to battling against the stone walls. His wife slipped inside, heralded by a shaft of silver moonlight. She closed the door, the atmosphere calming. The candle's flame sputtered in relief as it returned to its quiet consumption of wick.

He watched as Nicola stripped off her belt, then discarded her loose gowns. Now that he understood her better, he conceded to her need for those shapeless things. Nicola had no tolerance for any sort of bindings, even a gown's lacing. That she chose to tie herself so closely to him still astonished him. Not that he minded. A wife who cleaved only to him and vowed to love him until her life's ending was satisfying beyond any dream. This she had freely offered him; he had never asked it of her. He smiled. Such was Nicola's nature, the less he asked of her, the more she gave.

With her chemise removed, her pale skin gleamed like ivory in the candle's yellow glow. That gentle light lay taunting shadows along the feminine rise of her breasts. Deep within him, the part of him that never ceased to lust after her responded to the sight. He raised himself onto his forearm to better appreciate his wife's willowy form.

She stooped and caressed Roia. He heard the dull thud of his pet's tail against wooden floor, then the big dog groaned at having her ears rubbed. A month ago, Roia had again begun to seek her rest in their bedchamber. Gilliam couldn't decide if it was because Jos had adopted the pups, or that Roia had tired of being the plaything for so many youthful creatures.

When Nicola rose again, she did not come to join him in the bed. Instead, she turned to stare into the candle's flame. The meager light was enough to reveal the pain etched on her features. At least this time what hurt her had not driven her into that blankness.

"Is all well with Alexander?" He kept his voice quiet.

She started in surprise, turning swiftly to face him. Her pretty eyes were dark and filled with whatever it was that ached in her. "Aye, his head is pieced together, and he's bruised from head to toe. I stayed for a time to watch over him. The first hours are the worst in his sort of injury." She managed a tiny smile. "Once he's healed, I think his mother will beat him black and blue all over again for succumbing to the dares of others and trying to fetch himself a hawk's egg."

Gilliam laughed quietly. "Jos took his punishment like the man he will someday be. If all is good with Alexander, why are you so sad?"

She turned her back to him and bowed her head. "The reply came. 'Tis set as we planned, for the morrow at midday."

"Ah," he said softly, more in his own understanding than to acknowledge her words. It was not only worry over whether his meeting with de Ocslade would come to violence. 'Twas that the reeve's daughter betrayed her for a second time.

Gilliam watched her for a moment. If it were possible, he'd have gone to Thomas's daughter and begged the girl to leave before she did this treacherous deed. Nicola's heart, so huge as to accommodate Ashby and every soul within it, was breaking because one of her own would hurt her.

He eased from the bed, the ropes beneath the mattress squealing in protest as he moved. When he put his arms around her, her back to his chest, she molded herself to him, but she leaned her head against his shoulder, looking away from him. This left the slender line of her neck vulnerable to his mouth, and he did not resist his need to touch her. When he pressed his lips against her throat, she raised a hand to reach behind her and rest her fingers at his nape. As always, her touch set his skin to tingling.

He kissed her throat, then breathed against her cheek, "Will you tell me the details?"

"Love me first," she whispered. "I need to feel you alive and whole in my arms before I say what I must."

The need to fill her body with his eclipsed all else.

If she needed him to stave off her pain, he needed her desire for him to take as a promise against the morrow's outcome. The twining of their bodies would carry them past de Ocslade's threat and into the future he had planned.

She turned in his arms, keeping her fingers at his nape. As always, this caress of hers set his whole body to quivering with hunger. Until Nicola, he had never realized a simple touch could bring him to his knees. It was wondrous, the sensation devouring him and, dear God, there was such pleasure in being consumed.

Chapter Twenty-four

"My lord, what if you do more than spy Lord Ocslade? What if he sees you and you battle? Lady Nicola says he has the larger force. You need me to ride with you, my lord." Jos's plea came with all the force of one whose heart was breaking.

"My need is the greater one," Nicola said to the boy. "You must stay to guard me." She tried to lay her hand on his shoulder, but in his hurt, he jerked away from her.

"My lady, tell him there'll be no one there to see to his back without me." His words were earnest and pained.

Nicola only shook her head. "He has made his decision, and I cannot change him."

The sun was just rising. Gilliam and his twenty men left at this early hour not only on the pretense of doing business away from Ashby, but to gain themselves time to find the right concealment around the meeting place in the north woods.

Ashby's lord turned to his squire. "My lad, until you have mastered the sword the way you have that bow of yours, you cannot stand beside me. An archer has his purpose, but it takes him too long to reload, making him vulnerable to a swordsman. I have no wish to part company with you yet. Accept my decision with grace, for I am entrusting to you my lady's protection. This is a heavy responsibility, for her life is mine."

Gilliam finished belting his sword and scabbard over his surcoat, then tucked his gloves into his belt. As always, he left his mail hood dangling down his back. She drank in his image as if doing so for the last time, the wide sweep of brow, perfect line of his nose and wondrous shape of his mouth.

This was womanish thinking. Gilliam was no child, but a man of great power and ability. She ought to know, having been his sparring partner for the past months. Besides, there was no reason for this day to come to battle.

If only she could go armed into the glade, then she could be the one to see to his back. Instead, her role in the ruse trapped her into her everyday wear, with only a knife strapped to her calf for protection. How it would gall her to stand helplessly aside, should the day result in violence.

"I am watching you, my heart, and I think you are as bad as Jos." Gilliam reached out to draw her near to him.

" 'Tis this love of mine," she retorted, leaning up against him. His steel-coated arm around her back bit through the layers of her gowns to skin, but nothing could have caused her to move away from him. "It makes me feel soft and worried. Of course, you know how much I really hate this?"

"Aye, that I do," he said with a smile, touching his mouth to hers.

The caress was slow and gentle, with none of their usual passion. She let her lips cling to his for a long while, then stepped back to raise a hand to his face.

ler fingers traced the line of his brow, the strong
rust of his cheekbone, then the clean-shaven sweep
f his jaw. He caught her hand, his thumb moving
gainst the ring she wore.

"You are a pretty creature," she said. "I think I will
ake you home and keep you as my pet. Now, go, be-
ore this leave-taking turns me into naught but a weak-
need woman. Have a care, big man. Hugh will never
orgive you if you saddle him with me for as long as
e lives, however many moments that is."

He grinned. "I would never do that to another man."
'o the tune of Jos's single sob of frustration, Gilliam
valked to the hall door.

She and Jos stood where they were, both of them
taring out the open door. The sun lifted above the ho-
izon and rosy light filled the portal. A moment later,
Ashby's lord and all his men, save Walter, who
vatched the gate, thundered from the bailey.

When their hoofbeats were but an echo, Jos turned
n her, a frantic look in his eyes. "He has left me be-
ind."

"Aye, me as well," Nicola said. "Why, without me at
is back, he might well fall."

"You mock me," the boy said with the trace of a
rown.

"Nay, not at all," she replied with a quiet laugh.
'Tis silly, but it is how I feel."

"I, as well." He kicked at the rushes beneath his
eet. "I hate feeling helpless."

Once again, Jos reflected Nicola back to herself.
Oh, boy, we are two of a kind, you and I. Since we
annot have what we want, let us retreat to the fire, so
ve can sulk and fume together."

* * *

The hour before midday found Nicola pacing restlessly in the empty hall with the kennets baying and chasing her flying skirts. She stopped in the doorway. Jos stood nearby, blade in hand, practicing his stances just outside the hall.

Nicola glanced upward in frustration, seeking the time of day from a too-slow sun. The bright orb was hidden beneath a huge white cloud, chased on a chill wind. A great herd of others were sailing across the sky. She closed her eyes and leaned in the doorway.

The sounds of Ashby gathered around her. The swish of Jos's sword cleaving empty air, bees buzzing in the orchard, small birds trilling in the woodland. Millstones ground, one against the other, and the river splashed and laughed. She swore she heard the grass growing at her feet. How could the day drag so?

"Colette!" Tilda's frantic call came from the gate. Nicola leapt outside the hall to look.

Dressed in her fine gown, her cloak over her shoulders, Tilda fought to escape Walter's hold. "Nay, you will not stop me," she screamed, landing kicks and blows against the poor man. "Colette! Come to me, Colette!"

Nicola panicked; Tilda was too early. Beside her, Jos sheathed his sword. "Let her enter, Walter," she shouted.

Once freed, Tilda flew to her, her hair torn from its plait, her gown mussed. Tears stained her face. "My father," she breathed hysterically as she caught and tugged on her lady's hands. "Colette, come now. You must come save Papa."

Nicola stared at her. Gone was any sign of the sensual woman; in her place was a child torn to bits in worry for her sire. Where Nicola's heart wished to run,

er mind warned her to be wary and seek everywhere
or a trap. "What has happened to Thomas?"

"Her father seemed fine enough this morn when he
came to break his fast, my lady." Jos's quiet comment
was also cautious.

Tilda spoke over the boy's French words. "Oh,
Colette, I thought myself so cunning and now Hugh
has Papa. If you don't come right this moment to the
south meadow, Papa'll be dead for sure. Oh, dear God,
why did I do this thing?" Her face crumpling into self-
loathing, Tilda fell sobbing against Nicola.

"I think you'd better tell me what is what, Tilda."
The quiet firmness in Nicola's voice made her words a
command. "I'll not set foot from this place until I
know what you've done."

Tilda's head flew back, her face ragged. "I sought to
use you against Hugh, the way he used me against you.
It was wrong, I know, but I wanted vengeance on him.
Colette, when he wanted me no more, he gave me to
his nephew; I loved him, and he gave me away as if I
were no more to him than a shirt." There remained astonishment in Tilda that such a thing could have happened to her.

"Just how was I supposed to help you gain your
vengeance?" It was a cold question.

"But I told you," the girl protested. "Hugh would
finish your lord, making you a widow, then you would
kill Hugh. 'Twas what we agreed. It served us both,
giving you full control of Ashby, while I got my revenge on Hugh for his mistreatment."

"Aye, that was what you said," Nicola repeated,
stunned. "You told me. What you said was exactly
what you meant. It was not a way to twist me into
Hugh's custody." Her heart lifted.

"Why do you keep talking when we must hurry?" Tilda sobbed, again grabbing her lady's hands. "Hugh has taken Papa hostage to prevent me from betraying him to your lord. His man came to the house to say that if I do not bring you to meet him before a quarter hour's time, Hugh will kill Papa."

"Hugh does not trust you?" Nicola stared at her in surprise.

Tilda raised quaking shoulders. "He has no reason to trust me. Colette, come, please."

"My lady," Jos said quietly, "I cannot let you go to this place without an escort, and we must let my lord know what has occurred. He could yet arrive in time to see the nobleman."

He was right; their hopes for the day were not yet lost. "Aye, Jos, ride like the wind. There is a goodly three miles between where he waits and the south meadow, where Hugh now is."

"Nay, my lady, I'll send one of the stable boys. Go now, and I'll follow once I fetch my bow." There was no time to argue with him; he turned and sped into the hall.

Nicola grabbed the weeping Tilda's elbow, nigh on bearing the smaller girl from the bailey. "Walter," she called to the man as she passed him, "when Jos is gone, close the gates and hold them fast until I or my lord returns."

"Aye, my lady," the solder replied.

Jos's pony came clattering across on their heels. Hal was mounted bareback on the little horse, his brother, Rob, a year less than Hal's dozen, behind him. The smaller lad slid off the pony's back, and Hal set heels into the creature's sides. It cried out, but leapt into its fastest stride.

Rob raced past his lady and into the village. As he passed the William's smithy, he called out to that man's sons, asking them to come along with him. A moment later, the two boys came running after their friend.

Tilda jerked free of Nicola's hold. "Faster, Colette, or we'll be too late." She lifted her heels into a steady trot.

Nicola strode swiftly beside her. They passed the village green. Dickon, the potter's son, and two girls were tending to the geese and tossing a bit of wood between them in a game of catch. They watched as she and Tilda hurried by. In childish interest, they tagged along behind, forgetting their chore.

When this odd troupe reached the village's far edge, Nicola glanced behind her. There was no sign of Jos, but Dickon left his female companions behind to veer off to the west, dashing across a plowed expanse. His work seemed completely forgotten in some new game. Nicola shook her head. That would cost him a blow or two.

The south lea lay atop a hill, bordered on the north, east, and west by Ashby's wheat fields and on the south, below the hill's crest, by woodlands. The fields below it were already planted, leaving them peopled only by boys. The lads were clutched along the edges of the fields, pitching stones at the wood pidgeons and crows that came to steal the precious seeds. Nicola and Tilda moved slowly between them, walking only along the hedgerows and often backtracking to cross into the next, higher field. When they were almost at the summit, they came across John and another lad.

"Where do you go?" John asked, idly rattling his handful of stones.

"To the south meadow," Nicola replied, as if such a trip was a common thing for her.

"What do you know? We were to join the other lads on watch this day there for our meal. We'll come with you."

"Best you do not," she warned them.

"But we must," John replied with a grin. "They've got our bread and cheese."

There was no point in commanding them away. To do so would only pique their interest. Ah, well, once they saw the nobleman and his forces gathered there, they'd scatter to hide in the woods. The four of them crested the hill together.

The meadow spread out before them, lush and green, dotted with clutches of early blooming flowers. Ewes grazed peacefully, while their lambs, bright white against the new grass, leapt and danced in their own peculiar joy. As Tilda started through the lea, her feet sinking in the damp and springy earth, John grabbed his lady's hand.

"Jos is in yon oak," he pointed to the huge tree, its lower fork more than roomy enough for a boy to stand solidly within it. "We've come to protect him, should he need it."

Nicola stared at the lad in surprise. Jos was here already? To have arrived so quickly, he must have sprinted directly through the fields. Then the rest of John's statement registered. "Nay, lad. There's naught you can do against armed men. Stay well away."

"If there's naught we can do to help, we'll stay hidden," John said. "You should know that your lord's enemy has the reeve with them, but I think Old Thom is dead already. There are fourteen more men with the nobleman close within yon woods, but another twenty-five lurk farther into the depths. Jos sent Rob to warn Lord Ashby of this when he comes on the road. Have a care, my lady." John darted into the bushes that marked the beginning of the forest.

Nicola's heart stopped at the number of men. *Jesu Christus,* when Gilliam rode into the lea with their twenty, Hugh would fall on him and finish them all. She caught back her fear. That could only happen if Gilliam arrived in time to meet Hugh. Determination firmed in Nicola as she hurried to the oak. She'd just speed this little tête-à-tête to a rapid conclusion and send Hugh home. Gilliam would have to find another way.

"Why, Lady Ashby, I cannot tell you how surprised I am to see you here." Hugh's smooth voice came from the grove of trees about fifty yards from the oak. Helmeted and armed in his mail with his sword belt buckled atop his green surcoat, he rode his horse out into the meadow at a slow walk. His nephews, also armed in mail, followed. Behind them, came the remaining twelve wearing leather armor similar to Nicola's hauberk.

"Where is my father?" Tilda cried. These past months had much improved her French.

"Show the whore her father." Hugh called the command over his shoulder without looking behind him.

The final soldier rode slowly forward, in his hand a rope. At its end was Thomas's inert body, tearing up the moist sod as he was dragged along. Where Tilda screamed, Nicola fought to control her rage. Hugh needed to believe her humble and meek.

Tilda fell to her knees beside Thomas's body. "Oh, Papa, I am so sorry," she cried, her fingers working to loosen the knots that held his wrists in the rope.

Hugh drew his mount to a stop a good ten yards distant from Nicola. Helmed as he was, she could not see
much of his face, but she felt his stare. Bid by a simple
jerk of his head, his men enclosed her in a circle of
horses. She kept her focus on Hugh, alone.

"Thank God and his saints for bringing you to me."
She made it a woman's frail plea and punctuated it by
wringing her hands. "Please, my lord, I haven't long.
My husband is gone for the day, but he leaves me
under guard. If I am not soon returned, I'll be missed.
You must say you will help me."

Hugh took a moment to wrench off his helmet, but
left his coif tied about his head. The thick black lines
that were his eyebrows rose slowly over eyes just as
dark. There was a gleam of satisfaction in his gaze.
Then, he tilted his head to one side to peer at her, his
mouth pursed in interest. His perusal included every
inch of her long length.

"I would hardly have known you, my lady." It was
a quiet statement. "Marriage has changed you."

"Aye, so it has," she said with a quiver in her voice,
hoping to portray herself as a desperate wife. "Oh, my
lord, I have learned my lesson. Please, no longer damn
me for so rudely refusing your affections. I was arrogant and insufferable. Say you will forgive me."

Satisfaction grew in Hugh's expression. Against his
sallow complexion, his smiled gleamed brightly. "My
lady, who could deny one as lovely as you when you
ask so nicely. You are forgiven."

Nicola remembered to smile at him, then bowed her
head to hide her true reaction. Did Hugh believe her
dim-witted enough to forget he had called her an ugly
amazon? But, neither was Hugh dim-witted enough to
have forgotten her insults. "Your lordship is too kind to

me," she said from her meek position, "when my previous behavior toward you does not warrant your aid."

"Ah," the small knight said, "and here I find myself confused. Just how do you believe I can help you?"

Nicola raised her head, her brow creased in a very real worry. There was no sign of his previous smile left in Hugh's face. Had not Tilda's message told him all this? "My lord, I thought you knew. I wish to be free of my marriage. Would that I had accepted your offer last year. You showed more care for me then, than my husband does."

Hugh cocked a single brow. "It has taken you these many months to come to this decision?"

"Until Tilda returned home, I had no ally through whom to reach you. When Tilda said you might yet wish to wed me, well it made me believe—" She paused in sudden understanding. Hugh was making certain that 'twas she, not he, who suggested murder and remarriage. "I thought you might find some way to rid me of my husband. We would then be free to wed."

There, 'twas out. Now, all he need do was agree, then retreat to Ocslade. She willed him to hurry.

" 'Tis murder you have on your mind, is it?" Hugh's face remained free of any disgust, revulsion, or even pleasure at the thought of killing Gilliam.

"Nay," Nicola said, keeping her voice soft and feminine, " 'tis not murder when it is done in combat."

"I think the effort would be wasted. Your overlord will not have me vassal after I end his brother's life. It is said that if you scratch one FitzHenry, the others are after you like hounds at the hunt." It was a flat statement. Again, he was cautiously avoiding responsibility for what might happen.

"Are you refusing me, my lord?" 'Twas a prod on her part.

"I am only waiting to be convinced. Since you are plotting this, tell me how you think to wed me when your overlord will not have me?"

It came like a lightning bolt. "Throughout all this past winter, Ashby has been plagued by thieves. We thought they had moved on, since there've been no attacks since Easter. What if they had not, and my husband should come across them while hunting one day? Who can blame you for what thieves have done?"

Hugh watched her for a long moment, then a slow smile spread across his narrow face. "Well, now, this is indeed the day for surprises."

He turned in his saddle to stare back at the woman who had been his leman these past months. Tilda sat on the ground, her father's head cradled in her lap as she rocked and sobbed over him. "So, whore, what is your gain in this?"

When Tilda did not respond, Hugh jerked his head toward the man who had held Thomas's rope. "Make her answer."

The man reached out with a foot and tapped Tilda none too gently on her head. "Answer Lord Hugh, bitch," he said in English.

The girl looked up in confusion. Nicola shifted from foot to foot. This was taking too long. She willed Tilda to say something.

"My pardon, I was paying no heed. What was it you asked of me, my lord?" Both her fine French and the abject humility of the girl's voice startled Nicola.

"What's your gain in this, my lovely?" he sneered. "I have yet to see you do one thing that did not benefit you in some way." There was no sign in Hugh that he had ever held any affection for Tilda.

"None, my lord," she managed.

" 'Tis true, my lord," Nicola said, hoping to speed things along. "Tilda and I have been close since birth. She does this only to aid me. Such is the value of our love for each other."

Hugh returned his empty black gaze to her. "That creature loves no one but herself, she is not capable of more. This meeting of ours plagues me, Lady Ashby. Your lord husband has not left Ashby on any excuse for the past months, yet within five days of the whore's return, he is off on business."

Nicola's mind scrambled, seeking the right explanation. "As I said, the thieves had kept him trapped here. Believing them gone, since there have been no attacks for two weeks, my lord went to do what he could not achieve these past months."

"This sounds plausible enough," he agreed, nodding his head slowly. "Yet, I still find myself doubting. I have me an idea. Why do we not wait here until after the midday hour? That way, I will be certain."

"Certain of what?" Nicola clenched her fists to keep from screaming.

"Why, certain that your husband does not wait for me at our designated meeting place. 'Tis simple enough. If he is not there, he cannot ride back within Ashby's gates seeking you when you do not appear." His grin was the devil's own.

It took every bit of Nicola's strength to stave off her cry of despair. Hugh owned them. Gilliam would come for her with his small force, and he would die.

"Osbert, I think we've caught ourselves another hostage." Hugh said with a quick lift of his brows. "How much do you wager that Lady Ashby's sudden pallor says that her husband comes anon?"

"Why, Uncle, I think you are right," said one of the mailed men, his laugh mirthless.

The knight rode forward and drew his horse to a halt directly before Nicola. She blinked away her pain for Gilliam to present a woman's fearful mien. Her only hope remained in lulling them into complacency against her, praying that when the time came to act, she could be of some use to her husband. If only she had her sword and mail!

Enough of this knight was revealed beneath his helm and coif to suggest he resembled his uncle in his dark complexion and black eyes. However, instead of being small and slim, he was near her height with powerful shoulders. His gaze wandered over her, much as Hugh's had done.

"Now, Uncle, why did you tell me she was an ugly creature? I think I will not mind bedding her at all."

Nicola's eyes flew wide.

"Aye, I think I will enjoy comforting you in your grief, poor widow that you will soon be. If your overlord's pride would never let him accept my dear uncle as his vassal, his business sense will not deny him the joining of our houses. I will be a palatable substitute. Especially, since you will give me a son to be Ashby's heir." Osbert had the gall to wink at her. "You need not worry overmuch about pleasing me. I am a simple man. Tie me a woman to my bed, and I am happy, eh, whore?" He shot the question to Tilda.

"Aye, my lord," the girl replied with a tremble in her voice.

Again, Hugh turned in his saddle to look at Tilda. "My lovely, I might just see to it you receive those coins I promised you in November. You've done far better than I expected."

"I want no coins, my lord," Tilda said, her head bowed. "I have pleased you. That is sufficient reward."

"You need the coins. A Judas like you cannot survive without blood money. Osbert, against the chance of Lord Ashby's appearance, take Lady Ashby onto your saddle. Her husband will need to see we hold her."

Nicola's gaze darted frantically around the circle of men, until she once again won her calm by force of will. The knife on her calf burned against her skin. Aye, if she were calm and meek, she would win herself a chance to wreak some sort of havoc.

Osbert reached down a hand. Instead of fighting, Nicola helped him to raise her into his saddle, easing into a sideways seat in front of him. As he rearranged his reins, one leather strap at either side of her, she bowed meekly and stared at her leg. It would not take much of a reach to get to the knife, but once she had it, where could she use it against a man dressed in mail?

She raised her head to look at her captor. His eyes gleamed as he smiled slightly. The links of his mail were too small to allow her dagger to penetrate any one circle. She knew there were vents beneath each arm, but those would not be easy to reach, nor would an injury there necessarily render him helpless. Ah, but if she could get him to remove his coif, his throat would be vulnerable.

With a trembling smile, she screwed her expression into one she thought was terror. "I am very frightened, my lord." It was but a whisper. "Say you will not hurt me."

"If you do not fight me, I can be kind." His reassurance rang hollowly against his previous threat of tying her to his bed.

"Might I look upon your face? If I see proof of this kindness in your expression, I would be much at ease." Her fright seemed to please him, for he grinned broadly and wrenched off his helmet.

"Loosen my coif lacing, my lady, and look upon your new master."

The arrogance in his voice was a spear's thrust to her gut. Rage simmered just within her control as Nicola did as he commanded. She was careful to see that his hood lay all the way back, exposing the whole of his throat to her. Aye, he was her master, but only for the moment.

"Now, my lady, since we are not long from being united in marriage, why not kiss me and give me a try?" he asked with a laugh.

Nicola shook her head in a shy "nay," then bowed her head like a modest maiden. Her humble posture concealed her careful reach for the concealed dagger. The quarrel whirred so close to the back of her neck, she swore it shaved her hair from her nape. Osbert gagged and reeled in the saddle. Blood, warm and wet spattered Nicola's cheek. The knight's horse rose on its hind legs in reaction to its master's sudden relaxation. Nicola instantly grasped the reins, kicking her leg over the horse's head to sit astride, her skirts at her thighs. She didn't know whether to curse or bless Jos.

She glanced behind her. Osbert's life blood flowed from the torn vein in his neck, his eyes already going glassy in death's onset. His sword hilt was within reach. Nicola praised God as the blade came easily from its leather scabbard.

"To arms!" Hugh shouted, reeling his mount around to face the edge of the woods from whence the attack had come. When the next expected bolt did not arrive, Hugh glanced back at Nicola, then looked again, his lips twisting into a snarl of rage. "Take her!"

Nicola jabbed both heels into the beast's sides. The horse's sudden motion made Osbert's limp body tumble off the saddle. Sword lifted to strike, she sent the frightened horse barreling toward the soldiers ahead of her. Her blade met the first man's. His surprise and her womanhood made his swing sloppy. Her blow sent him flying from his saddle. It was distraction enough to escape their circle.

"Run, Tilda!" she screamed in English as her horse galloped toward the woodlands.

"Fetch her back, you idiots!" Hugh's shout was high-pitched in rage.

Nicola's horse entered the trees on a wide pathway, but she rode past the oaks into the thicker wood. Pulling the beast to a sudden halt, she slid off, then struck its hindquarters with the flat of her blade. The horse ran, dodging the trees and bushes.

Without hesitation, Nicola threw herself into a deep tangle of holly and bracken. Tall and thickly leaved, the holly offered sharp thorns along with concealment. It tore away her head cloth and scratched her face and hands as she drove herself deeply into it. She crouched as horses galloped past the bush, chasing the runaway steed.

There was a rustling beside her, and Dickon appeared. Nicola stared in surprise. "Jos wants to know if you are unhurt."

Only then did her hands begin to shake over how that lad had shot across the skin of her neck. "By our sweet lady's tits, you tell that boy if we live through this day, I will have his hide." It was an angry, fearful hiss.

Dickon grinned. "I will tell Jos you are well, my lady."

The horses returned to pass her hiding place at a much slower pace. "She's not on the steed, my lord," a man called.

"Damn that vixen! I will have her life for Osbert's." Hugh's cry was almost grieved. "Search the woods for both her and the whore. Bitch of Ashby!" he shouted out, "you will pay for Osbert's death with your own life."

"Well, well," Gilliam's deep voice boomed from the meadow's northern edge, "look who I meet this day. Once again, you trespass, seeking to steal from me my wife. This time, you die, little man."

Chapter Twenty-five

Nicola crept out of her hiding spot, sword in hand. "Go home, Dickon. Tell the folk there will be a battle here, and they must stay away." She reached down to gather up her hems and tuck them into her belt. Without hauberk and shield, she was trapped here in the woods, but if she needed to fight in her own defense, she would be ready.

"Aye, my lady." The lad crept out after her.

Nicola came to stand beneath the giant oak. She peered above her. Jos was not in the lower fork, but in a smaller one, higher up. The greater height offered him a clear line of sight and, although not as broad as the other, he yet had floor enough to set his foot in his bow and draw the string.

She looked around the massive bole; her heart caught and clung to the sight of her Gilliam atop that huge black beast of his. His helm was in place, disguising his face from her. He sat impossibly tall in his saddle, his great sword in hand, braced crosswise before him.

With Witasse snorting and sidling in excitement, Gilliam entered the meadow. Ashby's men spread themselves in an even line behind him, stretching across the lea. Sheep bleated, dashing wildly in every direction to avoid the horses. Nicola nodded in approval. Gilliam meant to keep Ocslade's men within range of Jos's bow. With one quarrel still in poor Osbert, his squire had eleven more. If Jos hit true, that was eleven men who would not fight. Eleven from forty was twenty-nine to Gilliam's twenty. Much better odds.

She took a moment to scan Hugh's ranks, seeking Tilda. There was no sign of her. Nicola sent a brief prayer winging skyward, not only for herself and her husband, but that Tilda had not been murdered.

When Gilliam was within five yards of Hugh, de Ocslade threw up his hand. One man blew a horn in alarm, and the rest charged. De Ocslade's men screamed at the top of their lungs as they threw themselves into battle. Gilliam's soldiers added their own shouts, bravely riding forward to encircle their enemy.

Someone grabbed Nicola's hand. She tore free, half raising her sword, before seeing that it was John.

"Come stand across from me along the pathway. We'll see if we can stop a few from reaching the lea," he said.

She glanced above her, meaning to shout a warning to Jos, but the boy had already turned. He aimed his bow at the open area through which the hidden men must pass if they chose this path. John and she crouched at either side of the wide pathway, the safest route out of the woods for a horse.

Their first foe appeared, trotting carefully through the close trees, his eyes focused on the meadow and not the greenery around him. Nicola rose, sword at the ready. Although his chest was well protected with padded leather, his leg was not. With all her might, she sent her blade into his horse's side, crushing the sol-

dier's lower leg to cripple him, even as she broke his
mount's ribs.

Another mounted man not as cautious as the first,
galloped toward them as the injured horse turned,
screaming in agony. The horses collided, oncoming
rider tumbling head over heels to lie still in the pathway. Nicola raced forward to make certain that the soldier could not fight, but the fall had done her work for
her. His neck was broken.

Another came, howling as he rode. John heaved a
good-size stone at him, striking the man in the head
and knocking his helm askew. Blood poured from his
broken nose as he slumped limply in his saddle.

His horse halted and stood quivering in fear. Nicola
ran to free one of the soldier's feet from his stirrup,
then shoved him off his mount. When he hit the
ground, she ended what the lad had started.

Three from twenty-five who hid. Another left the
woods with a quarrel in his shoulder.

A boy's terrified cry rang from the woodland's edge,
the sound cut off in awful finality. Nicola threw back
her head in despair.

The weight of it drove her into that terrible calm of
hers. All that lived in her now was the desire to kill
Hugh and his men for what a babe had sacrificed. She
strode along the path toward the field.

The gentle lea was awash with men, some mounted,
some on foot, others on their backs for all time. Sheep
bleated, swords clashed, Witasse screamed in rage.
Men's shouts mingled with the moans of the injured.

'Twas now fifteen of theirs against twenty-eight of
Hugh's. From above her another quarrel flew. A man
arched and fell, then did not rise. At the far edge of the
battleground, Witasse lifted himself onto his hindquart-

ers. Gilliam had dismounted to allow the horse to act in its own defense. The great beast lashed out in his blood-induced fury, trampling beneath his hooves those who sought to capture the costly steed. He roared toward another group of warriors, and men scattered.

Alfred stood in front of her, surrounded by three, death inescapable if she did not help. She swung. One of his foes lost his arm. She whirled from that blow into her next, drawing her sword upward as she turned, and buried the blade into the second opponent's unprotected back. Alfred finished the last.

Nicola started toward the next clutch of soldiers. "My lady, you're not armed! Stop, go no farther!" She heard Alfred's call, but his voice made no dent in her quiet.

Grinning like a madman, another simple soldier reached out to grab her arm. Fist clenched, Nicola brought her elbow crashing into his midsection. His eyes bulged for an instant before her blade followed her blow. He dropped away, and Alfred was suddenly at her side.

Nicola caught sight of the man who was responsible for all this. Hugh, yet mounted as his horse was not the weapon Witasse was, rode around the backs of five men, cursing and goading them into attacking those they had surrounded.

"To me!" Her husband's bellow from the center of that circle penetrated her calm. Gilliam needed her.

Nicola ran to him, Alfred hard-pressed to keep abreast of her. Her blade sliced into one man's back at his waist. He fell backward onto her arms; she stumbled beneath his weight. Alfred shoved the man off her. Nicola struggled to regain her footing.

A soldier turned to strike. Nicola automatically

raised her shield arm; it was empty. She threw a desperate block, but knew it would not deflect the blow. The man fell toward her, the steel-tipped quarrel having pierced both the front and back of his leather and padding.

Three of Ashby's men had joined their lord to form a ring of shields against Ocslade's greater number. "To me!" Hugh shouted, calling the remainder of his men to come overwhelm Ashby's few.

Nicola grimaced in a rage she could not feel. She snatched her dagger from its leg sheathe and darted beneath Hugh's blow to plunge the well-honed blade into his horse's neck. 'Twas no different than slaughtering a pig.

"You foul misbegotten bitch!"

Hugh swung at her. Despite the writhing of his steed, it was a well-aimed blow. Nicola stumbled in her escape. Alfred shoved her aside, taking what was meant for her.

Nicola scrambled to her feet. Hugh was down, his leg caught beneath his mount. He glared at her as she raised her sword, then grinned. Nicola leapt away instinctively, without thought.

"Uncle!" Hugh's other nephew's blade cleaved the air where Nicola had stood. A quarrel sped past him, missing only because his horse shied at that instant.

Hugh crawled from beneath his mount. "Henry, take that bowman!" he shouted, limping to join those who attacked Ashby's lord.

"Nay!" Gilliam bellowed with all the power of his voice, but he was yet trapped within the ring, five of his own men now forming a circle of shields with him against the ten who ringed them. "Defend Jos," he shouted to any of Ashby's soldiers free to do so.

"William, kill that bitch," Hugh screamed to his mounted nephew.

Ten yards from Nicola a man wrenched his bow from his back. She ran for him. The soldier leaned, placing his foot into the crossbow's curved arm; his back was exposed. She would die before he'd shoot her Jos. Hooves tore the turf behind her. She feinted away from the bowman. William rode on by, confounded by her swift and contrary movement.

The soldier had the quarrel in its trench, the bow stock to his eye as he sited the boy in the tree.

Sliding on the wet grass, Nicola shifted direction, sprinting for the archer. Again, William came for her. She heard Jos's quarrel as it whirred above her at the same time she saw the bowman release his trigger.

The knight behind her screamed in agony. His cry was echoed by Jos as the quarrel penetrated his body, toppling him out of the tree. Incapable of pain just now, Nicola avenged Jos's death by killing the bowman, then raced back to Gilliam. William's horse came trotting by, its master dragging from one stirrup. As the body turned, she saw the quarrel that had penetrated his face, stopped only by his helmet's back.

The circle of men around her own consisted of but Hugh and seven others. However, Ashby retained only two besides her love. Her husband glanced at her from behind his shield, upon which three men beat. "A shield, my love, then back to back," he called. "We stand or fall together."

She snatched up the shield Alfred had carried. When she started toward the circle, one of Ocslade's men turned to the attack.

"Nay," Hugh snarled. "Let her join them. We'll save her for the last and have some sport before it's done."

Nicola found her place beside her man. "Use my back and turn," Gilliam panted to her from over his shoulder. "Take the one to your left."

At his command, she rolled, bringing her sword up in her most deadly motion. The soldier held his small, round shield high in expectation of a man's overhand blow. Her sword tore through leather, her blow losing impact in the padding he wore beneath it, but still finding skin and bones to break. She kicked him off her blade.

Gilliam had used her motion to hide his own. His great sword flew crashing against one man's shield, then another's neck. One of their own cried out and fell.

"Again," he breathed. Once again, they turned in unison. Two more of de Ocslade's men dropped.

"Jesu," Hugh spit out in deep frustration and disbelief. Even with his leg injured, he was agile and skilled enough to wound the last of the Ashby soldiers. That left only Ashby's lord and lady. Hugh dropped back a step. His remaining three men did so as well.

Nicola turned slightly, her arms aching and her breath burning in her lungs. "Gilliam," she breathed. "I love you."

He stared past Hugh's shoulder as if startled. "We live," he panted with what sounded like a laugh. He drew back his blade.

De Ocslade prepared to meet Ashby's lord, sword to sword, only to arch, his mouth opening in surprise. He stumbled forward, turning instinctively to face his attacker. Gilliam's filthy blade roared down, the power of his blow cutting through mail and padding.

Hugh made no sound as he fell, only jerked and gasped as Gilliam freed his weapon from torn flesh

and twisted metal. Then, he was still. Standing just behind where Hugh had been was Tilda. The girl bore a
soldier's sword in her trembling hands.

There was no time to think. Even as Gilliam turned
on two of the remaining men, Nicola took the other.
Swords beat on shields a little longer before sending
the men to their just reward, then it was over.

The ensuing quiet was broken by the bleat of sheep,
Witasse's snorting breath, and the moans and cries of
the injured. In that instant, a lark lifted its voice in the
joy of spring.

Gilliam sank to sit on the ground, and Nicola followed suit, raising a trembling knee on which to lean
her head. Her gowns were heavy with blood, her arms
like lead, her legs quivering in exhaustion, and her
lungs aching. With her shoulder leaning against her
husband's back, she could feel him panting in exertion.
Her husband fell back to sprawl on the ground beside
her.

Nicola raised her head. Tilda yet stood rooted in
place, the blade now dangling from her fingers. The
girl's entire body trembled, and her brown eyes were
wide in shock and horror. "He killed my father," she
shuttered. "He killed Papa." Nicola could only nod in
response. The girl's eyes rolled up into her head, and
she dropped to the ground and lay still.

"My lord, do you yet live?"

Gilliam opened his eyes to look upon Father Reynard's homely face, the man's great beak of a nose
quivering in appalled concern.

"Aye," he said, incapable of more. From the beginning of the conflict through its remarkable end, he'd
held the faith that they would survive. Now that it was

over, he found himself incapable of believing they had triumphed.

Then he smiled. If someone had told him this morn that the reeve's daughter would save the day, he would have called him a liar for certain. His grin broadened in disbelief. 'Twas no less than a miracle.

The priest turned to Nicola. "My lady, do you yet survive?"

"Aye."

It was a sad sound, as if she wished the answer were otherwise. Gilliam struggled to sit up, his mail rattling against the effort, so he could look on her.

"God be praised," the priest said, blessing himself in the intensity of his relief. "Where are you injured?"

"Save for blisters, I am not hurt." Again, her voice was empty in sorrow.

Gilliam stripped off his gloves, then removed his helmet to better see her. Nicola lay on the grass, her head to one side. Tears made tracks through the filth on her face. She was covered in blood from head to toe, her sleeves so full of the stuff they hung heavily from her arms.

Reynard tried to wrestle her into a sitting position. "Come you quickly, then. We are taking the injured to the church. While the village women can tend most of them, there are several who demand your special skills."

"Leave her go, Father," Gilliam said, pushing the priest away from his wife. "She is exhausted and sick from the battle."

"My lord, their need is urgent," the churchman pleaded. "Only she can save those who are most gravely injured."

Gilliam turned his back on him, then touched Nicola's cheek. "Are you ill again?"

She shook her head, yet keeping her face turned away from him. " 'Tis easier, just as you said. The killing I did this day was simply what must be done, and that is all." The emptiness of her voice frightened him.

"What aches so in you? Do we not yet live and love?"

"Jos is dead. I saw him take the bolt and fall from the tree. Oh, Gilliam, my heart breaks. I had a hand in his death."

"He is not yet dead!" the priest cried, fair dancing in his agitation. "My lady, you must come this instant. The boy needs you for only you can fix him. So, too, does Alfred and one of the blacksmith's sons. You must come *now*." Reynard thrust out a hand to his lady, meaning to drag her to her feet if she did not rise on her own.

"Jos lives?" Nicola's look went wild with hope. Gilliam offered a hand to brace her as she struggled to her feet. "Take me to him."

Even with the priest's arm around her shoulders, she swayed in exhaustion. Gilliam set his hand at her hip to steady her. Father Reynard tried to walk away, but Nicola leaned so heavily against him, he staggered.

"Give me a moment, Father," she muttered, seeking to draw strength from her empty reserves.

"Love, I think you'll do him no good in your present state," Gilliam said, coming achingly and slowly to his own feet. He lay his hands on her shoulder. "You must rest."

"Nay," she cried out, throwing his hand from her shoulder as if she feared he might try to stop her. "Let me heal him." It was this that gave her the strength she sought. When she moved away, her footing grew steadier with each step.

Gilliam offered God a swift prayer of thanks, then tagged on his wishes for Jos's continued life. If the boy died, his wife's guilt would eat her alive. With his spiritual needs addressed, Gilliam turned, meaning to assess the damage. Even that simple motion made him dizzy. By the morrow, every muscle in his body would be alive in pain. He'd taken one blow across his back that he was certain had broken his skin. Why it had not broken bones was beyond him. Like this whole encounter, 'twas a miracle, no doubt about it.

The men of Ashby's village had come into the meadow. They turned bodies, seeking faces they knew among the dead. Walter came striding across the field toward him. "My lord, may God be praised. You live still!"

"Aye, that I do. Who do we have left?"

"I've seen Robert, Richard, and William all walk out, braced upon a peasant's shoulder. Philip lies yet stunned, waiting to be borne away. So, too, do Gilbert and Edwin, but they have other injuries as well. I saw Alfred as they took him to the church. He spoke to me, but I have little hope of his survival. The rest—" He paused and lifted his shoulders in eloquent description. "How many did Lord Ocslade bring?"

"Forty some," Gilliam said, releasing the lace that held his metal hood about his head. He pushed the thing back and took off the cap he wore beneath it, then ran his fingers through his hair.

"Holy Jesus," the man offered in admiration of their victory. "Alfred said I must tell you your lady is a berserker."

Gilliam shot him a sidelong glance, then remem-

366

Denise Domning

bered Nicola's blankness after the village woman's death. "I should have guessed. 'Tis a good thing I own her and need never face her, eh, Walter?"

"My lord, *only* you could own her," Walter said with a breath of amusement.

"That's true enough." Ashby's lord laughed. "Set the folk to gathering horses and stripping Ocslade's men of their armor. Not only does this day leave us to exist in peace, but Ashby is now far richer than dawn found us. Three sets of chain mail, hauberks, and swords aplenty, plus a stable full of horses. Not a bad day's work, I think me."

"Aye, my lord." Walter turned away to organize the peasants to these tasks.

Gilliam reached down for his sword, then went to one of the last men he'd killed. As he used that man's tunic to clean his blade well enough to sheathe it, the reeve's daughter moaned and came to her senses. He strode to her and offered his hand to help her rise.

"My lord," she said quietly, staring at him in consternation.

She was much prettier when her expression was not marred by a whore's leer. "Reeve's daughter, I owe you my thanks for this day's success. Because of you, my wife and I yet live. Do I dare tell you how astonished I was to see you racing up behind your lover, blade outstretched?" He smiled at her.

Her eyes filled suddenly. "He killed my father. I could not bear that he would kill Colette, as well." She raised her hands to cover her face. When she dropped them, gone was the pretty girl; the whore had returned. She eyed him speculatively, her expression growing soft with the promise of pleasure.

"Do not waste your time," Gilliam said, his remark made gentle by the love this girl claimed for Nicola.

The sultry look fell away, and the small woman shot him a bright smile. "Ah, well, 'twas worth a try. I think Colette was not honest when she spoke to me about her marriage to you, my lord."

He grinned in return. "I know she was not."

"I am not sure if I am happy or angry over this." The reeve's daughter frowned, her lips pursed as if she considered the issue, then she nodded. "I am happy."

"Now you must leave," he said quietly.

The commoner looked up at him. "You would not let me stay?"

"What is there here for you?"

"Nothing," the girl said in happy relief. "Aye, if I stay here, some other woman will have the life I want. I think I'll take me to a greater place than even Graistan, and find a kinder lord to keep me." She smiled up at him, pleased at her sinful thoughts.

Gilliam cocked a brow, then turned. "Walter, find this woman a fair palfrey, will you? She'll be needing a mount to take her on her travels."

"My lord, thank you," she cried in surprise. "This I did not expect."

He shook his head, refusing her thanks. "You have done me a great service, and for that I must see you rewarded."

The girl studied him, the fine planes of her face caught in hesitation. At last, she said, "I would not cheat you, my lord, when you intend me only kindness. I have already rewarded myself."

A whore *and* a thief, but an honest one. Gilliam grinned. "Have you?"

Her smile was gay, and mischief sparkled in her

brown eyes. For that brief instant, he saw the merry child who had won Nicola's heart. She turned her belt on her waist to reveal a heavy purse. "I thought Osbert and William would not be needing their coins any longer. I left what the others carried."

"Keep the coins with my blessing," he said, trying not to laugh. Walter brought her a small mare, yet fitted with its previous owner's saddle and bridle, then helped her to mount.

"You can ride?" Ashby's lord asked.

"Not well, but I think I shall improve," the girl replied. "My lord, will you bear a message to your wife for me?"

"With all gratitude."

"Tell her that I love her still, but cannot know how long this love of mine will last. Say to her that should I pass this way once more, under no circumstances is she to trust what I say." The girl's sudden smile was wicked with delight. "I am not the trustworthy sort."

This time, Gilliam did laugh. "Get you gone from my vale, little thief. I'll not tolerate your sort here."

She was still smiling as she set her heels into the horse and rode into the woodlands.

Epilogue

Nicola stared out over her crowded hall in pleasure. Not only was all of Ashby here for the spring ale, but the masons as well, along with Lord Coudray and his men, who had escorted the workmen. With the meal just ended, villagers and servants worked together to clear the tables. The morrow would find Mad Muriel and her son dining on lamb stew and duck brewet; the dogs received the remains of the roasted ox and sheep.

"My lady, that was truly a fine meal." Lord Coudray owned a rich baritone voice that made his every sentence sound like a song. He had shared a bench with her.

That this man was Gilliam's kin, there could be no doubt. His hair was just as golden, although it lacked the curl of her husband's fair locks. His eye color was a deeper blue, his nose had the same perfect length and width, his cheekbones high, and his jawline as strong. All in all, he should have been the more handsome of the two. Save that half his face was ruined.

The scars could be no more than a year old. The longest traveled from the top left of his brow, across the bridge of his nose, beneath the patch covering his right eye, then trailed off toward his ear. A second, smaller scar cut directly down from the shielded eye to curl into the corner of his mouth.

Still a little awestruck at entertaining so auspicious a man, Nicola said quietly, "I am very glad you enjoyed it, my lord sheriff."

"Geoff," he insisted, and he smiled at her. Even with the scar at his mouth's corner, it was a beautiful thing. His teeth were even and white, the curve of his lips infectuous. "Anyone who makes my brother as happy as you do cannot stand on ceremony."

"I am not happy," Gilliam said, speaking around her to his brother. "You are taking my bed for the next days, and she will not play bed games with me while we sleep in the hall."

"Gilliam," Nicola protested. "This is a private issue!"

Geoff laughed. "What is the matter with you, my mother's youngest son? This is a dangerous woman you taunt. I'd have a care with your tongue, were I you."

"She loves me too much to hurt me," Gilliam assured him.

"Humph," Nicola said, turning her back on him. "Do not be so sure."

"My lord, might I go sit with my friends?" Jos asked, coming to stand between her and Gilliam. He presented an odd image, dressed in his new formal attire, his arm yet caught in a sling while his shoulder healed, and naught but stubble atop his head. "Dickon wagers that my scar," he lowered his head to indicate the crooked line on his scalp, "is longer than Alexander's."

"Aye, go," Gilliam said with a smile.

"Not yet," Geoffrey said, reaching out to catch the boy by the sleeve and draw him closer.

Jos shot Nicola a worried glance. Despite all of their assurances, the boy strove to avoid Lord Geoffrey. He was certain his mother had convinced Lord Coudray that he was being abused at Ashby; Jos feared he would be forced to leave.

"I would drink to you, Jocelyn of Freyne." Hand still holding Jos's sleeve, Geoffrey reached for his cup. "To the infant of last autumn, who is no more, and to the warrior who used his skills to protect his lord and his lady, like a fine and loyal knight." He took a swallow of ale, then released the lad.

Jos blushed against the compliments. "My thanks, Lord Courday.

"Nay, my thanks to you, Jocelyn. I am right fond of my brother and grateful for what you did to help him. How glad I am I brought you to him."

Jos's cheeks grew redder still. "You will not take me away?"

Geoffrey's brow creased in confusion. "Why would I do that? You will stay here until you are knighted."

"My mother sent messages," Jos started, then sighed in relief. "My lord, please tell my mother that I am well and happy here. She must set her heart at ease over me."

"That I will do. Go to your friends now, Jocelyn."

As he darted away, he called over his shoulder, "Name's Jos, my lord."

Gilliam turned to sit astride his bench. "Come, love, there's room for you at the end now." He patted the spot between his thighs.

"Why do you carry messages to Jos's mother? Is she also your ward?" Nicola asked as she moved to sit be-

tween her husband's legs, her back against his chest.
This was a mistake. There was a tingling inside her
that suggested a week without lovemaking was impossible.

Geoff's jaw was suddenly tight. "Of a sort," he said
shortly. "It comes of my being sheriff. Pregnant wid-
ows must live at the shire's seat under the sheriff's
protection until their babes are delivered."

"Ah," Nicola said in understanding. This was a log-
ical way to protect a dead man's blood line. Not only
did it shield an unborn heir from scheming relatives, it
also assured that the babe was indeed born of his mother's body and was not some peasant's infant purchased
to replace a stillborn child.

"Ah, indeed," Geoff muttered. "I am praying she
drops the child while I am here. Better that my under-
sheriff sits at her side throughout her delivery than me.
Lady Elyssa has a way of raising my hackles that is
unsurpassed in any other woman."

"So, she is yet filling your moat with tears, is she?"
Gilliam asked with a quick laugh.

"Nay, she's given up tears and now insists on prying
into my private life." This sharp comment was followed by a sigh of resignation, and Geoff's shoulders
relaxed. "I should not complain so. She's a good
woman, who has restored Cecilia's voice. My daughter
has been without speech since her mother's death," he
added for Nicola's sake.

"Lady Elyssa has done this?" Gilliam asked in astonishment. "Then, fie on you for complaining over
her, or is it jealousy that goads you? You are as bad as
Rannulf and cannot abide to share your child's love.
'Tis a marvelous thing Jos's mother has done. Why, it
broke my heart to see my niece voiceless and shy in

June past, when she was always such a cheerful little lass. If you cannot thank Lady Elyssa on your own behalf, then thank her on mine."

"I did thank her," Geoff retorted. "Do not nag, Gilliam. I came here to escape my troubles, not dissect them."

"Aye, leave your brother in peace," Nicola said. "What sort of host chides his guest?" She leaned her head back against Gilliam's shoulder, her cheek resting against his throat. His arms around her tightened in response, then he raised his arms until his wrists were beneath her breasts.

She drew a sharp breath. Tingling turned into desire, and there was nothing weak-kneed about it.

Pipes squealed and drums beat as the musicians announced the first dance. There was a great stomping of feet to herald the dancers into the cleared space at the hall's center.

Nicola slid back on the bench as far as she could go between Gilliam's thighs. His long gown was bunched between his legs, keeping her from feeling his shaft against her lower back. His embrace tightened as he tried to accomplish the same thing. One week was definitely too long. She turned her head as if to look out at the dancers, her hair brushing across Gilliam's throat. It was his turn to gasp.

"Geoff, my wife and I will catch a breath of fresh air before the dancing starts," he said, his voice husky with his need for her.

Nicola cleared her throat to hide her laugh. The last thing she wanted to do was catch her breath. "Aye, I would like that," she said, rising from the bench.

Geoffrey aimed his gaze at her, then his brother, a faint air of amusement in his look. "As you will."

Gilliam grabbed her hand and nigh on pulled her out of the hall. Outside, the night was clear, the sky filled with stars, a waning moon already seeking its rest on the western horizon. Those of Geoffrey's men and Ashby's soldiery who were not interested in dancing had gathered in the bailey. Their fire was just coming to life, but their kegs of ale had been well tapped. Dice rattled in someone's cup. Walter crowed as he saw his lord and lady.

"I win! I told you they could not last a day!"

"Hold your tongue," Gilliam snarled at them as he and Nicola hurried their steps across the open expanse, "this is a private issue."

Nicola pulled him to a halt at the base of the tower stairs. "Gilliam, we cannot use the bed."

"Who's there?!" The cry came from around the corner of the cellar. Arnold, the master mason, appeared, lamp in hand. "Oh, 'tis you Lord Ashby, my lady." His brusque nod barely acknowledged her. "I expected another pair thinking to hide behind the cellar wall to couple. I've driven three away so far."

"Good work, Arnold," Gilliam said. "We want no fornicators at Ashby. What are you doing here?"

"Make some measurements. I do not hold much with frivolity. Waste of time." He stood, watching them as if waiting for something.

"Ah, well," Gilliam said, "I suppose we'll be going back to the hall and leave you to your work."

Arnold nodded as if this was a suitable answer. "Good night, my lord." He disappeared behind the wall again.

Nicola waited until he was out of earshot. "I've put fresh linens on the bed. We cannot use it," she hissed.

"He'll never notice, I vow," Gilliam whispered back.

He caught her to him, tugging off her head cloth to bury his hands in her hair.

Their mouths met in a frantic mating, her arms clutching him tightly to her. He lowered one hand to catch her breast, his thumb toying with the peak. She tore her mouth from his to kiss his throat, then his earlobe. Sweet Mary, but she wanted him right this moment.

" 'Tis wrong to abandon our guest this way," she breathed, trying to stop herself.

He caught her tightly to him, forcing her to rise to her toes. Nicola melted. She could feel his shaft even through their clothing. "Once and quickly, then. Best you put a whole week's worth of passion in it. I still won't play this game for others' benefit."

"Praise be to God," he murmured, then grabbed her by the hand. They dashed up the stair and into their darkened chamber. Gilliam pushed at the door, not taking time to see it properly shut.

Laces flew and gowns were discarded in record time. He grabbed her to him, and they fell onto the bed. Ropes squealed and posts squeaked. The footboard creaked.

His mouth burned a line down her throat; her fingers drew lines on his nape. As his hand caught her breast, she kissed his ear. Her thighs parted, and he entered her with one swift and wondrous thrust. She arched beneath him, wrapping her legs around his waist.

He rose above her on his elbows to spare her his weight. Not this time. She caught him around the neck, forcing his mouth to hers. Her kiss demanded that he take her with all his power. He groaned against her mouth and thrust again. Pleasure exploded in her.

The bed rocked, but Nicola was too far gone in her

own passion to notice. She freed his mouth and kissed his throat as her heels on his buttocks urged him to move again and again. There was an odd squeal in the room.

Gilliam gasped as she cried out. Feet braced against the bed's end, he poured himself into her, thrusting with all his might. And kicked off the footboard.

Ropes snapped, the end of the mattress dropped to the floor. The end bedposts clattered against the wall, curtain poles fell. The headboard started to drop atop them, then stopped, braced in midair by the curtain poles. Without the support of the footboard, the sideboards fell toward them and they were trapped in the sagging mattress.

"Mary Mother of God," Nicola cried out, her voice muffled by the curtains, "you broke the bed!" Gilliam shook in silent laughter.

"There is nothing humorous about this," Nicola protested, reaching up to push the bed curtain out of her face. "You great lummox, you broke the bed. Where is your brother going to sleep? Oh, *Jesu,* how are we going to explain this to him? I cannot believe you broke our bed!"

"Oh, Colette," he started, but could not get more out as he was laughing out loud now. When she made an irritated sound, he caught it back and managed to gasp out, " 'Tis Geoff's fault. The damn bed's too short for me. It's your fault, too. By God, but you drive me beyond sanity."

Of a sudden, it was funny. A tiny laugh bubbled out of her. "They will have to dig us out, I think."

"Nay, if I ease backward, I can slip out the end. I have it! We'll dress and hurry back to the hall. When it is time to bring Geoff out here, we'll act as if we had no idea how this had happened."

"Gilliam," Geoff said, his voice coming from the door, "it cannot work. I have caught you already."

"It was not my idea," Nicola protested, laughing in earnest. "I said the linens were clean and should stay that way."

"How?" Gilliam demanded.

"The master mason was working near the cellar and heard a terrible noise in this chamber. He rushed to the hall to fetch you or me, saying some couple used this chamber. I see he was right."

" 'Tis your fault. I told you the bed was too short," Gilliam said. "Now, go back to the hall, my mother's oldest son. We'll be back as soon as we are finished here." He grinned at his wife.

Nicola laughed. "Aye, but best be patient."

If you enjoyed
SPRING'S FURY,
you'll want to discover more
of Denise Domning's
magnificent medieval quartet,
featuring the four Graistan
brothers. Turn the page for
a description of
WINTER'S HEAT
and
SUMMER'S STORM,
both currently available in
paperback from Topaz. Also,
be sure to look for
AUTUMN'S FLAME,
the fourth and final book
of the quartet to be published
by Topaz in the fall
of 1996.

Summer's Storm

Lady Phillipa of Lindhurst had been a prisoner in her husband's castle since her arrival there as a child bride. His current absence gave her a respite from his cruelty and a chance to venture beyond the castle's iron gates. But her dread of returning paled in comparison to her terror of the handsome knight who suddenly rode his charger across field and fen and into her life.

For Temric, knight-errant and a powerful lord's bastard son, the sight of Phillipa's beauty awakened both a wrenching anguish and overwhelming desire. Long had dreamed of her, tormented by the knowledge she should have been his wife. It took but one kiss, and she understood that he had come to her rescue unbidden. She would go with him unafraid.

Just as fate made them lovers, the world made them outcasts. Condemned by king and kin and betrayed by those they trusted, Phillip and Temric would not be parted. If they were caught their lives would be forfeit. But one path remained: the way of true love and a plan so perilous it could bring death—or their most glorious dreams.

Winter's Heat

Her time in a nunnery had taught Lady Rowena many things, but not how to be a wife to the powerful lord who claimed her as his bride. Meeting him on their wedding day, her blue eyes defiantly locked with his, she vowed never to submit to this aloof, mysterious knight whose courtly charm barely concealed his ruthlessness.

His vast estates—and his bed—lacking a lady, Rannulf, Lord of Graistan, knew this convent-raised beauty brought a dowry he couldn't refuse. But the heat ignited by her touch reminded him that he had been a woman's fool once and would never be again. After one night of sweet consummation, he planned to coldly leave her and ride off to war, ignoring the desire that turned his blood to flame. . . .

"Denise Domning weaves a story that is at once startlingly realistic and deeply romantic. An impressive debut by a wonderfully talented writer . . . she has a marvelous future!"
—Rexanne Becnel